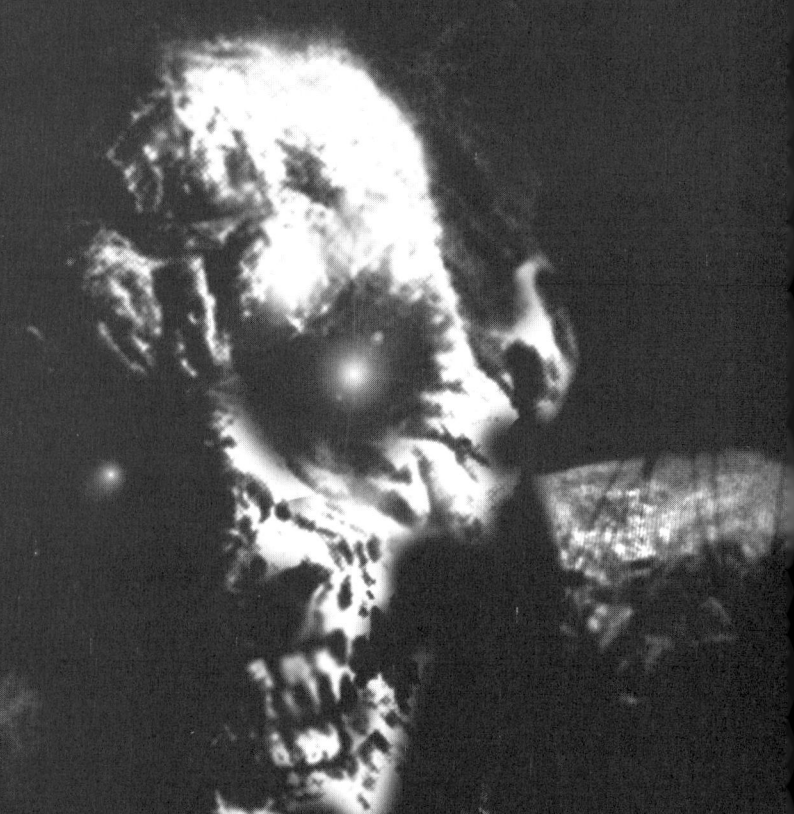

I don't know how or why ... but the dead ... they walk among us ... and they are Hungry

All Flesh Must Be Eaten

THE DEAD

A Roleplaying Game

EDEN STUDIOS PRESENTS A SHY/VASILAKOS PRODUCTION

All Flesh Must Be Eaten™

Produced by EDEN STUDIOS Directed by GEORGE VASILAKOS

Written by AL BRUNO III   CJ CARELLA   RICHARD DAKAN
JACK EMMERT   M. ALEXANDER JURKAT
AND GEORGE VASILAKOS

Editor M. ALEXANDER JURKAT

Director of Photography GEORGE VASILAKOS

Visual Effects STEPHEN BROTHERSTONE   MICHAEL OSADCIW
BRAD RIGNEY   CHRISTOPHER SHY
DAN SMITH AND GEORGE VASILAKOS

Cover Art CARLOS SAMUEL ARAYA

Playtesters STEPHAN AVERY   SHARI BAYLISS   ROB BECK
DEREK BELANGER   PAT DIXON   TROY DOWNING   DOUG JESSEE
SCOTT EGGERS   PAUL FRANKLIN   DEREK GUDER   BONNY LIANG
RYAN "CHICK" LYBARGER   SEAN REILLY   JIM ROOF
GERRY SARACCO   CHRIS SMITH   ADAM STEIN
JOHNATHAN STEPPE   JAY WROBEL   CRAIG YOUNGBLOOD
and TODD "THE UNDEAD PLAYTESTER" KRAUSE

Based on the Original Concept by
CHRISTOPHER SHY and GEORGE VASILAKOS

WWW.ALLFLESH.COM

Eden Studios
6 Dogwood Lane, Loudonville, NY 12211

All Flesh Must Be Eaten™, icons and personalities are © 1999-2009 Eden Studios
The Unisystem™ Game System © 1999-2009 CJ Carella.
All art © 1999-2009 Eden Studios.
All Rights reserved.

Produced and published by Eden Studios, Inc.
The Unisystem™ is used under exclusive license.

No part of this book may be reproduced without written permission from the publisher, except for review purposes. Any similarity to characters, situations, institutions, corporations, etc. (without satirical intent) is strictly fictional or coincidental. This book uses settings, characters and themes of a supernatural nature. All elements, mystical and supernatural, are fiction and intended for entertainment purposes only.

Reader discretion is advised.

Comments and questions can be directed via the Internet at www.allflesh.com, via e-mail at edenprod@aol.com or via letter with a self-addressed stamped envelope.

Ninth Revised Printing, october 2011
Stock EDN8020   ISBN 1-891153-31-5
Printed in Canada

Table of Contents

Chapter One: The Dead Rise................8

Chapter Two: Survivors....................22

Archetypes...68

Chapter Three: Shambling 101............80

Chapter Four: Implements of Destruction..120

Chapter Five: Anatomy of a Zombie.....142

Chapter Six: Worlds in Hell................160

Appendix...214

Index..246

FOREWORD

Everybody Loves Zombies

By Shane Lacy Hensley

A withered hand bursts up from the grave. The wet soil froths upward as the rest of an arm, then the decaying flesh of a gruesome skull, pushes itself from Hell. The grisly corpse rises from the dirt, and stands awkwardly on its twisted legs. It gazes about the cemetery -- spies its prey. A young woman and her husband mourn over her mother's grave. The zombie staggers forward. The woman screams, just as a hand from below explodes from the mound and latches onto her ankle!

You've seen it before, and you'll see it again. Great zombie movies like *Night of the Living Dead, Dawn of the Dead,* or *Evil Dead*. If you're reading this, you've probably seen all of those. And if you're a gamer, maybe you were just dying to play them. That's what *All Flesh Must Be Eaten* is all about.

When Eden Studios first announced this game, it was going to be nothing but a one-shot. A pet project. But like the undead, it just wouldn't die. Fans, stores, distributors, and even the freelancers wanted more. I saw the cover for *All Flesh Must Be Eaten* at Origins '99 and was hooked as well. I'm a big zombie fan, and when George Vasilakos asked me to write the foreword, I just about died (pun intended). Hell, I would have paid to write the foreword.

Things coming back from the grave are very popular these days. I can think of half a dozen properties based around this concept off the top of my head -- The Crow, Vampire: the Masquerade, Wraith: the Oblivion, Deadlands, Anne Rice's Vampire Chronicles, and even Buffy the Vampire Slayer and its new spinoff, Angel. Heard of a few of these? Thought you might have.

All these are good stories produced by talented and creative people, but why is the undead theme so popular? Why are we so fascinated with the things that don't stay where we plant them? Is it the millennium? Maybe. But I doubt it. I have my own theory about why everyone loves the undead so much. There's four reasons really, each one a little deeper than the first. Let me explain with an appropriate analogy -- the zombie's cozy little home, the grave.

On the surface, the most obvious reason to love zombies is as plain as the earthen mound on top of the grave. Any game, story, or movie with zombies is, by default, supernatural or fantastic. That means there's magic, or science so strange it might as well be magic. Gamers in particular love this stuff. All the really great roleplaying games -- from *Advanced Dungeons & Dragons* on -- have had zombies. Many fine games that didn't -- some that were much better conceived, written, and even presented -- have gone to the boneyard, in large part because they didn't have that fantastic element.

All Flesh Must Be Eaten

The second reason is shallow, but true. Think of it as the earth between the surface and the coffin. On my business card is the slug-line "Everybody Loves Zombies." Like the fine folks at Eden, I am a maker of roleplaying games, and zombies are an important part of our industry. Why is that? Partly, it's because if a game has zombies, it must have a fantastic element as well, as I said above. But "zombies" is a euphemism, too. What I really mean here is that a game (or any other medium) has to have some sort of gimmick. Something so cool a fan picks it up, grins like a skeleton, and just can't put it down until he's devoured every morsel. It's the undefinable "neatness factor." I call this the game's "zombies." The French would say it is the game's je ne sais quoi, an indefinable essence that makes it cool. There doesn't actually have to be groaning undead to make a game successful, but there does have to be some sort of hook, one sharp and jagged enough to snag a customer and drag him into the grave.

The third level is a little deeper, like the coffin itself, sitting deep beneath the soil. You can throw a few millennium-paranoia flowers on top if you want to, but I see "Y2K" as a catalyst more than a cause. Most of us do not dwell on our mortality on a daily basis, nor do I think most of us believe the end of the world is coming in a few months. But you can't watch the news without occasionally realizing that one day your life will be reduced to a small entry on page 9 of the local paper. Games like this, and properties like those I mentioned above, offer us a small taste of immortality. What if you could come back? What if the grave wasn't the end of the line? When I was younger and more people were religious, the promise of an afterlife dulled this quest for immortality. These days, religion is not as prevalent in twenty-somethings and younger. Is their quest for an afterlife transferring itself to a longing for physical immortality? Perhaps. I leave this to your personal philosophy.

Now let's go even deeper and open the coffin itself. That poor beggar inside has been waiting long enough. He's not so different from you or I. Maybe he smells a little worse (I hope!), and he eats brains, but we have something much stronger in common -- something in the soul. He claws his way out of the grave, struggles free of Hell itself. We claw our way out of the personal Hell we each find ourselves in sometimes. Whether it's business, love, family, or plain old complicated life, things get rough sometimes. Like the dead, we have two choices. Lay down and die, or rise up and fight back. "Rage against the dying of the light," to quote Dylan Thomas. The gaming industry is like that. Eleven months of the year are pretty rough. Then it's the con season and we all rise from the grave for one last shot.

Eden has always been a little smarter than the rest of the industry. I know, because I've been lurking in the graveyard for years. Now Eden is attacking, cutting their way through the gaming-horde-that-won't-die with incredible products like this one, smart leadership, and a stalwart team of slayers like George, Ricko, Al, CJ, Alex and Jack. I've read the bulk of *All Flesh Must Be Eaten*, and it's brilliant. Devour this book as our zombie friends would eat a nice, juicy brain.

Okay. Enough with the philosophy and accolades. Forget all this deep talk and go play the damn game. Partake in a tale of ravenous undead hordes and have fun like you used to when you first got into gaming. Forget about roleplaying your character's angst-ridden existence or acting out a star-crossed romance. Load your shotgun and blow out a zombie brain instead. Loot an abandoned mall while dodging groaning corpses looking for meat. Have fun. Be shallow -- it's easier to dig your way out of the grave that way anyway.

But maybe the next time life's got you down, think about those poor dumb zombies. If they can dig their way out of the ground -- battle their way back from the depths of Hell itself -- you can survive anything life has to throw at you. Just keep scratching, friend. There's daylight up there somewhere.

Groovy.

Shane Lacy Hensley

July 1999

Chapter One
The Dead Rise

"It has been established that persons who have been recently dead have been returning to life and committing acts of murder."

—Night of the Living Dead

0:00

. . . This account is for anyone who unearths the research center. I've set the computer's audio system to record whenever I speak or make a sound. The hard drive has enough space for thirty-six hours of audio, that is all I should need. Since mission control does not answer, I can only surmise that they too have been compromised.

My name is Professor Roy Hinkley. I leave our data and this audio journal in the hope that it will somehow aid whomever finds this place . . . I am the only remaining member of our research contingent. There were twelve of us at the start. A gathering of forensic specialists, neurologists, biologists, chemists, toxicologists and a pair of military consultants . . . we also had twenty-five infected cadavers to work with.

I prefer the term "infected cadaver" to the appellation the media is using -- zombie. It brings to mind cheap horror films and primitive superstition. If you take nothing else from my chronicle dear listener, know this -- this is a problem that can only be solved by science. Our assignment was to find some way to stop the walking undead before they swept humanity aside . . .

There were many early successes for our group. We determined the source of the infected cadaver outbreak was not the result of the wrath of a vengeful God, witchcraft, voodoo or something equally ludicrous. The source of the outbreak was radiation -- radiation carried on the back of a comet like rats carried plague-riddled vermin on their backs centuries ago.

The tragedy here is that we failed to realize the power of said radiation, the sheer scope of its reconstitutional abilities. Our procedures were as simple as they were methodical. At the beginning of every week, we would pull one of the infected cadavers from cold storage and begin a protracted series of tests. We analyzed everything from its hair to its basil ganglia and we were beginning to gain some understanding of how the radiation had animated previously lifeless tissue. I am utterly certain that if disaster had not befallen us we would have found a way to stop this nightmare in the beginning.

No wait. I have so little time and I still have not shared with you the intentions behind my audio record. You see, I was bitten by one of the infected cadavers and now the puzzling infection is going to run its course through me. There is no treatment but I hope that by chronicling my degeneration I may be able to aid science . . .

1:59

. . . I was bitten on the right hand, between the thumb and pointer finger. The bite was forceful enough of fracture the metacarpals. I've lost a good amount of skin and muscle tissue from the wound area. I've had it wrapped in bandages for some time now and I'm going to unwrap it now . . .

Chapter One

Fascinating. The bleeding has ceased but the area around the wound is darkening, almost like an abrasion on the surface of a piece of fruit. I briefly probed the area with a scalpel and found a spreading purulence. It resembles pus save that it has a reddish-black hue. It is thick with fibers that appear to be similar to some strains of thallophytic plant life. Is this how the infection will supplant my central nervous system? I wonder how it will affect the higher brain functions.

I wonder.

One of my fellow scientists, a garrulous little man named Wilkins, kept a cache of liquor in his rooms. I think I could use a drink . . . several drinks in fact . . .

2:26

. . . It appears that I will not be having that drink after all. I suppose this explains my lack of appetite as well. Mere moments after taking a sip from the bottle of rotgut Wilkins kept under his bed, I found myself wracked with nausea. At first, I attributed this loss of self-control to the low-quality swill I had foolishly imbibed, but as my retching metamorphosed into a bout of dry heaves I began to realize that something far more malignant was in effect . . . I made my way to the battlefield that had been our cafeteria and tried to see if I could consume a pair of crackers and a glass of water. If anything, the illness I felt at this was longer and more terrible. Just speaking about it makes me want to vomit all over again.

Much like rabies, it appears that the infection causes the sufferer's digestive system to reject all nourishment. I wonder if that is why the affected cadavers must feast upon living flesh . . .

7:39

. . . tried to sleep. Woke with a fever . . . 103 I think, it's hard to tell, my eyes are blurry. I kept dreaming of my loved ones, my wife, my parents, my . . .

Never mind. Such sentimental drivel doesn't exactly pertain to my thesis, does it?

To the point. Approximately nine hours after contracting the infection I find myself feverish. There is a slight ringing in my ears. I find myself ravenously hungry and the bruised area of my hand has now spread down the fingers and up to the head of the radius and the ulna. They look like dark threads working their way up my arm to my heart . . . My father died of a heart attack -- I wonder if this will feel similar . . . My hand occasionally clenches of its own volition. It's like watching a laboratory rat in its death throes . . .

8:28

. . . stupid really, we should have realized . . . we should have taken better precautions.

I pieced together what had happened by reviewing the security tapes. A medic and a neurologist were vivisecting one of the infected corpses. They had immobilized it by strapping it down to the table and then amputating its limbs and lower jaw. They removed, took samples from, and weighed the infected cadaver's organs. This was not simple sadism at work. We did this to see if the various nerve agents we were testing were having any effect at all. Besides, our main concern was testing and studying the infected cadavers' artificially stimulated nervous systems. Those excess tissues merely got in the way.

They threw the tissues into a container. After they were thoroughly and completely studied, the organs and the still struggling torso were taken to the incinerator and disposed of.

Those two scientists never got the chance to dispose of anything.

We should have guessed . . . I should have guessed that the neural matrix created by the alien radiation would not subscribe to the patterns of behavior used by Earthly life forms. This neural matrix was multi-tiered (dare I say holographic?) in nature. Unfettered by the powerful neurological impulses that ordinarily subsumed them, the discarded tissues somehow adapted themselves to operate on a fundamentally different level. Like the worm that when cut in half crawls in two separate directions.

And it looked something like a giant worm was attacking when the infected cadaver's small intestine looped itself around the throat of the neurologist and dragged him screaming into the fetid trash barrel.

The medic then made the mistake of fleeing the room, leaving the door open.

What happened next was like a butcher shop comedy. Somehow that infected cadaver, or I should say what remained of the infected cadaver, managed to free its monstrous kin from cold storage. Whether this was through dumb luck or an intelligence that had previously gone unnoticed, I can't say. By the time we realized what was going on we were being overrun . . .

9:31

. . . The ringing in my ears is getting louder, I can't stop sweating. The black lines stretch all the way to my chest. It feels like there's a fist in there slowly squeezing my lungs. My stomach is aching with hunger but everything I've tried to eat -- from ice cubes to raw hamburger -- will not stay down. At this rate I'll dehydrate before I succumb to the infection itself. Perhaps that's a mercy. If by some miracle Caroline Majors is still alive and a message can be gotten to her . . . tell her . . . tell her I was thinking of her . . .

10:37
. . . nuh . . . not want . . . nuh . . . can't . . . Jesus! . . . don't want to die . . . not like this . . . not like this . . . nuh . . .

18:07
. . . It's a miracle, a miracle! No more fever, the discoloration on my hand is fading -- and I can move my hand. Not as good as I used to but still . . . Perhaps the human auto immune system does have a way to combat the infection. I must see if I can contact the government!

But first I'm going to record my vital statistics and take a blood sample. Any information I can. The cure could be in my white blood cells just waiting to be released . . .

19:07
. . . My breathing is nothing more than a reflex action. I let my exuberance get the better of me. It doesn't make any sense! Why am I still here? Why am I still talking? . . .

20:18
. . . The fever was bad, worse than I ever expected. It killed me. You hear me talking but I'm an infected cadaver now. The brain dies last, like a fish in a tank nobody cleans . . .

21:02
. . . Stabbed meself -- No! Myself! Stabbed myself in tummy, blood but no pain. I like that, no pain but still here, falling apart like -- falling apart -- I'm going to get one of the guns offa the military soldiers that died in the cafeteria. Shot to head always works . . . scientifically proven . . .

22:24
. . . solider lying on back arms out like Jesus and Jesus say 'take of my body like bread' so I did it was cold and it filled my belly but then came out where the holes I made are. Maybe that's why I'm still hungry . . .

26:12
. . . god why? god why? god why? . . .

34:32
. . . they're huuuuhhh . . . muhore soldiers . . . huhhhhh . . . suh-hoon . . . uhm stuh-ill in muh muhnd buh-ut uh can't stuh-op! suh huh-ungry . . . uh-all uh huh-ave luh-ft is thu huh-unger . . .

Introduction

Zombies.

You know what they are. Walking dead. They claw their way out of their graves, the moonlight glistening in rotting eyes. They slowly stagger across the lawn possessed with an eternal hunger for human flesh.

And that smell. Don't forget the smell. As they approach your home, the evening wind blows the stench into the air. Your dog barks wildly, frenzied by the smell. You awaken from a restless sleep, look out your bedroom window and see staggering corpses walking toward your house. Half-asleep and half-dressed, you rush down the stairs to barricade the door and block off the windows.

You are halfway down the stairs when the first window shatters. Damn, they move fast for dead guys! You run into the living room and pry open your gun cabinet. As you fumble to load the gun, the front door collapses from the weight of a pair of rotting corpses. They shamble into the hallway, arms stretched out, reaching for you. You unload your shotgun into their chests. Blood sprays the wall as they are thrown back.

A window explodes besides you, showering you with broken glass. Decaying hands reach for you, tugging at your shirt and hair. You manage to pull free and run for the back door. As you open the door, you freeze. A rotting corpse stands before you, jaw falling off, worms boring out of its nose and ears. You pull the trigger. The corpse reels back as you blow a hole where its stomach was. It falls onto the porch . . . then starts to get right back up!

You try to rush past, but a zombie grabs your leg from behind. Your world turns upside down as you lose balance. You fall onto your back. Looking up, you see the zombie that you blew away in the hallway has made his way across the house and is clawing at your leg. He's not dead! Not even down . . . then, you remember. Gotta shoot them in the head!

As the zombie on the porch and the one from the hallway descend on you, you try to raise your shotgun. Shoot them in the head . . . it's the only way to be sure.

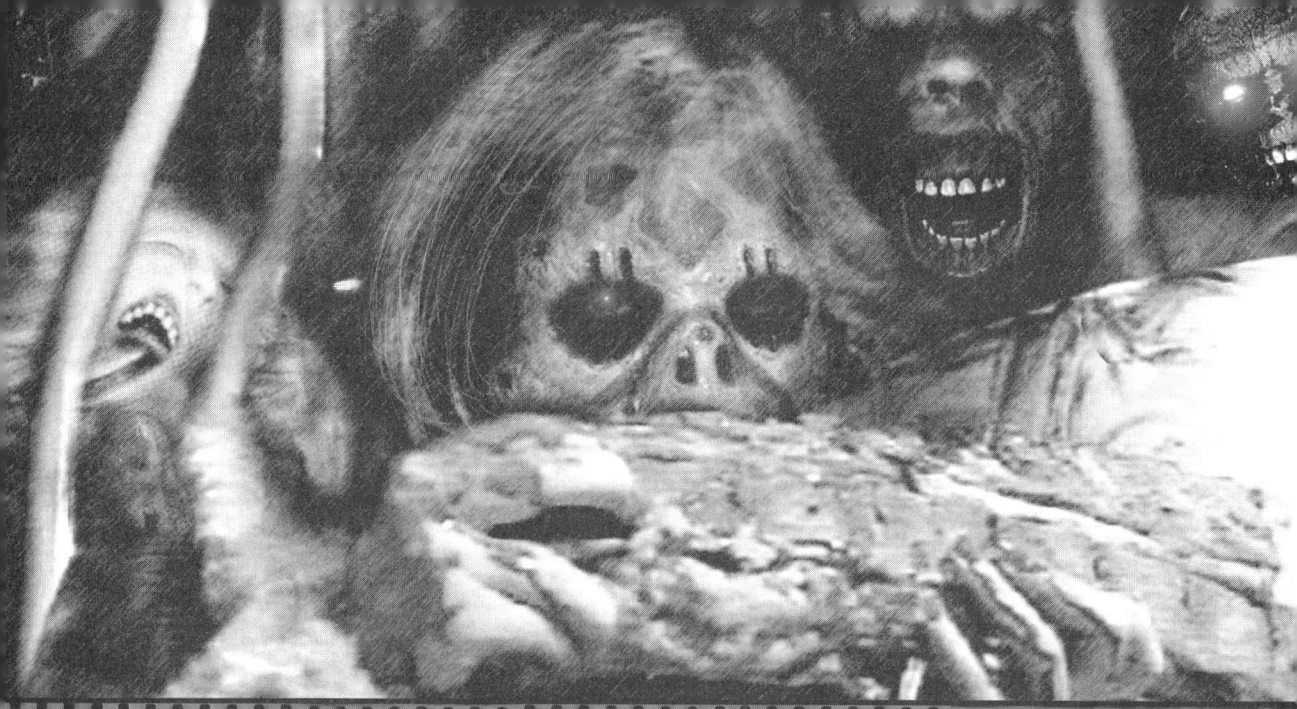

What's in a Name?

Although the movies do a good job of showing us these creatures in a graphic and visually impressive way, they do not really give us a good name for them. They have been called Ghouls, Flesh-eaters, Cannibals, and Zombies -- but these are not really what they are.

Ghoul is definitely no good. Ghouls are described in any occult book or dictionary as a creature or spirit that robs graves and feeds on the corpses. That doesn't apply here; indeed, it's exactly backwards. An example of a Ghoul is our friend Bela Lugosi. On several occasions in many of his movies, we find him stealing corpses to conduct unspeakable experiments. In this case, we might also call Dr. Frankenstein a Ghoul.

Flesh-eaters is a closely related name we could use, but it's still too broad. Everyday people can be considered Flesh-eaters. Most people eat hamburgers and steaks. Eating cooked flesh from a pig or cow doesn't make us a zombie. The main difference is that we are still alive, and not a walking corpse.

Cannibals doesn't seem to work either. In the film *Dawn of the Dead*, the scientists explained that "cannibalism, in the true sense of the word, implies an intra-species activity. These creatures cannot be considered human, they prey on humans, they do not prey on each other! They feed only on warm human flesh."

Zombie is not entirely accurate either. A Zombie or Jumbie (the name given to them in the Virgin Islands) is described by the Island experts as "a soulless human corpse, still dead, but taken from the grave and endowed by sorcery with a mechanical semblance of life." These creatures are brought to life by sorcerers called "Houngans" who bring the dead back to work as their eternal slaves. Zombies do not complain about their "living" conditions, they do not sleep, and they do not ask for a paycheck. Also, it is common knowledge by the Islanders that if you feed a zombie meat or salt, it will realize that it is dead and return to its grave. Now if this were the case, the zombie movies we know and love would not be anywhere near as entertaining. Can you envision the zombie rising out of its grave at night, a thin fog hugging the moist ground? It approaches two lovers embraced in the forest. It comes up behind the half-naked victim and takes a bite out of her back. Suddenly, it realizes it is dead and returns to its grave. Roll credits. End of movie.

In the end, most people would describe these shambling piles of rotting flesh as zombies, and for want of a better or more familiar term, that is the one we will use.

A Short History

Not many are aware of it, but the walking dead have a history, one that pre-dates the movies. The best place to start would probably be pre-medieval Europe. Legend and folklore have long held that sometimes, when a person dies with unfinished business, he may rise from the dead to finish it, or to seek revenge for some evil doing. There have been numerous stories that describe an evil murderer being killed by the dead. These walking dead sometimes devour their victims and continue to live as long as they can eat living flesh and blood.

The early European stories always described these flesh-eating, blood-sucking creatures as being dead-looking. Their appearance ranged from very fresh (just a blue-white pallor) to very rotten (black, bloated and stinking). Besides the obvious differences between these creatures and true Zombies (or Jumbies), these pre-medieval European creatures do not follow any master. They are slave to no one, except their eternal hunger. They rise from the grave and seek the living all on their own. They hunt flesh . . . living flesh.

These creatures do seem very much like our favorite grave-leaving, flesh hunters that starred in cult movies like George Romero's *Dead* trilogy, Richard Matheson's *Last Man on Earth*, *Oasis of the Zombies*, and *Night of the Zombies*. What do you think these hideous, rotting corpses bent on eating human flesh, sucking blood, and exacting revenge were called by the early Europeans? Wampyres! (Pronounced: vam-pie-er) Yes, that's right! Vampires! They are the original vampires that have been re-written and romanticized by writers for centuries.

In time, some very interesting Rumanian rulers were labeled "vampires" for their indulgent, bloody criminal-punishing techniques. They became the subjects of many fiction writers, immortalized to most in the classic *Dracula* by Bram Stoker. These writers drew from actual historical writings and local legends and, with a little imagination, creatively devised their own creatures. Modern literature is so completely saturated with this fictional image of the vampires, that when anyone says "vampire," we don't see the original decaying creatures for which the name Wampyre was created, we see the fictional fang-growing, gothic, aristocratic rulers of a crumbling European empire.

Paralleling this evolution, movie-zombies have gone from being depicted as actual Zombies, to Wampyres, to a strange blend of the two. They have become a risen abomination of humanity, out of control, with a lust for living flesh.

Actual Zombies can be found in such films as *White Zombie*, *I Walked With a Zombie*, and *Serpent and the Rainbow*. These films show us Voodoo in action. We have Voodoo priests that turn the dead, and sometimes the living, into Zombies. Another movie that shows Zombies as slaves of a master (in this case a master race from outer space) is Ed Wood's *Plan 9 From Outer Space*. It shows us aliens from outer space asking the age-old question, "Hey! What do voodoo priests got that we ain't got?"

In movies like *Dawn of the Dead*, we're not sure what raised the dead. In one of the scenes at the beginning of the film, there is a struggle between the SWAT team and some people in a room. If you look closely, you can see a table in the foreground that is covered with what appears to be a Voodoo altar of protection. In Lucio Fulci's film *Zombies*, the director shows you that Voodoo can "make the dead stand up and walk." You constantly hear the Voodoo drums being beaten in the distance. We never discover if the drums are the handy-work of the Houngans creating the Zombies or if these are the drums of the Islanders trying to ward off the evil that is plaguing them. The creatures in *Zombies* are more like the Wampyres of old, but with a Voodoo twist. What we do know is that the dead have "come back to suck the blood from the living." Houngan Zombies also have no way of creating other zombies. However, if a vampire bites you and doesn't rip you apart, you become a vampire. Just like in the movie *Zombies*. This is a prime example of the initial blending of Zombie and Wampyre lore.

In the early fifties, an American writer named Richard Matheson wrote a book of fiction based on the European Wampyres and the modern romantic Vampires. The creatures in his book *I Am Legend* looked like the dead, rotting Wampyres, but grow fangs, hate sunlight and garlic, and can be killed by driving a stake through their hearts. The strange twist of this story is that man created these Vam-pyres. They were mistakenly risen by science. I suppose they could be called Z-am-pyres.

Richard Matheson's book *I Am Legend* tells the story about how society is ever evolving. Sometimes when we evolve too quickly, we undergo a revolution. His Zampyres are nothing more than a group of revolutionaries bent on the destruction of the Old World. They can attain their goals by killing the main character, Robert Neville. Neville is the last true human on earth, hence the movie adaptation of the book *The Last Man on Earth*. Later there was another, starring Charlton Heston, called *The Omega Man*, but we won't go into that.

In 1968, George Romero released *Night of the Living Dead*. In this movie, the Earth was plagued by zombies (really Wampyres) -- a revolutionary force that wrenches control of the Earth from human society and ultimately replaces it with its own. Sound familiar? Yes, Romero was inspired by Matheson's *I Am Legend*.

Night of the Living Dead has its differences though. The origins of George's zombies are never explained. Neither light, garlic, mirrors, or stakes through the heart damage them. Only destroying their brain can kill them. The zombies in *Night of the Living Dead* are really Wampyres of the ancient world. They are here for unfinished business, and that business is to destroy the human race before it destroys itself and everything else!

More recently, the movies have devised new causes for the creation of our dead friends. These range far beyond a Voodoo priest's ranting and raving, or the desire to right a wrong done to them. In films like *Astro Zombies*, *Garden of the Dead*, *Let Sleeping Corpses Lie*, *Zombies 3*, and *Return of the Living Dead*, science either makes a very bad boo-boo, or intentionally creates zombies using something besides Voodoo magic.

In *Astro Zombies*, the creatures are created to work in the harsh conditions of outer space, but find themselves on Earth terrorizing young ladies.

In *Garden of the Dead*, some angry prisoners inhale formaldehyde to get high, die and return to destroy their captors.

In *Let Sleeping Corpses Lie*, entomologists create a machine that only affects the underdeveloped nervous systems of insects. This machine causes the insects to attack and devour themselves leaving our farms and gardens insect free without harmful poisons. Perfect, except for one thing we didn't count on. The nervous systems of the dead have decomposed to the level of insects. They are affected by the machine and begin eating human flesh.

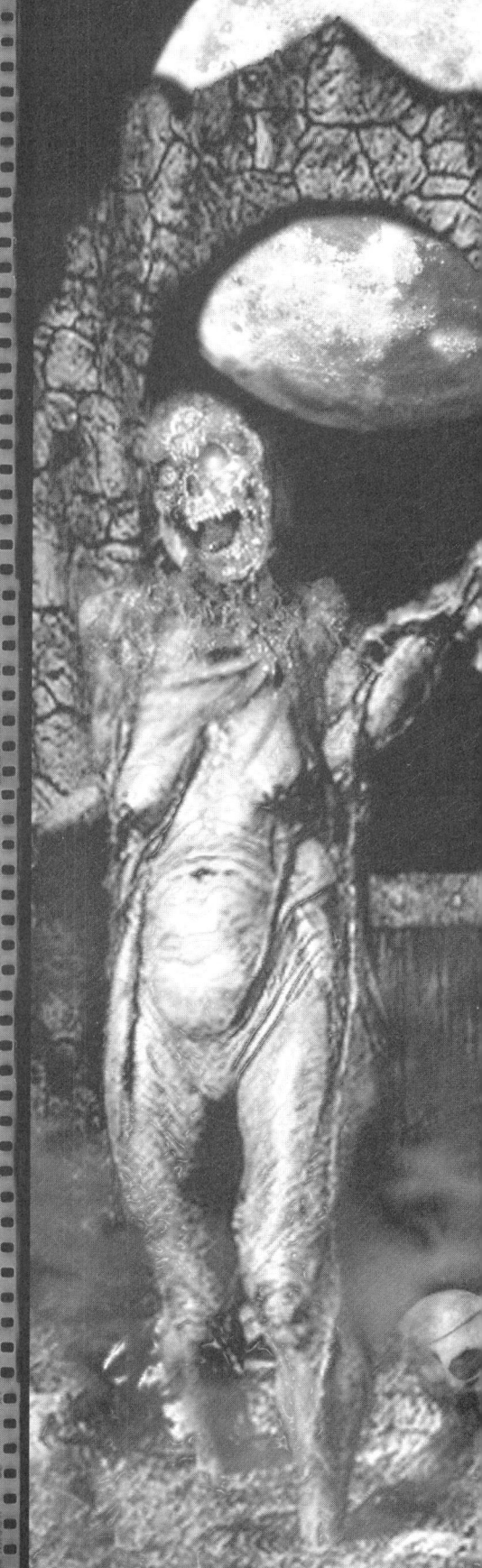

In *Zombies 3*, the germ warfare scientists in the military develop a means to create an army of the dead. These soldiers cannot be killed except by a shot to the head. The problem is that they also spread the germ through biting and scratching. Once the living are infected, they too become zombies. (The zombies in *Zombie 3* are some of the most spastic zombies ever shown on film next to those in *Return of the Living Dead*.)

Return of the Living Dead shows us how a military "screw-up" can put a dangerous germ warfare chemical into the hands of a couple of medical supply warehouse workers and ultimately destroy the world. The difference between all the Zombies/Wampyres depicted previously, and the dead in *Return of the Living Dead* is sheer aggressiveness! *Return* zombies are hell-bent for "BRAINS!" and cannot be killed. Hack off a limb and it will drag itself toward you for "BRAINS!" Thus, the legions of horror moviegoers have intertwined zombies and "BRAINS!" in a match made in Hell.

In sum, zombies in film have evolved from the reanimated slaves of Voodoo priests to Wampyres from ancient Europe, back to zombies raised by science, instead of Voodoo, that eat flesh like Wampyres and are totally out of control. George Romero once said, "I have always thought of the zombie as the 'blue-collar' monster." Zombies are the kind of horror that anyone can someday become! So, no matter how average, weak or insignificant you may have felt while alive, once dead, if you can manage to sit up, even for a moment, you too could strike fear into the hearts of the living!"

Now zombies have moved into the realm of gaming. Computer gaming got its first real taste of zombie horror in *Alone in the Dark*, a terrific, terrifying and revolutionary title. Then the *Resident Evil* series reared its gruesome head on the PlayStation. This is a captivating bit of "survival horror" that combined Special Forces teams, bad acting and brain-eating zombies. Indeed, this might be seen as the beginning of the survival horror game genre.

Now comes *All Flesh Must Be Eaten*, bringing survival horror to roleplaying. So, enough chatter! Read on and get playing. *All Flesh Must Be Eaten* should be something you can really sink your teeth into.

Chapter Summary

Chapter One: The Dead Rise presents these introductory remarks.

Chapter Two: Survivors details character generation. While *All Flesh Must Be Eaten* characters hale from diverse backgrounds and have a variety of strength and weaknesses, all are good at survival. This may be a result of innate toughness, or a guiding hand from above.

Chapter Three: Shambling 101 discusses game mechanics, from basic tests to combat to character development. All *Flesh Must Be Eaten* uses the Unisystem rules, found in other games such as CJ Carella's WitchCraft and Armageddon.

Chapter Four: Implements of Destruction describes a number of items useful for any character trying to survive in a world of zombie horror, from guns to vehicles to survival gear.

Chapter Five: Anatomy of a Zombie runs the gamut of zombie abilities. From locomotion to feeding to vulnerabilities, zombie capacities are described. Zombie Masters can mix and match these specific aspects to create unique zombies to terrorize their players.

Chapter Six: Worlds in Hell provides eleven entirely different campaign worlds. The world description, zombie menace and Story ideas vary widely in zombie lore. This chapter gives a thorough cross section of worlds for Zombie Masters to adopt.

How to Use All Flesh Must Be Eaten

All Flesh is essentially two books in one. Some parts are intended for the players and others are meant for the Zombie Masters.

The first four chapters are filled with material for players. From introductory notes to character creation to rules to equipment, Zombie Masters should allow their players full access to these chapters.

The last two chapters are reserved for Zombie Masters. The description of zombie abilities in Chapter Five is comprehensive enough that players should not be able to guess at any particular combination that a Zombie Master chooses. Nonetheless, it is always more horrifying if the players cannot be sure exactly what a zombie's capacities might be. The same is true for Chapter Six. Part of the thrill of any *All Flesh Must Be Eaten* campaign is discovering how the zombies came about and how to stop them (assuming they can be stopped). This is all detailed in Chapter Six and should be shared with the players only through game play.

The unique feature about *All Flesh Must Be Eaten* is its suitability for either extended play or short story arcs. Some may enjoy *All Flesh Must Be Eaten* like a traditional roleplaying game. The Zombie Master chooses a world background, or creates his own, and the players experience that world over time and build characters into major "players" in that world. Alternatively, the Zombie Master could set up an *All Flesh Must Be Eaten* campaign as a limited series of adventures revolving around the discovery of the cause of the zombies and (possibly) a way to stop them. Once the menace is halted, or the characters have all been eaten, another story arc with new characters and a new backstory may be started.

Conventions

Text Conventions

This book has different graphic features that identify the type of information presented. This text is standard text, and it is used for general explanations.

> Certain text is set off from the standard text in this manner. This is sidebar text and it contains additional, but tangential information, or supplemental charts and tables.

> Other text is set apart in this way. It details Supporting Cast or Adversaries that may be used in Stories at the Zombie Master's discretion.

Dice Notations

D10, D8, D6 and D4 mean a ten-sided die, an eight-sided die, a six-sided die and a four-sided die, respectively. When a number appears before the notation, that number of such dice should be rolled, and their results should be added together. For example, 2D6 means roll two six-sided dice, and generate a result between 2 and 12. Multipliers are expressed after the dice notation. For example, 3D10 x 4 means roll three ten-sided dice, add the results together, and multiply that total result by 4. This generates a number between 12 and 120. A number in parentheses after, or in the middle of, the notation is the average roll. This number is provided for those that want to avoid dice rolling and just get the result. So the notation D6 x 4(12) means that players who want to skip rolling just use the value 12. Some notations cannot provide a set number because their result depends on a variable factor. For example, D8(4) x Strength is used because the Strength value to be plugged into that notation will vary depending on who is acting.

Gender

Every roleplaying game struggles with the decision about third person pronouns and possessives. While the male reference (he, him, his) is customarily used for both male and female, there is no question that it is not entirely inclusive. On the other hand, the "he or she" structure is clumsy and unattractive. In an effort to "split the difference," this book uses male designations for even chapters, and female designations for odd chapters.

Measurements

This book primarily uses U.S. measurements (feet, yards, miles, pounds, etc.). Metric system equivalents appear in parentheses. In the interests of ease of use, the conversions are rounded relatively arbitrarily. For example, miles are multiplied by 1.5 to get kilometers (instead of 1.609), meters are equal to yards (instead of 1.094 yards), pounds are halved to get kilograms (instead of multiplied by 0.4536), and so on. If a Chronicler feels that more precision is necessary, she should take the U.S. measurements provided, and apply more exact formulas.

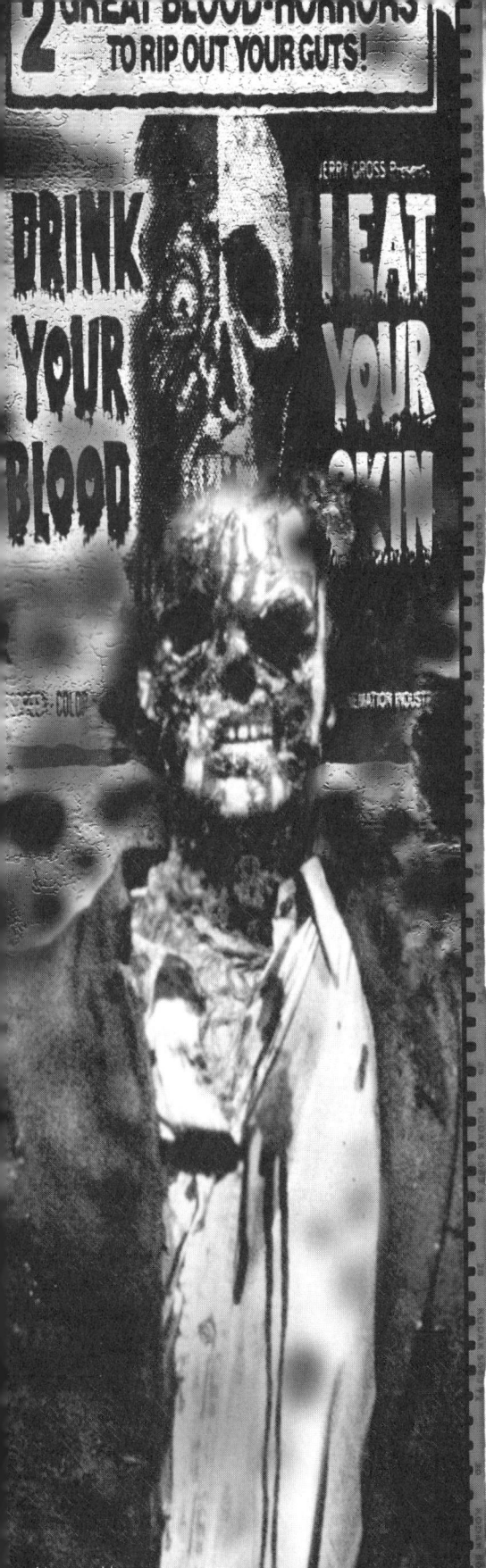

Roleplaying

This book contains a roleplaying game, its setting, and its rules. So what is a roleplaying game? Simply put, it is a combination of board game, strategy game, and improvisational theater. It is a more mature version of the games of "let's pretend" that we all played as children. The rules are meant to avoid the old disputes about exactly what happened ("I shot you! You're dead!" "Am not!"). To enforce the rules and provide a coherent setting, one of the participants assumes the role of Zombie Master (known as Game Master, Chronicler or Referee in other contexts). The rest of the players take the role of one character each, a Cast Member. The player controls the actions of that character, which are limited only by the rules, the character's abilities and limitations, and the player's imagination.

Roleplaying games have been around for more than two decades. They run the gamut from mindless combat scenarios to nearly ruleless, story-driven acting exercises. The Unisystem, the game rules of *All Flesh Must Be Eaten*, concentrates on the following elements. We consider these to be the main characteristics of a good roleplaying game.

Acting: Participants in a roleplaying game are acting out the part of a Cast Member, a fictional character (or, in the case of the Zombie Master, several characters). The character may be as similar or different from the player as desired. Some players prefer to take on the roles of heroic versions of themselves, while others want to "be in the shoes" of completely different people. Many elements of improvisational theater can be found in roleplaying. The player has to come up with the "lines" of her character as the storyline develops.

Storytelling: During a game, the Zombie Master and the players create a story, shaped by the actions of the Cast Members and the conflicts and situations provided by the Zombie Master. A Story is being experienced at the same time it is being written. Because there are a number of authors of this tale, however, the creators do not know exactly how it will end. Each character's actions impact on the result, as do the conflicts and drama injected into the story by the Zombie Master.

Uncertainty: The uncertainty of not knowing the end of the story is enhanced in many games by the use of dice, cards and other randomizing elements. This gives roleplaying an aspect similar to sporting events and games of chance: what will the outcome be? This provides an excitement similar to the feeling that many experience when watching a football game or a boxing match. The skills of the participants play a big role in what the results will be, but the final outcome remains uncertain until it is over. Some gamers prefer to reduce or even eliminate randomness altogether, preferring to let the needs of the story dictate the outcome. The Unisystem is designed to please both those who like the chance element, and those who wish to minimize it, or eliminate it outright.

Imagination and Creativity: Instead of being a passive form of entertainment, like watching television or reading a book, roleplaying exercises the players' imagination and creativity. Each shares the responsibility of producing a good and entertaining experience. Each brings humor, drama and suspense to the game. In roleplaying, the goal is not to win, but simply to have fun and help others have fun.

In sum, by playing a roleplaying game, the Zombie Master and the players weave a Story together. The adventures, triumphs, and tragedies of the characters are part of a larger tapestry. In effect, the gaming group is creating and experiencing a novel or play, experiencing the double thrill of the creative act and the enjoyment of reading a book or watching a movie.

The All Flesh Must Be Eaten RPG

All roleplaying games have at their hearts the "What if . . ?" question. In *All Flesh Must Be Eaten*, the question is "What if you were faced with a world gone to Hell, where ravenous undead sought living prey?" What if you had to fight for survival, sometimes against former friends and loved ones? Would you be curious to find out the cause of the horror? Would you delve into the heart of the zombie-infested areas to discover the truth? Would you brave death to end the threat? What if there were no cause, no solution? Would it be better to simply flee for safety to ensure the survival of the race. By taking on the role of an *All Flesh Must Be Eaten* character, players have the chance to answer these questions and more.

All Flesh Must Be Eaten is a game that combines elements of horror (there are walking dead in this world, and they feed on humans) with survival (characters have to rely on their skills and abilities to live through the night) and conflict (the characters may know the truth; what are they going to do about it?). The remainder of this book explains how to enter the worlds of survival horror and build Stories that challenge, amaze, thrill and delight players and Zombie Masters alike.

Chapter Two
Survivors

"I KNOW what's going on around me, and that's that a **bunch of zombies** have taken over the WORLD."

--Deadworld

Yeah, yeah, I know what those yahoos from the govamen' say, but I'm tellin' you that all zombies ain't dumb. Sure, most of'em are 'cause of the embalmin' fluid an' stuff we put in'em before they go in the ground. Must do somethin' to their brains -- makes'em shamble an' walk all stiff. Thing is tho', if you get one of'em what turned before they had a trip to the mortician . . .

Smart as a rabid fox an' twice as mean, I'll tell you what.

Perfect example, for ya. Back where it all started, back in that little town up north, they had this here undertaker. His name was Crawford or Crayford or somethin' like that. His family had always been the undertakers for the town, ever since his great, great grandfather. Thing is that this latest Crawford was a real piece of work, he went to some high-falutin' business school, an' he was all obsessed with the bottom line. Real piece of work.

So he does a few sleazy deals. He sells cheapass coffins at twice their price or better. He refuses to give anybody credit, an' if your check bounced? Well, lets just say that a few of Argos' poorer citizens woke up to find grandma or grandpa's nude corpse deposited on their front step. Nice huh?

Now when all the zombies started to come out of the ground in Argos, the boys an' me -- we'd already formed up one of'em there military-like gangs -- got deputized an' we were sent in to help the fancy-pants soldiers clean up. 'Course they sent us on all the fucked up missions. We went an' cleared out all the graveyards an' morgues. They went an' guarded all the lib'aries an' girls' schools. One of our missions is to burn down all the morchearies an' funeral homes. Easy enough round there, there was only one. Our good friend Mr. Crawford. Or was it Crayford?

Anyway, we get there an' sure enough, the place is ankle deep in walkin' dead. Now I say ankle deep because all four or six of the zombies we found were crawlin'. By this point, we had engagin'em down to a science. Half of us picked'em off usin' our scopes while the other half watched our backs.

Once they were down we moved in. I noticed somethin' strange, these zombies were carryin' tools, saws an' hammers an' scalpels. Up 'till then, the only thing I'd ever seen one of'em walkin' dead carryin' was its own guts to keep from trippin' on 'em. We knew about the embalmin' fluid makin' em stupid by now but this was not the kind of thing I wanted to see. If the zombies ever figured out how to fire a gun or work a backhoe . . . scarcely bears thinkin' about.

When we entered the funeral home we saw the place was trashed. You could smell gunfire in the air an' one of my compadres, Botnick, found a spent handgun beside an overturned desk. Another zombie came crawlin' in carryin' a fresh lookin' arm in his mouth. He looked like a damn dog bringin' in the paper. Except of course that this little doggie was squirmin' with maggots. We shot it in the head an' then started stompin' on the creepy crawlies as they tried to make their way to safety. I swear to god, when this is over I'm turnin' into a vegetarian.

So, I started to wonder why these zombies don't want to walk or nothin', so I told one of the boys to stop with the maggot polka an' take a look at its legs. Naturally none of 'em wanted to go there, so we made the new boy Botnick do it. He walked up to the dead zombie an' poked it in the leg with the butt of his rifle. Nothin' happened. Botnick prodded a little harder this time, an' still nothin' happened. Then he realized that the shoes had just been nailed onto the bottoms of this zombie's feet.

We were all a little curious, an' we all wanted to see what it would take to make the new boy cry, so we made him get one of the shoes off. After some pissin' an' moanin', he did just that . . . an' you know what he found?

No foot. Just a shoe nailed to the bone. It looked as though this zombie had been taken in a little. There was nothin' below the ankle.

Knowin' that somethin' weird was goin' on, we moved into the back room. We found more maggoty footprints comin' out of the embalmin' room, so we went there first an' cleaned up the last pair of livin' dead we were gonna find. Another one of my boys, Simmons his name was, he used to work in a Coroners office. He gave the place a once over an' tells me that these corpses have been gettin' flushed with plain old water, not embalmin' fluid. He told me that whoever owned this place was cuttin' corners, which is of course another way to say he was screwin' his customers.

Right about 'em we heard someone callin' for help. It took us a moment to figure out where it was comin' from 'cause we had to get Botnick to stop screamin' first. Guess the kid got a little spooked.

We followed the whimperin' into a big ol' storeroom stacked high with coffins. We started searchin' for who it was that was screamin'. But I'll be damned if we could find them. Now about this point I figured out two things. First that the screamer was comin' from inside one of these pine boxes an' second that these coffins were all the same color an' the same size. I mean exactly.

That was when I realized what was goin' on. I already knew from Simmons that this Crawford-Crayford guy was skimpin' on supplies. Just then, I had no doubt in my mind that he was usin' a one-size-fits-all policy with his coffins. It looked like some of his customers had come to state their dissatisfaction.

I thought about those saws an' that severed leg we saw the crawlin' zombies with.

I wondered how tall a man Crawford was. I wondered how much adjustin' the zombies had given him before lockin' him into one of his own cheapass coffins.

And lastly I wondered to myself if searchin' all these coffins an' rescuin' this dickhead would be worth the trouble.

In the end, we decided that we hadn't heard anythin', an' we burned the funeral home to the ground.

Introduction

Characters -- Survivors -- are perhaps the most important building blocks of any story. Without well-defined, compelling characters, the best plot line will fail to attract the reader or viewer's interest. So it is with a roleplaying game. Each player controls a character in the game. In effect, the player is both playing a part and scripting it. Each player makes the decisions for his character, and the Zombie Master and the other players come up with the consequences of those decisions. Through the give and take of this process, a Story is created.

Character creation is one of the parts of roleplaying that works most like writing a short story or a script. The player gets to create a fictional persona, someone he would like to portray in a game. This character can be heroic, cowardly, sensitive or silly. The Cast Member's habits, personality and typical behavior are completely in the player's hands. The character can be a carbon copy of the player, or an utterly different person. There are limitations, however. A character must fit the story, or in this case, the game setting. Rambo would be out of place in a Noel Coward play, and he would look silly and unrealistic in a Tom Clancy novel, for example. The scheming, treacherous and complex Iago could not jump from the pages of Othello into a four-color superhero story -- at least not as a main character (he would make a great villain, though).

This is not to say that all characters need to be heroes, or even the white-hat-wearing "good guys." They can be flawed, selfish or misguided. Generally, however, they should be similar to fictional characters in a story: interesting, fun to observe (and play) and, most importantly, crucial in the shaping of the Story, the final goal of any roleplaying game.

The Zombie Master will influence the character creation process. Ultimately, it is up to the Zombie Master to decide whether or not a given Cast Member is appropriate for a campaign. In some cases, he might decide that a character might not work for the current Story, or might be too powerful (or weak) for the tasks and troubles the Cast is likely to face.

Players should also try to keep in mind that roleplaying is a group activity. Creating a character for the exclusive purpose of dominating the game or hogging the spotlight may be fun for a particular player, but it will ruin everyone else's enjoyment -- and may lead to no games being played by anyone. If the Zombie Master disallows a character idea or conception, he probably has a good reason. Respect his judgment.

All Flesh Must Be Eaten

How to Create a Character

Would-be *All Flesh Must Be Eaten* players should be familiar with the setting of the game. *All Flesh Must Be Eaten* is a game of survival horror, but the specifics of the world will vary as the Zombie Master wishes. Once the Zombie Master has given some indication of the world background, players should think about what type of character, appropriate to that setting, would be desirable to play? Even then, the Zombie Master should be consulted. In some games, the Zombie Master may drastically restrict the choices available to players.

Some players may feel overwhelmed by too many choices. Although the Unisystem allows players to create a character fairly quickly, deciding what kind of character to play can take a while. Sometimes it helps if the Zombie Master takes the time to help each player with the creation of his character, before the first game is scheduled. If all else fails, the Archetypes (the ones in this book as well as those in future supplements) may help.

Archetypes

For those who wish to jump into the game right away, several Archetypes are available at the end of this chapter. These pre-created characters are almost ready to play. Once given a name, they can be played as is. Otherwise, they may be modified to suit the individual player's tastes. Finally, the templates may be used for inspiration to come up with a separate creation. For those ready to create their own personas from scratch, the remainder of the chapter provides the means to do so.

Character Elements

Cast Members in *All Flesh Must Be Eaten* have six basic elements. Some are conceptual (what type of character he is); others are numerical (what value Attributes he has). As the players make each selection, they narrow down the possibilities until they finally have a clearly defined individual, ready to play. The different elements are listed next, and are discussed in turn in the remainder of the chapter.

1. Character Type: This element provides a formula for purchasing all the character's other abilities. It grants a certain number of character points to be spent in several different areas: Attributes, Qualities, Skills and Metaphysics.

2. Attributes: The player must purchase the character's basic capacities, both mental and physical.

3. Qualities/Drawbacks: Although not required, characters are more interesting when they have some special abilities or detriments.

4. Skills: Each character has certain training. This is represented by their skills.

5. Metaphysics: For the Inspired, the precise supernatural powers must be purchased.

6. Possessions: These are the items the character owns at the beginning of the game.

Character Type

The Character Type determines the general combination of physical and/or mystical abilities of a character. In the Unisystem, the Attributes and traits of a character are established by allocating a number of character points. In essence, the player "buys" the levels in Attributes, Qualities and skills he wants. Since the player only has a limited number of points to "buy" things with, he has to make choices. For example, if the player makes a character too strong, he may not have enough points left over to buy a high Intelligence and other Attributes.

The Character Type defines how many points may be spent on each character element. The various components for which points are allocated are Attributes, Qualities (and Drawbacks), Skills and Metaphysics.

Three Character Types are presented in this book. Norms are for use in games that want to emphasize the horror of the survival genre. They are regular folk just trying to survive another day. They are above average, but only slightly. For a more heroic campaign that emphasizes action and taking the fight to the zombies, a Survivor or Inspired is the proper Character Type. Survivors are significantly above average in nearly all areas, but have no supernatural abilities. The Inspired do not have as many or as varied special abilities, but they do have access to supernatural powers.

Norm

"Hey, I'm just a regular person trying to get by for another day in a great, big world that doesn't care a rat's ass about me. Still, I thought I had things pretty well figured out. Then, things really went to hell!"

Norms are regular folk, living regular lives, plugging away day to day. They are slightly above average -- after all, no one wants to play a dweeb, but they shouldn't get cocky. Zombies are nasty creatures and the Norms better act together and plan carefully if they want to survive the night.

In games oriented toward putting a real scare into the players, Norms should be the only Character Type available. More heroic and action oriented settings should use the Survivor and Inspired Types. Check with your Zombie Master for direction here.

Norms begin with 14 points for Attributes, 5 points for Qualities (and up to 10 points in Drawbacks) and 30 points for Skills. Norms may not purchase the Gift or Inspiration Qualities.

Survivors

"I don't know what is going on, and I don't care. There may be a logical explanation for this, but for now I'm going to shoot anything that doesn't look right. It's bad, yeah, but make no mistake, I'll survive this. I'll survive anything!"

Survivors are tougher, smarter and stronger than normal. They have to be -- normal humans are very hard pressed to survive the zombie masses. Survivors are extraordinary individuals (perhaps with a few Attributes near or at the human maximum), whose great physical or mental prowess allows them to live, and even bring the fight to the shambling undead.

In some games, Survivors may be mixed with Norms to add an extra punch, as long as the players don't mind characters with differing power levels. In almost all heroic or action-oriented games, Survivors will be the most common character. Check with your Zombie Master for more information.

Survivors start out with 20 points for Attributes, 15 points for Qualities (and up to 10 points in Drawbacks) and 35 points for Skills. Survivors may not purchase the Gift or Inspiration Qualities.

Inspired

"I know the world's gone to Hell. I know only the smart and tough survive. Clearly, we need to fight to survive. At the same time, we cannot lose our faith. Sometimes, you need more than muscles and guns and cars to survive. As long as I remain strong and continue to believe, I've got just a little edge for those special occasions."

The Inspired are characters with a touch of supernatural power. Most believe that this power comes from Above, though some hear a "calling" from Nature, Spirits or the cosmos. Regardless of its actual source, the Inspired can call upon this power in times of need. Often, it's just what is needed to survive another day in Hell.

The Inspired are generally not as naturally blessed or skilled as Survivors. They make up for this through faith, and the power it provides them. Inspired may not be appropriate for all worlds. The Zombie Master will provide direction on this matter.

The Inspired have 20 points for Attributes, 10 points for Qualities (and up to 10 points in Drawbacks), 25 points for Skills and 15 points for Metaphysics. The Inspired must buy the Gift and Inspiration using Quality or Metaphysics Points.

Chapter Two

Optional Skill Point Generation System

The basic skill point generation system allocates Skill category points depending on the Character Type chosen. This optional method takes into account the character's age, intelligence and social background. This system tends to give characters more Skill points, but is a bit more elaborate and time-consuming. If the players and Zombie Master decide to adopt the optional system, drop the Skill point allocations from all the Character Types discussed previously, and use the following formula.

Character Type: Norms get 25 points. Survivors get 30 points. The Inspired get 20.

Intelligence: 3 points per level of the character's Intelligence Attribute. Characters with 0 Intelligence or less get only one point.

Age: Starting characters are assumed to be 18-30 years old (player's discretion). Younger characters subtract 5 points from their total Skill points. Every 10 years after 30, characters add 5 Skill points but subtract 2 levels from Attributes (these subtractions can be taken from any Attribute).

For example, Jory's character is a 50-year old Survivor with an Intelligence of 5. His base Skill points are 30, and with his high intelligence he gets an additional 15 points. Due to his age, the character has an extra 10 points to put into skills, but he loses 4 Attribute levels. Although he originally had Strength 3, Dexterity 3, Constitution 3, Perception 3, Intelligence 5, and Willpower 3, Jory decides to reduce the character's Strength, Constitution, Perception and Willpower to 2. He now has a total of 55 Skill points.

Social Level or Resources: Characters with a positive Social Level or Resources take the highest level in either of those qualities and add 1 Skill point per level. Characters with Resources of 0 or below do not get a bonus or penalty.

For example, Grygori is a 23-year old Survivor with Intelligence 3 and Resources 1. He gets 30 points for being a Survivor, 9 points for Intelligence, 0 points for age, and 1 point for status, for a total of 40 Skill points.

Unisystem Cast Members

When employing Cast Members across Unisystem games, such as *All Flesh Must Be Eaten*, *WitchCraft* or *Armageddon*, Zombie Masters should consider play balance. Other than Norms, *All Flesh Must Be Eaten* Cast Members are based on a 70-point total. In *WitchCraft*, the most common Cast Members are built with 80 character points in total. In *Armageddon*, that total can be much higher.

Attributes

Attributes are inborn characteristics of a character: his physical strength, intelligence, senses and so on. By selecting a set of Attributes, players define the limits of what the character can do. For example, if a player "buys" a very low Dexterity for his character, he should not be surprised if the character routinely fails to do anything that requires grace and manual coordination. As Attributes are bought, the player can start getting a sense of what the character is like. Is he strong but dumb, quick but weak, sharp and perceptive but weak-willed?

When determining a character's Attributes (and in general, when creating the character), it is suggested that players use a pencil to write the numbers down. This enables players to make changes as they continue through the character creation process.

Two kinds of Attributes are used in *All Flesh Must Be Eaten*: Primary Attributes and Secondary Attributes. The basic difference is that Primary Attributes are purchased using Attribute and other character points. Secondary Attributes are calculated from a character's Primary Attributes.

Buying Attributes

During character creation, Cast Members get an number of points to distribute to their Primary Attributes based on the Character Type chosen (see earlier in this chapter). Attributes can be "bought" at up to a level 5 on a one-to-one basis (i.e., a Strength of 3 would cost 3 points, a Strength of 4 would cost a total of 4 points, and so on). Attributes after level 5 are much more expensive: 3 points per additional level. Cast Members cannot raise an Attribute past level 6, the absolute maximum for humans (buying an attribute up to level 6 would cost 8 points).

The six Attributes that may be purchased using character points are Strength, Dexterity, Constitution, Intelligence, Perception and Willpower. Each Primary Attribute is described in turn.

Strength

A measure of the physical power of the character, Strength determines how much damage the character inflicts with hand-to-hand weapons, how much weight he can carry, and how powerful he is. It also helps determine how much damage and exertion the character can withstand before collapsing.

Strength is useful to people who do a lot of heavy lifting or anybody likely to enter close combat. Characters apt to have a high Strength include athletes, manual workers, and soldiers. A low Strength indicates either small size and body weight, or just a lack of exercise.

A character may high jump (Strength x 10) inches (x 2.5 cm) and broad jump (Strength) yards (meters). Double these numbers with a good running start.

A chart detailing how much a character of any given Strength can lift is located nearby. This is the weight someone of that Strength can lift without much effort. Higher weights can be lifted with some effort (assume a maximum lifting weight -- for brief periods -- equal to double the Lifting Capacity).

A character can "push the limits" and try to lift more by passing a Simple Strength Test. Every Success Level achieved allows the character to lift an additional 10% of his maximum lifting weight. This effort costs the character D4(2) points of Endurance for every Success Level in the Test. A failure on the Strength Test causes D4(2) Life Points of damage -- the character strained himself and tore something up . . .

Strength Table

Strength	Lifting Capacity
1-5	50 lbs/25 kg x Strength (Strength 5: 250 lbs/125 kg)
6-10	200 lbs/100 kg (Strength - 5) + 250 lbs/125 kg
11-15	500 lbs/250 kg x (Strength - 10) + 1,250 lbs/625 kg
16-20	1,000 lbs/500 kg x (Strength - 15) + 5,000 lbs/2,500 kg

Reduce the maximum weight by one tenth when throwing something.

Dexterity

Dexterity is a measure of the character's coordination, agility, and gracefulness. It is used to determine how proficient a character is with any Task that requires motor control and precision. This ranges from performing card tricks to picking pockets to punching somebody in the face (Dexterity helps the punch land; Strength determines how much the punch hurt the other guy). Any Task where the character's speed and coordination matter is influenced by Dexterity. A high Dexterity is common among dancers, gymnasts, or pickpockets. People with low Dexterity are clumsy and ungraceful.

Constitution

This Attribute determines how physically hardy or healthy the character is. Constitution is important when it comes to resisting diseases, damage, and fatigue. This Attribute is used (along with Strength) to determine how much physical injury the character can survive and still remain functional. Constitution also comes into play with physical skills that involve endurance, like swimming, long-distance running and the like.

Intelligence

This Attribute determines the character's ability to learn, correlate and memorize information. The higher a character's Intelligence, the easier it is to improve scholastic skills. Also, this Attribute is used to understand and interpret information. Note that Intelligence and education are two separate things. A person can be brilliant but illiterate. Education is covered in the Skills section, which determines what a character has learned in his life.

Perception

Perception governs the five senses of the character. It gives a general overview of the sharpness of the character's ability to sense things. This Attribute is used to find clues, notice things, and avoid getting surprised. Also, Perception determines the character's intuition and alertness. A character with a low Perception would be nearly oblivious to what is going on around him.

Willpower

This Attribute measures the mental strength and self-control of the character, and his ability to resist fear, intimidation, and temptation. Willpower is important for some of the Inspired's Miracles. It is also important for Norms and Survivors, for it can be used to resist magical coercion, psychic mind control, and the influence of panic, among other things.

The Meaning of Numbers

When creating a character, the player assigns a value to each of the six Primary Attributes, typically ranging from 1 to 5, with the human maximum being a 6. This is done, as stated before, by "buying" an Attribute value with the available character points. This value represents the limits of the character with that Attribute. The higher the Attribute value, the more accomplished the character is in that area. The following paragraphs express some guidelines for Attribute levels 1 to 5.

Level 1: The character is below average in that Attribute. A Strength of 1 indicates a poor physique, either a petite or flabby, sedentary person. A Dexterity of 1 indicates clumsiness, a character who is likely to drop things, not to be trusted with delicate manual work unless the person has trained very hard to do so. An Intelligence of 1 is below average -- not mentally challenged, but certainly a bit slow on the uptake. A Perception of 1 is the trait of a character who is not very aware of his surroundings, and likely to miss what's going on around him. Characters with a Constitution of 1 are delicate and often in poor health: they are the ones who get sick first, and their low physiques may be caused by abuse of drugs, tobacco or alcohol. A Willpower of 1 depicts a person who is easily influenced by others, a follower, and somebody who is likely to succumb to temptation.

Level 2: This is the average for human beings. Most people in any given group have Attributes in this range, typically with one or two Attributes at levels 1 or 3.

Level 3: This is above average but not extraordinary. A Strength and Constitution of 3 show some athletic aptitude, probably belonging to somebody

> ### Very Low or Very High Attributes
>
> Most humans have Attributes in the 1-5 range. A 0 level represents very low Attributes, and a -1 indicates subhuman levels for humans above the age of five. A 6 in an Attribute is the peak of human achievement; even a medium-sized city rarely has more than a handful of people with such high Attributes.
>
> Note that these limits apply only to humans. It would be dumb to expect that a horse or an elephant would have the same Attribute limitations as human beings. Most large creatures have a Strength of 7-12 (including horses, bears, and apes). Massive creatures, like whales or elephants, have Strengths of 15-20 or higher. By the same token, graceful animals like cats, birds of prey and the like have an average Dexterity of 4-7. Constitution is one of the few Attributes that does not exceed human levels very much. Some large animals like elephants are somewhat delicate. They have more Life Points than humans, but shock and disease are just as likely to bring them down.
>
> Supernatural beings like zombies are beyond human limits. Some of these creatures have superhuman physical Attributes, and long-lived entities may have extraordinary mental ones as well. Only the power of faith, or the strength of numbers and weaponry, give humans any chance of standing up to such beings.

who works out regularly and vigorously, or a natural athlete who has not taken time to develop his talent. Characters with a Dexterity of 3 are graceful individuals. Intelligence 3 indicates a bright person who can easily learn new skills, if he has the temperament to do so. With a Perception of 3, the character has good senses and intuition, and is not easily fooled or confused. A character with a Willpower of 3 is rarely convinced or bullied under normal circumstances.

Level 4: An Attribute at level 4 is well above average. Very few people -- perhaps one out of every ten in a random group -- have an Attribute at this level. Strength and Constitution 4 can be found only in athletes, including the best football players in a large high school, or college campus, extensively trained Special Forces soldiers, and other people who spend a large amount of time and effort keeping in shape. A Dexterity of 4 would only be common among gymnasts, acrobats, dancers and other talented individuals. Mental Attributes at level 4 indicate near genius (Intelligence), very acute senses and intuition (Perception), or an "iron will" (Willpower).

Level 5: This is the "practical" human limit. While people with Attributes at level 5 are not "record breakers," they are among the best and the brightest representatives of humanity. In a small or medium-sized community, only a handful of people will have one or two Attributes at this level, and they are likely to be well-known for their strength, wisdom or toughness. Cities, large college campuses, and groupings of Survivors have more of these extraordinary individuals, but even there they will not be common.

Secondary Attributes

Once the six Primary Attributes are determined, some quick calculations are used to figure out the Secondary Attributes. Secondary Attributes are not bought; they are determined by plugging the Primary Attributes into the formulas given below.

With the exception of Speed, which basically determines how fast a character can run at an all-out dash, the other Secondary Attributes determine a pool of points. Certain factors (injury, fatigue, fear or the use of magic) temporarily increase or decrease the amount of points in each pool. For example, Life Points determine a character's current health. If an injury is sustained, the health (the Life Points) of the character is lowered; healing the damage will eventually raise the pool back to its original level. The more severe the damage, the more points are removed from the Life Points pool.

The Secondary Attributes are Life Points, Endurance Points, Speed and the Essence Pool.

Life Points

This Attribute determines the physical health of the character. The Strength and Constitution of the character are the determining factors. A big, muscle-bound athlete can survive more punishment than a pencil-necked, cold-catching nerd. On the other hand, a bullet to the head or a solid whack with an ax will probably kill either character with the same ease. Life Points indicate the amount of physical damage the character can take before being unable to function. Other things that drain Life Points include disease, extreme fatigue, and some supernatural attacks.

Formula: Add Constitution and Strength together, multiply by four, and add 10 to the result. The formula is best written as ((Constitution + Strength) x 4) + 10. The human range is 18 to 58.

Determining Secondary Attributes with Low Primary Attributes

Some characters have Attributes of 0 or even in the negative numbers. These levels represent Attributes that are far below average. Special rules for determining Secondary Attributes are required in this case. When dealing with low Primary Attributes, treat them as being equal to 1 for determination purposes. If the Attribute is negative, then subtract it from the resulting Secondary Attribute.

For example, Dell is a frail and sickly boy with a Strength of -1 and a Constitution of 0. To determine Dell's Life Points, treat the -1 and 0 as "1s", resulting in a base of 18 Life Points (2 x 4 plus the base 10). Then reduce this to 17 Life Points -- the negative value is subtracted from the total.

The special rule for treating 0s and negative numbers in Secondary Attributes only applies to those that involve multiplication (Life Points, Endurance Points and Speed). Essence is calculated as normal.

Endurance Points

Endurance Points measure the character's ability to withstand fatigue and exertion before collapsing. Like Life Points, Endurance Points use Constitution and Strength, but they also use Willpower, taking into account that some people can push themselves past normal physical limits through the sheer force of will. The more Endurance Points a character has, the longer he can run, lift things, swim, etc. As the character exerts himself, he starts losing Endurance Points. When Endurance Points are reduced to 0, the character sooner or later passes out from exhaustion (see Endurance Point Loss, p. 114). In some cases, light damage from non-lethal attacks is subtracted from Endurance Points instead of Life Points.

Formula: Add Constitution, Strength and Willpower together, multiply by three, and add 5 to the result. The formula is best written as ((Constitution + Strength + Willpower) x 3) + 5. The human range is 14 to 59.

Speed

This Attribute represents how fast a person can run at maximum speed. It only comes into play on the few occasions when running speed will be a consideration, such as when a character is chasing or being chased by somebody.

Formula: (Constitution + Dexterity) x 2 is the speed in miles per hour (for kilometers per hour change the multiplier to 3). The human range is 4 to 24 mph (6 to 36 kph). Half that amount is the number of yards (meters) that the character runs in a second.

Essence Pools

Essence is the amount of spiritual energy the character has within himself. It measures, basically, the strength of the character's soul and life force. Essence is also the binding force of reality. This means that inside each human being are the building blocks of Creation. Inspired Miracles can channel Essence for a variety of powerful effects.

Although Essence is used primarily in the performance of Miracles, it can also be temporarily drained by strong emotions (like fear and hatred), and by the attacks of some supernatural creatures. Totally draining a human being of Essence can lead to his death.

Formula: Add the character's Primary Attributes together. The Inspired often have extra Essence, due to their greater control over the flows of primal energy. This extra Essence is purchased during character creation (see the Increased Essence Pool Quality, p. 48).

Qualities and Drawbacks

Qualities are innate characteristics that give the character an advantage or positive trait. Drawbacks are characteristics that somehow limit or detract from the character. Both Qualities and Drawbacks serve to round out the character, and can be helpful both to roleplay and to "succeed" in the course of a game.

Qualities are desirable traits, and therefore they "cost" character points. Drawbacks, on the other hand, are limiting factors, and as a "reward" for acquiring them, the character gains extra points. Points acquired from Drawbacks can be used in any point category -- Attributes, Qualities, Skills and Metaphysics.

For point categories other than Attributes, Drawback points may be added on a one-for-one basis. Purchasing Attribute points using Drawbacks is much more expensive. The cost to raise an Attribute one level is equal to the value of that level. For example, raising an Attribute from 3 to 4 costs 4 Drawback points, from level 4 to 5 costs 5 Drawback points, and so on. Further, the costs are cumulative. Raising one Attribute from 3 to 5 costs 9 Drawback points.

Categories

Qualities and Drawbacks are labeled by category. For the most part, these categories are descriptive and do not affect play. In certain instances, however, the category does matter. The major example is Supernatural Qualities; generally only the Inspired can have Supernatural Qualities. Some Supernatural Drawbacks can be inflicted on Norms or Survivors, at the Zombie Master's discretion. The following categories are used: Mental, Physical, Social and Supernatural. While the majority of the Qualities and Drawbacks are alphabetized by name, the Supernatural category has been separated from the rest and included at the end. Charts in the Appendix organize the Qualities and Drawbacks by category for easy reference during character generation.

Numerical Qualities/Drawbacks

Some Qualities and Drawbacks are expressed in numerical ways: the most common examples include Attractiveness, Charisma and Resources. These are similar to Attributes, since these Qualities and Drawbacks change the character in positive or negative ways. As a result, they are represented as bonuses or penalties. For example, a Charisma Quality of +2 represents a bonus of 2 levels on any Task or Test that involves influencing or manipulating people through social skills, while a Resources Drawback of -2 indicates very low income and few possessions, well below the national average.

Bringing a trait below the average gives the character extra points to put into other character elements. These traits have an average value of 0; so if a player does not want to deal with any numerical Quality, simply assume that is has a base value of 0.

Qualities and Drawbacks During Play

Some Qualities and Drawbacks may be acquired or lost during the course of a game. In some cases, a Quality or Drawback might change. For example, a scarring wound could reduce the character's Attractiveness, or a change in fortune might increase or reduce the character's Resources or Status Level. When such a change occurs, no experience points are needed to purchase them. If the player wants to purposefully change a Quality or Drawback, he must spend experience points and come up with a good reason for the change (see Experience, 118).

Creating New Qualities/Drawbacks

The list below is far from exhaustive, although it covers most of the basics. In many cases, a "new" Quality or Drawback can be an extension or variation of an existing one. The value of the characteristic should be balanced out by the benefits or penalties it grants the character. Most Qualities or Drawbacks should be worth between 1 and 3 points; only the most powerful or crippling of them should have a value of 4 or higher.

List of Qualities and Drawbacks

The following Qualities and Drawbacks may be taken by any *All Flesh Must Be Eaten* character, as long as the Zombie Master approves.

Acute/Impaired Senses
2-point Physical Quality or Drawback

This Quality/Drawback must be purchased separately for each sense: sight, hearing, touch, smell or taste. Normally, the five senses are represented by the Perception Attribute. Acute or Impaired senses indicate one or more senses that are higher or lower than normal for a person with that Perception Attribute.

When bought as a Quality, an Acute Sense gives the character a +3 bonus to any Perception-related Test or Task that relies on that sense. If acquired as a Drawback, an Impaired Sense gives a similar -3 penalty to Perception-based Tests or Tasks.

Some Impaired Senses (hearing and sight in particular) can be easily corrected in the modern age through the use of glasses, hearing aids and similar devices. If the impairment is eliminated by the use of such devices, the Zombie Master should reduce the value of the Drawback to 1 point. It is possible to have more than one type of Acute or Impaired Sense, or, for example, to have Acute Hearing and Impaired Eyesight, or a similar combination of senses. For obvious reasons, a character cannot select both the Impaired and Acute versions of the same sense.

Addiction
Variable Mental Drawback

An addict craves a substance and must have it, even against his better judgement. Most addictive substances eventually impact on his health. Many of them are also illegal, and using or purchasing them may land the character in jail should he be discovered. Those concerns matter little to the addict, however; when the craving hits, he can rarely resist it. He often does things he would normally never consider in order to satisfy his need, from cheating and stealing to committing serious crimes to selling his body or even betraying his friends.

When an addicted character hasn't gotten his usual "fix," he suffers from debilitating withdrawal symptoms. Most mental actions (e.g., any Tasks or Tests using Intelligence, Perception or Willpower) are at a penalty equal to the value of the Drawback (so, a character with a 2-point Addiction suffers a -2 penalty to most mental actions) until the addict can get what he needs. The most severe drugs (like heroin) also produce strong physical effects; such addicts have a penalty of -3 to all physical actions in addition to the above penalty on mental actions.

The value of this Drawback is determined by the severity of the addiction and the relative effects of the drug or substance. A detailed description of the effects of different addictive substances would fill an entire book or more. Chroniclers should adjudicate the game effects of a "high" on a character. This can range from a small action penalty for being slightly "buzzed," to the complete stupor of a heroin trip. In the game, as in real life, drugs are dangerous and unpredictable, and an addict character is often unable to control himself.

The Addiction Point Value Table gives guidelines for the value of a given type of addiction. Zombie Masters should modify these values as desired.

Addiction Point Value Table

Habitual drinking or smoking: 1 point.

Heavy drinking or smoking, light use of marijuana or LSD: 2 points

Heavy use of marijuana or LSD: 3 points

Alcoholism, habitual use of barbiturates or cocaine: 4 points

Habitual use of heroin, heavy use of barbiturates or cocaine: 5 points

Heavy use of heroin: 6 points

Unlike most Drawbacks, this problem cannot be easily overcome. Generally, the best a character can hope to do is to deny his craving "one day at a time." Getting rid of this Drawback should never be a matter of saving up enough points to "buy it off." Resisting the craving requires a series of daily Willpower Tests. For each Willpower Test up to the level of the character's Willpower, these Tests are Simple. For each one after that, the Tests are Difficult. All Tests suffer a penalty equal to the point value of the Drawback, plus an additional -1 to -4 depending on the strength of the drug and its availability (tobacco is so available and addictive that Willpower Tests are at a minimum penalty of -4 or even higher). Once the character accumulates 10 Success Levels in succession from successful Willpower Tests, one character point may be spent to reduce the strength of the addiction by one point. Another 10 Success Levels in succession are needed for the next point, and so on, until the Drawback is eliminated. If any Test is failed during the course of accumulating the 10 Success Levels, all Success Levels are lost, and the accumulation process must begin again.

For example, Joshua has a level 3 Willpower, and a 2-point Addiction to marijuana. He starts to kick the habit, and begins making daily, Simple Willpower Tests. These Tests have a -2 penalty for the level of the Addiction, and a further -1 for the drugs availability and potency (Zombie Master's judgment). For three days, Joshua rolls a 6, 8 and 15 (see the Rule of 10, p. 93). Adding his Willpower doubled (6), and subtracting his penalties (-3), the results are 9 (one Success Level), 11 (two Success Levels) and 18 (five Success Levels). This amounts to eight Success Levels. Joshua only needs two more Success Levels to bring the Addiction down to a 1-point Drawback. Unfortunately for Joshua, however, the going gets tougher, and Difficult Willpower Tests are now required. The next day, Joshua rolls a 4. Adding his Willpower (2 -- no doubling) and subtracting his penalties (still -3), the result is 3. This failure sends Joshua in desperate search of a "fix." If he decides to try and kick the habit again, a new series of Willpower Tests must be begun with no Success Levels accumulated.

This struggle should be a major part of the character's roleplaying. A convincing depiction of the torments of the addict may be rewarded with bonuses to the Willpower Tests.

Adversary
Variable Social Drawback

At some time in the past, the character has made an enemy, or he belongs to a group, race or nation that automatically attracts the enmity of others. An Adversary is more than somebody who dislikes the character, however. He, she or they wish nothing less than the destruction of the target, either by killing or ruining him.

The more powerful the Adversary, the higher the value of this Drawback. Chroniclers should determine if an Adversary is appropriate to the game in question. If the Adversary is unlikely to appear frequently, the Chronicler can reduce the point value or disallow it altogether. Individuals are worth 1 to 3 points as Adversaries, depending on their resources and abilities. A normal person would be worth 1 point; a Green Beret or a multimillionaire would be worth 3 points. An organization may be worth 2 to 5 points, depending on its power. A gang of thugs would be worth 2 points, the police department of a city would be worth 3 to 4 points (depending on its size and competence), and a large national agency like the CIA would be worth 5 points or more.

The player should have a good reason why his character has earned the enmity of the Adversary. The Zombie Master can then weave this enemy into the plot of the Story in any way he sees fit.

Artistic Talent
3-point Mental Quality

Some people have a natural gift for producing astounding works of art, even if they lack formal training. Geniuses like Mozart and Picasso had the ability to create true art seemingly without effort. A character with this Quality has the talent to become a famous artist. Artistic Talent affects only one form of artistic expression, such as Painting/Drawing, Sculpture, Singing, etc. It is possible to buy this Quality multiple times; each additional purchase grants the bonuses to an additional type of Fine Arts. Further, Essence bonuses (see below) are cumulative.

Whenever a work of art is created, the character receives a +3 bonus to all related Task attempts. Additionally, even if the Task is failed, a minimum of one Success Level is always acquired -- even a failure by the truly talented still has artistic merit.

In most *All Flesh Must Be Eaten* settings, true artists have very strong souls. A character with Artistic Talent adds 12 Essence Points to his pool, to represent the power of his spirit. In some worlds, this also makes artists more likely to be targeted by entities that feed on Essence, which may explain the often tortured existences of true artists.

Attractiveness
Variable Physical Quality or Drawback

This Quality or Drawback determines the character's looks (or lack thereof). The average person has an Attractiveness of 0, which means the person looks plain and undistinguished unless he takes steps to enhance his appearance (clothing, makeup and poise always make a difference). Positive values in Attractiveness indicate pleasing features, while negative values indicate ugliness, scars, or unpleasant characteristics. The character's Attractiveness value can be added to or subtracted from any Test or Task that involves making an impression on other people. In some cases, negative Attractiveness values can be useful. When trying to intimidate or scare people, positive Attractiveness values have no effect, but negative ones count as bonuses! For example, a character with an Attractiveness of -3 would add +3 to any Task where intimidating people is a factor.

Note that the physical Attributes of a character determine exactly how his Attractiveness is expressed. For example, a character with Strength and Constitution of 3 or 4 and a Attractiveness of 4 appears extremely athletic, likely tanned from outdoor exercise, with a well-muscled body. A character with a Constitution of 1 with the same Attractiveness rating is probably a delicate-looking, pale person with almost doll-like features.

Purchasing Attractiveness costs 1 point per level if bought as a Quality, or adds 1 extra character point if acquired as a Drawback. After character creation, Attractiveness can change only by events that modify the character's entire appearance, either through scarring or plastic surgery.

Attractiveness can range from -5 to +5 in humans. A +1 or +2 make the person stand out in a crowd and attract attention unless the character somehow hides his features. At +3 or +4, the character can easily make a living through looks alone, as a model or entertainer. At +5, the character would be as comely as the top models, beauty pageant contestants and movie stars in the world. On the other hand, at -1 or -2, the person has homely features, or unsightly blemishes or scars. At -3 or -4, the character's features are downright repulsive. At -5, people will be taken aback by the character's appearance; looking at him will be a source of discomfort. Beings with inhuman features can have levels as low as -10.

Charisma
Variable Mental Quality or Drawback

This trait represents the personal magnetism and leadership qualities of the person, ranging from -5 to +5. A character with a Charisma in the negative range is instinctively disliked by most people he meets. People are naturally inclined to antagonize or avoid him. Charisma can be added to any Task where the character is trying to influence other people. Negative Charisma, of course, reduces the chance that any attempt to influence people will work.

Clown
1-point Mental Drawback

The Clown refuses to take things seriously, and is always coming up with jokes and wisecracks, even during the most inappropriate moments. Perhaps the character is deeply insecure and tries to gain other people's acceptance through humor, or he simply delights in keeping people off-balance with his comments. The biggest problem these characters have is that they cannot keep their mouths shut even when they know a joke will only work against them.

Clowns are generally accepted and liked during situations where their quirky humor is not out of place (parties and other social gatherings, or among friends). Their sense of humor gets them in trouble during tense and dangerous situations. Another problem the Clown faces is that people often do not take him seriously even when they should.

Contacts
Variable Social Quality

The character has friends or allies who can provide him with information, warnings and even help, should he require it. The more helpful the contact is, the higher the Quality's point value. For any and all Contacts, the Zombie Master determines whether or not the Contact is available at any given time. Generally, the more time the character has to reach or get word to his Contact, the more likely the Contact is to come through.

A Contact that only provides rumors and hearsay is worth 1 point. If the Contact usually provides reliable information and will help the character out in small ways (offering a ride, letting the character spend the night at the Contact's apartment), this Quality is worth 2 points. Actual allies who will help the character in any way they can are worth 3 to 5 points, depending on the Contact's resources.

Covetous
1- to 3-point Mental Drawback

A Covetous character wants certain things and is prepared to go to great lengths to acquire them. He may be motivated by love of money, lust for sensual satisfaction, hunger for power, or the search for glory. Whatever he desires, be it fame, fortune or influence, he will do almost anything to get it, limited only by any sense of caution or morality he may have -- and in some cases, not even by that. A Covetous character usually refrains from breaking his own moral code or the laws of the land in the pursuit of his goals, but if a golden opportunity presents itself, the temptation may be just too great.

There are four types of covetousness, based on what the character wants: Greedy (money and wealth), Lecherous (sexually attractive people), Ambitious (power and influence), and Conspicuous (fame and renown). It is possible to covet two or more of those things, but each additional source of desire adds but a single point to the value of this Drawback.

The Covetous Drawback has three levels of severity, worth 1, 2 and 3 points respectively.

Level 1: The first level is relatively mild. The character knows what he wants, and he spends a great deal of time and effort to attain his goals, but he won't break his own rules or those of society to do so. His desire otherwise dominates his life, however. Most of his actions should be directed towards achieving his objective, directly or indirectly.

Level 2: The second level is stronger -- presented with enough temptation, the character may act even if it goes against his better judgement or morality. He may resist if the action he contemplates is truly wrong and reprehensible -- stealing credit for a heroic deed performed by a friend, for example -- but resisting requires a Simple Willpower Test, at a penalty of -1 to -3 if the temptation and possible rewards are great.

Level 3: The third level is the strongest -- a desire so strong that it often overwhelms any scruples the character may have. When presented with temptation, he can only avoid acting by passing a Difficult Willpower Test, with penalties ranging from -1 to -5 depending on the size of the "prize." For a high enough reward, the character will turn on friends or loved ones, and even betray his cause or principles.

Cowardly
1- to 3-point Mental Drawback

A Cowardly character is easily scared and intimidated. Furthermore, he is very reluctant to take any risks; putting his neck on the line always strikes him as incredibly foolhardy. Note that this does not mean that a Cowardly character will not fight if necessary. Such a character usually tries to stack the odds in his favor, however, before resorting to violence. He would have no compunction (except as determined by other Drawbacks) against attacking others if circumstances minimized the danger. A coward can hide his Drawback from others very easily, as long as he is not involved in a situation that is clearly dangerous. Only then may his limitations become apparent.

This Drawback has three levels of intensity, worth 1, 2 and 3 points respectively. The level of the Drawback acts as a modifier to any Willpower Test or Task to resist fear, intimidation or bullying. For example, a character with a 2-point Cowardly Drawback incurs a -2 penalty to any Fear Test (see Getting Scared, p. 96).

Level 1: At the first level, the character avoids taking unnecessary risks, but fights when cornered (or when he thinks he has the upper hand). Simple Willpower Tests are necessary to avoid fleeing or surrendering when confronted by what the character considers to be superior foes. The same goes for taking even small chances, like confronting the boss, asking for a raise, complaining about some problem, or the like.

Level 2: The second level of this drawback is stronger. The character needs to pass a Simple Willpower Test to fight back even when he thinks the odds are in his favor, and needs to pass a Difficult Willpower Test to avoid fleeing dangerous situations, or taking chances.

Level 3: The last level is the worst, requiring Difficult Willpower Tests to get involved in confrontations or risky situations even when the character has a good chance of succeeding. Truly dangerous or heroic acts are simply impossible; the character never knowingly or willingly endangers himself, and may actually even betray his friends if he thinks he will save himself in the process.

Cruel
1- or 3-point Mental Drawback

Cruel people enjoy making other people suffer. The truly evil derive satisfaction from anybody's pain. Some people are perfectly normal and nice most of the time, but when angered or given offense, make their enemies pay -- and love doing it.

This Drawback has two levels or degrees of intensity. The second level is best restricted to villains, as it indicates a serious mental problem that may make most characters unsuitable for the typical campaign. As always, the Zombie Master has the final say.

Level 1: This character would never hurt a friend or a loved one. Enemies, especially those who have really angered him, are a different matter. He enjoys inflicting pain (mental or physical) on those he feels "deserve what they get." Characters with this level of cruelty are capable of committing atrocities under the right circumstances, but will not go out of their way to find opportunities. This is a 1-point Drawback.

Level 2: This person is a true sadist, and never passes up the chance to inflict pain on others. Even friends and loved ones are not safe from him. When it comes to enemies or those who get in his way, he enjoys nothing so much as their utter destruction or humiliation. When no enemies are available, he uses his "talents" on those around her. This is a 3-point Drawback; people with this Drawback will rarely keep any friendships, and will quickly gain enemies.

Delusions
Variable Mental Drawback

Delusions are beliefs that have no basis in reality. The character refuses to abandon such beliefs even in the face of overwhelming evidence to the contrary, or at best comes up with rationalizations to explain away any contradictions. Some examples are given below.

Prejudice: The belief that a group of people (racial, ethnic or national) has certain characteristics (positive or negative). While everyone has some prejudices in some way or another, a delusional person staunchly holds to these beliefs. In some cases, the person refuses to trust or befriend any member of such a group, regardless of the merits of the individual person. Such a Delusion is worth 1 to 3 points, depending on how intense the belief is, how large a group it applies to, and how it dominates the character's life. At the 1-point level, the character could be an "Archie Bunker"-type bigot; at 3 points, he would be a rabid white supremacist.

Delusions of Grandeur: This person thinks he is somebody far greater and more powerful than she really is. In extreme cases, the character thinks that he is a historical or mythological figure like Napoleon or Sherlock Holmes. The more common type has an exaggerated sense of overconfidence: "I am a genius, but nobody understands me -- which is why the best job I've held is cashier at a 7-11" (1 point); "I am the Messiah; prepare for the Second Coming!" (3 points).

Phobia: A Phobia (however defined) counts as a Delusion, worth -1 to -3 points depending on the severity. So, claustrophobia would be worth -1 if the character is uncomfortable in enclosed spaces and -3 if the character is unable to enter an elevator without suffering an anxiety attack.

Weird Delusions: Any strange belief that flies in the face of reality. Some examples: "Aliens talk to me through my wristwatch," "I have to wear this tin foil cap so the laser satellites don't make me kill again," "Dogs are the Spawn of Satan, and must be destroyed." The value depends more on what the character does about the Delusion than about the Delusion itself. For example, if the character in the last example simply refuses to pet dogs, and avoids being next to a dog, a 1-point Delusion would be sufficient. If he tells people about his beliefs all the time, and keeps pestering any dog-owning friends and neighbors about the dangers of keeping such monsters around, a 2-point Delusion would be appropriate. If he carries his insanity to its "logical" conclusion and starts hurting or killing dogs, the Delusion is worth 3 points and he is likely to get in trouble with the law (assuming any law men are left alive).

Emotional Problems
Variable Mental Drawback

Those with Emotional Problems react in unreasonable ways to some situations and problems. The reaction can be anger, pain or anguish, typically more extreme than normal. Maybe a traumatic event in this life (or even in a previous life) has made them this way. These emotional problems can be triggered by distressful but relatively ordinary events in normal life; they prompt a very strong reaction from a disturbed character. Some situations that can trigger emotional problems are discussed below.

Fear of Rejection: This person is afraid of rejection, and when he experiences rejection (or thinks he has been rejected), he feels hurt and angry. People with this problem may be afraid to make friends or approach people they are attracted to, and if their fears come true, will harbor a great deal or resentment and anger. This is a 1-point Drawback.

Depression: This character's emotional problems make the very act of living seem like a hard chore. Common symptoms of Depression include sleep problems (either oversleeping or bouts of insomnia), severe procrastination (to the point that the sufferer may lose his job), and a lack of interest in anything. A character with Depression is at -2 to most Tasks, and tends to avoid becoming involved in anything. This is a 2-point Drawback. A severe shock may snap someone out of this state for a while (a life-threatening crisis will do it), but the character will sink back into inactivity afterwards. Certain drugs and psychiatric treatment can reduce the effect of this problem (which will also reduce its value).

Emotional Dependency: These types tend to be "clingy" and overly dependent on others. Once they make a friend, they want to hang around him all the time. When involved in a relationship, they are excessively needy. This behavior tends to annoy people around them. This is a 1-point Drawback.

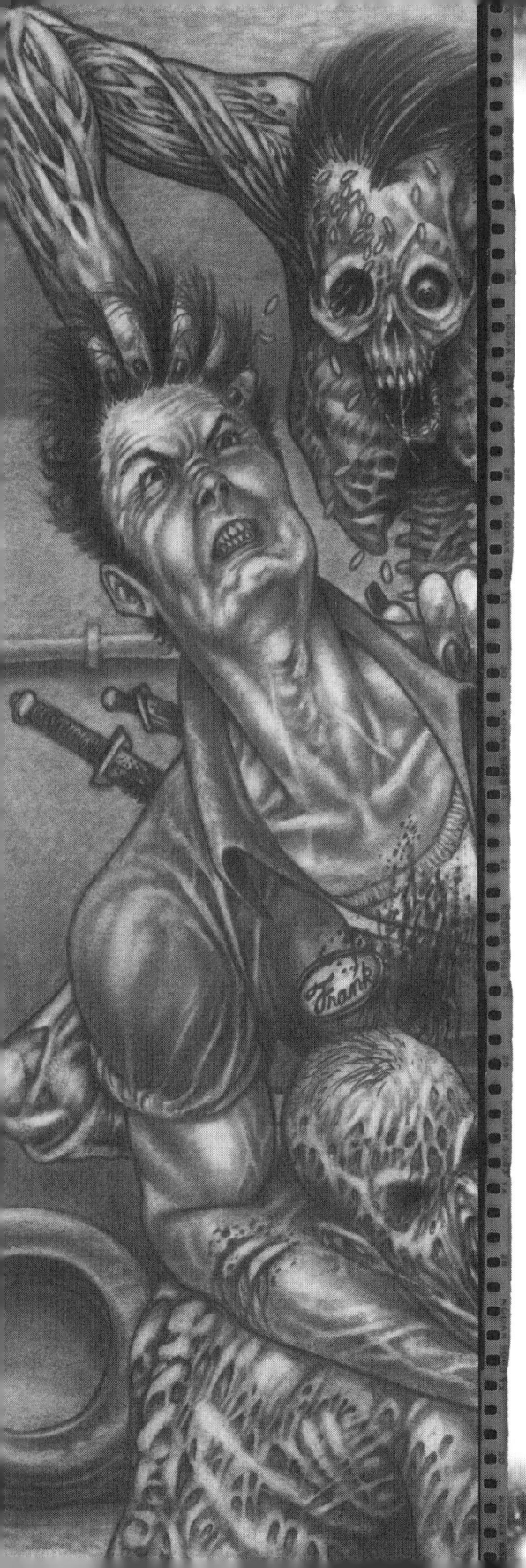

Fear of Commitment: Whenever this character starts feeling too close to somebody, he becomes afraid and starts pulling back. Maybe he is afraid that if he lets somebody get too close, they will hurt him, and it's not worth the pain. Or perhaps he fears that if he reveals too much about himself, the other person will see the "real him" and will be appalled or disgusted. This makes it very difficult to have a healthy relationship with either friends or lovers. This problem is a 1-point Drawback.

Overcoming an Emotional Problem: A common theme in fiction involves characters who in the course of the plot manage to overcome their flaws. Emotional Problems can be overcome by characters during play. This should always be roleplayed. If the player was able to convey the inner struggle of his character over the course of several Stories, the Zombie Master might allow him to eliminate the Drawback without having to "pay" any Experience Points to do so (see Experience, p. 118).

Fast Reaction Time
2-point Mental Quality

Unlike most people, who are easily surprised and blindsided, these quick individuals can often anticipate their enemy's moves and counteract them. They almost never "freeze" in a dangerous situation. In combat, contact sports or other physical confrontations, characters with this Quality can act first without needing to check for initiative, restricted by common sense (Fast Reaction Time will not help the target of a sniper half a mile away, for example). This Quality also provides a bonus of +1 on Willpower Tests to resist fear.

Hard to Kill
1- to 5-point Physical Quality

Characters with this Quality are extremely tough, and can withstand an amazing amount of damage before going down. Even after being severely wounded, medical attention has a good chance of reviving them, scarred but alive. This Quality is bought in levels. Level 5 is the highest possible for human beings. Each level of Hard to Kill adds 3 Life Points to the character's Pool. Additionally, each level adds a +1 bonus to Survival Tests (see Survival and Conciousness, p. 112). For obvious reasons, this is a very useful Quality for Survivors and the Inspired.

Honorable
1- to 3-point Mental Drawback

The Honorable character follows a code of honor, and will not break it lightly, if at all. The more restrictive and rigid the code is, the higher its value. The character with the code of honor should almost never break its rules, no matter what the cause. In a life-or-death situation where honor must be ignored, the character might do so, but even then a Difficult Willpower Test is necessary to pass the psychological barriers reinforcing the code of honor. Players whose characters ignore honor for the sake of convenience should be penalized for poor roleplaying. The levels of the Honorable Drawback are discussed below.

Level 1: These characters do not lie or betray friends or loved ones, or people they respect. Anybody else, especially people from groups they dislike or are prejudiced against, are fair game. This is a 1-point Drawback.

Level 2: This code of honor is more complex, and applies to everyone, friend or foe. The character always keeps his word and does his best to fulfill any promises he makes. He will not betray the trust of others once he has accepted it. Note that the character may be reluctant to give his word except in a good cause, because once it has been given he will abide by it. This is a 2-point Drawback.

Level 3: This person lives by a strict set of rules that control most of his actions towards others. In addition to all the other restrictions above, he will refuse to participate in acts of betrayal such as ambushes, striking a helpless or unsuspecting foe, or cheating in any way. Lying is anathema, and he will only lie in cases of extreme need. Even then, he will feel guilty and will not do a very good job at deceiving; any tasks requiring lying will have a -2 to -6 penalty, determined by the Zombie Master.

Humorless
1-point Mental Drawback

The Humorless character lacks the ability to laugh at life, and takes everything with the utmost seriousness. Other people's attempts at humor leave him cold or annoy him. Most people find this facet of his personality to be unattractive or bothersome. Clowns and practical jokers most likely select the Humorless as their favorite target.

Lazy
2-point Mental Drawback

This character just does not like to work and is always looking for ways to avoid hard work. This limits how much he can learn or accomplish in life. A Lazy character must roleplay an unwillingness to work, except in situations where the work is extremely important, and even then he will try to shirk his duties or select the easiest task. More importantly, the character has a hard time learning skills, due to his inability to spend the required time and effort.

When determining and improving skills for a Lazy character, the character point cost becomes higher after reaching a certain level. This level is determined by the character's Attributes. A Lazy but intelligent or dexterous person can learn a great deal with little effort -- at least at first. Skills are purchased normally until their level is equal to the Attribute most commonly associated with them. Combat and physical skills would be linked to Dexterity, technical and scholastic skills would be associated with Intelligence, and so on. After reaching that level, any further improvement costs double the normal cost. Lazy people are unlikely to ever excel at anything.

For example, Gert is a near genius-level woman (Intelligence 4) who has never had to work very hard to be successful. She could have been a great computer programmer, but has instead settled for being a very good one. Gert's Computer Programming Skill can be bought up to level 4 in a normal manner. After level 4, however, the cost to raise the skill is doubled. It takes 10 points to raise the skill to level 5, and 12 points to raise to level 6! Indeed, Gert never goes beyond level 4, too lazy to transcend this limit.

Minority
1-point Social Drawback

A Minority character is considered a second-class citizen because of race, ethnic group or religion. He is a member of a small or disadvantaged group, disliked by the mainstream. People of the dominant group tend to act in negative ways towards him; many will be automatically suspicious, fearful or annoyed at him for no reason other than what he is. This Drawback has a 1-point value to reflect the relatively enlightened early 21st-century America, where people cannot be denied service in a restaurant because of the color of their skin (in most places, at least). In other settings, where prejudice has the full weight of the law and tradition behind it, this Drawback might be worth 2 to 3 points.

Multiple Identities
2 points/Identity Social Quality

Some characters have more than one identity. This false person comes complete with such records as a birth certificate, a social security number, and a credit rating. Only characters with criminal, espionage or law enforcement connections are likely to have this Quality, because convincing papers require access to good forgeries and computer records. Each fake identity costs 2 character points. Note that characters traveling under aliases or who have purchased a fake driver's license do not need to purchase this Quality. Each Multiple Identity grants a set of papers and records that pass all but the closest scrutiny. Most police organizations will be fooled by the fake identity; an all-out investigation by such agencies as the FBI or NSA would reveal the truth.

Nerves of Steel
3-point Mental Quality

A character with this Quality is almost impossible to scare. Whether he is too dumb or too tough to be frightened is open to question, but he can keep his cool even in the face of unspeakable horror. Only the most bizarre and terrifying situations make an impression on a fearless character, and even then he has a good chance of not succumbing to panic. The character must make Fear Tests (see Getting Scared, p. 96) only when confronted with the strangest supernatural manifestations, and gains a +4 bonus to his roll even then.

Obsession
2-point Mental Drawback

A particular person or task dominates the character's life, to the exclusion of most other things. To pursue his Obsession, he will go to almost any lengths (as limited by his morality). He may neglect other duties, both personal and professional, to pursue that which fascinates him. The Obsession may be a person (who may or may not be aware of his feelings, but who almost certainly is upset about their intensity) or a task (like getting revenge on somebody, or performing some important or notorious feat).

Paranoid
2-point Mental Drawback

"They" are out to get you. Trust no one. Everything is a conspiracy, everyone is keeping secrets. This character never knows when somebody is going to turn against him. A paranoid character expects treachery at every turn, and rarely trusts even his friends and relatives. Note that in the some worlds, where secret organizations have run centuries-old conspiracies, being paranoid is somewhat healthy. However, a character with this Drawback sees conspiracies and danger everywhere, including places where there are none. This makes his stories and beliefs less likely to be believed, even when they are true. Paranoid characters often suffer from Delusions and Emotional Problems (their point values are determined separately).

Photographic Memory
2-point Mental Quality

Those with photographic memories have an uncanny ability to remember things. After reading a book, they can quote passages without missing a word, and they almost never forget anything. The Zombie Master will provide information that the character would remember whenever it is necessary. Also, characters with this Quality receive a +1 bonus on any skill where memorizing facts is useful; most scholastic skills fall under this category. Furthermore, any Tasks where memory can play a role gain a +1 to +3 bonus, at the Zombie Master's discretion.

Physical Disability
Variable Physical Drawback

This Drawback covers any physical problems affecting the limbs of the character. A disabled character may suffer from limb loss, spinal column damage, and any number of tragic impairments. The possibilities are discussed below.

Missing or Crippled Arm/Hand: The hand in question cannot be used to grab or hold objects. Any Test or Task requiring two hands is at a disadvantage (-3 or worse) or simply impossible. This is a 2-point Drawback. A character with a prosthetic hand can overcome some of these problems, reducing the Drawback to 1 point in value.

Missing or Crippled Leg/Foot: The character is unable to walk or run normally. With the help of crutches or a cane, he can move at up to one-third the normal Speed value of the character. Hand-to-hand combat Tasks are at -2. This is a 3-point Drawback. Prosthetics can reduce the penalties, increasing speed to up to half-normal, and reducing combat penalties to -1. This reduces the Drawback value to 2 points.

Missing or Crippled Arms: Both arms are missing or crippled. The character cannot use any tools normally. Some people with this handicap have learned to use their feet with great skill to compensate for their loss. This is a 4-point Drawback.

Missing or Crippled Legs: The character is unable to walk. Without the help of a wheelchair, the best he can do is crawl or roll on the ground. This is a 4-point Drawback.

Paraplegic: Both arms and legs are crippled or missing, or the character is paralyzed from the neck down. Almost all physical activities are impossible. A special wheelchair, operated with the neck or mouth, can help the character move around (if the unfortunate has access to such instruments). Someone needs to take care of all the basic needs of the character, from feeding to changing him. This highly debilitating trait is an 8-point Drawback.

Reckless
2-point Mental Drawback

A Reckless character is supremely overconfident and impulsive, willing to take incredible risks, often without thinking of the consequences. Most of the time, he never looks before he leaps -- and gets into all kinds of trouble as a result. A Reckless character prefers to act first and think about it later. He says what's on his mind with no consideration for diplomacy or courtesy, rushes into dangerous situations, and rarely wastes time on second thoughts. Reckless does not necessarily mean suicidal, however. Acting on impulse no doubt puts the character in jeopardy, but doing something that is clearly lethal is not role-playing, it's just stupid.

Recurring Nightmares
1-point Mental Drawback

This character is plagued by terrifying dreams that relive some traumatic experience or are just frightening and disturbing. Every night, the Zombie Master may check to see if the character suffers from the nightmare. This may be done at the Zombie Master's discretion, or may be rolled randomly (a roll of 1 on a D10 means the character experiences a nightmare that night). On any night when the character is afflicted by the nightmare, he loses D4(2) Endurance Points as the result of his inability to go back to sleep.

Resistance
1-point per level Physical Quality

Some people are innately better at ignoring the bad things that life (or the unliving) throw at them. This ability allows the character to fend off the effects of a particular type of harm. Each type of Resistance Quality must be purchased separately. Some examples are presented below, but others may be devised by Zombie Masters and players.

For Resistance (Disease), the Quality level is added to Constitution when resisting Contagion Strength. For Resistance (Poison), the Quality level adds to any Constitution Test required, and decreases the damage caused per Turn (to a minimum of 1). It could also be viewed as an "iron-clad stomach," and offer protection against eating bad or "off" food. Resistance (Fatigue) decreases any Endurance Point loss by its level (to a minimum of 1 per time period involved). A Resistance Quality for pain would decrease the penalties associated with severe wounds, and add to the Willpower and Constitution Test necessary to avoid being stunned (see The Effects of Injury, p. 111).

Resources
Variable Social Quality or Drawback (2 points /level, positive or negative)

The character's level of Resources determines how much material wealth he has access to. This trait varies widely. Some levels are described below.

Destitute (-5): The character has no money, the clothes on his back, maybe ten dollars' worth of stuff and maybe a shopping cart. Lucky to scrounge a few dollars a month.

Miserable (-4): Owns about $100 worth of property (including the clothes on his back). May live in public housing, or might be homeless. Lucky to scrounge $100 a month.

Poor (-3): Owns some $500 in property and lives in low-income housing. Has an income of $500 a month or what he gets from welfare.

Hurting (-2): Owns about $1,000 in property, and lives in a small apartment in a bad part of town. Has an income of about $1,000 a month before taxes.

Below Average (-1): Owns $5,000 in property (including an old vehicle, perhaps) and lives in an apartment. Has a pre-tax income of $1,500 a month.

Average (0): Owns $15,000 in property. Has an income of $2,500 a month before taxes.

Middle Class (+1): Owns $50,000 in property (will usually include a house or condominium, not to mention vehicles). Has an income of $5,000 a month before taxes.

Well-off (+2): Owns $300,000 in property. Has an income of $10,000 a month before taxes.

Wealthy (+3): Owns $700,000 in property. Has an income of $40,000 a month.

Rich (+4): Owns $2,000,000 in property. Has an income of $50,000 a month

Multimillionaire (+5): Owns $5 million in property. Has an income of $200,000 a month.

Each additional level adds an additional $5 million in property and $200,000 to monthly income.

Secret
Variable Social Drawback

There exists a dangerous and hidden fact about the character. The more damaging the secret if it became known, the higher the value of the Drawback. For example, damage to one's reputation and livelihood would be worth 1 point; a threat to the person's well-being (he might be arrested or deported if the truth were known) is worth 2 points; if the secret could cost the character his life, it is worth 3 points.

Showoff
2-point Mental Drawback

The whole world is the Showoff's audience, and he loves to perform for it. He never misses a chance to cast the spotlight on himself or his accomplishments, while quickly excusing or covering up his mistakes. A Showoff loves to get public acclaim, or at least the respect of his peers. Most of the time, he simply makes sure people notice him, but on occasion he might try a bit too hard to attract attention to himself and his deeds. This Drawback is slightly more complex than the Covetous: Conspicuous Drawback, and the Showoff is less likely to betray his principles in order to hog the spotlight.

Situational Awareness
2-point Mental Quality

The observant almost always know what is going on around them, and can react with uncanny quickness to the unexpected. These characters gain a +2 bonus to any Perception-based rolls to sense trouble or danger in the immediate surroundings. It is very hard to sneak up on them; the same bonus applies to resist any Stealth Tasks to approach them.

Status
Variable Social Quality or Drawback (1 point /level, positive or negative)

This trait represents the standing of the character in the eyes of the people around him. It includes any fame, glory or notoriety the character might have. Note that wealth and Status are often linked; a character gets a bonus to his Status equal to one-half his Resources level (if positive). 0 is middle-class American; -5 is a homeless person, +10 is a member of an ancient noble house, a movie mega-star, or the hero of millions.

Talentless
2-point Mental Drawback

The Talentless individual is totally lacking in creativity and artistic talent. Maybe he is too stolid and practical, or maybe he just doesn't have the imagination to do anything artistic. This Drawback does not just affect his ability in the arts, but also in many social skills where flair and creativity are necessary.

A Talentless character has a -3 penalty when trying to do anything artistic. This penalty does not affect Tasks where other people's art is judged; many expert critics are Talentless. When he does try to do something himself, however, the best he can hope for is a mediocre result. In addition to the penalty, the character can never get more than one Success Level in artistic pursuits, regardless of how high his skill or roll are. People with this Drawback also make poor liars, charmers or social butterflies. The same penalty applies to such skills as Intimidation, Seduction and Smooth Talking -- a lack of creativity affects the ability to influence others.

Zealot
3-point Mental Drawback

A zealot is a person whose beliefs (political, religious or personal) are so strong that they dominate his life and behavior. Zealots are willing to sacrifice anything, including their lives (or the lives of others) in service to the ideals they hold dear. These characters are dangerous to themselves and others, and show a total disregard for the law whenever the law conflicts with their beliefs.

Supernatural Qualities and Drawbacks

When available, Supernatural Qualities are purchased using Quality or Metaphysics Points. Some Supernatural Qualities require the Gift Quality before they may be purchased. Unless otherwise desired, only Accursed, Good Luck/Bad Luck and Old Soul should be available to Norms and Survivors.

Accursed
Variable Supernatural Drawback

The character has been afflicted by a powerful curse, one that may haunt him until the end of his days. The actual elements of the curse, and how difficult it is to remove it, determine the point value of this Drawback. For the most part, it is the result of a misdeed the character committed in the past, and atonement for the misdeed is a major step (but may not be the only one) needed to remove the curse.

A curse of this magnitude is only possible for the worst crimes and injuries. The Zombie Master and the player may work together in deciding the origins of the curse, or the Zombie Master may craft it himself. In the latter case, the origin of and the solution to the curse should remain a mystery to the character.

Depending on its severity, a curse can be worth anywhere between 1 and 10 points. A 10-point curse would be a terrible thing, something that would utterly ruin any chance of the character leading a normal or happy life, or which might kill the victim at any moment. Some rules of thumb to determine the power of the curse are given below. As usual, the Zombie Master is the final judge as to what is appropriate to a campaign setting.

A major inconvenience or annoyance is worth 1 point. For example, the character seems to attract flies, fleas and vermin; milk sours quickly in the presence of the victim; little accidents plague the accursed one.

Something more dramatic and harmful would be worth 2 to 3 points. For example, people tend to be distrustful and angry at the character for no apparent reason (-2 to -3 on all attempts to influence people), or the character can never accumulate a lot of money without losing it (this would preclude any Resource level above 0). Alternatively, people around the character are plagued by small accidents and annoying incidents. In this case, personal involvement is as important as that of physical proximity. A close friend of the victim suffers from the effects of the curse regardless of how far away he is. By the same token, all the people sharing a subway car with the accursed person also suffer from it.

Severe or life-threatening curses will be worth 4 to 5 points. For examples, every day, an accident, mishap or random occurrence will endanger the character's life -- a car skips a red light when the character is crossing the street, a gang shootout breaks out in front of him, or a similar dangerous chance event occurs. If the character is alert, he might survive the mishap without injury, but every day, he has to live with the knowledge that sometime, somewhere, something dangerous and terrible is going to happen.

The difficulty in getting rid of a curse may add 1 to 5 points to its value. If undoing or atoning for a past misdeed is the only requisite, no additional points are awarded. If the misdeed is not known, add 1 point, as the character must spend time finding out why he was cursed. If the undoing process is extremely complex, or involves illegal activities (in some cases, killing the one who cursed the character is necessary), add 2 to 3 points. If a long quest culminating in a difficult magical ceremony, divine intervention, or a similar extraordinary factor is necessary, add 4 to 5 points. And some curses cannot be removed by any means. This adds 6 points to the value of the curse, but no measure will be effective in eliminating it.

Gift

5-point Supernatural Quality

The Gift denotes a connection with the Otherworlds, a connection that allows the character to sense things that are hidden from others. All the Gifted have the ability to perceive the presence of supernatural energies or creatures. By succeeding at a Simple Perception Test, a Gifted character can sense if a supernatural being is near, and can detect strong flows of Essence in an area or object. This sensing is not precise. It does not tell the character exactly what or who is emanating an excess of magical energies, although the Success Level of the Test gives the Gifted character more information.

Good/Bad Luck

1 point/level Supernatural Quality or Drawback

If a character enjoys Good Luck, Fortune smiles on him far more often than most people. Sometimes, he pulls off amazing stunts that by rights he should find impossible to perform. Whenever he needs a break, there is a good chance that circumstances will conspire to give him one. If the character suffers from Bad Luck, on the other hand, Murphy's Law ("if anything can go wrong, it will") always applies to everything he does.

In game terms, each level of Luck counts as a +1 bonus (or -1 penalty) that can be applied to a Task or Test, once per game session. Multiple levels can be added together for a big bonus on one Task/Test, or spread around several different actions. For example, if a character has 3 levels of Good Luck, he can get a +3 bonus on one action, a +1 bonus to three actions, or a +2 bonus for one and a +1 bonus for another.

With Good Luck, the player decides when it comes into play. Bad Luck, however, is in the hands of the Zombie Master, who chooses when it affects a given Task or Test. Zombie Masters should exercise caution and good judgement when applying Bad Luck. If they use Bad Luck for meaningless rolls, then the Drawback becomes little more than a minor inconvenience. On the other hand, applying Bad Luck to Survival Tests or other critical rolls generates resentment among players. Make the Bad Luck count, but don't abuse the characters.

For example, Jenna has a 2-point Bad Luck Drawback. At one point in the Story, Jenna takes aim with her gun as a potential source attempts to flee the area. The character's mission will be much harder if the source escapes, but Jenna is in no immediate danger, so the Zombie Master tells Jenna that a startled bird flies in front of her, spoiling her aim. A -2 penalty is applied to Jenna's shot.

Increased Essence Pool

1/5-point Supernatural Quality (1/2 point after character creation)

While all human beings have Essence, the Inspired generally have a greater amount. Their connection to the Otherworlds has strengthened their souls, making them living beacons of energy. Having a large Essence Pool is both a blessing and a curse. While

Essence can be used to affect the world in many ways, it also attracts the attention of evil and supernatural beings who feed on other's Essence.

Spending 1 point during character creation adds 5 points to the character's Essence Pool. This can be done multiple times. After character creation, every 2 Essence Points costs 1 experience point. This makes it more cost effective to build up Essence when creating the character, representing the relatively slow improvement of the Inspired's powers during the course of their lives. Essence can be purchased after any game session where Essence were used, to indicate a strengthening of the character's spirit.

Any character with the Gift Quality can increase his Essence Pool.

Inspiration
5-point Supernatural Quality

The Inspired can transcend the limits of the flesh, and become a tool of a Greater Power. They are Inspired to fight the forces of darkness, and dedicate their lives to this purpose.

The Inspired may use their own inner strength under the delusion that their power comes from without, or they may truly be the instruments of an omnipotent being. The important thing is that they must hold dearly to the tenets of their faith, and must never go against them.

If an Inspired character breaks a commandment or hesitates in his faith, he temporarily (or even permanently) loses the capability to perform miracles. Furthermore, the powers of the Inspired can only be used in ways that serve the Higher Power the character worships. Characters with Inspiration are able to channel Essence using their link to a Higher Power. Most Inspired consider this Higher Power to be the "True God."

The Gift Quality is a prerequisite to purchasing Inspiration. An extended discussion of Inspiration powers can be found later in this chapter (see p. 62).

Old Soul
4 points/level Supernatural Quality

The character has been reborn many times. As a result, his soul has become stronger. Characters with Old Souls tend to be very mature and precocious for their age. It would be nice to believe that age invariably provides wisdom, but Old Souls are equally likely to be depraved or insightful, cruel or kind. Whatever their orientation, it will usually be more extreme, having been refined over several lifetimes.

This Quality can be acquired multiple times during character creation (but it cannot be acquired afterwards). Each "level" represents some 3-5 previous lives lived before the character's current incarnation. The player can determine who these former selves were, where they lived, and what they know, or he can leave such information in the hands of the Zombie Master. From a roleplaying point of view, creating a "past lives tree" can be interesting.

Each level adds 6 points to the character's Essence Pool, even if the character is not Inspired. This may make Old Souls very attractive to certain supernatural predators. Additionally, each level also adds 1 character point to the Attribute Point Pool; these character points can only be used to increase mental Attributes (Intelligence, Perception and Willpower). Successive lives tend to increase the character's overall insights and understanding -- for good or ill. For example, Mandy has 3 levels of the Old Soul Quality. This gives her 3 more points to put into her mental Attributes, and 18 more Essence Points.

Old Souls are sometimes able to tap into the knowledge of their previous lives. These attempts require the character to pass a single Test using both Willpower and Intelligence as modifiers, and each attempt drains the character of 1 Essence Point, which is regained normally. When attempting to perform an unskilled Task, the character may receive a flash of knowledge from one of his previous lives. If the player took the time to decide what his character's previous lives knew, then the character gains, for that one Task, a skill level equivalent to the character's Old Soul level, but only the skills that the character knew in his previous lives are available. If the previous lives are not known, then the character uses only one half of the Old Soul level (rounded down), but virtually any skill might be known. The only exception would be high-tech Skills that a previous life would be unlikely to know. Asking one's ancestral memories how to hack into a computer system is not likely to work very well . . .

For example, Mandy, with 3 levels of Old Soul has about 10 past incarnations. The player decided to take the time to figure out who those people were. They include five peasants from different time periods (the Zombie Master insisted on at least that many characters being peasants, since most people in pre-modern times tilled the soil for a living), a Confederate soldier, a Mongol raider, a Medieval Italian Princess, and a Wicce from the Victorian Era. In the course of an adventure, Mandy needs to ride a horse, and she does not know how, but her Mongol past life was an expert. If she passes the Willpower and Intelligence Test, she can ride the horse with an effective skill of 3, at the cost of 1 Essence point. The skill will be in effect for as long as the ride lasts; if later in the day she needs to ride a horse, a new Test and an expenditure of Essence are required. If the player had not fleshed out the past incarnations, Mandy would have been able to ride the horse, but with a skill of only 1.

Skills

Skills are learned abilities, the result of training, study or experience. In general, anything that can be taught is considered a skill. The character's background, education and life experiences determine what skills he would be likely to have.

Buying Skills

To acquire skills, use the character points allocated to the Skills category (as determined by the Character Type). Most skills are deemed Regular Skills, and cost 1 point per level from levels 1 to 5. After level 5, each additional level costs 3 points. For example, Lorna wants her character to have the Driving Skill. She decides that the character is an excellent driver -- in fact, he could race cars for a living! Such expertise would require a skill of 5 or higher. Lorna decides to go for broke and give the character a Driving Skill of 7. This would cost her 5 points for the first 5 levels, and 6 points for the other two levels, for a total of 11 character points. Lorna's character will be an ace driver, but he will not have very many skills in other categories.

Special Skills

Certain skills are more difficult to learn, requiring more time and greater dedication. They are called Special Skills, and include Martial Arts, Medicine and others. Special Skills cost 2 points per level until level 5, and 5 points per level thereafter, unless otherwise specified in the skill description.

The Meaning of Numbers

Like most numbers in the Unisystem, high is good and low is bad. The higher a skill level is, the more proficient the character is at using that skill. In general, a level 1 indicates a beginner or amateur, somebody who has just learned the rudiments of the skill.

A level 2 or 3 represents general competency -- the ability to perform average tasks with ease. A level 4 or 5 indicates extreme competence in the subject, the result of a lot of study or practice. Higher levels indicate true mastery of the skill or craft, and the ability to perform the most difficult tasks with relative ease.

Skill Types

Skill Types are required for some skills and represent broad areas of knowledge within the more generic skill category. For example, within the Guns Skill are the Handgun, Rifle, and Shotgun Types. Types most often come into play with broad scholastic skills, such as Humanities, Science and Language. Types must be chosen each time the more generic skill is taken, and cost no character points.

Skill Specialties

Both fiction and real life display many examples of people who specialize in a specific aspect or field of study within a skill. A history student may specialize in the early medieval period, for example, or an occultist may know a great deal more about zombies than anything else.

In game terms, Specialties costs 1 character point, and result in a +2 bonus to Tasks involving that field of expertise. This is written as a separate skill. For example, a character could purchase Occult Knowledge 3 for 6 Skill category character points. By specializing with 1 Skill category point, the character could gain Occult Knowledge (Symbology) 5.

Specialties are raised by improving the base skill. For example, if the character's Occult Knowledge Skill rises from 3 to 4, his Occult Knowledge (Symbology) Skill goes up to 6. Specialties may not be raised without increasing the base skill level. Purchasing a new Specialty after character creation costs 6 experience points.

Specialties should be distinguished from Types, which cost no character points. For example, a character might take Humanities (History) at level 3 during character creation. This costs the usual 3 Skill points. If he chooses to specialize, he might learn Humanities (Pre-Columbian History). This costs 1 point and piggybacks on her History Skill; the Specialty skill level is 5.

Learning New Skills

A character can learn new skills after character creation, during the course of play. This can be done in two ways: through formal study or training, or by hands-on experience. The first option is more time consuming, but is the sure way to do it.

Learning new skills from scratch is usually more difficult than improving pre-existing skills. This is why it is generally better to have a character with a wide variety of skills at relatively low levels than an overspecialized character with only a few skills. The latter character will have trouble learning new things. The costs of learning new skills and improving old ones are detailed in Experience (p. 118).

Using Common Sense

The guidelines provided in the list of skills below, like all the rules in this book, should always take a second seat to plain common sense. If a player is trying to twist the letter of the rules to wring some unreasonable advantage, Zombie Masters should let common sense prevail.

Skill List

The following sections discuss a number of skills that may be purchased by *All Flesh Must Be Eaten* characters. These skills are listed in the Appendix for easy reference during character generation.

Acrobatics (Special)

The ability to perform tumbles, somersaults and other complex maneuvers. This skill teaches balance, flexibility and speed. Use Acrobatics and Dexterity for most Tasks. This skill is commonly known by circus performers, dancers, martial artists, gymnasts, and athletes. Also, Acrobatics can be used instead of the Dodge Skill to avoid attacks.

Acting

The ability to play a role and successfully counterfeit behaviors, emotions and other character traits. A talented actor can weep on demand, or convincingly display an array of emotions. This skill is useful to both legitimate artists and criminals and con men. Use Intelligence and Acting to give a good performance, and Perception and Acting to spot or judge someone else's act.

Beautician

This is the ability to use make-up, hair dressing, and cosmetics to enhance a person's appearance. Use Intelligence and Beautician for the Task; each Success Level adds a +1 to a person's Attractiveness by hiding blemishes and enhancing a person's good points. Modifiers to these Tasks include the materials available (a +2 in a fully stocked beauty salon, -2 or worse with improvised materials) and the subject's basic Attractiveness level.

Beautician Skills can also be used to help change a person's appearance (Beautician and Intelligence). A skilled character can use hair dyes, contacts and make-up to change a person's look greatly. This skill can be used to replace the Disguise Skill, or can add a +1 bonus to Disguise Tasks for each level of success in the Beautician and Intelligence Task.

Using Beautician and Perception allows the character to see how extensively a person is made up, and may be used to identify a disguise (this Task is resisted by the disguiser's own Intelligence and Beautician or Disguise Skills).

Brawling

Brawling covers basic street fighting, karate-parlor "martial arts" training, and similar combat skills. In hand-to-hand combat, Dexterity and Brawling are used for kicks, punches, and similar maneuvers. Strength and Brawling are used for take-downs, wrestling and slamming people around.

Bureaucracy

This skill provides familiarity with the organization of, and procedures used by, bureaucratic institutions. With this skill, the character can find ways to improve an organization's service and performance, or otherwise obtain their services or products more efficiently. Use Intelligence and Bureaucracy to devise ways to make a large group or organization more (or less) efficient; use Willpower and Bureaucracy to "cut through red tape."

Cheating

The skill of breaking the rules and tricking an opponent. Mostly used in games of chance and other forms of gambling. Use Intelligence and Cheating to perform the trick, or Perception and Cheating to spot such a trick.

Climbing

A character with the Climbing Skill knows how to best use any surface to get to the top. Climbing Tasks use Dexterity, Strength or Constitution, depending on the type of climb attempted.

Computer Hacking

This is the skill to penetrate computer systems through a modem, overcome protection and password programs, and steal information or inflict damage on the system. Most tasks use Intelligence and Computer Hacking, although spotting a specific type of defense or password system may use Perception and Computer Hacking instead.

Creating New Skills

It is impossible to account for every possible skill in this book. Chroniclers and players who do not find a skill here should feel free to come up with their own. When creating a new skill, a few questions must be answered.

Is the skill very difficult to learn (i.e., any discipline requiring several years of training)? If so, then it should be a Special Skill, with a higher point cost. Does the skill require a person to specialize (which means the skill will be broken into several separate Types) or is specialization optional or additional (in which the Specialty rules apply)?

And finally, what Attributes are commonly used with the skill in question, and under what circumstances? Normally, physical activities rely on Dexterity and in some cases Perception, scholastic disciplines rely mainly on Intelligence, and so on.

Computer Programming

The skill to write a set of commands in one of the many computer languages. Writing a program uses Intelligence and Computer Programming; Perception and Computer Programming is used to recognize elements of another program.

Computers

This is the basic skill with computers, including how to use a keyboard and mouse, basic commands, and so on. As computers become more "user-friendly," Zombie Masters can assume that most Computer Tasks are Routine or Easy, except where they involve unfamiliar programs and operating systems.

Craft (Type)

The Craft Skill covers numerous types of skills such as those employed by carpenters, seamstresses, weavers, weaponsmiths, woodworkers, etc. When the Craft Skill is purchased, a particular Skill Type must be specified. Characters may further want to specialize. For example, Gunsmith is the Specialty of the Craft (Weaponsmith) Skill focusing on guns. Bowyer would likewise relate to bows.

Intelligence and Craft is used to conceive and plan an item. Dexterity and Craft is tested to create the item, or repair a damaged item. Perception and Craft serves to appraise an item. The Fine Arts, Electronics, Engineering, Mechanic and other Skills may be used to supplement the Craft Skill. Note that devising and creating a particular item may be a time consuming and difficult task. Often, it is far easier to simply buy a mass produced item.

Dancing (Type)

This skill is not necessary to gyrate to a catchy tune. Dancing represents training in a form of dance, and includes anything from ballet to tribal rituals to high accomplishment on the disco floor. The character must indicate the specific Type of Dancing he is familiar with. Other Types have a default level equal to the Dancing level -2. Dancing and Dexterity are used to actually dance; Dancing and Perception are used to recognize a type of dance and to judge the quality of another's performance.

Demolitions

The ability to set and disarm explosives. Use Intelligence and Demolitions to set up an explosive charge, Perception and Demolitions to understand the setup of an unfamiliar bomb, and Intelligence and Demolitions (resisted by the bomber's own Intelligence and Demolitions) to disarm an enemy bomb. Zombie Masters may restrict this skill to those with access to military or espionage training.

Disguise

The ability to change one's appearance using wigs, make-up and clothing. High-tech spies can also use rubber masks, implants and other gadgets to completely alter their face and even body (such high-tech aids may give bonuses of +2 to +6, at the Zombie Master's discretion). Use Intelligence and Disguise to apply a disguise, and Perception and Disguise to spot somebody else's disguise.

Dodge

This is a basic combat skill, representing the ability to move out of the way of attacks. Dodges include sidestepping a blow, "hitting the dirt" to avoid gunfire, ducking behind cover, etc. As a skill, Dodge is learned by people with some practice in diving for cover. Dodge is used with Dexterity for most Tasks.

Driving (Type)

The skill to control any land vehicle of the specific Type. Each kind of vehicle (Car, Truck, Tracked Vehicle, and Motorcycle, among others) requires a separate Driving Skill Type. Most driving Tasks use Dexterity and Driving.

Electronic Surveillance

The skill to set up, use and detect electronic "bugs" -- sophisticated microphones and even cameras hidden in a location to spy on or detect people. Use Intelligence and Electronic Surveillance to set up and use a "bug," and Perception and Electronic Surveillance to detect one (resisted by the operator's original Intelligence and Electronic Surveillance Task result). Zombie Masters may wish to restrict this skill to those with military or espionage backgrounds.

Electronics

This skill allows a character to build and repair all manner of electronic devices and tools, and grants the character knowledge about electronic systems and the like. The difficulty of repairing an electronic device depends on how intricate the device is, and how damaged it is. Constructing an electronic item is also more difficult the more advanced and complex the device. Zombie Masters should apply a penalty or bonus depending on these factors. Finally, an electronic tool kit must be available for all but the most rudimentary repairs. A lab or workshop may also be required. All repair or construction attempts take time, ranging from a couple of hours to days. This too should be determined by the Zombie Master.

Understanding an existing electronic device calls for a Perception and Electronics Task; repairing or constructing a device requires an Intelligence and Electronics Task. It should be noted that this skill and the Mechanic Skill complement one another, and are often used together.

Engineer (Type)

This skill reflects the general knowledge of structural design, material strengths, and construction techniques in a variety of fields and applications. Examples of the Types of Engineering Skill include Architecture, Civil, Construction, Mechanical, Electrical, and Biological. In some games, the Zombie Master may just lump them all into one category, depending on how big a role such skills play in the course of a Story. Alternatively, separation between Engineering Skill Types (and even Specialties) may be important to the storyline. Planning or devising an object, structure or device within the character's Engineering Type demands an Intelligence and Engineering Task.

Escapism

This is the ability to escape from ropes, handcuffs and other restraints. Most of these Tasks use Dexterity and Escapism, with each attempt taking between 1 and 5 minutes, depending on the complexity of the bonds. A simple rope tie would have no modifier, but complex knots might have penalties of -1 to -5, police handcuffs involve a penalty of -4, and a straitjacket/strap/chain combo might have penalties of -5 to -8. Expert escape artists also use visualization techniques -- they carefully think about their method of escape before attempting it. This is an Intelligence and Escapism Task that takes two minutes; each Success Level adds a +1 to an immediately subsequent Dexterity and Escapism Task.

Fine Arts (Type)

There are many Types of Fine Arts Skill, such as Drawing, Painting, Computer Graphics, etc. In some games, the Zombie Master may lump them all into one category, depending on how big a role such skills play in the course of a Story. Alternatively, separation between Fine Arts Skill Types (and even Specialties) may be important to the storyline.

Rolls to conceptualize a work of art, or to produce it from memory, improvisation or imagination require Intelligence and Fine Arts. Rendering a concept that is recorded, such as using models or plans, requires Dexterity and Fine Arts. Appreciating another's work uses Perception and Fine Arts.

The Success Levels of a Fine Arts Task indicate how good the artistic expression is. Regardless of the final Task result, the Success Levels cannot exceed the skill level of the artist. For example, a character with Fine Arts (Drawing) 2 cannot accumulate more than 2 Success Levels on a drawing.

First Aid

This skill allows a character to treat basic injuries, and use such techniques as CPR and the Heimlich Maneuver. A successful Intelligence and First Aid Task heals some damage to an injured person (see Medical Healing, p. 113). Typical Tasks include identifying the problem (use Perception and First Aid), performing First Aid (Intelligence and First Aid), and using CPR or applying the Heimlich Maneuver (Dexterity and First Aid).

Gambling

This is the knowledge of most common games of chance, their rules and techniques, and the best strategies to win the games. A character needs both Gambling and Cheating to effectively break the rules.

Guns (Type)

This skill allows the character to use one type of firearm. The most common Types include Handgun (pistols and revolvers), Rifle, Shotgun, Submachine Gun, and Assault Rifle. If the skill is taken for one Type, the character can use other types of guns, but at a -2 penalty to all Tasks.

Dexterity and Guns are used to fire the weapon. Aiming rolls use Perception and Guns; each Success Level adds +1 to the Guns Skill on the next shot fired at the aimed target.

Haggling

The skill provides the character with the ability to deal for goods and services, or otherwise bring two or more parties to some common ground. It may be applied when buying, selling or bartering goods or services. Often used in a Resisted Task, each level of success modifies the price of the subject by 10%. It may also be used for less tangible exchanges, such a political dealmaking. In such circumstances, the Zombie Master should adjudicate the result given the goal and the levels of success. Haggling can also be used to determine whether the character is being misled or conned. Use Willpower and Haggling to get the best deal; use Perception and Haggling to spot a con.

Hand Weapon (Type)

Each basic type of weapon is a separate skill. Hand Weapon Skill Types include Axe, Club, Foil/Rapier, Knife, Spear, Staff and Sword. Pre-modern missile weapons like Bow and Crossbow are also Types. They must be learned separately. When using an unfamiliar weapon, use the most closely related Hand Weapon Skill at -2 to -4 (depending on how dissimilar the weapons are).

Humanities (Type)

Each of the various Humanities disciplines (archeology, anthropology, economics, history, law, political science, sociology, theology, etc.) counts as a separate Humanities Skill Type. In some games, the Zombie Master may just lump them all into one category, depending on how big a role such skills play in the course of a Story. Alternatively, separation between Humanities Skill Types (and even Specialties) may be important to the storyline, and a variety of penalties may be applied when trying to use a specific Type outside its range. In any event, most Humanities Tasks use Intelligence or Perception and Humanities.

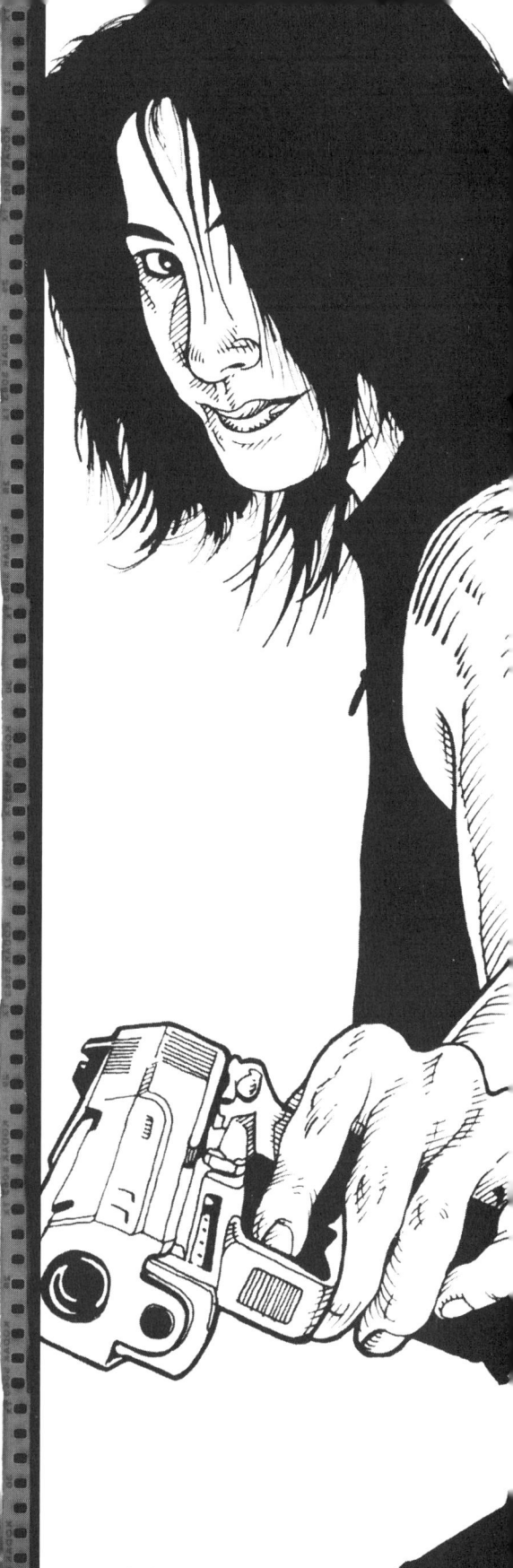

Humanities Skill Types can include many Specialties. For example, Humanities (Law) includes a number of different subjects, any one of which may be a Specialty (i.e., corporate law, environmental law, criminal law, etc.). Other than giving a character the normal +2 Task bonus for Specialties, Zombie Masters may wish to penalize Tasks attempted outside the specialization. For example, a character with Humanities (Ancient History) gains a +2 bonus for Tasks involving the Spartan wars, but may incur a -1 penalty for a question concerning the Renaissance, or a -3 penalty for a question about World War I.

Instruction

Teaching is a skill and an art. The subject matter is important but conveying that information in an interesting, stimulating and comprehensive manner is the heart of the Instruction Skill.

The first step in using the Instruction Skill is to pick a subject matter to teach. This may be any skill known by the teacher, but it must be at least two levels higher than the student's level.

If the required skill level is possessed, the teacher and student must spend a certain period of time on lessons. Every week of game time that the two spend at least 10 hours studying the skill, the teacher can attempt an Intelligence and Instruction Task. The Success Levels of this Task are cumulative; for example, if the teacher and student spend three weeks working on the skill, the Success Levels of all three rolls are added together. When the teacher accumulates five Success Levels in the Task, the student gets 1 Experience Point toward improving that skill.

For example, Rolando is an accomplished singer (level 5), and a decent teacher (level 3). Maria wants to learn to sing better; she has Singing 1. Rolando's Singing Skill is more than two levels higher than Maria's, so he may teach her. After they spend a good deal of time working together during one week, Rolando tests his Instruction Skill. He rolls a 6, adds 3 for the skill level, and 2 for his Intelligence for a total of 11, or 2 Success Levels. The next week, they study together again, and Rolando rolls particularly well -- gaining three Success Levels. Maria gains 1 experience point dedicated to the Singing Skill.

Intimidation

The skill to make people afraid, Intimidation is used by bullies or others in most confrontational situations. A good Intimidation Task result may stop a fight before it starts by convincing the opponent that he doesn't want to mess with the character. Use Willpower and Intimidation for "real" intimidation attempts, or Intelligence and Intimidation to bluff.

Language (Type)

Every character is assumed to have level 5 in their native or primary language. Each additional language must be purchased as a separate Skill Type. The skill level in a language determines not only basic fluency, but the "thickness" of the character's accent (see the Language Skill Level Table nearby). Most of the time, the character need not pass a Task to see if he communicates; as long as the character knows the language, assume that he can talk in it without needing to roll. A Task roll would be necessary in situations involving highly technical or scholarly speech (which may use a lot of words the character doesn't know) or when dealing with extreme regional accents or slang.

Lock Picking (Type)

This skill covers all the basics in breaking and entering. There are two Types: Mechanical and Electronic. Most Tasks use Lock Picking and Dexterity, modified by the difficulty of the lock. Lock Picking (Electronic) uses Perception and Intelligence for the most part, to spot and neutralize electronic locks and security systems.

Martial Arts (Special)

This is the skill of using an advanced system of hand-to-hand combat. Characters with Martial Arts can do more damage with their hands and feet. Kicks and punches performed with the Martial Arts Skill have a damage bonus equal to the character's skill level. So, a character with Martial Arts level 3 does an additional 3 points of damage with a kick or punch. This bonus is added when the rest of the damage has been calculated, after any multipliers and dice rolls.

Chapter Two

Language Skill Level Table

Skill Level	Fluency
1	Very thick accent and frequent grammatical mistakes; the character will be immediately identified as a foreigner, and may be misunderstood.
2	Thick accent but largely fluent; the character should have no problems being understood.
3	Slight accent; native speakers will realize this is not the character's first language.
4	Full fluency, only a Resisted Test (listener's Simple Perception versus speaker's Simple Intelligence) will spot the character's accent.
5	Complete mastery; the character can pass for a native without problems.
6+	Dialects; character can perfectly imitate regional accents and dialects in addition to the main version of the language.

Mechanic

This skill allows a character to build and repair all manner of mechanical devices and tools, and grants him knowledge about mechanical systems and the like. The difficulty of repairing a mechanism depends on how intricate the device is, and how damaged it is. Zombie Masters should apply a penalty or bonus depending on these factors. Constructing a mechanical item is also more difficult the more advanced and complex the device. Again, modifiers should be imposed by the Zombie Master. Finally, a mechanical tool kit must be available for all but the most rudimentary repairs. A lab or workshop may also be required. All repair or construction attempts take time, ranging from a couple of hours to days. This too should be determined by the Zombie Master.

Understanding an existing mechanical device calls for a Perception and Mechanic Task; repairing or constructing a mechanism requires an Intelligence and Mechanic Task. It should be noted that this skill and the Electronics Skill complement one another, and often are used together to make repairs to an item or to construct an item.

Medicine (Special)

This skill covers medical knowledge, including basic surgery skills, diagnosis and general medicine. Most doctors also specialize in one type of medicine, such as cardiovascular, surgery, or neurosurgery. These are treated as Specialty Skills.

Diagnosis Tasks use Perception and Medicine, general treatment calls for Intelligence and Medicine, and surgery uses Dexterity and Medicine.

Myth and Legend (Type)

This is the knowledge of t.he mythology and folklore of a specific culture or nation. This skill can be used to identify supernatural creatures, but the information gleaned from myth and legend may be completely wrong or at least very inaccurate. Each culture or nation is a separate Skill Type.

Notice

Notice represents the degree of alertness a person has about him. A character with this skill can use it with Perception to see what is happening around him, or with Intelligence to remember something he noticed some time ago. A character with Notice can use it with Perception to spot or hear another character using Stealth.

Occult Knowledge (Special)

This is the skill of true arcane knowledge. It covers most of the basic Metaphysical facts of whatever world serves as the background for the game, including a working knowledge of Essence and other specific supernatural features.

Myth and Legends is a comparatively broader skill covering a variety of topics. Much of that information with be contradictory, false or misinterpreted. Occult Knowledge, on the other hand, is less inclusive (the character will not know as much), but that information, at least as relates to Essence and mystical powers, will be essentially true. The character may also know some information about a number of cults and supernatural creatures, although some of that information may be flawed or incomplete.

Pick Pocket

The skill of taking another person's hard-earned money or things without him noticing it. Most rolls use Dexterity and Pick Pocket, resisted by the victim's Perception and the highest of his Notice, Streetwise or Pick Pocket Skills (if any, or Perception alone -- not doubled -- otherwise).

Piloting (Type)

The skill to control any aircraft or water vehicle of the specific type. Each type of vehicle (propeller plane, jet plane, sailboat, ocean liner) requires a separate Piloting Skill Type. Most Piloting Tasks use Dexterity and Piloting, or Intelligence and Piloting for very large vessels.

Play Instrument (Type)

The character is able to play a musical instrument of one type, chosen when the skill is taken. The character may choose more than one type of instrument to play, but each instrument is counted as a separate Skill Type. At the higher levels of the skill, the character is more proficient in tonal quality, rhythm, and improvisation. In order to play for pleasure, the character would use Dexterity and Play Instrument. If performing a complex piece of music, the attempt would use Intelligence and Play Instrument. If the character is performing a long piece of music, use Constitution and Play Instrument. In all circumstances the quality of the performance is reflected in the levels of success. No matter what the ultimate roll, no musician may enjoy more Success Levels than he has skill levels.

Questioning

This is the ability to interrogate, spot lies, and otherwise extract the truth from people. This skill is quickly learned by police officers, private investigators, and investigative reporters. Most interrogations should be roleplayed. If a Task or Test is needed, how well the player roleplayed the interview should give him bonuses or penalties of +5 to -5, at the Zombie Master's discretion. Tricking somebody into revealing something uses the questioner's Intelligence and Questioning, resisted by a Simple Intelligence Test. Spotting a lie uses Perception and Questioning, also resisted by a Simple Intelligence Test. Breaking a victim's will to resist uses Willpower and Questioning, resisted by a Simple Willpower Test. The use of torture and drugs may give bonuses of +1 to +6 to the questioner's Task.

Research/Investigation

This skill allows a character to search out information or follow a series of clues and leads to a reasonable conclusion through deduction, source checking, going to libraries, searching on the Internet, and the like. Alternatively, this skill can be used by the character to do legwork -- running down leads on a story, questioning contacts and sources of information (the latter would incur some penalties; this aspect would best be left to the Questioning Skill).

In all cases, the use of this skill takes time. The amount of time is determined by the Zombie Master, based on the nature of the search being undertaken by the character. Most uses of this skill involve Intelligence and Research Tasks. In other cases, it is possible that Constitution and Research (in the case of searching through dusty old tomes for long periods of time or walking the length and breadth of a library for the better part of a day), or Perception and Research (in the case of researching obscure facts in voluminous materials, such as finding a certain name in a room full of documents) can be used.

Riding (Type)

The skill to ride horses, carts, chariots and other animals or animal-driven vehicles. Each type of animal or vehicle requires a separate Riding Skill Type.

Rituals (Type)

The skill to perform rituals and ceremonies of a particular culture, religion or mystical group (each counts as a separate Skill Type). Rituals that require dancing or other complex physical activity use Dexterity and Rituals; most others use Intelligence and Rituals to remember all the appropriate steps or activities involved.

Running (Type)

There are two Types of Running. The first one is Running (Marathon). This skill covers running for endurance and distance. A good marathoner can cover ten or more miles (15 or more kilometers) without stopping. An official marathon usually covers 25 miles (40 kilometers). The best runners can cover that distance in about two hours. A character with Running (Marathon) can use this skill and his Constitution Attribute to resist the effects of fatigue after a long period of extensive physical activity. Also, add 1 Endurance Point to the character's pool for every level in Running (Marathon).

Running (Dash) trains the character to increase speed for short distances. On a dead run, use Constitution and Running (Dash) to increase maximum running speed. Each Success Level acquired adds +1 to the character's Speed Secondary Attribute.

Sciences (Type)

Each science (biology, chemistry, astronomy, mathematics, physics, etc.) counts as a separate Science Skill Type. In some games, the Zombie Master may just lump them all into one category, depending on how big a role such skills would play in the course of a Story. Alternatively, separation between Science Skill Types (and even Specialties) may be important to the storyline, and a variety of penalties may be applied when trying to use a specific Type outside its range. See the description of the Humanities Skill for more information (p. 55). Most Sciences Tasks use Intelligence or Perception.

Seduction

The ability to make oneself sexually attractive to other people by saying the right things and putting on the right act. Intelligence is used, modified by any Charisma or Attractiveness bonuses or penalties the character might have. Other skills may give bonuses to Seduction attempts. For example, previous Tasks using Beautician and Smooth Talking add their Success Levels to the Seduction attempt.

Singing

While everybody can try to sing, this skill is necessary to do it right. This skill reflects the training of the character's voice. Use Constitution and Singing for the quality of the song, Intelligence and Singing to remember every verse of a long or complex song, and Perception and Singing to recognize and measure the quality of someone else's singing.

Sleight of Hand

This is the ability to perform sleight of hand and legerdemain, and is known mainly by stage magicians. With this skill, a character can fool the audience into looking at one thing while she does something else. Most Sleight of Hand Tasks use Dexterity, and are resisted by a Perception Test (Simple or Difficult depending on the circumstances) or a Perception and Notice Task. To plan a complex magical trick (e.g., sawing a woman in half, diverse death traps) requires an Intelligence and Sleight of Hand Task, often supplemented by assorted Craft Skills to actually build the contraptions or gadgets needed.

Smooth Talking

This skill allows the character to lie convincingly or to confuse and deceive others. This skill is commonly known by con men, salesmen and politicians. Use Intelligence and Smooth Talking for most Tasks.

Sport (Type)

This skill covers all types of competitive sports, from football to ping pong. Each Sport must be learned as a separate Type. Depending on the Task, use Strength or Dexterity and Sport. For example, a football pass would use Dexterity and Sport (Football); a tackle would use Strength and Sport (Football). To come up with a good strategy or game plan, use Intelligence and Sport; to spot a rules violation, use Perception and Sport.

Stealth

The ability to move quietly and to take advantage of cover and concealment. Most Task rolls use Dexterity and Stealth; Perception is used to find good hiding places.

Storytelling

This skill allows a character to sway or influence an audience, be it one individual or a group of people, from one emotion to the next by means of a tale. It can be used for the purpose of educating an individual or a group of people, as well as merely for entertainment. In some cultures, storytelling is the means by which knowledge and lore are passed down, and so the skill has uses for some primitive societies, but is also quite useful under certain circumstances when dealing with Myth and Legend and Occult Knowledge and the like. The character may tell a tale that is true or fictional, although the audience will generally not know the difference. The character must constantly be aware of how the listeners are reacting to the tale and thus may alter his pacing, volume, or even change the course of the story to elicit a better or greater response.

Storytellers use Willpower and Storytelling Tasks. The Success Level dictates the effectiveness or entertainment value of the story. If the people listening to the story are familiar with the tale, they may resist the attempt of the storyteller character to influence them with a Difficult Willpower Test.

Streetwise

The general knowledge of the lore and rules of the streets. A character with this skill knows how to behave in a given situation, knows the names and most of the faces of the more notorious local members of the underworld, and can identify most illegal transactions and operations. Use Intelligence and Streetwise to recognize a local street name, gang color or criminal, and Perception and Streetwise to spot trouble or detect criminal activities nearby.

Surveillance

This is the ability to follow and keep people under observation. A character with Surveillance can attempt to keep sight of a target while following him through a crowded street, and remaining unobserved. By the same token, this skill allows a person to know if he is being followed or observed. Use Surveillance and Perception for either activity.

Survival (Type)

This is the skill of living off the land. Each kind of terrain requires a separate Skill Type. Attempts to use a Survival Skill in the wrong place or type of terrain are at a -3 penalty. Common Types include Forest, Mountain, Jungle, Desert and Arctic.

Swimming

Swimming is the skill that allows a character to stay afloat and to move in the water without drowning. Floating is an Average difficulty Constitution and Swimming Task when fully clothed; it becomes Easy with little or no clothing (see Modifiers to Tasks and Tests, p. 94). Each 2/1 EV (see p. 126) of equipment or weight effectively reduces a character's Swimming Skill level by one.

If the Task is failed, the character sinks and drowns in a number of Turns equal to his Constitution. Shedding clothing or equipment (which requires one Turn) allows a character to attempt the Task anew.

If the character succeeds, he stays afloat and may swim at a speed equal to his Swimming Skill in yards (meters) per Turn. Swimming is an exhausting activity. Floating with little clothing uses 1 Endurance Point per 10 minutes. Floating while fully clothed uses 1 Endurance Point per minute. Swimming unclothed takes 1 Endurance Point per minute at half-speed and 5 Endurance Points per minute at full speed. Those who swim clothed, or who carry equipment when they swim, use double the Endurance cost and move at half speed. Towing another person while Swimming imposes a -1 modifier, doubles the Endurance cost, and halves the swimmer's speed.

Throwing (Type)

This skill has three basic types, but others may be added as desired. Thrown (Knife) includes all small-sized edged weapons. Thrown (Axe) covers any top-heavy object with a longish handle, such as maces, baseball bats and similar projectiles. Thrown (Sphere) provides expertise in targeting rocks, grenades or any such hand-sized object. The latter also defaults directly to Sport (Baseball), if that skill is possessed. All skill Tasks use Strength and Thrown.

Tracking

This is the skill used to follow the trail of an animal or person, usually in wilderness terrain, but also in an urban setting if snow or dust are present in enough quantity to leave a trail. Most Tracking Tasks use Perception and Tracking; attempts to hide one's tracks use Intelligence and Tracking.

Trance (Special)

Trance is often used by those that claim to be shamans and mystics. It enables the character to enter a meditative state that transcends physical limitations. Among other things, someone in a trance can withstand pain, hunger and thirst better than the average human being. A trance is also helpful when sensing the influence of the supernatural.

To enter into a trance, use Willpower and Trance. If successful, the character becomes extremely focused on the task at hand, which gives him a -2 penalty on all non-related Perception Tests. On the other hand, the character is not affected by pain and shock penalties, and he gains a +2 bonus on all Tasks and Tests he is concentrating on. A character in Trance also regains Essence more rapidly; characters gain double the normal Essence amount per hour of meditation.

Traps

This is the knowledge to detect, disarm and set traps, snares and the like. It is commonly known by Special Forces soldiers, guerrillas, hunters, trappers and others. Use Traps and Intelligence to devise a trap, Traps and Perception to detect a trap, and Traps and Dexterity to disarm a trap.

Unconventional Medicine (Type)

This skill covers all methods of healing not widely accepted by Western Science, including herbal medicine, acupuncture, etc., each of which is considered a different Skill Type. The effectiveness of each type of unconventional medicine is determined by the Zombie Master. If the skill is effective in treating disease and injury, use the same skills and effects as the conventional Medicine Skill (see p. 57).

Veterinary Medicine

Just like the Medicine Skill, but applies to animals. A Veterinarian can treat humans, but is at a -3 penalty to all Task rolls, and despite the results of rolls, cannot gain more than two Success Levels.

Weight Lifting

When trying to exceed Strength limits (see Strength Table, p. 30), Weight Lifting is very helpful. Use Strength and Weight Lifting instead of Strength times two, or, if the Strength Attribute is higher than the Weight Lifting Skill, add one-third of the Weight Lifting Skill level (rounded up) to the base number.

Writing (Type)

This skill allows the character to construct and write entertaining and/or meaningful written accounts and narratives. The character is able to write text in a convincing manner to suit whatever goal or presentation is required. Types of skills would include Academic (learned expositions of the arts, humanities or sciences), Advocacy (legal arguments, ad copy or promotional materials), Creative (such as novels, poems or plays), Journalistic (informative discussions of newsworthy topics), and Technical (precise descriptions using nomenclature specific to a certain technology).

Using an Intelligence and Writing Task, the character is able to write documents, items, notes, or whatever the type of specialization implies. The quality of the writing depends on the Success Levels obtained. The Success Level of such a work cannot exceed the writer's skill, however. Using a Perception and Writing Task, the character can critique writing of the style with which he is familiar.

Metaphysics

Metaphysics are the special Powers that the Inspired and certain supernatural beings can wield. The only Metaphysics available to Cast Members at this point is the power of Inspiration.

Inspiration

This is the power of pure unbridled faith -- the belief in a Greater Power and the will to perform great works in the name of that Power. Its wielders claim to serve the Creator directly. Detractors claim the powers are within the faithful themselves, and have no external source. Whatever the truth is, the Inspired can perform incredible feats, called Miracles. These Miracles are special abilities gained through mystical revelation.

The Inspired have access to an assortment of abilities allegedly derived from the connection of the character to the Creating Agency. Some occultists claim that these powers come from inside the Inspired, and are nothing more than the channeling of their own Essence to fuel their religious fanaticism. No matter who is right, without their Faith, the Inspired would not be able to perform their incredible feats. To use a Miracle, the character must firmly believe that he is fighting the forces of evil in the name of his God. Otherwise, he will be left with nothing but his own meager strength.

Acquiring Miracles

Miracles are learned through mystical revelation by the Inspired. To acquire Miracles, the character must first buy the Inspiration Quality. Miracles cost 5 character points each during character creation, and 10 points apiece afterward. Additionally, the Inspired often have a large Essence Pool as a result of their connection to the Creator.

Using Miracles

The Inspired use Miracles by channeling Essence into the effects they desire. The Inspired can use up his entire Essence Pool in one Miracle if it seems necessary. Essence is regained at the rate of 1 point per Willpower level every 5 minutes.

Miracles cannot be used at the whim of their wielder. Only extreme situations, where lives are at stake or supernatural powers have manifested openly, warrant the use of Miracles. An Inspired who tries to call upon the Strength of Ten to win a bar fight will fail; even worse, the blasphemy of trying to use God's powers to do profane work may cost the Inspired his powers, perhaps permanently! In most cases, the Inspired must try to solve their problems through mundane means. Only when confronting beings who are clearly agents of an unnatural powers will using one's abilities be justified. Even trying to fight mundane evil may not warrant using Miracles.

Within these parameters, the use of Miracles is relatively easy. If enough Essence is available to power the Miracle, it automatically manifests itself. Some Miracles need additional Tests or Tasks to fulfill the intended goal, but there are no Miracle-related skills.

The Denial

In addition to their repertoire of Miracles, all the Inspired can use their Essence to neutralize any supernatural power that uses Essence. The Denial (as this power is called) consists of projecting Essence against the supernatural being using the special power. If the Inspired used up more Essence than the target did, the power fails.

When Miracles Clash

What happens when the Inspired of two different religions run up against each other? In the past, such individuals might face off, each confident of being the servant of the one True God. Even then, however, more often than not, Miracles of either side would not work against another Inspired, regardless of their religious persuasion. In recent times, this is almost always the case.

It may appear (and many Inspired believe this) that the members of every monotheistic religion are worshipping the same Deity, and that their differences are meaningless in His/Her/Its Eyes. Inspired who have publicly said such things, however, have often found themselves excommunicated or shunned as a result.

Tests of Faith

Inspired Miracles can be lost at any moment. Should the character lose his Faith, his powers become nothing but memories. Falling from Grace is a terrible tragedy for the Inspired, and in the strange and vicious worlds of *All Flesh Must Be Eaten*, it is easy to do so. Pride (which "Goeth before the Fall"), temptation, greed, lust and cynicism are among the many pitfalls that await the Inspired in their war against the forces of darkness. Some beings -- not all zombies are mindless -- take a perverse delight in tricking the Inspired into making that fatal mistake which costs them their state of Grace.

Sometimes the moral dilemmas are truly harrowing. Should the Inspired save an innocent or take the opportunity to destroy a being that, left to its own devices, will surely kill again? Should the character break his word if given to a supernatural monster, even if the monster seeks to twist the meaning of the promise? Is accepting a reward for one's actions a sign of greed, or is turning it down one of pride? The Inspired have to come up with the right answer or risk losing it all.

Zombie Masters should throw these and similar quandaries in the path of Inspired characters, although they should take care not to purposefully trip up the characters. The temptation of the Inspired can make for powerful Story devices, but try not to be too cruel implementing them. Touching up on a few books on philosophy and morality might not be a bad idea so as to prepare interesting and devious tricks.

Miracles

These are some of the most common Miracles among the Inspired. Additional Miracles will be published in subsequent *All Flesh Must Be Eaten* books, and may be devised by creative Zombie Masters and players.

Blessing

Essence can be used to alter probability or imbue certain items with special abilities. When providing Luck, each 3 Essence spent grants the Cast Member a +1 bonus to any one Test or Task. The bonuses remain until used and may be used all on the same Test/Task or spread among separate ones. Note that the bonuses are only effective if used for a Test/Task that advances the Lord's causes, or helps preserve the Inspired's existence. Essence spent in this manner may not be regained until the Blessing benefits end. For example, an Inspired who gives himself a +5 Luck bonus has his own Essence Pool depleted by 15 points until the bonuses are used up.

When used to empower objects, 10 Essence is spent to change the very character of the item. Particularly large items may require more Essence to bless (in the Zombie Master's discretion). The actual effects of a blessed object vary by world, but some zombies are particularly susceptible to blessed items (see Chapter Five: Anatomy of A Zombie, p. 149).

The Binding

This is the power to restrain zombies and other supernatural beings, at least temporarily, by using Essence. The Inspired orders the creature to halt in the name of his God. This power is used to prevent monsters from attacking or fleeing while the Inspired metes out justice. The Binding only works against supernatural creatures, not other Inspired.

This Miracle costs 2 Essence Points per Strength and Willpower level of the supernatural creature (or Essence equal to one half the Power Level if available). The Inspired may not know how much Essence is necessary. If he does not have enough, his Essence Pool is drained and the Miracle does not take place.

In addition to the Essence cost, the Inspired must win a Resisted Test involving Simple Willpower rolls from both the Inspired and the creature. If the being is not truly evil (as determined by the Inspired's religion or the Zombie Master), it gains a bonus of +2 to +5 in the Resisted Test. If the Inspired wins, the creature is bound in place for 1 Turn per Success Level on the Willpower Test; during that time, the creature may not attack or defend itself, and is rooted in place.

Divine Sight

This Miracle allows the Inspired to find the Truth in everything he sees. Although this ability is very useful in uncovering the presence of the supernatural, the Divine Sight sometimes shines a light on some unwanted truths as well. While the Miracle is activated, the Inspired can not only see invisible spiritual entities and the strange auras of supernatural beings, but it also shows the true nature of human beings. In a world of hypocrisy and lies, this ability often shows taint among pillars of the community, respected leaders of Church and State, and other seemingly benign and honest people. Inspired with the ability to invoke the Divine Sight sometimes remove themselves from their original Church, unable to deal with the complacency and greed that can mar such institutions. Many start to develop a cynicism that clashes badly with the Faith necessary to carry on the good fight.

Activating this Miracle costs 5 Essence Points, and it lasts 10 minutes. Unless the creature or person is protected from scrying or mental probing (and such protection will be perceived by the Divine Sight), his nature, personality and goals will be clearly seen by the Inspired.

The Touch of Healing

This is the ability to cure wounds, disease and disabilities. In the past, most Inspired people were healers; now far too many are warriors. The Miracle costs 1 Essence Point to heal D4(2) points of damage. Mild diseases cost 2 points, Moderate ones 5 points, Serious diseases cost 15 points, and the cost is 25 points for a Terminal disease (see Disease, p. 108).

The Touch of Healing may only be used under extraordinary circumstances, and is generally used only on the faithful. The Inspired may elect to make exceptions for non-believers who are nonetheless fighting the good fight (interestingly enough, some among the Inspired are actually a lot more tolerant than the mundane leaders of many Churches).

becomes inured to pain and fatigue, gains inhuman levels of strength, and can fight until killed. This display of power is only possible under the most extreme situations, however. To try to invoke it when there are any other options is considered sinful. Only when facing overwhelming odds should the Strength of Ten be summoned.

This Miracle costs 15 Essence Points. The Inspired gains +5 to Strength (which also raises his Life Points by 20 points), and is immune to shock and pain until the battle is over. This means the character can keep fighting even when reduced to 0 Life Points or below (he still needs to pass Survival Tests after reaching -10 Life Points to stay alive, however). Once invoked, the power lasts until the threat is gone or until the Inspired succeeds in martyring himself.

Holy Fire

This powerful Miracle calls down divine retribution upon the forces of evil. This retribution comes in the form of a blast of blinding white flames, or a bolt of lightning striking from above. This attack can only be attempted on supernatural beings. Sometimes, if the being in question is not truly evil or is somehow part of the mysterious ways of the Deity, the blast will not inflict full damage, or will inflict no damage at all. Such an event clearly demonstrates that the Inspired is not meant to destroy the creature -- for the time being, at least.

This power costs 20 Essence Points and inflicts D8(4) points of regular damage times twice the Willpower of the Inspired. For example, an Inspired with a Willpower of 4 inflicts D8 x 8(32) points of damage. Any being within line of sight can be targeted. No attack roll is necessary; the power zeroes in on the selected target. Mundane body armor will not protect against this attack, but supernatural protective powers may.

Strength of Ten

This is the ability that allows the Inspired, when confronted with evil, to summon the strength of the righteous, temporarily transforming him into a nearly unstoppable warrior of vengeance. The Inspired

Visions

Through this Miracle, the Inspired opens himself to the Deity for guidance and advice. The Inspired is often visited by flashes of insight about places and people; these insights may come in the form of dreams or sudden visions that may strike at any time or without warning. Sometimes, the Inspired will pray for guidance and be rewarded with a Sign of some kind. Most of the time, the visions are ambiguous and need interpretation. For example, the Inspired might see the face of a man, a famous politician. Is the man a tool of evil, or is he being threatened by the forces of evil? The Inspired would have to find out somehow.

This ability costs 5 Essence Points when the Inspired actively seeks guidance. The Inspired's prayers may not be answered, depending on what the Zombie Master feels is appropriate to the moment, although such attempts should usually be successful -- provided the Inspired is appropriately humble in his petitions. When the Zombie Master sees fit to visit a spontaneous Vision upon a character, there should be no Essence Point cost.

The actual details of the visions will vary widely. Some may be a single image, while others may give more clues as to places, people, and circumstances. The nature of visions should always be determined by the needs of the Story.

Prayers

In some of the worlds of *All Flesh Must Be Eaten*, a simple prayer has more power than most scoffers could imagine. As a focus of the faith and willpower of a person, Prayers can be used to help convert Essence into Miracles, and even to gather Essence. Norms and Survivors with enough piety and strength of will (one will not work without the other) can also make use of Prayers to focus some of their Essence into actual defenses or even attacks against supernatural horrors.

Prayers only have an effect if the character's life shows enough devotion and respect to his religion. Most people only pay lip service to their beliefs; that will not do at all. In the course of a game, however, a character might "discover religion" as part of the often traumatic events that make up most Stories. A character undergoing such a revelation might be able to make use of Prayers.

Inspired and Prayers

The Inspired may find additional strength through Prayers. If the character spends at least an hour in deep prayer and meditation, he may find himself replenishing Essence at double the normal rate. The use of prayers in the course of a Miracle is considered to be part and parcel of such a Miracle. A Christian Inspired would be expected to quote from the Bible, just as a Muslim one might recite a line from the Qur'am. This conveys no special bonuses or penalties, beyond the increased Essence recovery.

Norms, Survivors and Prayers

Norms and Survivors are the main beneficiaries of the power of Prayer. The ancient chants of religious scriptures hold a great deal of power for those who truly Believe. A faithful character who prays may gain unexpected strength in his time of need. In game terms, treat this as a Task using Willpower and Humanities (Theology) or Rituals. Modifiers for the character's piety range from -10 (for a foxhole convert who is just trying to save his skin) to +10 (for a truly saintly individual, very rare in today's world). Each level of success in the Task releases a point of Essence from the character's Essence Pool. Each Essence Point released confers a +1 bonus to any Test or Task that contributes to the survival or advancement of the faithful. Alternatively, each Essence Point grants a +2 bonus on any Resisted Task or Test against a supernatural or mystical ability of any kind.

Holy Symbols

From the legends of antiquity to Hollywood movies, the power of holy symbols is part and parcel of many stories about the supernatural. The myth goes that anybody with a cross has nothing to fear from a vampire, or that by wielding the right holy symbol a righteous man can banish demons and scare off spirits. There is a grain of truth in such tales, but only a grain. The power lies not in the symbol, but within its wielder. A character using a holy symbol (be it a Cross, an Ankh or any similar object) to protect himself must pass a Simple Willpower Test, with the same modifiers used in Prayer Tasks (see above). Each Success Level allows the character to focus 1 Essence Point through the holy symbol. Supernatural beings confronting the charged holy symbol must make a Difficult Willpower Test, at -1 per Essence Point focused through the symbol, or feel pain and fear when faced with it. The creatures will hesitate to come near the wielder, let alone attack him; even if the monster does not flee the symbol, all its actions will be at a -4 penalty.

Chapter Two

Possessions

This is everything the character owns. In most *All Flesh Must Be Eaten* games, a detailed inventory of a character's possessions is not necessary. A character with average Resources owns a TV set, a phone, and a number of items of clothing -- at least before the world goes to Hell. He lives in a rental apartment or room. Most characters also own a vehicle of some sort. The Resources Quality/Drawback helps determine what a character is likely to own. A multimillionaire may own boats, airplanes and helicopters, while a destitute character will have to make do with a purloined shopping cart.

Items particularly useful to characters are discussed in Chapter Four: Implements of Destruction.

Finishing Touches

After the player has determined all the basic elements, he is pretty much finished with creating the character. All that is left is a few final touches that make the character come alive and seem like more than just a collection of numbers on a piece of paper. Note that these "finishing touches" can be done just as easily at the beginning as at the end of the character creation process. Sometimes, the last touches can wait until the player starts roleplaying the character. Some players need to start playing before they get a "feel" for the role. As always, each player should do whatever works best for him.

Name

First, of course, is the character's name. This simple touch can add a number of roleplaying elements. The character's first and last name can indicate ethnic background (an Italian name conjures images of growing up in an ethnic neighborhood in New York, for example) and the kind of family that raised the character (a Biblical name might indicate a strict Christian background, while a name like "Moonlight" might indicate the character's parents were Hippies). Some characters may adopt nicknames or "street names" in addition to their given names. Maybe they hate the name their parents gave them. It is easy to come up with any old name, but having it mean something can add to the fun.

Appearance

The character's appearance and demeanor are also important elements. Whether or not a character is attractive and charismatic is determined by any Qualities or Drawbacks purchased during character creation, but the description makes the numbers come to life. Beyond obvious things like hair and eye color and general physique, there are subtler elements that can help the Zombie Master and the other players get a better "handle" on the character.

Does the character walk in a timid, stooped position, or does he swagger around like she owns the world? Does he have any nervous ticks or other habitual behaviors? Does he smile a lot, or does he have a grim demeanor? The character's appearance should take into account his Attributes, Qualities and Drawbacks -- a character who is Paranoid may have a tendency to look behind him every once in a while, or maybe he always insists on being the last one to enter any room.

Age

Beginning characters are assumed to be between 18 and 30 years old. Within this range, the exact age is entirely up to the player and Zombie Master. For those wishing to play younger or older characters, the Optional Skill Point Generation System sidebar gives some ideas how to modify characteristics.

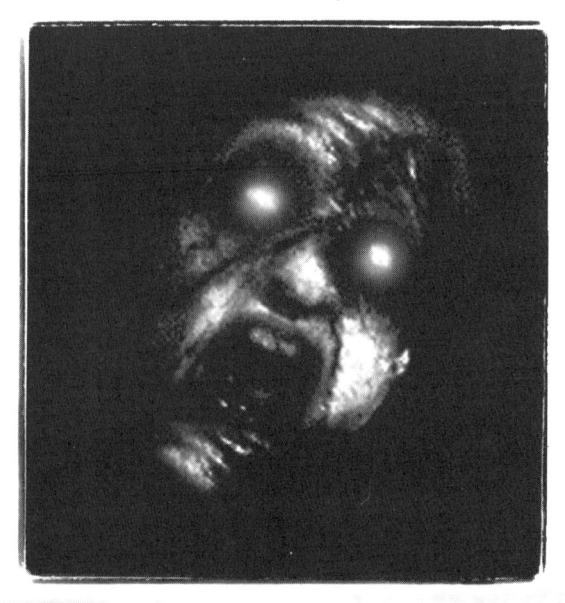

All Flesh Must Be Eaten

Athlete
Survivor

Str 5 **Dex** 4 **Con** 4
Int 2 **Per** 3 **Wil** 2
LPs 52
EPs 38
Spd 16
Essence 20

Qualities/Drawbacks
Attractiveness 2 (2)
Charisma 1 (1)
Fast Reaction Time (2)
Good Luck 3 (3)
Hard to Kill 2 (2)
Resources 1 (2)
Situational Awareness (2)
Status 1 (1)

Skills
Brawling 3
Climbing 2
Dodge 3
Driving (Car) 2
Guns (Shotgun) 2
Hand Weapon (Hockey Stick) 2
Intimidation 2
Running (Dash) 2
Seduction 1
Sport (Basketball) 3
Sport (Football) 3
Sport (Lacrosse) 3
Swimming 1
Weightlifting 1

Gear
Binoculars, Pick-up Truck, Hockey Stick

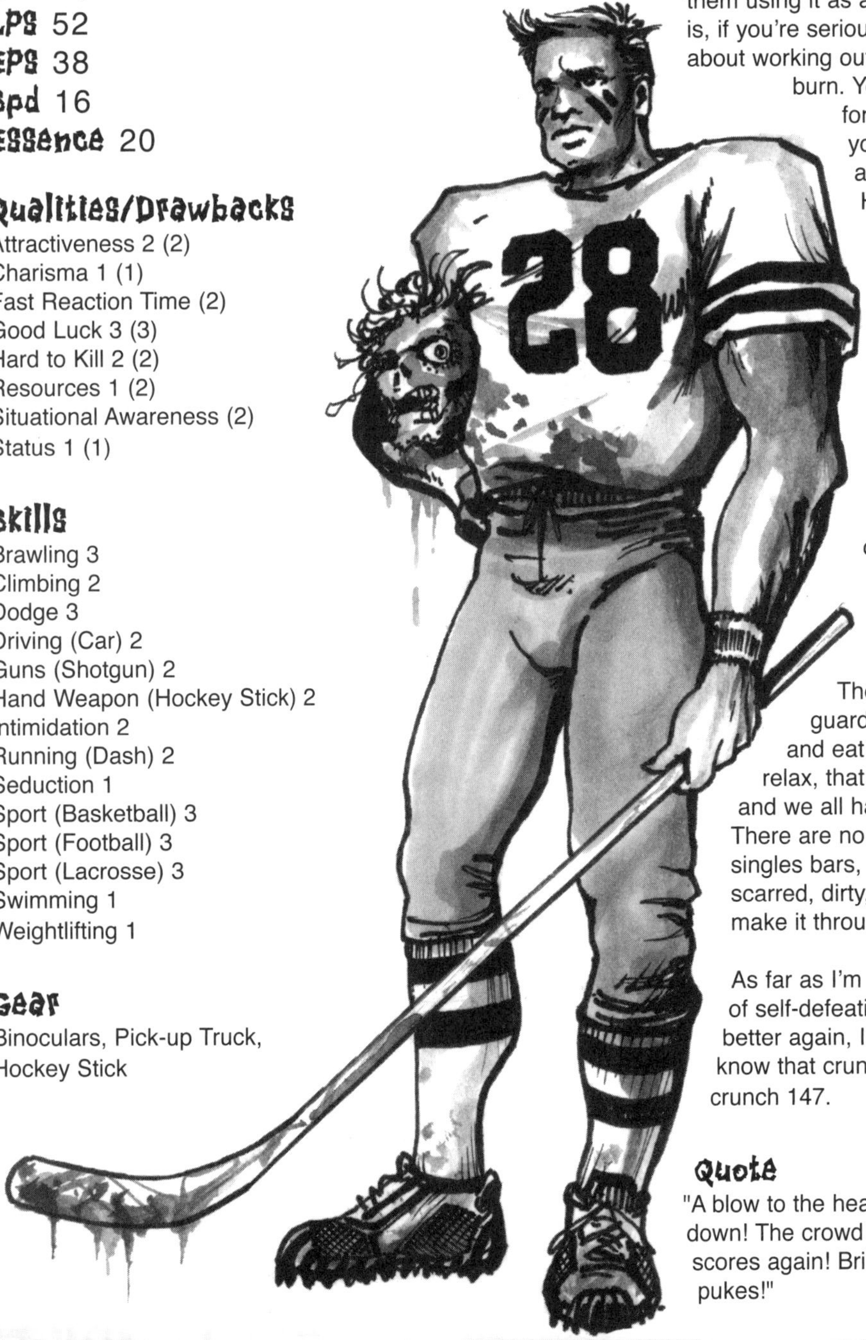

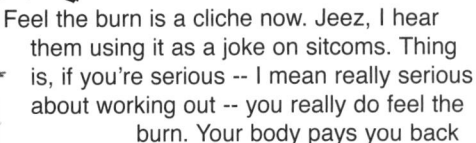

Personality
Feel the burn is a cliche now. Jeez, I hear them using it as a joke on sitcoms. Thing is, if you're serious -- I mean really serious about working out -- you really do feel the burn. Your body pays you back for treating it right by giving you this high that no amount of pot, beer or Hostess Fruit Pies can match.

Of course, it's much harder to stick to a schedule now. We're always moving, always looking out for food, ammo and defensible shelter. So I have this rule, every night, no matter where we make camp, I do a full set of reps before I eat or turn in.

The others think I'm nuts. The minute they can let their guard down, they booze it up and eat like pigs. They tell me to relax, that the world has changed and we all have to change with it. There are no more supermodels and singles bars, there's just groups of scarred, dirty, terrified people trying to make it through another day.

As far as I'm concerned, that's a load of self-defeating crap. Things will get better again, I know that as sure as I know that crunch 146 is followed by crunch 147.

Quote
"A blow to the head! The pussface goes down! The crowd goes wild! He swings, he scores again! Bring it on, you lame-ass pukes!"

All Flesh Must Be Eaten

Biker
Survivor

Str 6 **Dex** 2 **Con** 3
Int 2 **Per** 2 **Wil** 3
LPs 58
EPs 41
Spd 10
Essence 18

Qualities/Drawbacks
Contacts (Biker Gang) (3)
Contacts (Fence) (2)
Hard to Kill 4 (4)
Nerves of Steel (3)
Status (Gang Leader) 3 (3)

Skills
Brawling 4
Cheating 2
Demolitions 1
Dodge 2
Driving (Motorcycle) 4
Driving (Truck) 2
Gambling 1
Guns (Handgun) 3
Guns (Shotgun) 2
Hand Weapon (Club) 2
Hand Weapon (Knife) 3
Intimidation 2
Mechanic 3
Streetwise 2
Weight Lifting 2

Gear
Cutting Torch, Knife, Leather Jacket, Motorcycle, Sleeping Bag, Shotgun, Toolkit

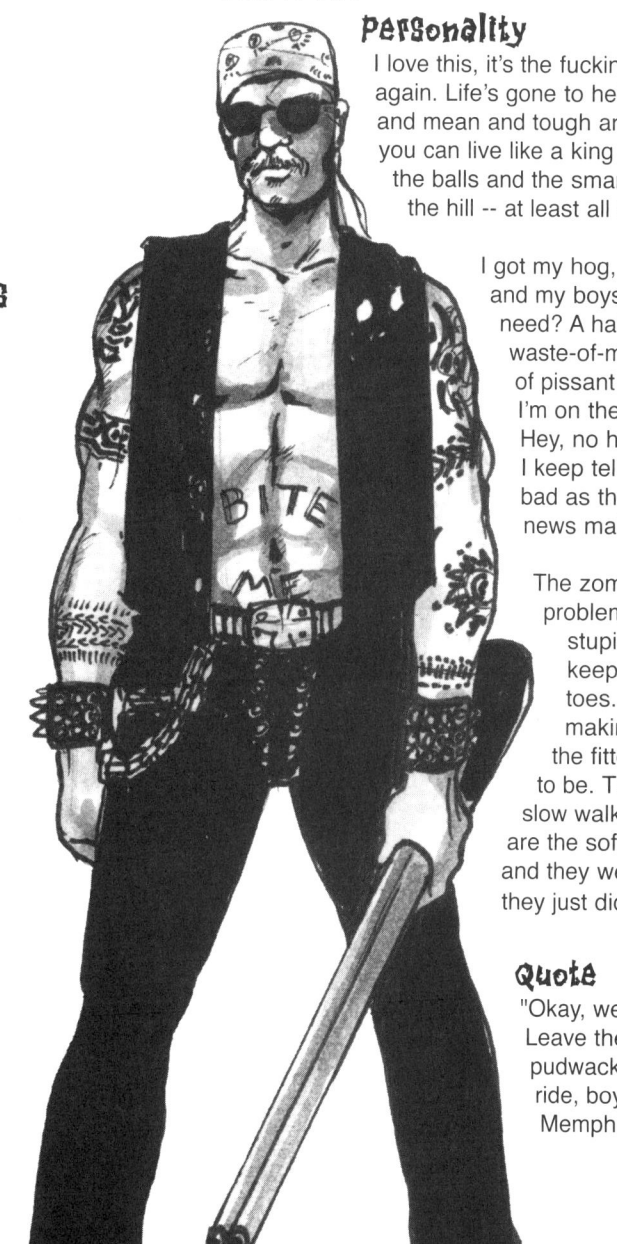

Personality
I love this, it's the fuckin' wild west all over again. Life's gone to hell, and only the strong and mean and tough are left standing. Hell, you can live like a king out here if you've got the balls and the smarts. That's me, king of the hill -- at least all the hills around here.

I got my hog, my shotgun, my gal, and my boys. What else do I need? A haircut, a nine-to-five-waste-of-my-life-make-work kind of pissant job? I don't think so. I'm on the road, wind in my hair. Hey, no helmet laws now, right? I keep telling you, life's not as bad as the weenies on the news make out.

The zombies? They're only a problem if you are slow or stupid. Otherwise, they keep you on your fuckin' toes. I figure they are just making sure it's survival of the fittest, like it's supposed to be. The only people those slow walkin' pudwackers get are the soft middle class bozos and they were already dead . . . they just didn't know it.

Quote
"Okay, we got what we need. Leave the rest for the pudwackers. Mount up and ride, boys. Tomorrow, we're in Memphis."

Archetypes

All Flesh Must Be Eaten™
Cheerleader
Survivor

Str 2 **Dex** 5 **Con** 3
Int 3 **Per** 3 **Wil** 4
LPs 36
EPs 32
Spd 16
Essence 32

Qualities/Drawbacks
Artistic Talent (Dance) (3)
Attractiveness 4 (4)
Fast Reaction Time (2)
Hard to Kill 2 (2)
Resources 2 (4)
Status 1 (0)

Skills
Acrobatics 3
Acting 2
Beautician 2
Brawling 2
Dancing 3
Dodge 2
Driving (Car) 2
Guns (Handgun) 2
Haggling 2
Hand Weapon (Baton) 2
Notice 2
Running (Dash) 1
Seduction 3
Singing 2
Smooth Talking 2
Streetwise 1
Swimming 1

Gear
Baton, Cellular Phone, Camera, Jeep

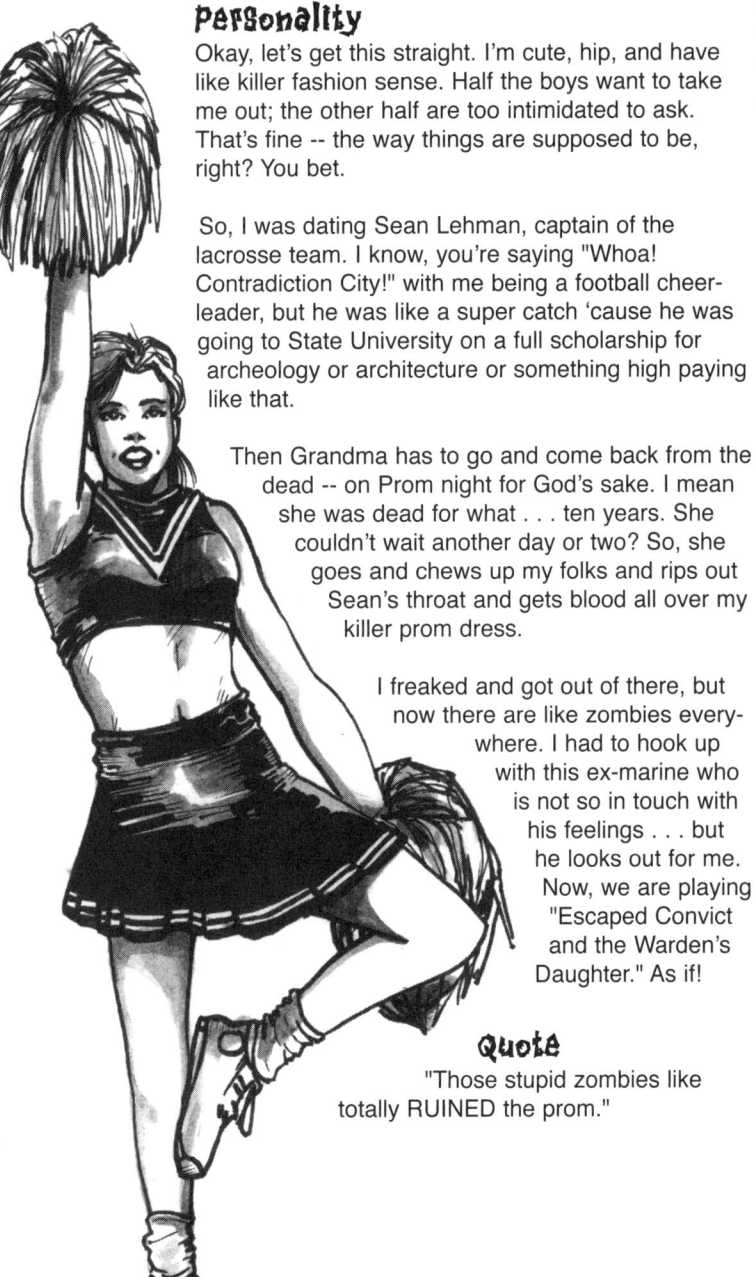

Personality
Okay, let's get this straight. I'm cute, hip, and have like killer fashion sense. Half the boys want to take me out; the other half are too intimidated to ask. That's fine -- the way things are supposed to be, right? You bet.

So, I was dating Sean Lehman, captain of the lacrosse team. I know, you're saying "Whoa! Contradiction City!" with me being a football cheerleader, but he was like a super catch 'cause he was going to State University on a full scholarship for archeology or architecture or something high paying like that.

Then Grandma has to go and come back from the dead -- on Prom night for God's sake. I mean she was dead for what . . . ten years. She couldn't wait another day or two? So, she goes and chews up my folks and rips out Sean's throat and gets blood all over my killer prom dress.

I freaked and got out of there, but now there are like zombies everywhere. I had to hook up with this ex-marine who is not so in touch with his feelings . . . but he looks out for me. Now, we are playing "Escaped Convict and the Warden's Daughter." As if!

Quote
"Those stupid zombies like totally RUINED the prom."

Archetypes

All Flesh Must Be Eaten
Detective
Norm

Str 2 **Dex** 2 **Con** 3
Int 2 **Per** 3 **Wil** 2
LPs 36
EPs 26
Spd 10
Essence 14

Qualities/Drawbacks
Addiction (Alcohol) (-1)
Addiction (Smoking) (-2)
Contacts (Police) 3 (3)
Hard to Kill 2 (2)
Nerves of Steel (3)

Skills
Brawling 2
Bureaucracy 1
Computers 1
Driving (Car) 2
Electronic Surveillance 2
First Aid 1
Guns (Handgun) 2
Guns (Shotgun) 1
Humanities (Criminal Law) 2
Intimidation 2
Notice 2
Questioning 3
Research/Investigation 3
Stealth 2
Streetwise 2
Surveillance 3

Gear
Handgun, Chainsaw

Personality
The only reason I became a PI was because I lost my police job. Now, don't get it wrong here, I wasn't let go because I was crooked or because I went nuts. See this star-shaped scar on my hand? Got home late at night and was slipping off my shoulder holster and . . . well, the damn thing went off and ruined my hand. Stupid, but the truth.

Thing is, being a PI wasn't like being a cop. I used to love walking into a crime scene and trying to figure out what happened. As a PI, all you do is sleazy spy work, like trailing lying spouses gettin' a little extra on the side. That work gets old fast.

Thing is nowadays I'm getting to do real detective work again. Dealing with our smelly dead friends has strained the local and national authorities to the limit. PIs like me are suddenly important again. You want to find out who stole your stuff? You want to find out who killed your son? I'm your man.

Yeah, I know that someday my nosing around is going to get me killed, but it's worth it having that cop feeling again. In a world where the dead outnumber the living ten to one, it's good to feel alive.

Quote
"The dame had legs that wouldn't quit, they kept flopping around like dead fish. I restarted the chainsaw and cut that zombie bitch into smaller pieces."

Archetypes

Goth Chick
Inspired

Str 3 **Dex** 3 **Con** 3
Int 3 **Per** 4 **Wil** 4
LPs 34
EPs 35
Spd 12
Essence 42

Qualities/Drawbacks
Artistic Talent (3)
Inspiration (5)
Gift (5)
Increased Essence (2)

Skills
Acting 2
Brawling 1
Computer Hacking 1
Computers 2
Dancing (Industrial) 2
Dodge 2
Escapism 2
Fine Arts (Sculpture) 2
Guns (Handgun) 1
Myth and Legend 2
Occult Knowledge (Vampires) 2
Seduction 2
Stealth 2
Streetwise 1
Writing (Poetry) 1

Metaphysics
Visions
Binding

Gear
Anne Rice Novel, Camera, Cellular Phone, Handcuffs

Personality
I remember the first time I saw one. It was at some rave out in the desert -- I wasn't too hot on the crap techno music the DJ's were pushing, but my friend Ginny said there'd be free nitrous oxide. That's cool.

All of a sudden, people started coming out of the desert at us. They were moving all spastic, but I thought it was just the strobe.

I remember watching as the strobe made it seem like a bunch of photographs. Pic one: She closes on Ginny. Ginny doesn't see. Pic two: She embraces Ginny. She's white like marble. Pic three: Ginny's eyes go wide. I hear flesh ripping. It was so Anne Rice! Pic four: The biter pulls Ginny's head back to a weird angle. She looks more yellow now, and Ginny's flesh is hanging from her cracked teeth. Pic five: Ginny's screaming. Spraying blood reflects lustrous in the light. Ginny, wherever you are, forgive me, but it was so beautiful. Like something off the Cranes first album.

'Course it's gross, but hey I seem to have some power over them. I figure, if zombies are real, why not vampires?

Quote
"God this sucks . . . there's like a billion zombies and not like one vampire."

All Flesh Must Be Eaten

Hacker
Norm

Str 2 Dex 2 Con 2
Int 4 Per 2 Wil 2
LPs 26
EPs 23
Spd 8
Essence 14

Qualities/Drawbacks
Attractiveness -1 (-1)
Contacts (Hackers) 2 (2)
Multiple Identities 1 (2)
Resources 1 (2)

Skills
Bureaucracy 1
Cheating 2
Computer Hacking 3
Computer Programming 3
Computers 3
Dodge 1
Driving (Car) 1
Electronics 4
Guns (Handgun) 2
Notice 2
Research/Investigation 3
Sciences (Mathematics) 3
Streetwise 2

Gear
Handgun, Laptop Computer

Personality
Subjects: Project Romero
Path: <obscured>
From: "The Ace" ace@university.edu
Newsgroup: alt.conspiracy.zombies.menace

I only hacked into the Pentagon because I heard they got gigabytes of porn hidden in there. I figured, it's the Pentagon, they got to have something sweet -- not too demure, not too sleazy. Tasteful, if you know what I mean.

Anyway, I found a file called the Romero Project. It was too intriguing to pass up. Besides, I knew a Laura Romero in college and she was quite the hottie. I swear, I spent hours trying to crack that file, but no go. 'Course, that just made me want it more. You know how it is. No friggin' piece of code was going to stop me.

Then my hard drive seized up. No big deal, we are talking Windows here, right? Wrong. I rebooted and watched as the machine efficiently shredded everything -- from the Temp directories to the Bios. Damnedest virus I ever saw.

Very impressive. As I reinstalled my OS (and then re-reinstalled it -- so damned impressive), the reference clicked. George Romero -- the zombie movie guy.

So I'm thinking this whole zombie mess was created by the military. Hell, it all could be a field test! I'll check out more and <file ends>

Quote
"Hardware, software, bullshit! The real Y2K bug is flesh-eating geeks!"

Archetypes

All Flesh Must Be Eaten

Police Officer
Survivor

Str 3 **Dex** 2 **Con** 4
Int 3 **Per** 4 **Wil** 4
LPs 50
EPs 38
Spd 12
Essence 20

Qualities/Drawbacks
Contacts (Police) 3 (3)
Contacts (Underworld) 2 (2)
Hard to Kill 4 (4)
Nerves of Steel (3)
Situational Awareness (2)

Skills
Brawling 3
Computers 1
Dodge 2
Drive: Car 3
First Aid 2
Guns (Handgun) 4
Guns (Shotgun) 3
Hand Weapon (Club) 3
Intimidation 2
Questioning 2
Streetwise 2
Surveillance 2
Swimming 1

Gear
Class IIIa Vest, First Aid Kit, Flare Gun, Flashlight, Handcuffs, Handgun, Squad Car (Sedan), Vehicle Radio

Personality
Don't bug me. Uniform doesn't mean anything anymore. I'm not a public servant anymore. I'm just a man with a gun trying to survive. I can't help you. I got my own problems now.

No, you listen to me. My granddad was a cop, my father, my uncles, all cops. Back then, cops were the law and cops had respect. By the time I became a cop, it was a whole 'nother game. Sensitivity classes, social working, civilian review board, police brutality suits. They curse you and spit at you and hate you -- just 'cause of the uniform.

Fine. I took the oath, I did the job. I worked my butt off to take care of my buddies, and make my family proud.

But zombies? Fucking zombies, I didn't sign up for. I'm outta here. Got my ammo and supplies and squad car. As far as I'm concerned, the city can take care of itself.

Look I don't care about your wife and kid. I'm not surprised they're surround by zombies. There's zombies everywhere.

You're kidding. Don't tell me you don't even have a gun.

All right, all right. Take this shotgun and let's go. I can't believe I'm doing this -- again.

Quote
"I shot the guy and he wouldn't stay down! Good thing the cameraman from COPS tripped."

Archetypes

All Flesh Must Be Eaten

Priest
Inspired

Str 3 Dex 3 Con 3
Int 3 Per 3 Wil 5
LPs 34
EPs 38
Spd 12
Essence 35

Qualities/Drawbacks
Inspiration (5)
Gift (5)
Honorable 3 (-3)
Increased Essence Pool (3)

Skills
Driving (Motorcycle) 2
First Aid 3
Guns (Handgun) 1
Humanities (Theology) 4
Instruction 2
Language (Latin) 2
Myth and Legend 2
Notice 2
Occult Knowledge 2
Singing 2
Science (Psychology) 1
Storytelling 2

Metaphysics
Holy Fire
Touch of Healing
Divine Sight

Gear
First Aid Kit, Flashlight, Holy Book

Personality
Such an event so close to the 2000th anniversary of Our Savior's birth certainly gives one pause. Many of our more evangelical brethren have taken this to be a portent of the Rapture. They speak of Armageddon and quote from the Revelation.

Despite what the seminarians teach, I have always taken that book of the Bible to be nothing more than a metaphor, a disguised critique of the Roman Empire. There is nothing in it that mentions flesh-eating zombies. In fact, the only flesh-eating in the Bible is the Eucharist. So, what does a man of the cloth make of all this?

The Vatican is strangely silent, but they've always been a cautious bunch. I for one believe it's all the work of Satan. When we see such dark wonders, we question our faith. We see rotted bodies shambling around, and wonder where is the Lord? This is humankind's greatest test -- we must strive to be worthy.

We fail to realize that He is beside us, as always. You may laugh, but I have seen with my own eyes as I have healed the suffering and called forth fire to burn the monstrosities.

And it's done wonders for sermon attendance, let me tell you.

Quote
"The Lord is my point man, I shall not want."

Archetypes

Reporter
Norm

Str 2 **Dex** 2 **Con** 2
Int 2 **Per** 3 **Wil** 3
LPs 26
EPs 26
Spd 8
Essence 14

Qualities/Drawbacks
Contacts (Criminal) 2 (2)
Contacts (Police) 2 (2)
Contacts (Media) 3 (3)
Obsession (Finding the Truth) (-2)

Skills
Brawling 1
Bureaucracy 1
Computers 2
Disguise 1
Dodge 2
Driving (Car) 2
Electronic Surveillance 2
Guns (Handgun) 2
Haggling 1
Questioning 2
Research/Investigation 3
Smooth Talking 2
Stealth 2
Streetwise 2
Surveillance 3
Writing (Reporting) 2

Gear
Cellular Phone, Laptop Computer, Notepad, Tape Recorder

Personality
What better story is there than the end of the world? There are so many different angles. There's the human-interest angle -- ZOMBIES ATE MY DAUGHTER! -- always popular with the Reader's Digest crowd. There's the conspiracy angle -- IS THE GOVERNMENT RESPONSIBLE FOR THE ZOMBIE MENACE? -- they eat that kind of stuff up in the Midwest. And let's not forget the celebrity angle -- ZOMBIES RAMPAGE BALDWIN COMPOUND! NATIONAL GUARD DECLARES SEARCH FOR SURVIVORS NOT IN NATIONAL INTEREST. That was a hoot!

I thought that for as long as the crisis lasted, I could write about it. At first, I worked for a paper, but the building got overrun. We moved to a copy store, but in six months that was gone. Then we found a library with a working phone line and started posting information on the newsgroup alt.conspiracy.zombie.menace.

Now, most of the staff is gone from flesh-eaters, looters and trigger-happy GIs. I guess it's just as well. I can't write anymore. I'm burnt out. It's hard to keep going when you're part of the endangered species.

Quote
"Why am I taking notes? Someday these corpses are going to be put back in the ground. When that happens, I'm gonna be the first person to tell the story. If that ain't worth a Pulitzer, I don't know what is."

All Flesh Must Be Eaten

Scientist
Norm

Str 2 **Dex** 2 **Con** 2
Int 4 **Per** 2 **Wil** 2
LPs 26
EPs 23
Spd 8
Essence 14

Qualities/Drawbacks
Contacts (University) 3 (3)
Photographic Memory (2)

Skills
Bureaucracy 1
Computer Programming 2
Computers 2
Driving (Car) 1
Electronics 2
Engineer (Biological) 2
Engineer (Electronic) 2
Guns (Handgun) 1
Humanities (Psychology) 2
Research/Investigation 3
Sciences (Biology) 4
Sciences (Chemistry) 4
Sciences (Mathematics) 2
Writing (Scientific) 2

Gear
Doctor's Bag, Biohazard Suit, Flare Gun, Laptop Computer, Multitool, Specimen Jars and Tools

Personality
Gentlemen, it is my opinion that the zombie situation can be addressed if we stop reacting to them with superstitious frenzy. Such behavior is ill-suited for these desperate times. Zombies are a scientific problem. They are no more supernatural than global warming.

I understand that many are uncomfortable with my report. Although it appears to be madness, it is difficult to dispute my hypothesis that the OrganoCore fertilizer-spawned creatures can only be entirely neutralized through the utter reformation of our environment. The necessary mega-tonnage of nuclear weapons can be easily accessed and directed at a land mass such as the Himalayas to fill the atmosphere with sufficient ash to black out the sun's radiation.

Of course, only a small portion of humankind can be saved from the proposed nuclear winter. The appendix breaks down the recommended sectors of society. I am sure that general agreement may be had in this forum on targeting those in the top 10% IQ and supermodels. Naturally, others may be harder to convince.

Quote
"In the end, cold hard science will get us out of this."

Archetypes

All Flesh Must Be Eaten
Soldier/SWAT

Survivor

Str 3 **Dex** 4 **Con** 4
Int 3 **Per** 3 **Wil** 3
LPs 47
EPs 35
Spd 16
Essence 20

Qualities/Drawbacks
Fast Reaction Time (2)
Hard to Kill (3)
Nerves of Steel (3)
Situational Awareness (2)

Skills
Brawling 2
Climbing 1
Computers 1
Demolitions 2
Dodge 2
Driving (Car) 2
First Aid 1
Guns (Auto Rifle) 4
Guns (Handgun) 2
Guns (Gren. Launcher) 2#
Guns (Lt. Machine Gun) 2#
Guns (Shotgun) 2*
Guns (Submachine Gun) 2*
Head Weapon (Bayonet/Rifle) 3#
Stealth 2
Survival (Forest) 2
Swimming 2
*SWAT Only   #Soldier Only
With only slight modification, this archetype could be used for a Militia member or a Survivalist.

Gear
Assault Rifle, Class IV Vest, Class II Helmet, Combat Webbing, Flashlight, Grenades

Personality
Honor. Duty. Sacrifice. All that shit. I bought it though, that's why I signed up. One C.O. said women can't make good soldiers because we are too emotional. Guess he never heard of Lorena Bobbit or Charlie Manson's girls, eh? I stayed in and moved up -- showed them all.

Then the PHADE virus happened -- AIDS redesigned by a pissed-off Stephen King. We started rounding up the infected citizens at medical research camps. I got assigned head of security at one of them. It made me proud -- soldiering is about saving people, not just killing them.

Talk about a combat post. We had zombies coming at us all night, every night. We lost soldiers, but we did our job -- we gave the scientists time to find a cure.

Then the order came down. Liquidate the infected. Yeah, it was ugly, but I told myself -- cold, murderous logic was the only solution. Just like that, we were going door to door. We gave the children lollipops for being brave when they got their "shots". We zipped up the body bags and tossed them into the furnace.

Good soldier, I kept thinking, good soldier.

Quote
"We've got the zombies contained to a 3 block radius. Call in an airstrike. Yes, I know there are still civilians in there, Corporal. Make the call."

Archetypes

All Flesh Must Be Eaten

Video Store Clerk
Norm

Str 2 **Dex** 2 **Con** 3
Int 2 **Per** 2 **Wil** 3
LPs 33
EPs 29
Spd 10
Essence 14

Qualities/Drawbacks
Contacts (Criminal) 1 (1)
Contacts (Law) 1 (1)
Hard to Kill 1 (1)
Photographic Memory (2)

Skills
Brawling 2
Cheating 2
Computer Hacking 3
Computers 3
Dodge 2
Driving (Car) 2
Driving (Skateboard) 2
Electronics 2
Fine Arts (Cinema) 3
Guns (Handgun) 2
Haggling 2
Myth and Legend (Zombies) 3
Play Instrument (Guitar) 1
Sport (Extreme) 1

Gear
Backpack, Dr. Who Videos, Handgun, Video Camera

Personality
You ever seen that trick they do with the zoom and dolly cam? You know, where the dolly pulls out as the lens zooms in? Makes the guy in the middle of the frame look as if the whole world is collapsing in around him? That's what it felt like the first time I saw the undead coming at me.

Let me set the scene. Was working the late shift at Newton Plaza. Business had been quiet what with all the wandering gangs rampaging. Police were pretty tight-lipped about it all. Was all very Assault on Precinct 13.

Anyway, I hear a squeeeeee noise, then many squeeee noises -- like someone running their sweaty palms over a plate glass window. I look around and I see lots -- I mean dozens -- of people pressed against the store windows. And these folks do not look healthy. Was something out of a Fulci film. Couldn't move until the glass shattered. Then I booked, but fast.

I was like Dustin Hoffman in Marathon Man. When I got home, the zombies were moving up the stairs of my apartment building. I headed them off at the pass by using the elevator. It was a long shot, but I had to save my Dr. Who collection. Not to mention my girlfriend.

Quote
"I had to choose, save my girlfriend or my Dr. Who collection. I know Jenny would have understood. The survivors will thank me when it's all over."

Archetypes

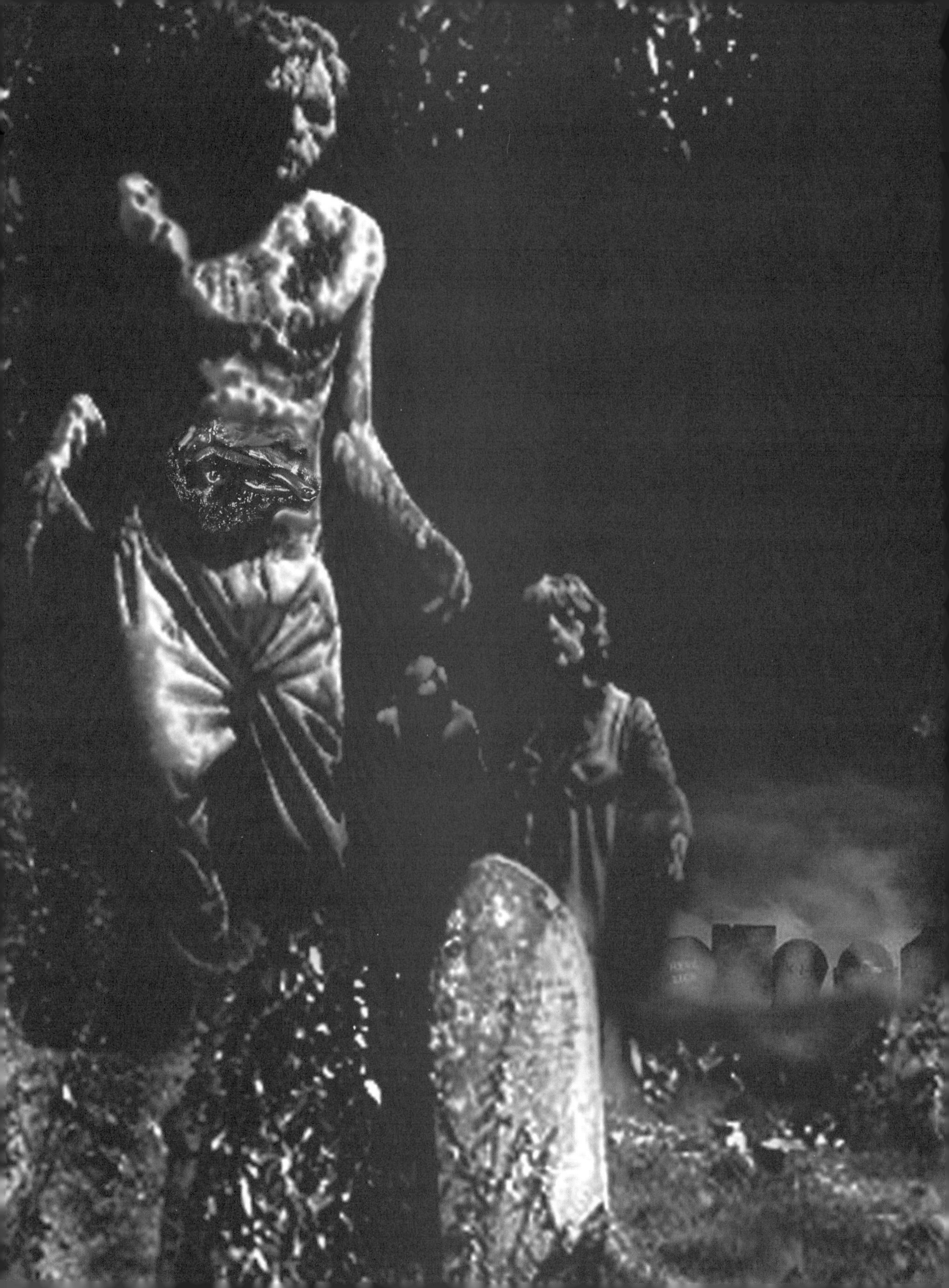

Chapter Three
Shambling 101

"How do you KILL something that's already DEAD?"

-- Return of the Living Dead

There are rules to surviving out here. Today I broke all of them. That's why I'm stuck here in this room listening to dead men scratch at the walls. I wonder how long it will be before one of those rotting fingers finds a handhold and starts pulling. I keep myself from nodding off by imagining a swarm of hands tearing through one of the windows, or the door flying off its hinges to reveal a wall of rotting zombie faces.

Thing is, though, I think that the waiting will get to me first. The sound of the floor boards creaking as they shamble past, and the smell -- God what a stink! Like roadkill in the hot summer air, so sweetly sour that with every breath it leaves you on the verge of gagging. And the scratching, we mustn't forget about the never-ending goddamn scratching. That's why I'm writing in this journal that I was planning to use as toilet paper. Hopefully, it will keep me sane long enough for me to . . . Oh wait, I'm getting ahead of myself.

Let's get back to the rules.

Rule one: never underestimate the enemy.

This was the number one problem in the early days. People would see the zombies coming and instead of thinking tactically they would stand their ground and keep firing. After all, isn't there's always time to run? Besides it only takes one head shot and no more deadboy!

We lost half the national guard that way.

First of all there isn't always time to run, because if you see one zombie there's usually at least four of them you're NOT seeing. So while you're blasting away at deadboy #1, deadboy #2 is coming up from the other direction to put the bite on your ass.

Second of all, contrary to popular belief, it doesn't take a simple head shot to kill a zombie. It's got to be through the brain. Half the freakin' amateurs these days don't realize that and completely loose their shit when the zombie they just shot still dogs them, sans face.

Perfect example is the screw up that got us here. The CO of my Guard unit -- swear to god I don't know where they're finding these people -- has us out sweeping the perimeter for deadboys. He sent us into what's left of Culver City. College-boy figures that since it's the dead of winter the zombies will be less active.

Yeah right.

At first, things were pretty quiet. We found a few of their nests and took them out with a little of the old shake and bake (incendiary grenades for those who don't know). Thing is you can never be too sure. I've seen some of those bastards walk through the flames like it was nothing.

We also scrounged for supplies wherever we could. It's not a rule, but it's a good policy to remember that you can never have too much ammo or Spam.

It was dusk, and we were ready to go. When all of a sudden there's this howl in the air, like a whole chorus of the deadboys are screaming at once. I knew what that meant, so did a few of the old-timers in our unit.

A Zombie Master was out there.

Rule two: never, under any circumstances, engage a Zombie Master with less than an entire division.

We didn't have too much choice about breaking this rule. A wall of white swept over us from the east, something half-snowstorm and half-avalanche. Blinded, we're all shouting, trying to stay together. Some of the newbies are panicking, our C.O. especially, firing off random shots into the squall. I know better, I just hold my position.

This is just foreplay.

Just as fast as the storm was on us, it's gone. The only difference now is that we're all knee deep in snow and there's a small army of the deadboys advancing on us. It was like they just came out of nowhere. I hear our new C.O. sobbing, he's telling us to fall back to the transport.

Here's where I broke rule three: there is strength in numbers. You see, I knew from bitter experience that the first thing a Zombie Master is gonna do is take out your means of rapid retreat. I also knew that our 90-day wonder wasn't going to listen to me in his current state of mind.

So I deserted. Running through the snow wasn't easy, and I had to pop a couple of the deadboys that were somehow burrowing through the snow after me.

I still don't know where the hell they learned that little trick.

I figured the best thing to do was to hole up and let the zombies fight it out with the other members of my unit. Once they've fed they tend to get lethargic, kinda like a real person twenty minutes after Thanksgiving dinner. As soon as the screaming stopped, I'd slip out.

You probably guessed, that's rule four: don't let yourself get cornered.

I found a building that didn't look like it had been used. It looked like some kind of a hospital clinic, one of those little one-floor jobbies that people with no medical insurance had to go to.

The sounds of the firefight were just starting to reach me when I got inside and shoved as much crap as I could in front of the door. It wasn't much of a barricade but it would delay them long enough for me to get out the back if I needed too.

Before I could relax I did a quick room-to-room search. I made sure to check the basement first, the deadboys love crawlspaces for some reason. The battle was still continuing. I could hear them fighting it out from street to street. Right then I half made up my mind to get back out there and die with the rest of my team.

The rustling made me forget all that.

It wasn't until I came up from the basement that I first heard it. My hands went icy with sweat as I continued the search. I half-expected to find the Zombie Master sitting in the waiting room, flipping through an old copy of NEWSWEEK.

Instead I found some girl, barely twenty years old, she's going through the storage room. Blood was dripping from the circular, four inch gash in her forearm.

"What happened?" I asked.

She screamed at the sound of my voice and raised her good arm up to protect herself. In another time, she might have been pretty, but life out here had harshened her features. Malnutrition had made her slim though, and I liked 'em slim.

I asked again, "What happed to you?"

"I -- I got bit."

Poor thing. I didn't think I could do what had to be done, but the training took over and I put her down with a single clean shot to the head. Rule five: bit is as good as dead. I don't know what the zombies house for saliva but within thirty-six hours of being bit most people turn into zombies themselves. And let me tell you it is not an easy death, it's like rabies and the Ebola virus all swept into one. You hemorrhage, shit yourself and go mad, then its gets bad.

Some of the doctors on base have been experimenting with anti-toxins and amputations to stop the infection, but they've had very limited success. Until its perfected, if someone you know is bit, take them down.

I don't care if its your girlfriend, your Mom or your best friend. Take them down.

If you don't, you're signing two death warrants instead of one.

After putting another shot into her for good measure, I shut myself into one of the rooms, lay down on the cool metal table and waited for the sound of my friends dying to go away.

A crash woke me up. I wanted to kick myself, of all the stupid things -- to fall asleep here and now . . . I was up and on my feet in seconds, M-16 in hand.

For a moment I was relieved, the men from my squad had found me. For a moment I stood there, frozen in place, not knowing if I should smile or grovel. Then the smell hit me, and the nonsensical groaning noises they were making. My eyes adjusted to the light. Their uniforms were in tatters. Their eyes were dead, like something out of a taxidermist shop. Their torsos and throats were ripped open, things glistening and black lolled out.

There must have been at least a dozen of them between me and the door. There was no way I was going out at the bottom of a freakin' zombie dogpile. I'd have probably been dead right there if not for the fact that half of them were busy chowing down on the girl I had shot earlier. I opened fire, the muzzle flash of my M-16, lighting the room with a strobe like effect.

They all saw me now.

I got lucky. The first few shots were head shots. Several zombies dropped, clearing a path for me. I barreled for the door only to find more of the bastards shambling inside.

Right, the back door then. I turned and fired into the sea of blank faces. How had they found me? Was it dumb luck? Or something more?

Halfway through the clinic I ran out of bullets.

And that is the last rule -- rule six: always save the last bullet for yourself.

Upending the gun I started using it as a club. The back door collapsed and more of the deadboys staggered in. Trapped, I did the only thing I could, I dove into the basement and locked the door behind me. It looked like a strong door and a good old-fashioned bolt lock. I knew that would hold them for a while.

That was I think two days or so ago, and my dead friends have shown no sign of leaving. They just wait and scratch at the doors and windows idly, like they know they've got all the time in the world.

Luckily this place is pretty secure. They must have had a problem with break-ins. I searched the place over and found nothing of use, no food, no ammo. The only thing I did find was a canister of medical waste that makes mewling sounds.

That's how I figured out this place used to be an abortion clinic.

So now I wait. How long can I survive without food and water? I'm sure they covered it in Basic but I'll be damned if I can remember now. I figure I've got a few more days before they lack of water gets the better of me.

That's assuming the doors and windows hold of course.

I've got no choice. I've got to try and fight my way out, using my M-16 as a club. And I've got to do it soon. But I'm going to wait one more day, maybe two.

When I go out there, I want to be just as hungry as they are.

Introduction

Like all games, the **Unisystem** has rules. They help the Zombie Master determine what happens at certain points of the Story. The **Unisystem** is also designed to offer several options to the players.

The main rule is that *All Flesh Must Be Eaten* players should do what works best for them. If a rule does not satisfy, is too complicated, requires too much detail, or is just plain unpopular, change it. Be sure that the entire gaming group knows of any changes beforehand, however. This minimizes complaints and arguments that detract from everyone's enjoyment of the game.

Running A Game

Usually, roleplaying games unfold in this way: the Zombie Master describes the situation, and then asks the players what their Cast Members are doing. Dialogue is conducted normally. A typical descriptive set-up might go as follows.

Zombie Master: *You are driving your car down a lonely country road. It's dark outside, and your car's headlights are barely enough to break the darkness in front of you. It almost feels like you are the only people on Earth. As you go around a bend in the road, you notice a pickup truck stopped by the roadside, a couple of hundred feet away. A person -- it's too dark to see if it is a man or a woman -- is by the vehicle. He or she notices your vehicle and starts waving. What do you do?*

In this example, three Cast Members are in a car, each controlled by a separate player. Each character has a chance to do something, although the driver has the most choices -- she could stop the car by the pickup truck, slow down and see what is happening, speed up and avoid the accident entirely, or anything else. The other Cast Members could talk to the driver, or look around for anything suspicious, for example.

In this case, and throughout most games, the Zombie Master presents a situation. When she asks "What do you do?" it is the Cast Members' turn to start contributing to the story. Sometimes the players take the initiative, informing the Zombie Master of their plans or intentions; in that case the Zombie Master describes the consequences of those actions. Through this interaction, the Story that is the game's end result is crafted.

Using the Rules

In most *All Flesh Must Be Eaten* games, a great deal of the characters' actions do not require rules, rolling dice, consulting charts or determining Success Levels. Common examples of such "ruleless" actions are discussed below.

Talking: Unless the character is gagged, mute or trying to speak in a foreign language she does not know very well, speech is always possible. A player need only recite the character's "lines."

Routine Actions: These include anything that any person can do, such at picking up objects, walking from one place to another, opening and closing unlocked doors. Any action that a normal person can perform with little or no effort requires only that the player announce that her character is going to do it.

Traveling: Getting there is not always half the fun. Just like in movies and books, the Zombie Master can "cut" any long, tedious actions. For example, if the characters are traveling to Europe by plane, and the real action awaits them there, the Zombie Master can sum up their trip in a few sentences:

You bought tickets for the first available flight; subtract the cost from your funds. The plane was half-empty, and it took off late at night, so most of the passengers were asleep for most of the trip. You enjoyed a few hours of rest, and now you are at the airport, going through Customs.

In general, if the rules are not required, don't use them. The feeling that the players are telling a Story should be disrupted as little as possible.

Only when the outcome of an action is in doubt, and the results of that action are important, should the rules come into play. The rules answer the question "What happened?"

Generally, the outcome of an action depends on the Attributes or skills of the characters (all those numbers on the character sheet), the circumstances (which may impose bonuses and penalties), and good old luck (determined by the result of a dice roll or card draw, unless the Story-Driven Method is used).

Dice

Dice are the most commonly used tools in gaming and, in this author's opinion, still the best method to determine random outcomes. Regardless of which method a Zombie Master chooses, the dice system is considered the default method in these rules. If the card method is used, for example, simply replace the words "roll" or "dice" with "draw" or "card."

When dice are used, the **Unisystem** relies on four different kinds: ten-sided, eight-sided, six-sided and four-sided. Such dice can be found in any good hobby or gaming store, and in many comic books stores. Dice are denoted by placing a "D" in front of their numerical value. So, a D4 indicates a four-sided die.

Ten-sided dice (D10s): Used for Task/Test determination and to determine the damage that weapons do, D10s are the most commonly used dice. Entire game sessions can come and go without using any dice other than the D10s. They can be replaced in a very rough sense by using two six-sided dice and subtracting two from the roll (treat a result of '0' as a '1').

Eight- and four-sided dice (D8s and D4s): In the **Unisystem**, these dice are only used to determine damage. Different damage types represent different weapon types. It stands to reason, for example, that a bigger weapon (like an axe) will do more damage than a smaller weapon (like a switchblade) when wielded by someone with the same strength. So, the smaller weapon uses a smaller damage die.

For example, a switchblade would do D4 times the Strength Attribute of the wielder in damage, while an axe inflicts D10 times the attacker's Strength. Dice rolls can be reduced or eliminated by using an average damage value (equal to half the value of the die used). This means that a weapon always does the same amount of damage in the hands of any particular warrior. For example, a switchblade always does 2 points of damage times the Strength of the wielder. This saves the trouble of rolling dice, but removes the random element of very low or very high damage.

Six-sided dice (D6s): These are the most common dice available, easily "borrowed" from any number of easily obtained board games. If D10s are not readily available, D6s can be used as a replacement.

Diceless Roleplaying

The base or "default" method of resolving actions in the **Unisystem** is through the use of dice. Not everyone likes dice -- indeed, a few people actively hate them. Some dislike the idea of letting pure chance determine the outcome of a Story; others would like a more elegant way to simulate randomness. To accommodate as many different playing styles as possible, the **Unisystem** has been designed to be usable in several different ways. In addition to the dice-based rules, the game can be played in two other ways: using regular playing cards, and eliminating randomness altogether.

Using Cards instead of Dice

For gamers who want to keep randomness when determining results, cards can be used instead of dice. Each player should start the game with a standard deck of 54 playing cards. The cards should be shuffled at the beginning of each game. When determining an action, draw a card instead of rolling dice.

Aces are treated as 1s. Numbered cards use their value. If a face card is drawn, consider the result to be a "5" and draw again. If the next card is another face card, the final result is considered to be a "10". Otherwise, the draw result is considered to be a 5. If an Ace is drawn, use the Rule of 1. If a natural 10 (but not two face cards) is drawn, use the Rule of 10 (see p. 93).

Jokers are generally discarded. However, if the Zombie Master wants to add an unexpected element, the following rule can be used. If a Joker is drawn, draw another card. If the new card is black, a mishap has occurred. The attempted Task or Test fails in some unexpected and spectacular way, which is left to the Zombie Master's imagination. If the second card is red, the action is automatically successful, usually owing to luck rather than skill (again, the Zombie Master can use his imagination to give the result an interesting and creative meaning).

Those are the only differences in the basic game. All the other rules described in this book apply normally. Damage rolls are either replaced with the set damage numbers written in parentheses, or the dice are kept for that part of the game.

Player-Controlled Outcomes

With card-based gaming, the Zombie Master can allow the players more control over their "luck" when performing Tasks or Tests. This is a special subsystem that can only be used with cards.

At the beginning of the game, each player draws a "hand" of six cards from the deck. The player then decides which card she will use on a given Task or Test. If the player thinks the attempt is important and she really wants to succeed at it, she plays the best card in her hand. The player, however, cannot draw new cards until her entire hand is "dealt."

Unless the player's hand is downright terrible, she will be able to choose which Tasks are successful, simply by using her highest value cards on a specific Task or Test. Of course, if the player uses up her best cards too quickly, she may be stuck with a couple of aces at a critical point of the Story!

When the Rule of 10, the Rule of 1, or face cards come into play, the second card is drawn from the deck, not the hand. Also, if the player initiates an action, the Zombie Master may require her to draw from the deck. This eliminates instances of players using up low cards in meaningless actions.

This subsystem is particularly appropriate for dramatic moments. Nobody wants to "fumble" when trying to cast the Invocation that might decide the fate of an entire city, for example. It also encourages strategic thinking; the player must decide when to play her best cards, and when to accept failure with good grace. By taking into account the needs of the Story, the player may decide her Cast Member should fail at certain points, adding to the drama of the game.

This optional rule requires that the players spend some time deciding what cards to use in a given situation -- they still do not know how difficult the situation may be, or what the opposition may draw against them. It usually helps move the Story along in a dramatically appropriate way, as the Cast Member tends to have "good luck" when the Story calls for it more often than not. On the other hand, this method cuts down on the uncertainty of the moment, and may end up having the players think more about strategy than the flow of the Story.

Story-Driven Roleplaying

For Zombie Masters and players who want to avoid random rolls or card drawing, the **Unisystem** can be used in the Story-Driven Method. The Zombie Master assigns outcomes dependent on the flow of the Story and the basic abilities of the player.

Task Resolution

The Story-Driven Method games use a straight number comparison. If the character's appropriate Attributes and skills are equal to or greater than the Difficulty Number (see the table nearby), the Task or Test is successful. The Zombie Master determines the Difficulty Number based on the needs of the Story, and how detailed and creative the player is in describing her Cast Member's action. If the roleplaying part of the action is good enough, the numbers involved should not be a factor, and the action should be successful automatically.

For example, Bertha the Witch, played by Holly, wants to talk (using her Smooth Talking Skill) a security guard into letting her sneak into a private party. Holly gives a great performance as Bertha, vamping it up and weaving a wild but believable tale. The Zombie Master does not bother comparing numbers or results, but simply plays the guard, who, with a stunned smile on his face, lets her pass.

In another example, Boris, a desperate Survivor, is played by Louise. He is trying to break into a warehouse to secure some supplies. The Zombie Master decides that this is a Difficult Task, and asks Louise to tell her Boris' combined Dexterity and Lock Picking Skill. Boris' Dexterity is a 4; his Lock Picking is a 5. The total of 9 is better than what is required for a Difficult task (usually a 6 to 8), so Boris is successful.

When two characters are using skills against each other, the higher combination of Attribute and skill wins. Only special circumstances alter this. A weaker fighter who goes on the defensive and is extra careful may last for a while before being defeated by his stronger enemy. A player who comes up with a good "dirty trick" or tactic may prevail against superior odds. Again, it is description, narrative skills and the Zombie Master's judgment that are the final determinants of most outcomes.

Difficulty Numbers Table

Type of Task	Difficulty Number
Easy	1-2
Challenging	3-5
Difficult	6-8
Very Difficult	9-10
Heroic	11-12
Impossible	13-15

Diceless Damage

In the Story-Driven Method of the **Unisystem**, damage can be applied using the fixed values (listed in parentheses in all weapon or damage descriptions). Alternatively, damage can be adjusted to suit the dramatic needs of the game. Here, a light wound is a cut on a limb, a nasty bruise, a cracked rib. It is not immediately incapacitating, but requires medical or supernatural help or it may worsen in time. Most weapons that inflict an average of less than 10 points of damage cause light wounds.

A serious wound can do a number of things. It can drop the target immediately (the victim may or may not survive the ordeal) or it can kill the victim if no medical help is available (the victim may still continue to move and act for several minutes or even hours, however). Being shot or stabbed in the torso area is the most common serious wound. The Zombie Master decides if the victim falls down, either as the result of physical shock, or just the psychological realization that she has been injured, or whether the victim carries on with her actions (people have been known to continue fighting or running even after sustaining mortal wounds). As a rule of thumb, any weapon whose average damage is 10-20 points inflicts serious wounds on a direct hit. Consider most handguns, regardless of their average damage, to inflict serious wounds in the torso area. Even small caliber bullets can do a lot of damage by bouncing around the victim's body.

A critical wound instantly drops the victim, and in all probability kills her. Critical wounds include beheading, a large caliber bullet hit to the head, being cut in half by a train, and similar mass trauma.

Using the Random Element

It is often easy to get caught up in the mechanics of the game and lose track of the Story. This may lead to players eventually getting bored of the game altogether. To make sure that this does not affect their games, Zombie Masters should take into account the following considerations.

When to Roll

Sometimes Zombie Masters and players fall into "roll-playing" mode -- rolling dice for all kinds of actions, even those that really don't matter. When a player wants to roll to see how nicely her Cast Member can park a car (unless there is some storyline reason why this is important), roll-playing has crept in. Rolls should be made when the outcome of an action has an impact on the Story, especially if success is doubtful. Rolls can add to the excitement and tension of the game, because nobody, including the Zombie Master, knows what the final outcome will be. Will the Inspired finish her Invocation before the zombie can bite her? This is the type of situation where a roll may help heighten the mood.

Rolls Don't Rule

There is another type of situation to consider: it was supposed to be a minor encounter -- a single zombie surprised two Cast Members. A fight ensued, and the Zombie Master got lucky, rolling several 10s in a row for the zombie's attack. All of a sudden, enough damage has been inflicted on a Cast Member to kill her -- thus ruining the main storyline.

Zombie Masters should sometimes consider "altering" roll results if those results are both highly unlikely and disruptive to the basic plot. In the example above, perhaps the outcome rolls could be "adjusted" to represent minor wounds or just a scary near miss. It helps if the Zombie Master makes her rolls out of sight of the players.

However, if it becomes common knowledge that the Zombie Master ignores roll results to keep the Story going, a great deal of the uncertainty and thrill of the roleplaying game is lost. The Zombie Master should keep this practice to a minimum -- so that when she needs to use it her players do not catch on.

The Basic Rule

Unless the Story-Driven Method is employed, all actions are resolved in one basic manner. Roll a ten-sided die (D10) and add the Attribute and/or skill numbers the Zombie Master deems applicable. Tell the result to the Zombie Master, who adds or subtracts any modifiers (for example, noticing something is more difficult in darkness than in broad daylight). If the final result is a 9 or higher, the action succeeds. If the result is less than 9, the attempt failed. The higher the total value, the more successful the action is (in some cases, just being successful is enough; in others, the degree of success may have some significance). This basic rule applies when using skills, engaging in combat, working magic, and so forth.

Tasks Using Skills and Attributes

Most actions, from sneaking around in the dark to writing the Great American Novel, are considered to be Tasks. A Task always uses one Attribute and one skill. The Zombie Master decides which Attribute and skill are appropriate to the action at hand. The die is rolled, and the applicable Attribute, skill and modifiers are added to the result. The higher the traits used are, the greater the chance of success.

For example, Tracy is playing a Goth high school student named Miranda. She wants her Cast Member to identify the foul-smelling, humanoid creature prowling in the school courtyard. The Zombie Master tells Tracy to use Miranda's Perception (to see how good a look Miranda got of the creature) and Notice Skill (the character's practice in picking up things that slip by most people). Miranda's Perception is 4; her Notice is a whopping 2. Tracy rolls a D10, getting a result of 6. This result, added to her skill and Attribute levels, produces a total of 12. Since it is dark outside, the Zombie Master applies a penalty of -3 to the Task, reducing the total to 9. That is enough to be successful. The Zombie Master says "Miranda, you realize that the shambling figure is a high school student who was killed last year in a drunk driving accident. But he's dead . . . and walking! With part of his head split open, he staggers toward you. What do you do now?"

Tests Using Attributes Alone

Some actions use only a character's Attributes; no skills are applicable. Some examples include lifting things (which uses Strength), remembering something (which uses Intelligence), and so on. These situations are known as Attribute Tests, or just Tests.

There are two types of Test: Simple and Difficult. Simple Tests are relatively easy things -- lifting an object using your entire body, for example. To resolve a Simple Attribute Test, roll and add the Attribute involved, doubled. For example, a character with a Strength of 2 adds 4 to the roll.

Difficult Tests are more challenging; lifting something with only one hand, for example, makes for a Difficult Strength Test. In those cases, only the value of the Attribute involved (do not double it) is added. This, of course, reduces the chances of success.

For example, Ashe is wandering through a forest at night, alone. What Ashe does not know is that a zombie is prowling these selfsame woods, and is closing in on him. The Zombie Master tells Ashe to roll a D10 and add his Cast Member's Perception Attribute, doubled. The woods are pretty quiet, and zombies are not known for their subtlety. The creature is not even trying to be quiet, making this a Simple Attribute Test. Ashe's Perception is 4, which doubled adds a total of 8 to the die roll. Ashe rolls the die and comes up with a 7, for a total of 15. The Zombie Master says "Ashe, you hear a guttural growling noise behind you. Something is rushing through the forest towards you. It should reach you in less than a minute. It's so loud you heard from it some distance away. What do you do?"

Determining What Attributes to Use

The Zombie Master often has to quickly decide what Attribute to use on a given Task or Test. For most situations, the relevant Attribute is described in the skill description, the Story write-up, or somewhere else in the book. For tense, dramatic situations, however, the Zombie Master should avoid slowing the game down by thumbing through all that material, and let common sense guide the choice. The following rules of thumb should be enough to judge what Attribute should be used in a given Task or Test.

Strength: Strength works when something requiring brute force is involved. Physical skills like Sports, Climbing or Swimming sometimes require Strength.

Dexterity: This is one of the most commonly used Attributes. Dexterity applies to any Task or Test requiring accuracy, physical balance, quickness, and eye-hand coordination.

Constitution: Constitution is mostly used in physical Tasks involving long-term endurance and vitality, or in Tests against diseases and toxins.

Intelligence: Anything that primarily involves memory and reasoning uses Intelligence. Remembering a name, understanding a difficult concept or idea, solving a mathematics problem or a puzzle -- all use Intelligence.

Perception: There is some overlap between Intelligence and Perception. When in doubt, the Zombie Master can have the player use the higher of the two (or the lower for a difficult Task or Test). Generally, Perception is used to spot, recognize or identify things. The overlap with Intelligence comes from the fact that memory is used to recognize and identify things. In general, if the Task or Test involves any of the five senses, use Perception.

Willpower: This Attribute is most commonly used defensively -- to resist other skills, powers or abilities. It is also used on Tasks or Tests where a character is trying to intimidate another. Willpower helps a person maintain eye contact during a staring contest, for example.

Unskilled Attempts

Sometimes, a character must try to do something she is not trained to do. Unskilled attempts always have a hefty penalty, but very gifted or talented people may be able to succeed even on the first attempt. Use the appropriate Attribute (do not double it), with a minimum -2 penalty (in addition to any other modifiers). Furthermore, the level of success of the Task (see later in this chapter) can never be too high. No matter how high the total outcome roll is, only a Decent outcome (second Success Level) will result from the attempt.

Some skills require so much training and preparation that untrained people have no chance of performing them. A penalty of -6 to -10 can be applied if the character is trying to perform very complex skills. For example, trying to perform surgery with no help other than a few medical manuals incurs a -10 penalty. Alternatively, the Zombie Master may rule that the attempt automatically fails (or, to keep the players in suspense, she may let them make rolls -- who knows, they might get lucky).

For example, Eric is playing the part of Nick, a 14-year old. Nick is riding with his father in a car. Suddenly, his father slumps over the steering wheel, unconscious (unknown to Eric/Nick, his father was bitten by a zombie when they escaped the gas station, and now the zombie virus has taken its toll). The terrified 14-year old tries to stop the car before it crashes off the road. This Task would normally be resolved by using the Driving Skill and the Dexterity Attribute, but Nick has no Driving Skill! A penalty of -2 is assigned for the lack of a skill. Nick has a Dexterity of 4, so he only adds 2 (his 4 Attribute, minus 2) to the roll of a D10. If the total is 9 or higher (which would require the die roll to be a 7 or higher), Nick manages to hit the brakes and stop the car without causing an accident. Otherwise, his panicked attempts may cause the car to swerve, go into a spin, or worse.

Resisted Tasks/Tests

Sometimes, a character tries to do something and another character (either a Cast Member or one of the Supporting Cast) tries to stop or hinder her. Similarly, an attempted action may be noticed or foiled by the target or victim of the action. When this happens, a Resisted Task or Test must be resolved.

Resisted Tasks or Tests use the same basic rule mentioned above. Both sides in the contest get to roll and add the appropriate Attribute or skill. If both fail (no one rolls over 9), neither side accomplishes the effect desired. If one fails and the other succeeds, the successful character prevails. If both succeed, the results are then compared, and the higher total result, after adding and subtracting all modifiers, is the winner of the contest. Some examples of Resisted Tasks and Tests are discussed below.

Arm Wrestling: This requires both sides to make Simple Strength Tests; the higher successful result wins the contest. For dramatic purposes, the contest might be spread over more than one roll (two out of three, or three out of five, for example).

Pursuit on Foot: Both sides use Dexterity and Constitution. If one person started running first, she gets to add a +2 to the roll. Also, the side with the higher Speed gets to add the difference between the two Speeds. Just subtract the lower Speed from the higher one, and add the result to the faster character's roll. The winner manages to either catch up with or lose the pursuer, depending on her intention.

Sneaking: The person doing the sneaking uses Dexterity and Stealth. The target uses either Perception and Notice or a Simple Perception Test.

Combat: Combat is described in more detail later in this chapter. Many combat actions consist of Resisted Tasks or Tests.

The Role of Luck

Sometimes, people perform feats they should normally not be able to accomplish. By the same token, even the most accomplished person occasionally fumbles or screws up relatively simple Tasks. When a roll (before adding or subtracting any modifiers) comes out as a 1 or 10, there is a chance that something really good or bad is about happen.

The Rule of 10

On a roll of 10, roll again, subtract 5, and add the result (if higher than 0) to 10. So, if the second roll is 6, 7, 8 or 9, the final result is 11, 12, 13 or 14, respectively. If the second roll is 5 or less, nothing is added and the final roll remains 10. If another 10 is rolled, add 5 to the roll (for a total of 15), and roll again. If a player rolls a string of 10s, she keeps adding 5 to the result and rolling again.

For example, Malcom, played by Jason, is trying to leap between two buildings, using his meager Strength of 1 and Dexterity of 2. The Zombie Master imposes a -5 penalty because the two buildings are fairly far apart. Knowing his Cast Member is almost certainly doomed, Jason rolls the bones. He gets a 10. "Roll again," the Zombie Master says. Jason rolls a second time, getting a 10! His total roll is a 15 so far, but he gets to roll a third time. This time the roll is a 3 -- no effect. The 15, plus Malcom's Dexterity and Strength, gives Malcom an 18, which is reduced to 13 by the -5 penalty -- enough to be successful. "You leap further than you could have imagined," the Zombie Master explains. "For a few moments, you actually feel like you are flying, and then you land well past the building's edge. You feel shaky and weak-kneed, and you know deep in your heart that you may not duplicate this feat in a hundred years."

The Rule of 1

On a roll of 1, roll again, subtract 5, and if the result is negative, a negative roll replaces the first roll. If the result is positive, the roll remains 1. If the second roll is between 5 and 10, the final result remains 1. If the second roll is 2, 3, or 4, the final result is -3, -2 or -1, respectively. If the second roll is 1, the prior roll is replaced with -5, and the player must roll again (applying the same rule).

For example, Robin the police officer, played by Jennifer, is wrestling with a zombie. Robin's Strength is 4. The fiend she is grappling with is relatively strong, Strength 5. Robin is trying to overpower the undead. Both sides use their Strength, doubled, in the Resisted Test. Confident of her Cast Member's abilities (an 8 against a 10 before the dice hit the table), Jennifer rolls her D10 -- and rolls a 1. Her second roll is a 3, resulting in a replacement roll of -2, which gives her a total of 6 (her base 8, minus 2). The Zombie Master rolls for the fiend. The die roll is a 7, which produces a total of 17. "Your grip slips: the creature breaks free and tosses you across the room," the Zombie Master describes. "Grinning macabrely, the monster lunges at you. What do you do?"

Role of Luck Table
Result After Second Roll

Second Roll	Rule of 10	Rule of 1
1	10	-5, roll again
2	10	-3
3	10	-2
4	10	-1
5	10	1
6	11	1
7	12	1
8	13	1
9	14	1
10	15, roll again	1

Alternative Rule

For those desiring something a bit simpler, the second roll should be D6-1. If the first roll was 10, add the result. If the first roll was 1, subtract the result. If the second roll is a 6, add or subtract 5, and roll again.

This option requires the use of a different die, and increases the chance of a higher or lower final result, but the change is not so significant that it is unbalancing.

Zombie Master's Discretion

The Zombie Master is the final arbiter of what a roll means. Some Zombie Masters apply the rules to the letter, and always consult the Outcome Table. Others simply decide on the spot what a roll means. Most use some combination of the two. Remember, maintaining the flow of the game is always more important than the rules. Slowing down the game to look up rules for a relatively minor action is not worth it. Wing it, and keep the game alive, immediate and interesting.

Modifiers

Most of the time, Tasks and Tests only account for the appropriate skills and Attributes. Sometimes, however, circumstances make some Tasks or Tests easier or more difficult. A ladder is a lot easier to climb than a greased pole. Shooting at a target in the dark is a lot harder than at high noon. If the Zombie Master feels that a Task or Test is made easier or more difficult because of circumstances, she can add modifiers, positive or negative, to any result. Assigning modifiers is something that should be done only when absolutely necessary, as it may slow down the game. The Zombie Master determines what circumstances are important enough to create modifiers, and decides how they affect an outcome.

Base Modifiers Table

Routine: No roll needed

Easy: +5 or more to the roll

Moderate: +3 to +4 to the roll

Average: +1 to +2 to the roll

Challenging (includes most combat rolls): No modifier

Difficult: -1 to -2 to the roll

Very Difficult: -3 to -5 to the roll

Heroic: -6 to -9 to the roll

Near-Impossible: -10 or worse

The Outcome Table

Sometimes, just being successful at a Test or Task is not enough. The degree of success may have an impact on the game or on future actions. This is particularly true in social interaction rolls, where a high level of success may impact future interactions with people previously impressed. It also applies to artistic endeavors, where the Success Level determines how good a work is produced. Furthermore, in combat, a particularly good or lucky blow or shot may end a fight right then and there.

When the degree or level of success of a Task is important, the Zombie Master may consult the Outcome Table nearby. This table serves as a guideline of how good a total roll is, and how impressive the character's actions were. An imaginative Zombie Master can use the results to add to the drama of the Story. For example, a highly successful display of combat skill may cause enemies to surrender or flee, too intimidated to continue fighting. A particularly successful performance may gain a character new friends and admirers. The Outcome Table is meant as a playing aid, not a restrictive law. The Table can be used as often or seldom as the Zombie Master desires.

Chapter Three

Outcome Table

A result of 9 generally means the attempt was accomplished (that's good enough in most cases). When the degree of the success needs to be measured, however, Success Levels depend on the final result (a roll including all positive and negative modifiers).

9-10: First Level (Adequate): The Task or Test got done. If an artistic endeavor, it is just adequate, and critics/audiences are likely to give it "ho-hum" responses. A complex and involved Task takes the maximum required time to complete. An attempted maneuver was barely accomplished, and might appear to be the result of luck rather than skill. Social skills produce minimal benefits for the character.

Combat: Attack does normal damage.

11-12: Second Level (Decent): The Task or Test was accomplished with relative ease and even some flair. Artistic results are above average, resulting in a warm reaction from many, but not most. Complex and involved Tasks take 10% less than the maximum required time. Attempted maneuvers are skillfully accomplished. Social skills manage to gain some benefits for the character (including a +1 to further attempts on the same people under similar situations).

Combat: Attack does normal damage.

13-14: Third Level (Good): The Task or Test was completed with ease. Artistic results are largely appreciated by connoisseurs and well-liked by the public (although some critics will be able to find something wrong). Complex and involved Tasks take 25% (one fourth) less time than normally required. Attempted maneuvers are done with seeming effortlessness, apparently the result of great skill. Social skills are not only successful, the character will be at +2 on future attempts on the same people (this is not cumulative with subsequent high rolls -- use the highest bonus only).

Combat: This is the roll needed to hit a relatively small and specifically targeted area, or to accomplish a tricky shot or strikes (for strikes against specific body parts, see p. 104)

15-16: Fourth Level (Very Good): The Task or Test was very successful. Artistic endeavors are rewarded with a great deal of appreciation from the intended audience. Complex and involved Tasks can be finished in half the time. Social skills produce a lasting impression on the people involved, resulting in a bonus of +3 on all future attempts in that skill involving the same people.

Combat: Increase the damage rolled by 1 before applying the Multiplier.

17-20: Fifth Level (Excellent): The Task or Test produced excellent results. Any artistic endeavor impresses the audience greatly, leading to a great deal of recognition and fame. Social skills have a future bonus of +4, as above.

Combat: Increase the damage rolled by 2 before applying the Multiplier.

21-23: Sixth Level (Extraordinary): The Task or Test produced amazing results, accomplishing far more than was intended. Artists gain fame after one such roll, but all their future accomplishments will be measured against this one, which may lead to the "one-shot wonder" label. Social skills gain a future bonus of +5, as above.

Combat: Increase the damage rolled by 3 before applying the Multiplier.

24+: Further Levels (Mind-boggling): For every +3 to the total above 23, increase the Success Level by 1, and the Social skills future bonus by 1.

Combat: Add +1 to the damage rolled for every additional Success Level.

Damage Modification Example: Luigi punches an opponent and his attack roll is a 17 (fifth level of success: +2 damage bonus). Luigi's normal punch damage is D4 x 3. Given his Success Levels, the damage is modified to (D4+2) x 3, or 9 to 18 points. Even on a bad damage roll, the attack inflicts a decent amount of damage.

Getting Scared

In the dark and dangerous settings of *All Flesh Must Be Eaten*, characters often experience frightful events. Indeed, in a world where the dead have risen from the ground and walk among us, it's pretty likely that someone will see a decomposing corpse walking. In such places, even the strong hearted get scared once in a while.

Fear Tests

When facing a fearsome creature or otherwise experiencing fright first-hand, Norms and Survivors must pass a Difficult Willpower Test. Inspired require only a Simple Willpower Test. If the Fear Test is failed, the victim succumbs to panic. Most of the time, the character will "freeze up" for at least a Turn. Alternatively, she may run away. Zombie Masters who want to add more detail can consult the Fear Table (see next page).

Fear Modifiers

Certain circumstances make it easier for the character to feel afraid. Very gory and gruesome events add penalties of -1 to -4, depending on how graphic the violence is. Hideous creatures may bring penalties of -1 to -5. Some beings have alien or thoroughly evil auras that inspire a deep, instinctual fear in people: such creatures may bring penalties of -2 to -8 to all Fear Tests! Some of the undead creature descriptions in Chapter Six: Worlds in Hell include specific modifiers to Fear Tests.

Essence Loss Because of Fear

Losing one's nerve often results in a temporary Essence loss. If Essence is reduced below 0 because of a terrifying experience, the character will be mentally scarred by the ordeal. Maybe seeing the same creature again will drive the character into screaming hysterics – or maybe she will be obsessed with finding it and killing it and all its kind. See the rules for Essence loss later in this chapter for more information (see p. 114), or consult the Fear Table.

Using the Fear Table

The nearby Fear Table can be used when a character fails a Fear Test. Roll a D10, subtract the Willpower of the character, and apply any Fear Test penalties as bonuses. So, a -4 penalty to a Fear Test would count as +4 bonus to the Fear Table roll.

If the result is less than 9, the victim was simply scared for a few seconds but was able to recover. If the total is equal to a 9 or higher, consult the Fear Table. The table uses the Success Levels to determine how badly the character suffered as the result of the terrible shock.

The Zombie Master can use the Fear Table for guidance and inspiration, but she should not let dice rolls rule the game. If a result seems inappropriate at the moment or to the character, the Zombie Master should devise her own outcome or result of the fear.

Time

Like any other story, a roleplaying game is a narrative that occurs over a specific length of time. Some games have detailed breakdowns of game turns, rounds or phases. The **Unisystem** use everyday measures of time (seconds, minutes, hours and days), saving the more arbitrary Turn measure (1-5 seconds) for combat and similar tense situations.

Additionally, a distinction must be made between Game Time and Real Time. "Game Time" is the "fictional time" of the story. "Real Time" is what the players and Zombie Master spend playing the game. Game Time is as fluid as the Zombie Master decides it to be. A decisive event taking only a few minutes of Game Time may require the players to spend several hours of Real Time to resolve. For example, a combat with multiple participants may take seconds in Game Time, but many minutes in Real Time because character's lives are at stake. By the same token, a period of hours, days or even years can be made to "flash by" in Real Time if the story demands it. "Well, after four days of continual rituals, you are ready for the final ceremony." Most of the **Unisystem** rules use Game Time, and are designed to take as little Real Time as possible.

Fear Table

Success Level	Effect
1	**Shakes:** All the character's actions suffer a -2 penalty for 2 Turns. Lose 1 Essence point.
2	**Flight:** Victim runs away screaming for 1 Turn. If cornered, the victim may fight or react in a more rational way. Lose 2 Essence points.
3	**Physical reaction:** Fear causes a messy physical reaction (often involving bodily functions best left to the imagination). Not only is this embarrassing, but it imposes a -1 penalty to all actions for D4(2) turns. Lose D4(2) Essence points.
4	**Paralyzed:** The character cannot move for D4(2) Turns. Only intervention by other characters (who may shake her, slap her or otherwise force her to act) will allow her to take any action. Lose D6(3) Essence points.
5	**Faint:** The shock and fear are so severe that the character collapses, unconscious. A Difficult Constitution Test is required to recover consciousness; this can be attempted every minute, or whenever somebody tries to stir the character. Lose D10 x 4 (20) Endurance points and D8(4) Essence points.
6	**Total Hysterics:** The victim becomes a screaming, babbling, totally useless maniac for D8(4) Turns. Lose D10(5) Essence points.
7+	**It Gets Worse:** Higher results are left to the Zombie Master's imagination. They may include life-threatening effects like heart attacks or comas, or a bout of temporary insanity lasting hours, or worse. . .

Combat

All Flesh Must Be Eaten is a game about survival, there is always a chance that confrontations will become a life and death struggle. However, *All Flesh Must Be Eaten* is not a war game. There are no detailed movement rules and strict damage systems. Combat is handled just like any other Task. A character attempts to do what she wants (in combat, this usually entails inflicting bodily harm on others). Whether she is successful depends on her skill, what the target is doing to stop her (if anything), and the luck of the dice (or the determination of the Zombie Master in the Story-Driven Method).

Turns

Combat in the **Unisystem** can be as formal or as informal as the Zombie Master desires. To simplify things, action is broken down into Turns. A Turn is a short length of time, about 1 to 5 seconds of Game Time in length. Basically, this is enough time for a normal person to perform one combat Task, like slashing at an enemy, firing a handgun, diving for cover, etc. The main reason for using Turns is to keep things organized; in a Turn, every character gets a chance to do something, and may have something happen to her in return.

The Zombie Master determines what action or actions are possible in a Turn. While people can theoretically do a lot of things in just a couple of seconds, combat situations are highly stressful times. Something as simple as reloading a pistol can be delayed by adrenaline-induced trembling. It is easy to swing a baseball bat around, but actually delivering an aimed blow at a target requires concentration and deliberation. Remember, this applies both to the Cast Members and the Supporting Cast. While most zombies are exempt from such emotions, human opponents should also suffer from fear, "buck fever" and other combat impairments. Common sense is the most important thing. Always remember that an extended action (emptying a gun at a target, for example) may prevent the character from doing anything else (like diving for cover if somebody shoots back) during a given combat Turn.

Running Combats

Each Turn gives enough time for all characters involved to perform or attempt to perform a desired action (within limits; some actions may take several Turns). The Turn may be broken down into six steps (see the nearby Turn Steps sidebar).

Ideally, an entire combat Turn should take no more than a couple of minutes of Real Time (very large groups entering combat will, of course, stretch that length of time). The Zombie Master should eliminate any step she feels will needlessly slow down a combat situation. Determining initiative is often a matter of common sense. Intentions can be summed up in a sentence or two, unless the Zombie Master and the players enjoy a detailed description of action scenes. The actual dice-rolling is meant to be fairly quick; an attack-defense sequence can be solved in two rolls.

Turn Steps

1. **Intentions:** The Zombie Master asks each player what her character intends to do during the next Turn.

2. **Initiative:** The Zombie Master determines who gets to attack first, or allows it to be determined randomly.

3. **Performance:** Attack, defense and non-combat Tasks or Tests are performed, starting with the character with the highest Initiative.

4. **Damage:** Any damage inflicted by the results of the Performance step is applied to the target or targets (this can end the fight right then and there).

5. **Repeat:** Further Tasks are resolved and damage inflicted until each character has had a chance to act during the Turn.

6. **End:** The Turn ends and the process starts again back at step 1.

It is the Zombie Master's job to describe the action. Rather than just say "You hit, and inflicted ten points of damage," descriptions should be more like "You slashed the guy in the arm. From the way the blood spurts out, you cut him deeply -- the man yelps in pain and backpedals away." Keep the imagery lively; make the players feel that their Cast Members are in a dangerous situation. It is particularly effective when a Cast Member blasts a large hole in a zombie, and it doesn't seem to make any difference to the shambling horror. It just keeps on coming.

Intentions
What Will Be Attempted

At the beginning of each Turn, the Zombie Master asks the players what their Cast Members intentions are. Each player gets to state actions. This could be something as simple as "I duck for cover" or "I hit him with my baseball bat" or as complex as "I aim at the walking undead's head" or "I jump behind a crate, toss a grenade, and pray."

The Zombie Master decides if the intention is possible, if it will take one Turn or less, and what skills are necessary. The Zombie Master can point out to the player any risks or problems the action may bring about -- if the player's Cast Member would know or understand those risks. Some Zombie Masters let a player's intentions stand even if they are stupid or suicidal; others try to "coach" their players through every action. Both extremes are bad. There is nothing wrong with reminding a player of something she may have forgotten in the "heat of battle" (again, if it is something that her Cast Member would have noticed). On the other hand, some players may resent being told what to do all the time.

Initiative
Who Goes First

Most of the time, this should be a matter of common sense; the party or person who initiates the violence usually goes first at the beginning of a fight. After the first Turn of the fight, Initiative depends on what happened in the previous Turn. Typically, the combatant who actually managed to land a blow or hurt his target gets to go first. The Zombie Master can always decide who attacks first based on the particular circumstances at the time.

Initiative can also be determined randomly. To do so, each player who has a Cast Member in the situation rolls a ten-sided die and adds the character's Dexterity. The highest result wins the Initiative for that Turn, and makes the first move. The remaining characters act in descending order of Initiative.

Note that certain Qualities and abilities can affect a character's Initiative.

As noted, some circumstances may also determine Initiative. Characters with ranged weapons usually get to attack before those holding hand weapons or no weapons at all. A magical or psychic attack, which requires only a thought to activate, will go before hand-to-hand or ranged attacks under most circumstances. Also, a guy who sucker punches somebody gets to go first. A sniper firing on an unaware target half a mile away automatically gets Initiative. As always, the Zombie Master has the last word.

Group Initiative

To speed up play, the Zombie Master may decide to allow each discrete side of a combat or tense situation to roll for Initiative instead of each character. Generally, this means only two rolls are made (one for the Cast Members and one for the Supporting Cast). The character on each side with the highest Dexterity provides the roll bonus.

This method, while faster, is less realistic. Furthermore, it allows all members of one side to attack or act before anyone on the other side attacks or acts. If the "bad guys" outnumber the Cast Members and gain Initiative, it could prove to be very deadly.

Performance: Who Does What

The Performance step lumps together any Tasks or Tests required for the actions declared during the Intentions step. As such, a great many things can happen during this step. Several are discussed below. For all others, Zombie Masters should determine which Task or Test must be performed (if any), and then interpret the results of those attempts.

Multiple Actions

In general, each character may take one action without penalty in a Turn. More than one action may be performed, however. The main limitation is skill; dividing concentration is difficult. Each additional action taken in a Turn has a cumulative -2 penalty. In other words, taking one extra action is done at a -2 penalty, a third action is at -4, and so on.

In close combat, things work slightly differently. In that circumstance, characters may perform one attack and one defense Task or Test each Turn at no penalty. Any actions beyond that attack and defense is at a cumulative -2.

For example, Jin the Kung Fu expert, played by Dan, is facing three zombies. The ugly monsters all attack him at almost the same time. Jin punches one of them, and tries to evade their attacks. His attack and one defensive move are free. The second defensive move is at -2, and the last one is at -4 -- not surprisingly, the last attack strikes home, and the zombie inflicts a nasty wound on the martial artist.

Close Combat

Close combat is any fight conducted at arm's length by people using fists, feet, or hand weapons (such as knives, swords and sticks). In close combat, the character with Initiative gets the chance to strike first. The target may attempt a defensive maneuver, like blocking the attack with a hand weapon of her own, dodging or jumping out of the way, or the like.

Striking at an enemy is a Task: use the character's appropriate skill (Brawling, Martial Arts, Hand Weapon) and Dexterity. If the enemy has a hand weapon of her own, she can try to parry the attack, using her own Weapon Skill and Dexterity. Characters with Martial Arts can parry hand weapons with their bare hands; those with Brawling or no close combat skills cannot. Instead of parrying, the defender may dodge out of the way. This uses Dexterity and the Dodge Skill (if the character has it), or must be resolved as a Difficult Dexterity Test (if not). So, even an unarmed, unskilled person may try to get out of the way of an attack by passing a Difficult Dexterity Test.

An attack and defense set is resolved as a Resisted Task. If the successful attacker gets a higher result than the defender, her blow lands and inflicts damage. If the defender ties or gets a higher result, she manages to deflect or dodge the attack. Some modifiers may be applied for light (see the Ranged Combat Modifiers Table, p. 102) and other circumstances at the Zombie Master's discretion. Otherwise, that's all there is to it.

All Flesh Must Be Eaten

Detailed Close Combat Rules

Some players may want more detail to their fights than simple attack and defense rolls. These optional rules are meant to accommodate this element. Zombie Masters should reward good intention descriptions with a few bonuses in the appropriate Task rolls.

Defensive Posture: The character remains on the defensive, forsaking any chance to attack in favor of protection. A character using this tactic gets a +3 bonus on all defensive Tasks or Tests she performs on that Turn. This is a good tactic for trying to keep a superior enemy busy while waiting for reinforcements to arrive, or to gauge an opponent's skill before making a move (judging the opponent's skill may require a Task involving Perception and the appropriate Weapon Skill -- although if the attacker manages to hit despite the defensive posture, no Task roll is necessary).

Aggressive Posture: The character goes all-out in her attack, abandoning any hope of defense to smash the enemy. This gives a +2 bonus on all attack Tasks performed that round, but no defensive Task may be made. This is a good tactic if the enemy is unarmed or if the character thinks she can take any damage inflicted by her opponent. Most of the time, though, it is too risky.

Feinting: A feint is a false attack meant to distract the enemy and lower her defenses against the real strike. The feint is resolved as a Resisted Task -- the attacker's Intelligence and close combat skill against the opponent's Perception and close combat skill. The attacker's and defender's close combat skill need not be the same. The attacker might attempt the feint using Brawling Skill, while the defender attempts to read the feint using a Martial Arts Skill, for example. If the attacker wins the contest, she gets a +1 bonus on her next attack Task for each Success Level in the feint Task.

Improvised Weapons

Sometimes, a weapon is not at hand during a dangerous situation, and one must use an improvised weapon (a broken bottle, a table leg, chair, etc.). It will, however, be less effective than a real, balanced weapon.

When using an improvised weapon, the character uses the closest Weapon Skill she has. Anything that involves thrusting sharp objects (broken bottles, forks, icepicks, etc.) uses the Hand Weapon (Knife) skill (or Sword skill, but at a -2 penalty due to the shorter reach). A longer, swung object could use Hand Weapon (Club or Sword or similar weapon) skill. If no related Hand Weapon skill is available, use a Difficult Dexterity Test to strike or defend. Used defensively, a chair or similar large object actually acts like a shield, giving the character a +1 to +2 bonus to her parry roll. The Zombie Master should assign penalties for large, heavy and clumsy improvised weapons (-1 to -3 in most cases).

Ranged Combat

Ranged combat involves any sort of missile weapon, from a thrown stone to a machine gun. The attacker with Initiative gets to fire at the target; this Task involves the attacker's appropriate ranged combat skill and Dexterity. Range, lighting and other modifiers affect the Task.

Defenses: In ranged combat, the target has precious few choices. She can stand his ground and fire back, hoping the attacker will miss, or she can duck for cover. Ducking for cover uses Dodge and Dexterity. If the result is greater than or equal to the attacker's Task result, the target was able to hit the ground or jump behind cover in time to avoid the shot. The only problem with that tactic is that it is the only action the target can take on that Turn. That is why most firefights are dominated by the group that fires first; the targets are pinned down and cannot fight back.

Aiming: A character who wishes to shoot can also take some time to aim her weapon. This delays her attack to the end of the Turn (giving the target a chance to fire first, move behind cover, or perform other actions), but it makes the attack more likely to hit. Aiming is a Task involving the character's Perception and Weapon Skill; each Success Level adds a +1 bonus to her attempt to strike.

Modifiers: Modifiers to ranged weapon attacks are listed on the table nearby. Note that range affects the Task. Ranges for various weapons are listed in the Weapons Table (see p. 134). If looking for modifiers takes too long, the Zombie Master should feel free to dispense with them, or determine them on the spot.

Firing Multiple Shots

One to five seconds is a long time for modern automatic and semi-automatic firearms. An average submachine gun has a cyclic rate (the number of bullets fired if the trigger is kept pressed) of over 600 rounds per minute -- 10 shots are fired in one second! Even a semi-automatic pistol or double-action revolver (which fire as fast as the trigger is pulled) can be emptied in under five seconds. The main drawback of firing multiple shots is that most rounds miss the target. While rapid-firing, most automatic weapons experience "muzzle climb" as the gun bucks and fires higher and higher up. Semi-automatics also experience aim-ruining recoil.

Semi-Automatic Multiple Shots: Any weapon that fires a shot every time the trigger is pulled can fire multiple times in a Turn. Each successive shot gains a cumulative -1 penalty (i.e., the second shot is at -1 to hit, the third shot is at -2, and so on). If the gun has a heavy recoil (a .44 magnum, for example), the penalty is a cumulative -2.

Automatic Fire -- Bursts: The most controllable automatic fire is short bursts of three to five shots. A burst fires at no penalty. Each Success Level in the Task means the attacker scores a hit, up to the total number of bullets in the burst. For example, a shooter firing a three-shot burst who scores two Success Levels hits with two bullets, each doing damage separately. Success Levels only affect the number of hits, not the damage (no damage multipliers from the Outcome Table apply). If she racks up three Success Levels or more, all three rounds strike the target. If firing multiple bursts, each successive burst suffers a cumulative -3 penalty.

Automatic Fire -- Rock 'n Roll: Here, the shooter keeps the trigger depressed and "hoses" the target with a stream of bullets. Most the bullets are going to go high as the gun's muzzle is forced up by the constant recoil. Each group of ten shots counts as a "group;" make a strike Task for each group. Each Success Level means one bullet hits. Again, Success Levels only affect the number of hits, not the damage. Each group after the first is at a cumulative -4 penalty.

Ranged Combat Modifiers Table

Point-Blank Range: +1 to Strike Tasks, and add 1 to the Damage Multiplier.

Short Range: No modifier.

Medium Range: -1 to Strike Tasks.

Long Range: -3 to Strike Tasks, and reduce Damage Multiplier by 1.

Extreme Range: -6 to Strike Tasks, and reduce Damage Multiplier by 2.

Poor Lighting Conditions (A dark alley, candlelight, moonlight): -1 to Strike Tasks.*

Bad Lighting Conditions (Moonless night): -4 to Strike Tasks.*

Total Darkness: Use a D10 roll with no other modifiers; only a natural roll of 9 or higher strikes the target. If a character makes a Difficult Perception Test, she can add each Success Level to the D10 roll, accounting for the use of senses other than sight to spot the target.*

Multiple Shots: -1 for each additional shot, or -2 if the weapon has a heavy recoil.

Gun Scopes: A telescopic scope will add +2 to +5 to any Aiming Tasks.

* Lighting modifiers also apply to close combat attacks.

Automatic Fire -- Suppressive Fire: Automatic fire can be used to "sweep" an area, suppressing any targets there (i.e., making them kiss the ground and pray for deliverance) and hitting anybody stupid enough to stick their head into the "beaten zone" (the area the shots are spraying). No roll is made, just the intention to spray an area with gunfire. Rather than have to look at cones of fire and complicated formulas to determine the area covered, assume that most automatic small arms sweep an area the size of a doorway or two. Anybody straying into the area will be struck by D4(2) shots.

Shotguns

For the most part, shotguns use two types of missiles: shot (small pellets contained in a cartridge), and slugs (solid shot). Shot scatters, creating a "cone" of bullets that spreads over distance. It is thus easier to hit a target with shot than with a normal bullet. Characters using a shotgun loaded with birdshot (the smallest pellets) gain a +2 bonus to strike targets at any range; with buckshot (larger pellets) apply a +1 bonus. Slugs are treated like normal bullets. Shotgun damage is treated later in this chapter (p. 105).

Keeping Your Cool

A factor rarely taken into account in most games is the ability (or lack thereof) of people to remain controlled and calm while under fire. Most people who are shot at tend to freeze or panic. Only the very brave, the very stupid, and combat veterans are likely to keep their cool and do the right thing when every instinct in their bodies is telling them to start running, NOW! Zombie Masters wishing to run a heroic game are free to dispense with this factor, although its use may discourage hot-headed players from getting their Cast Members into firefights at the drop of a hat.

When being shot at, a character must pass a Simple Willpower Test to continue carrying out her original intention. A failed result means the character freezes or hesitates, and loses any chance to act in that Turn. This rule also applies to the Supporting Cast, so sometimes it is a good idea to fire blindly in the general direction of one's enemies, if only to make them "keep their heads down."

Damage
How Much Does It Hurt

Once a character hits a target (or the enemy hits the Cast Member), the damage inflicted must be determined. Damage works differently than Task resolution. Damage is measured in points, which are marked off the character's Life Points, or a zombie's Dead Points. If Life Points are reduced to 0 or below, the character is critically injured and is at risk of dying. The effects of damage are explained later in this chapter (see p. 111).

Most forms of damage in the **Unisystem** are determining by rolling a die; the result is then multiplied by a set number (called, for obvious reasons, the Multiplier). For example, a .22 pistol does D4 x 2 points of damage. In this case, the 2 is the Multiplier, and to determine damage a four-sided die is rolled and the result is multiplied by 2.

Why express damage in this manner? First, the Multiplier can get modified in a number of situations. In the case of the pistol, a bullet hitting at point-blank range does more damage than one fired from a hundred yards away. At point-blank, the Multiplier is increased; at longer ranges, it drops. Also, some weapons have a variable Multiplier. Most hand weapons, for example, do damage based on the Strength of the wielder. A baseball bat wielded by a ten-year-old does not do as much damage as the same bat in the hands of a champion weightlifter. To figure the bat damage, the base damage (D8) uses the Strength of the wielder as a Multiplier.

Finally, although multiple dice could be rolled and the results added together, using a Multiplier increases the chances that maximum and minimum damage will be inflicted. When rolling several dice, low rolls tend to "cancel out" high rolls, usually resulting in an average damage roll.

Damage values for normal punches, kicks and a number of different weapons are presented in Chapter Four: Implements of Destruction. Damage suffered by other forms of injury appear later in this chapter.

Reducing Dice Rolling

The "default" Unisystem relies on two types of dice rolls: outcome rolls, which use a D10 and add modifiers, skills and Attributes, and damage and armor rolls, which usually require rolling a die and multiplying it by a set value. The second type of roll is used only in combat situations. Some gamers may prefer to reduce the randomness of combat, or simply reduce the number of dice rolled. The quickie way of eliminating damage and armor rolls is to use the "average" value of a die roll (actually, a little below average). This value is listed in parentheses next to each damage roll in the Weapons Tables. Instead of rolling damage or armor dice, simply apply the set number each time a hit is scored.

Oh, God -- I've Been Shot!

When people are injured (and they realize it -- some people may be unaware of even mortal wounds for some time), their first reaction is usually shock and fear. Even if the wound is not lethal, the typical person will collapse, scream and do a number of useless things. Only people driven by rage, drugs or pure determination (or too stupid to know better) will carry on with a fight despite their wounds. To simulate this, the Zombie Master may require characters who have been injured in combat to pass a Simple Willpower Test before continuing their fight. A penalty equal to the damage taken by the character may be applied to the Test. This penalty is left to the discretion of the Zombie Master -- a dramatic fight should not be slowed down because the protagonist was wounded. In such cases, the Zombie Master can rule that the character is so determined (and pumped full of adrenaline) that she shrugs off any wound that does not kill her.

Targeting Body Parts

These rules can be used for dramatic purposes, but add more complexity to combat. The following chart determines the penalty to the attack, and the modifier to the damage inflicted. Damage bonuses occur after penetration (if the target is not wearing armor, all damage is modified accordingly).

Head: -4 to hit. Blunt damage is doubled; slashing/piercing is tripled. Bullet damage is modified by two levels (i.e., armor-piercing bullets inflict triple damage, normal bullets inflict four times damage, etc.). Endurance Point damage (in non-lethal combat) is quadrupled.

Neck/Throat: -5 to hit. Blunt damage is doubled; slashing/piercing damage is quadrupled. A slashing attack on this area that does enough damage to kill the victim results in decapitation. Bullet damage is modified by one level (armor-piercing bullets inflict double damage, and so on).

Arms/Legs: -2 to hit. Damage in excess of Life Points/3 cripples the limb; extra damage is lost.

Hand/Wrist/Foot/Ankle: -4 to hit. Damage in excess of Life Points/4 cripples the area. Extra damage is lost.

Vital Points (heart, lungs, spine, kidneys, etc.): -2 to hit. Blunt damage is doubled; slashing/piercing damage is tripled. Bullet damage is modified by one level (see Neck/Throat bullet damage).

Special Weapon Types and Damages

Not all weapons are created equal. Some inflict harm differently than others. Of course, many of these special damage features are only applicable against other humans; they may be useless against zombies (see Flesh Notes, p. 147). Damage formulas that do not contain special notations like those below are consider to inflict regular damage.

Two-Handed Weapons: Close combat weapons used two-handed raise the effective Strength of the wielder by 1. For example, a Strength 3 character wielding a two-handed axe has an effective Strength of 4 for purposes of damage.

Slashing/Stabbing Weapons: Edged or pointed weapons have a better chance of inflicting permanent damage on their victims. An edge can slice muscle tissue and even chop through bone. A point can reach deep in a target's vital organs. To simulate this, any stabbing or slashing damage that is applied to a target (after taking into account any armor reductions) is doubled. Blunt weapons (from fists to dropping safes) do not enjoy this benefit, although they often do more general damage.

Normal Bullets: A normal jacketed bullet tends to corkscrew and ricochet inside the human body, shattering bone, piercing vital organs and doing assorted forms of mayhem. Thus, normal bullet damage is doubled after penetrating armor.

Hollow-Point Bullets: Expanding bullets create a greater wound cavity and tend to spend more of their energy inside the victim's body as the bullet flattens and mushrooms inside flesh. Armor can easily stop these bullets. Double any Armor and Barrier Value between the target and the bullet, but any damage that gets through is tripled.

Armor-Piercing Bullets: These high-velocity, solid rounds punch through armor and obstacles, but they also tend to punch through the target in a relatively flat trajectory, doing reduced damage. Armor-piercing rounds halve any Armor or Barrier Value in their path, but the damage inflicted is not modified.

Shotguns: Slugs are treated like normal bullets, with damage doubled when hitting flesh (there are also hollow-point slugs, which do triple damage, as above). Shot damage does not double, and any armor worn is doubly effective against it (even heavy clothing affords some protection against the lighter birdshot used in hunting shotguns). On the other hand, shot spreads over a wider area, making it easier to hit the target (see earlier in this chapter, p. 103).

Explosives: Explosions inflict damage in two ways. First is the shockwave, which is nothing more than gas or air traveling at tremendous speeds. More dangerous are the fragments the shockwave throws around at bullet speed. Fragments come from either debris created by anything the shockwave encounters (bricks, earth, rocks), or from specially designed metal casings or shrapnel (the metal case of most bombs is designed to break into jagged metal fragments to inflict maximum damage; some pipe bombs are filled with nails or ball bearings for the same reason). The shockwave damage is rapidly reduced by distance; fragment damage is not.

To make matters simpler, explosive damage in *All Flesh Must Be Eaten* is expressed as one value, which takes into consideration both fragmentation and shockwave damage. Simple concussive devices do less damage than fragmentary ones. There are three areas of effect: Ground Zero (very close to the explosion), General Effect (the area of most widespread damage after Ground Zero), and the Maximum Range (the area after which the explosion ceases to inflict significant damage). The ranges of most common explosives are listed in Chapter Four: Implements of Destruction (p. 136-137). These measures are not strictly scientific and accurate, but any more detail will bog most games down needlessly; some Zombie Masters may wish to simplify matters by only using the General Effect Damage. Body armor is largely ineffective against concussion (Ground Zero damage); only fully sealed armor (like that used by Ordinance Disposal teams) protects with its full Armor Value at any range; normal body armor protects with half its Armor Value at Ground Zero, and normal AV at other ranges.

Another form of explosive damage is that used in rockets and anti-tank weapons. These weapons use the Shaped-Charge Effect to better penetrate armor (of vehicles and other hard targets). Generally, those missiles divide the Armor or Barrier Values of a target by a number, usually 3 to 5, depending on the effectiveness of the weapon. Anti-tank weapons are not described in this book, but will appear in future **Unisystem** sourcebooks.

Poison

Poisons are foreign substances that, when introduced into a person's body, cause harm, injury or death. They include manufactured chemicals and substances secreted or injected by animals or supernatural creatures. In the real world, some poisons can kill a person instantly, while others have varying degrees of lethality. As a weapon, poison is often unreliable and can be as dangerous to the wielder as to the intended victim.

In game terms, poisons all have a Delivery Method (how the poison is applied) and a Strength Rating (its lethality). The Delivery Method is either ingested (eaten), injected or contact. Some poisons may be applied in more than one way, but their effectiveness may vary according to how they are delivered.

The Strength Rating determines how much damage the poison inflicts, or how difficult it is to resist its effects. The Strength Rating of a poison depends on the type of toxin. There are three basic kinds of poisons: corrosive, irritant and narcotic (also known as nerve poisons). Each kind has its own characteristics.

Corrosive poisons include a number of acids, and several common cleaning fluids. They can burn the skin directly, inflicting a number of points of damage (see the nearby Corrosive Damage Table) every turn the person is exposed (being splashed with the liquid means the victim is exposed until the corrosive is washed off with water). If ingested, they do the same damage until the poison is neutralized with an antidote, or ejected by vomiting.

Irritants include such poisons as arsenic; they are more slow-acting, and require multiple doses. Instead of direct damage, the poison slowly drains Life Points, typically one point per every two Strength Rating of the poison, for every dose ingested. For example, if the poison has a Strength Rating of 1, damage occurs after two doses. This Life Point damage can only be healed if the poison is purged from the system. When the victim's Life Points are reduced to 0, the victim may die (a Survival Test postpones death).

Narcotic, or nerve poisons include curare, chloroform and strychnine. They directly depress the victim's nervous system and such functions as breathing.

Corrosive Damage Table

Poison Strength Rating	Damage
1	1 point
2	1D4(2)
3	1D6(3)
4	1D8(4)
5	1D10(5)
6	1D6 x 2(6)

They can induce unconsciousness, paralysis, or death. These poisons do not inflict damage directly. Instead, they use a Simple Strength Test against a Simple Constitution Test by of the victim. If the poison's Strength wins the contest, the victim suffers the poison's specific effects. Typically they include drowsiness or unconsciousness (for weak narcotics) to heart or respiratory arrest (resulting in death by suffocation unless first aid or medical care are immediately provided).

Some sample poisons are discussed below. Zombie Masters can devise game mechanics for other poisons based on these examples.

Cobra Venom: This powerful corrosive neurotoxin has an average fatality rate. The Delivery Method is injection. Depending on the species, this venom has a Strength of 3 to 6. Each bite injects one dose, and inflicts Corrosive damage based on its Strength for 5 turns. For example, the bite of a relatively weak cobra (Strength 4 venom) would inflict D8(4) points of damage for 5 Turns. If the bite is drained, the venom does half damage. After administration, an antitoxin prevents further damage. A cobra can bite more than once in a 24-hour period, but the strength of the venom drops one level per subsequent bite, as the dosage is reduced. In the example above, the cobra's next bite would do D6(3) points of damage. On the other hand, if the cobra bit the same person twice or more, the damage is cumulative.

Some cobras can spit venom. It is treated as a Strength 1 Corrosive (1 point). If the venom hits a victim's eyes, she must pass a Difficult Constitution Test or be blinded for 1 hour. After that, a Simple Constitution Test at +4 must be passed, or the blindness becomes permanent.

Arsenic: This irritant poison can be found in some insecticides and weed killers. In the ancient world, arsenic oxide, which is colorless and flavorless, was a favored poison, although its effects take a long time and people can actually develop an immunity by ingesting small doses.

The Delivery Method is ingestion. A large dose of arsenic has a Strength of 6, and inflicts 3 points of damage per hour until the poison is removed (usually by inducing vomiting, although a full stomach pump in a hospital is preferred). Smaller doses have a Strength of 2, and inflict 1 point of damage per day. Symptoms of gradual poisoning (ingesting one small dose daily for 5 or more days) include weakness (reduce Strength by 1 and Endurance Points by 10), stomach problems, slight disorientation (reduce Intelligence by 1) and a greenish pigmentation of the skin. Each dose adds to the daily damage (after 5 days of gradual poisoning, the victim would suffer from 5 points of damage per day). Medical attention will quickly eliminate all traces of arsenic from a person's system, however.

Curare: Curare is a nerve poison that paralyzes and may kill. The natives of the Amazon use it to bring down large game, often dropping small deer in their tracks with one arrow or blowgun hit.

Curare may be administered through poisoned darts or other injection, with each application having a Strength 4 dose. Additional darts or doses increase this Strength by 1 level (i.e., three hits with darts has a combined Strength of 6). If the victim fails a Resisted Simple Constitution Test against the poison's Simple Strength Test, the victim's Dexterity is reduced by 1 level per Success Level of the poison's Strength Test. If Dexterity is reduced to 0, the victim is totally paralyzed and unable to move. If the Success Levels of the poison are greater than the victim's Constitution +1 (three Success Levels for the average Constitution 2 person), the victim's heart stops, and she dies in 20 minutes unless medical or magical healing is applied. Even if the victim wins the Resisted Test, her Dexterity is reduced by 1 level per dose! The effects of curare (if the victim survives) last for 6 - Constitution hours (minimum 1 hour).

Supernatural Healing and Poisons

Any supernatural power that heals injuries can undo the damage inflicted by corrosive and irritant poisons. If the poison is still in the victim's system, it must be removed or the damage or effect continues even if the previous damage was cured. The Touch of Healing Miracle undoes the effects of any poison and removes them from the body of the victim, at the cost of 10 Essence Points.

Disease

Diseases have three major game characteristics: Vector (how the disease is transmitted), Contagion Strength (how easy it is to catch it) and Severity (how much damage it inflicts).

Vectors include airborne (the virus or bacteria can survive in the air for some time, infecting anyone who breathes it), vermin (an insect, like lice or mosquito, transmits the disease), body contact (the person must be in some form of casual contact, touching, for example, or sharing sleeping quarters), waste (drinking or eating things contaminated with the waste products of the diseased; this may also be caused by insects who contaminate food or drink), bodily fluids (transmitted through intimate contact, blood transfusions, and so on), and, of course, zombies.

If the character is exposed to the disease, Contagion Strength is used in a Resisted Test (Contagion Strength doubled versus the victim's Constitution doubled) to see if she catches the disease. Prolonged exposure, weakness (from wounds or exhaustion) and so on may produce penalties of -1 to -6 to the Constitution Test.

The Severity (Mild, Moderate, Serious or Terminal) determines how much damage the disease inflicts. Many diseases simply produce weakness and are not fatal except under very bad circumstances, while others are invariably fatal. Severity effects include Task penalties (due to the debilitating effect of the disease), as well as Endurance and Life Point Loss. Mild Diseases inflict no permanent damage. Moderate Diseases incapacitate the character and may inflict damage, especially if not treated. Serious Diseases inflict damage and may have lethal effects. Terminal diseases kill. There are simply too many types of diseases with different symptoms and effects to cover them adequately here. Zombie Masters wishing to introduce disease in their game may want to do some research and then use the guidelines here to put them in gaming terms.

Some sample diseases are discussed below.

The Common Cold: This disease is typically airborne, has a Contagion Strength of 6 (very easy to catch), and relatively mild Severity (-1 to -2 to all Tasks for a day or two). Reduce Endurance by one-third while the person is sick.

Ebola: Transmitted through body contact (although an airborne version might be concocted by some germ warfare lab some day), and has an incubation period of a few days. Contagion Strength is 4-6, and the Severity is Terminal. When the symptoms appear, the patient suffers a -1 penalty to all Attributes; a further -1 is imposed per day (cumulative). Symptoms include fever, pain and aches similar to the flu. In a day or two, internal bleeding begins (lose 6 Life Points on the first day, and an additional D10+6 points per day thereafter). Survival requires a Difficult Constitution Task at -4 (one roll allowed).

Other Sources of Injury

Drowning: Without preparation, a human being can hold her breath for 1.5 (2.5 with preparation) minutes plus D10(5) x Constitution seconds. After that, the person will pass out and die in a couple of minutes.

Manual strangulation does 1 point of damage per 2 levels of Strength (rounded down). A strangling rope doe 1 point of damage per level of Strength.

Falls: A falling character takes D6(3) points of damage for every yard (meter) drop, to a maximum of D6(3) x 50 (terminal velocity). Note that a few people have survived falls from great heights. This damage is usually bruises and broken bones.

Fire: Being exposed to fire inflicts D4(2) points of damage per Turn. Being engulfed in fire does D6(3) points of damage every Turn. A character who takes more than 5 points of fire damage has experienced severe second-degree burns or one third-degree burn. One who suffers 15 points of fire damage has second- and third-degree burns over a large area of her body; this may cause permanent or crippling injuries.

Armor

Since the time of the first caveman, people have been trying to use all kinds of materials to protect themselves against attack damage. Heavy cloth, leather, wood, metal, ceramics and plastic have all been used at one time or another to turn spear points or bullets, to cushion blows and to, hopefully, render the wearer immune to harm. Most people in the modern era, with the exception of police officers and some criminals, rarely own or wear any sort of armor. But armor can be found.

The protection of any suit has an Armor Value (listed in the Armor Value Table, p. 138). Armor Values are expressed much like Damage effects, with a variable number (typically a die roll), a Multiplier, and a flat value added to the roll. This represents the fact that no suit of armor offers the exact same protection over every inch of the body. When a character is struck, roll the base die times the Multiplier, add the flat value, and subtract the result from the number of damage points inflicted. If the armor result is greater than or equal to the damage result, the character suffers no injury.

Armor Types and Layering

Characters may wear different types of armor over different parts of the body (a helmet and a light Kevlar suit, for example). If the optional Targeting Specific Body Parts rules (see p. 104) are used, then simply use the armor value that applies to that specific area.

Some characters may want to wear two types of armor on top of one another; this is especially true in historical/fantasy scenarios where armor and padding types may be combined. Modern armor is not meant to be layered; wearing a Kevlar vest over another Kevlar vest will be extremely uncomfortable, and only possible when the lightest form of Kevlar is used. It is also not as effective as it would appear at first glance. In general, when layering armor, add the average value of the weakest armor, halved, to the Armor Value of the heavier layer, and increase Encumbrance by 1 step (i.e., none becomes light, light becomes medium, etc.).

Encumbrance

One of the problems with wearing armor is that it slows a character down and makes some things (like being quiet, or reacting quickly to danger) difficult. These problems are measured by the Encumbrance Value of armor. Encumbrance Values are discussed in detail in Chapter Four: Implements of Destruction (see p. 126).

Breaking Things

In game terms, all objects (doors, bottles, cars, tanks) have a Damage Capacity, Armor Value and a Barrier Value. The Damage Capacity is how many points of damage it takes to either destroy them or simply render them useless. Basically, the Damage Capacity of an object fulfills the same role as Life Points do for living beings. Armor Value is how much damage can be absorbed by the object without taking any damage. Barrier Value indicates how much protection they afford to someone hiding behind them. In effect, the Barrier Value acts as "armor" that an attack must punch through in order to hurt whatever is behind those objects.

The Damage Capacity and Barrier Value are two different things. It takes more damage to totally destroy a door than to fire a bullet through it (and injure whoever is behind it), for example. For the most part, the Damage Capacity measures how much it takes to make the object stop functioning, or to blast a large hole (a yard/meter radius opening in the case of a wall) in it.

Generally, the Zombie Master should only worry about the Damage Capacity of objects when the Story absolutely demands it. If people want to smash a plate glass window, they should simply do it without rolling damage. On the other hand, if the characters are using an axe to break down a door before the fire raging behind them consumes the house they are trapped in, a few rolls to see how long it takes them to escape can heighten the tension.

For example, Lucas is a cop with Strength 4, attempting to kick open a door, just like on TV. His Kick Damage is D4 x 5(10). He makes a Strike Task (with a +5 bonus, since the door is not exactly dodging away), and gets a +2 bonus to damage. Lucas' player rolls a 3, raised to 5 because of the bonus, for a total of 25 points. The door lock has an Armor Value of 6 and 15 damage points, so it is broken, and the door swings open. If he had kicked a reinforced lock (AV 20; DC 30), not only would he not have broken the door, the Zombie Master would have been well within his rights to have Lucas take the damage he inflicted -- promptly breaking every bone in his foot!

In another example, the perp inside sees Lucas through the peephole and decides to shoot him through the door! The perp fires a .45 pistol at point-blank range (only the door and some two yards of air stand between him and Lucas). Total damage rolled is 32 points. The door has a Barrier Value of 12, so 20 points get through and Lucas (who was not wearing body armor) takes a total of 40 points (bullet damage doubles); he drops to the ground, unconscious but still alive. If the door had not been in the way, he would have taken a total of 64 points (32 points doubled), and he'd probably be taking a dirtnap. Of course, if the thug had tried to shoot through one inch (2.5cm) of steel (Barrier Value of 80), his shot would have bounced off, with a decent chance of ricocheting right back at him!

Armor Value and Damage Capacity of Common Objects

Object	Armor Value	Damage Capacity	Barrier Value
Wine Glass	0	1	0
Glass Bottle	1	5	0
Window	1	3-5	1
Dresser	3	5-10	6
Desk	5	30	6
Personal Computer	4	10-20	5
Door	5	30	10-12
Door Lock	6-8	10-20	--
Reinforced Door	10-15	40-60	20-30
Reinforced Lock	20-25	30-50	--
Wood Wall	5 + 1 per inch	20 per inch	8 + 1 per inch
Brick Wall	9 + 1 per inch	30 per inch	12 + 2 per inch
Concrete Wall	18 + 2 per inch	50 per inch	20 + 5 per inch
Ferroconcrete Wall	20 +5 per inch	75 per inch	50 + 10 per inch
Steel Wall	30 +5 per inch	100 per inch	60 + 20 per inch

Note: Inches may be multiplied by 2.5 to get an equivalent measurement in centimeters.

All Flesh Must Be Eaten

Injury

Damage in the **Unisystem** is measured in Life Points, representing the character's vitality and toughness. As Life Points are depleted, the ability of the character to continue moving and performing actions is impaired. If they are reduced to below 0, the victim is incapacitated and in danger of dying.

When describing a person's injuries, the Zombie Master is encouraged to go beyond the numbers and use creativity. As a rule of thumb, a wound inflicting less than 2 points is superficial -- a cut or a bruise. One doing 3 to 5 points is deep but not life-threatening, except against weak or sickly individuals. A wound doing 6 to 10 points is severe -- a stab in the stomach, a deep cut in an arm or leg causing massive hemorrhage, cracked or broken bones. Life-threatening injuries -- a chest wound, a head injury, damage to a major organ or a wound that cripples or crushes a limb -- are in the 11 to 15 point range.

The Effects of Injury

During combat or other tense situations, adrenaline keeps all but the most serious wounds from affecting the character's performance.

A character reduced to less than 5 Life Points is severely hurt. It will be difficult to do anything unless the character is driven by adrenaline into pushing himself. Most actions suffer a -1 to -5 penalty due to pain and shock.

At 0 points or below, the character is knocked down, stunned and semi-conscious. A Willpower and Constitution Test is necessary for the character to get back on her feet. Such a Test is penalized by the amount by which she is reduced below zero. When reaching -10 points or worse, there is a chance the character will die (see Survival Tests, page 112).

Knocking People Out

Hitting people over the head or punching them in the face to knock them out or stun them is never as easy as it appears in the movies. Hitting people on the head is as likely to kill them as knock them out -- loss of consciousness is often a sign of a severe, life-threatening injury. A punch on the jaw may knock somebody out, or may just break the person's jaw (and, incidentally, the knuckles of the person doing the punching).

However, some Zombie Masters may apply "cinematic" rules to their games, allowing characters to engage in non-lethal brawls and attempts to capture people without harming them (or, by the same token, allowing the Zombie Master's minions to capture Cast Members without inflicting permanent damage). The following optional rules can be used for this purpose.

If the player announces her Cast Member is making a non-lethal attack, and is using a blunt instrument, any damage inflicted is applied to the Endurance Points of the victim, instead of her Life Points. This allows characters to get punched repeatedly, pass out and be fine in a few hours. If the Zombie Master wants to make a minimal concession to reality, she may rule that every 4 points of Endurance Damage inflicted in this manner imposes 1 Life Point of actual injury. Thus, a character who gets knocked out will still nurse some bruises and cracked ribs after the fight.

Survival and Consciousness Tests

When a character has been reduced to negative 10 Life Points, she may be killed instantly. To see if this happens, the character makes a Survival Test. Survival Tests are a special form of Attribute Test, using Willpower and Constitution, at a penalty of -1 for every 10 Life Points below 0 (rounded down) the character currently suffers.

This Survival Test only determines whether or not the character drops dead right then and there. Passing the Test does not mean the character is out of the woods. Unless medical attention is available, the character may still die in a few minutes. Every minute that is spent without receiving medical help, a new Survival Test is required, at a cumulative -1 penalty.

Characters with First Aid or medical skills can stabilize the victim with a successful Task. Characters without First Aid or other medical skills can try to help by bandaging any visible wounds. Whether this works under the circumstances is left entirely up to the Zombie Master.

If the character survives the Survival Test, she must still check to see if she remains conscious. A Consciousness Test is run exactly as a Survival Test is, except the modifier is equal to the amount of negative points imposed!

For example, Tiny (46 Life Points) is hit by a burst of submachine gun fire. After all damage is accounted for, he is at -24 points. His Constitution is 5, and his Willpower is 3, for a base Survival Test score of 8. This is reduced by -2 because he is at over 20 points below 0, to a total of 6. Tiny must roll a 3 or higher on a D10 for the required total of 9. He rolls a 6 (for a total result of 12), and survives.

To stay conscious, however, Tiny needs to make a similar Test, but at a -24 penalty! Not surprisingly, he fails and collapses, unconscious.

Every minute, he needs to roll his Survival Test again, first at a -3 penalty (the original -2 plus an additional -1), then at -4, and so on, until he finally dies or receives medical help.

Recuperation

Medical care and time are needed to recover from any injury. Unless seriously injured, however, time is the most important factor.

Resuscitation

Even if the character is dying, modern medicine and the Inspired can try to bring the victim back from the threshold of death. Once again, common sense is the rule. A multiple gunshot victim might survive if no major brain damage was inflicted, but somebody who was decapitated, or burned to a crisp in a gasoline explosion is not likely to benefit from any help in this world.

A character who fails a Survival Test can be brought back to life if extensive medical help (like that available in a modern Emergency Room) is made available within Constitution x 2 minutes. If paramedics are available, this length of time may be extended by an additional minute for each Success Level the paramedic gets on a First Aid Task.

The medical team in the hospital will try to revive the patient (anybody who's watched the TV show ER knows the drill). The doctor in charge performs a Medicine Task (typical doctors at an Emergency Room have a Medicine Skill of 4 and an Intelligence of 3). Each Success Level gives the patient a +1 bonus on a new Survival Test. The advanced lifesaving techniques of the hospital add an additional +3 bonus. The recently dead character must now pass a new Survival Test, at a penalty of -1 for every 5 points she is below 0, plus all the bonuses described above. If she passes the Test, she lives. Otherwise . . .

Regaining Life Points

All right, so a character got injured but survived. What next? The human body can recover from an amazing amount of damage, but, movie and fiction claims to the contrary, people who get shot or stabbed cannot just get up and keep moving -- not without risking death. Also, a few bandages and blood transfusions cannot restore somebody to full health immediately. The Zombie Master can modify the guidelines below to make her world as "Hollywood" or realistic as she likes, of course. The default rules, however, assume that getting injured is a "Bad Thing." Avoiding injury is much safer than betting a character's Life Points against the tender mercies of guns and knives.

Medical Healing

A First Aid and Intelligence Task restores 1 Life Point per Success Level obtained. Performing First Aid on oneself is possible, but with a -2 modifier. One Task is allowed for each wound inflicted. This requires players to keep track of how many wounds their characters suffered in addition to Life Point depletion. If the bookkeeping slows the game down, ditch it, and just allow one First Aid Task per combat.

A character recovers 1 Life Point per Constitution level per day of rest under medical care until she reaches 0 points or higher. After that point, she regains a fixed 2 Life Points per day. Following on the example discussed previously, Tiny Tim (46 Life Points normally; -24 after injury) would recover 5 points per day in a hospital until reaching 0 Life Points (this would take 5 days of intensive care). Then he would have to spend another 23 days in bed to fully recover. In total, this is almost a month of bed rest (and that only because he has such a high Constitution; a normal person reduced to -24 points, provided she survived at all, would spend well over a month in the hospital).

Without proper medical care, a character injured below 0 Life Points risks dying from complications such as infection and blood loss. While recovering without medical care, a character must pass a Survival Test every day. She recovers 1 Life Point per level of success (to a maximum of 1 Life Point per Constitution Level). If she fails the Test, she loses 1 Life Point instead!

Endurance Point Loss

Endurance Points measure the character's ability to resist fatigue after extended exertions. Hard work, like actively avoiding zombies for long periods of time, drains 1 Endurance Point every ten minutes. Very hard labor (running at top speed while carrying a sack of rocks) drains D4(2) Endurance Points per minute. Bursts of frenzied activity, like very intensive close combat, drain Endurance at a higher rate, burning as much as D4(2) points in one Turn.

Endurance Loss Table

Hard Work	1 per 10 minutes
Very Hard Work	D4(2) per minutes
Frenzied Activity	D4(2) per Turn

Endurance "damage" may also occur due to "nonlethal" attacks (see Knocking People Out, p. 112).

Characters must get at least seven hours of sleep in a 24-hour period. Anything less and they lose 1 Endurance Point per hour of missed sleep. For example, if the character regularly sleeps five hours a night she will lose 2 pounts each day -- points that require some extra sleep to regain. Further, for each hour past 24 that a character stays awake, 1 more Endurance Point is lost. So, a character who stays awake for 36 straight hours loses 19 Endurance Points.

Effects of Endurance Loss

At 5 Endurance Points or less, the character feels groggy and dizzy. All actions incur a -2 penalty. If a character's Endurance is reduced to 0 or below for any reason, she is in danger of falling unconscious. A Survival Test is necessary to remain on her feet, at a -1 penalty for every 5 points below 0 (round up). This Test is repeated every Turn -- eventually, the character will fall unconscious.

Regaining Endurance Points

Characters recover 1 Endurance Point per Constitution level per half hour of sleep, or the same amount for every hour of rest. Endurance Points lost due to lack of sleep can only be regained by sleeping.

Essence Pool Loss

The characters who need to worry about Essence losses the most are the Inspired. Nonetheless, shock and terror may release Essence Points from all Cast Members (see Getting Scared, p. 96).

For those who want to roleplay the mental exhaustion caused by the stress of battling zombies, another drain on Essence may be employed. In stressful non-combat situations, such as being locked in a barn surrounded by zombies, Norms and Survivors loose D4(2) Essence Points an hour, and no Essence is regained during that time. The Inspired suffer the same loss but regain their Willpower in Essence per hour, offsetting that loss. In a combat situation, 2 Essence Points are lost per Turn for ranged combat, and 3 points per Turn for close combat.

Effects of Essence Loss

A character reduced to half her Essence Pool feels numb, and it may be hard to elicit any strong emotional reactions from her. Also, mental Tasks are performed at a -1 penalty until the Essence Pool is restored to half capacity.

At 1 or 0 Essence, the victim falls into a deep depression. All Tasks and Tests suffer a -3 penalty, and it is difficult to concentrate or care about anything. If Essence is reduced below 0, the victim must pass a Difficult Willpower Test, at -1 for every 5 Essence Points below 0. If she fails, she temporarily loses one level in one mental Attribute (the Zombie Master may let the player choose), or she temporarily gains a Mental Drawback worth at least 2 points.

If Essence is reduced below -30 Essence, the character must pass a Survival Test, with a -1 penalty for every 10 points below -30. Characters killed by Essence drain have no apparent cause of death. Medical science will diagnose only "heart failure".

Regaining Essence Points

Inspired can regain lost Essence in a matter of minutes (equal to their Willpower per 5 minutes). Others are limited to regaining 1 Essence Point for each Willpower level, every hour.

Vehicle Rules

Vehicle combat (i.e., any combat where one or more vehicles are involved) is handled mostly like normal combat, with a few modifications. Since the **Unisystem** is not a wargame, the rules don't concern themselves with complex movement and range modifiers. Instead, vehicle combat is handled in a more cinematic nature – think Star Wars, not Harpoon. As with all rules, the set below should only be used when the Story calls for it.

Vehicle Attributes

Vehicles have a number of Attributes, comparable to a character's Attributes, that determine its capabilities. Most of the time, they are only used in combat or other action-oriented events (the ubiquitous car chase, for example). Worrying about Handling during a routine trip to work is mostly a waste of time.

Weight: The average unloaded weight in pounds. For cargo vehicles, a separate entry indicates its cargo capacity. Halve this value to convert to kilograms.

Speed: In miles per hour, this Attribute is divided into maximum speed, and average cruising speed. Multiply by 1.5 to get kilometers per hour. Halve Speed to get yards (meters) per second.

Acceleration: This is how many miles per hour the vehicle can increase its speed per Turn. All vehicles can safely brake 30mph per Turn. More serious braking requires a Task with a modifier of -1 per 5mph of braking over the safe maximum.

Range: Basically, how many miles a vehicle may travel is a function of how many miles per gallon it gets, and how much fuel it can carry. For aircraft, effective range is often half its maximum range, with half the range being the "point of no return." At that point, the aircraft does not have enough fuel to return to base (assuming it needs to return to its point of origin, of course). Range can vary enormously from those averages, though. Aircraft in particular can burn a lot of fuel just performing complex acrobatics or going at maximum speed.

Toughness: This is a general measure of the vehicle's ruggedness, redundant systems and damage control systems. It determines how long a vehicle can continue to function even after being heavily damaged. Most vehicles are relatively delicate machines; break enough parts and they'll stop working. Others, like high-tech tanks, can survive a great deal of punishment. This attribute is roughly equivalent to a human being's Constitution Attribute. Toughness is rated from 1 to 6, with extraordinary vehicles having values of 7 or higher.

Handling: This is a measure of the vehicle's maneuverability and responsiveness to the driver/pilot -- within the vehicle's capabilities, of course. A tank, no matter how good its Handling, is not going to be able to maneuver in close quarters as well as even the clumsiest motorcycle. Handling is comparable to a human being's Dexterity. For some driving and piloting tasks, Handling replaces or modifies the pilot's Dexterity.

Damage Capacity (DC): This is a rough estimate of how much damage a vehicle can take before it is destroyed or inoperable. Obviously, damage to a critical component disables a vehicle long before its Damage Capacity is depleted, but, for general purposes, most civilian vehicles have a DC of 30 plus 3 for every 500 pounds (250 kg) of weight, rounded down. Military vehicles have a base Damage Capacity of 50 plus 5 for every 500 pounds (250 kg) of weight. So, a 2,000-pound car would have a damage capacity of 42 points, and a 30-ton tank would have a Damage Capacity of 650. Some large components like turrets, wings and the like have their own Damage Capacity, typically ranging from 20% to 100% of the DC of the main body. Generally, damage modifiers (like slashing or stabbing damage, or modifiers for bullet type; see p. 105) do not apply to vehicles, which take only the basic damage rolled or generated.

Armor Value (AV): Almost all vehicles are somewhat harder to hurt than normal people. The metal, wood or plastic of their hulls is strong enough to deflect some attacks, and, in the case of armored vehicles, armor plating is added for increased protection. Most cars have an AV of 2 to 10, depending on how sturdy their hulls are. Cars can be made "bulletproof" by adding layers of Kevlar and other materials to their construction. Typical armored cars have the equivalent of 5 to 20mm of steel plate (see below).

To determine the AV of military vehicles, take the armor thickness of a given location (usually expressed in millimeters of steel armor, even when it is not really steel) and use the following formula:

Less than 25mm: Multiply the total thickness in millimeters by 3, and add a variable of D8 x (Armor Thickness/5). So, a vehicle with 10mm of steel armor equivalent would have an AV of 30 + D8 x 2 (38).

25mm (1 inch): 25mm of steel armor has an AV of 75 + D10 x 2 (85)

Over 25 mm: Take the armor's thickness (in millimeters) and add 50 to the total. To this is added a variable number equal to D10 x (Thickness/25). So, for example, a tank with a frontal armor thickness of 200mm (8 inches) would have a total AV or 250 + D10 x 8 (290).

Accuracy: This Attribute applies only to vehicles with weapon systems, and measures such things as radar, laser or other range-finding and targeting systems. Accuracy sometimes replaces or modifies Dexterity when firing vehicle-mounted weapons. Many primitive or simple weapon systems have no specific sights or aiming mechanisms; in those cases, the character uses Dexterity and Weapon Skill, often with a penalty.

Vehicles In Action

Most of the time, using a vehicle involves no Tasks or Tests. The character, provided she has the appropriate Driving or Piloting skill, gets in and goes wherever she wants. During stressful moments (pursuing an enemy, or realizing that the car's brakes have been cut), Dexterity and Driving/Piloting Tasks are needed. For the most part, this should be dictated by the Zombie Master as the individual situation demands, but some possibilities are discussed below.

Driving at High Speed: Speed kills, as the saying goes. Going at very high speeds in a lone, straight stretch of highway is no problem. Problems only occur when the character has to do something besides go in a straight line. Maneuvering at speeds over 50 mph (75 kph) requires a Dexterity and Driving Task (if the character's Dexterity exceeds the Handling rating of the vehicle, use the Handling rating instead). Potential modifiers include -1 per 10 miles an hour over 50; -2 for attempting to swerve or taking a sharp curve; -1 to -3 for sudden attempts to maneuver (avoiding a deer jumping right in front of a car would be at a -3 penalty). Fast Reaction Time gives characters a +2 bonus to these maneuvers. The results of failure can range from a partial spin to rolling the car over, crashing against an obstacle, or worse, depending on the circumstances (see Collisions below).

Chases: These work largely like normal foot chases (see Resisted Tasks/Tests, p. 92). Make Resisted Dexterity and Driving/Piloting Tasks (if the character's Dexterity exceeds the Handling rating of the vehicle, use the Handling rating instead). The first person/vehicle to start moving gains a +1 to the Task. The faster vehicle receives a +1 bonus for every 5mph it is moving above the other vehicle's speed. If going at very high speeds, both sides should also need to succeed at a couple of Tasks using the High Speed modifiers above, to ensure nothing happened to them during the chase. A chase should last at least a minute or two. To make things dramatic, the Zombie Master can dictate that the pursuer needs to accumulate a number of Success Levels above the pursued's own Success Levels, with Tasks being rolled every minute of the chase. The Zombie Master should be descriptive of the chase, and if it is taking place in a crowded highway or city streets, should throw in a number of complications (pedestrians, other cars, highway patrolmen) to spice things up.

Collisions: When a vehicle hits something, it does damage to both the target and itself. Base damage is equal to D10(5) times a factor equal to the vehicle's weight (in tons) and 1/10 the vehicle's speed (or the differential in speeds if a vehicle hits a moving object) in miles per hour (or 1/15 the speed in kph), rounding up. For example, a 2-ton truck going at 50 mph inflicts D10 x 7 (2 for the weight plus 5 for the speed) points of damage. If the vehicle is very large, like a sailing vessel, damage uses only the speed of the vehicle, not its weight, for the multiplier.

If the target is far lighter than the vehicle (car versus pedestrian), the vehicle takes only a third of the damage rolled. If the target is somewhat smaller (truck versus car), the heavier vehicle takes half damage. If the impact is against a much heavier object (a tank or a concrete wall), the vehicle takes D10+2 multiplied by (Speed/10) as above. All collision damage subtracts the Armor Value of the vehicle before being applied to its Damage Capacity. Additional damage from a collision may occur if one of the vehicles catches on fire or explodes. This happens very rarely with cars (Hollywood conceits to the contrary -- cars are designed not to explode), but more frequently for aircraft. Explosions are covered under the Vehicle Combat rules below.

Passengers inside a vehicle involved in a collision take half damage if not wearing seat belts and 1/5 damage if they are. Air bags provide an additional AV of 20 against the collision damage, except for small children and small people, who may take an additional D6 x 2 points of damage from the air bad itself.

Malfunctioning Vehicles: If the vehicle is damaged somehow, has been sabotaged, or suffers some dangerous or catastrophic malfunction (loses its brakes, loses all four aircraft engines, and so on), a Dexterity and Driving/Piloting roll is needed to try to stop or bring down the vehicle before any mishaps happen. Modifiers range from -1 (one flat tire) to -6 (all engines are off-line in an aircraft). In some cases, a severe malfunction will not be an issue -- a malfunctioning car can be stopped fairly easily, unless it was going very fast (in which case, apply the High Speed modifiers).

Ground Vehicle Combat

Most vehicle combat (with the rare exception of ramming attacks) involves ranged weapons. These attacks range from people with guns firing from the inside of a vehicle to complex weapon systems like missiles or laser-aimed cannon.

Shooting From Vehicle: Firing from a moving platform with hand weapons has a base penalty of -3, with another -2 if the vehicle is moving faster than 30mph (45kph).

Using Vehicle-Mounted Weapons: Early vehicle weapons were not stabilized, and had fairly primitive aiming mechanisms. World War II tanks, for example, had to stop and fire to have any hope of hitting the target. For those vehicles, penalties are as above, with the additional complication that the gunner's Dexterity cannot exceed the weapon's Accuracy rating. For stabilized vehicles, the penalties are limited to -2 if the vehicle is moving over 30mph.

Dodging: Most military vehicles cannot Dodge attacks; they are too big and too slow. Lighter vehicles such as motorcycles and car-sized targets may attempt to drive fast enough to avoid an attack; this is treated like a Resisted Task, with the target's Dexterity and Driving/Piloting skill versus the attacker's Dexterity and weapon skill, or Accuracy, depending on the weapon.

Air Combat

Air combat is a highly complex set of maneuvers, where the ability to see or sense the target is as important as the ability to destroy it. To reflect air combat accurately would require so many rules as to make the game very difficult to play (unless it is a computer game, where most of the calculations are made by the machine). Described below are a few cinematic rules for fast and furious air combat.

Dogfighting: This type of combat was a lot more common in the days before guided missiles, when men were able to see the destruction of the enemy through their gun sights. Dogfighting combat is a Resisted Task, using the Dexterity and Piloting Skill of the two combatants. If one aircraft has a higher Handling rating than the other, add the difference between the two to the more maneuverable vessel. Situational Awareness adds +2 to the Task; Fast Reaction Time adds +1. The winner manages to get on the target's "six" (six o'clock, right behind it) and can shoot it.

Playing Chicken: This occurs when two aircraft fly at each other, firing and seeing who turns away (or is destroyed) first. The two aircraft can fire at each other for one or two Turns, depending on their speed and weapon range. If neither ship is destroyed, the two characters engage in a Resisted Willpower Test; Nerves of Steel bonuses apply. The loser turns away, and the winner can now engage him with impunity for one Turn.

Experience

People change with time. In the **Unisystem**, characters live and learn and become more experienced as they participate in the Stories created in the course of the game. After several such Stories, the character will be more skilled and powerful than she was when she began. This is also borne out in fiction: the Hobbits from the *Lord of the Rings* trilogy were much tougher, stronger and experienced at the end of their heroic quest.

Character improvement is represented in the **Unisystem** by experience points. Experience points are awarded to each player at the end of every gaming session. The better the game and the player's performance were, the more points should be awarded. With these points, the players can improve their Cast Members' Attributes, skills and other elements.

This experience point system is used for all **Unisystem** games, both dice-driven or diceless.

Awarding Experience

During or at the end of each roleplaying session, the Zombie Master awards each player with experience points. Outlined nearby are some guidelines as to how many experience points should be awarded for a playing session: average awards are 2 to 6 points.

Improving Characters

So what do players do with all these experience points? They work much like the character points used to create the Cast Member. They can be used to raise Attribute and skill levels, to acquire new Qualities or reduce or eliminate Drawbacks, or to increase Metaphysical abilities. The cost of these improvements is different than the cost of acquiring them during character creation, however. After a Cast Member has been defined, it is a lot harder to advance in some areas. To determine how to improve characteristics, refer to the nearby Character Improvement Table (see p. 119).

Improving Attributes

Unlike skills and powers, Attributes represent relatively fixed qualities of a Cast Member. As a result, after character generation, Attributes may be improved no more than one level. If the Attribute was 5 or less before improvement, the one level increase costs 5 experience points. If the Attribute was 6 or greater before improvement, the one level increase costs 10 experience points.

Reasons For Improvement

Having enough experience points to raise a characteristic is usually not enough. There must also be an explanation as to why the Cast Member improved in that area, and usually those reasons are determined in the course of the game. If the Cast Member used a skill or Attribute repeatedly in the previous few game sessions, it would make sense for that skill or Attribute to get better. To learn a brand-new skill, the Cast Member must have spent some time working on that skill before being allowed to spend the points to acquire it. To acquire a Quality, eliminate a Drawback or gain new Metaphysical powers, there must have been a series of events or circumstances that make it sensible for the characteristic to arise or disappear.

Experience Point Awards

Being There: All Cast Members who participated in the game session receive 1 point.

Good Roleplaying: 1 point per instance.

Advancing the Storyline While Remaining in Character: 1 to 3 points. This rewards players whose roleplaying, planning and Cast Member actions helped develop the Story.

Heroic Roleplaying: 1 to 3 points. Given to players whose Cast Members remained true to themselves even when it meant they would suffer for it. The heroic type who risks his life for others, or even the coward who runs or surrenders when the wise course would be to fight are good examples of this.

Ingenuity Award: 1 to 3 points. Given to players who used impressive and unexpected tactics and problem-solving to deal with a plot device. This, however, only applies if the devious plan or tactics were true to the Cast Member (not the player). If the village idiot suddenly starts having spurts of Machiavellian brilliance for no good reason, then no award should be given.

Saving Experience Points

The player does not have to spend all earned experience points right away. She can elect to save them for a later date, perhaps waiting to have enough points to raise a specific characters.

Character Improvement Table

Improvement	Point Cost
Attribute	see text on p. 118
Existing Skill	The cost of the next level (e.g., to go from level 3 to 4 costs 4 points)
Existing Special Skill	The cost of the next level + 1 (e.g., to go from level 3 to 4 costs 5 points)
New Skill	6 points for level 1
New Specialty	6 points
New Special Skill	8 points for level 1
Quality	Same as per character creation
Remove Drawback	Pay off the original value of the Drawback
New Inspired Miracles	10 points per new Miracle

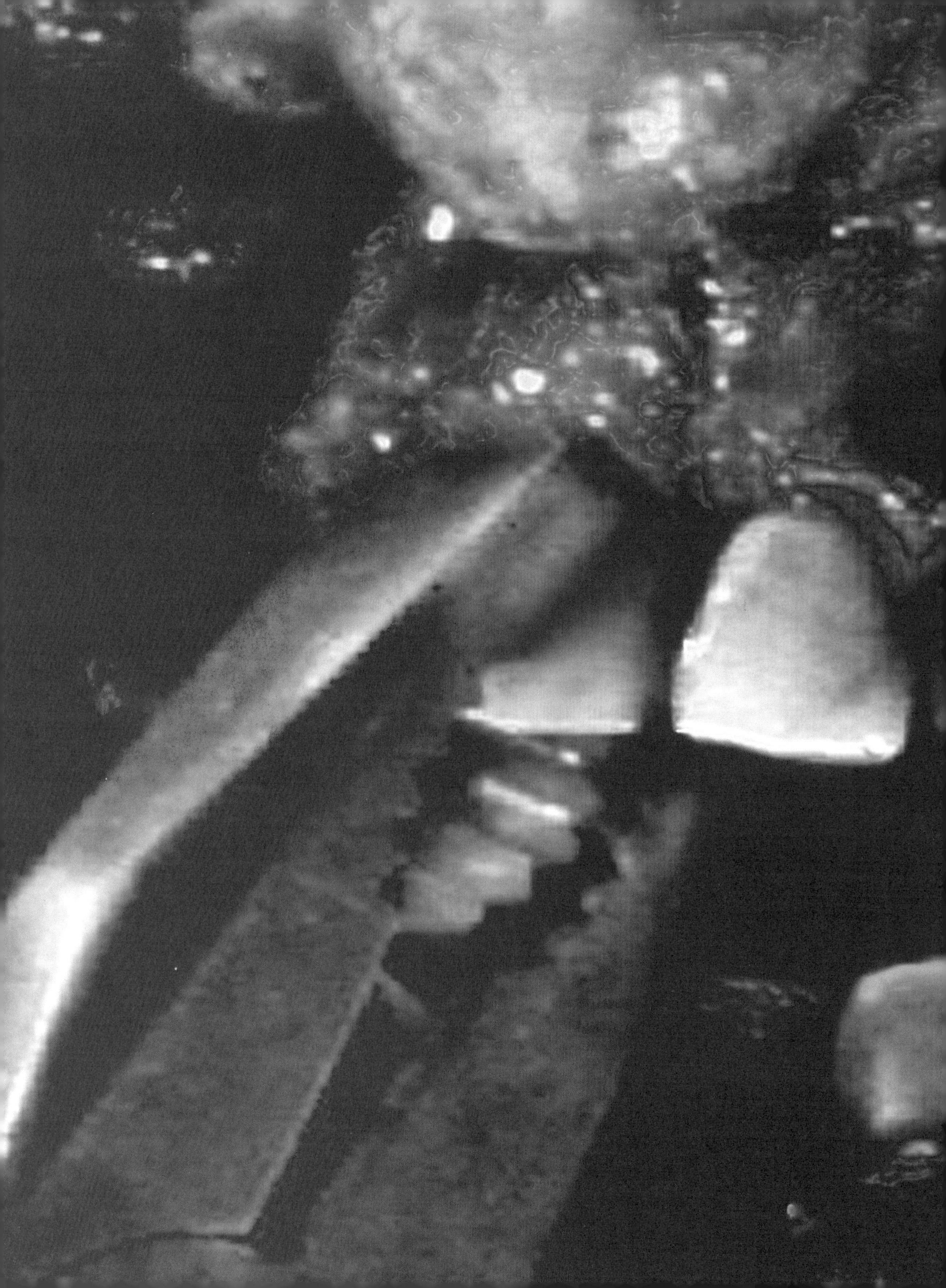

Chapter Four
Implements of Destruction

This is my boomstick! It's a 12 gauge double barreled Remington S-Mart's top-of-the-line. You can find this in the sporting goods department. Shop S-mart Shop S-mart

--Army of Darkness

The mottled gray flesh puckered around the tip of the scalpel and slowly gave way. Blood, long gone cold, welled up half-heartedly around the edges of the wound. With practiced ease, Dr. Gerald Becker drew the blade across the corpse's chest, opening it from shoulder to shoulder. Angling the blade downward, he made an incision from sternum to pubis. Returning the scalpel to the tray table, he grabbed the rib spreader.

This, he thought, *is where one of these DOD bastards faints.*

But, as the bony cage snapped and yawned open, none of the Department of Defense agents fainted or even so much as stifled a gag.

Gerald wished he had a nurse to help him, or at least an orderly, but Special Agent Douglas and his team had wanted witnesses kept to a minimum. A textbook example of bureaucratic thinking -- half the town suspects something is going on, this would only confirm those thoughts. He glanced briefly at the morgue, with its doors lolling off their hinges and windows shattered. Hell, half the hospital *knows* something is going on now.

With the ribs spread wide, Gerald lifted the lungs from the chest cavity, letting them hang over the edge. Then he removed the heart, liver, and stomach. He piled the organs in a scale beside the tray table, and stepped back. "There's your evidence gentlemen."

The four men stepped forward in unison, and peered into the chest cavity. They could pass for brothers -- each of them was tall and broad-shouldered, with dark, military-style haircuts and stark expressions on their nondescript faces. They each wore charcoal-colored suits beneath their trenchcoats. Only the leader of the four, Special Agent Douglas, wore a hat, a battered gray fedora. Gerald wondered if he was self-conscious about going bald, a lot of these macho types were.

After they had stared intently for about five minutes, Special Agent Douglas asked, "How did you find out about this?"

Gerald couldn't believe how calm they were acting. When he'd first seen one of those things, he'd made a sound somewhere between a scream and a moan. "As you know, I was dispatched here to investigate an outbreak of what appeared to be a new strain of Cholera. Kriely is a small town and they lost half the underage and elderly population to the disease."

Special Agent Douglas adjusted his hat and commented, "I've read your report on the subject."

Gerald wondered, *Sixty people dead in a 48-hour period and that's all you can say? Is there ice water in your veins?* He looked back to the other three DOD agents, they were watching him -- no, not watching, studying him, like he was a student and they were a team of professors hell bent on flunking him.

"Please continue, Doctor Becker."

"When I arrived here I got right to work. I didn't notice anything odd at first. I was too busy trying to explain and deal with this new strain of Cholera. It wasn't until my third night here that I noticed something odd."

Special Agent Douglas stared into one of the refrigerated cabinets used for storing bodies. Its door had been torn off and there were bloody fingertrails all along the inside of the cubicle. Gerald shivered at the sight and continued speaking, "It was night and I was walking back to my motel. I was tired and I wasn't really paying attention. I collided with someone walking the other direction. We both fell flat on our asses. I, of course, was quick to apologize and help the other person up. When I got a good look at his face I realized that I'd seen him before. Here. In the morgue. I'd done an autopsy on him less then twenty four hours beforehand!"

"Did you tell this to anyone? The local police or the hospital staff?" Special Agent Douglas queried.

Gerald shot him a glare, "Tell them what? That the dead were coming back to life?"

"What did you do next?"

"I knew that custody of the remains had been entrusted to the town's funeral home, so, in spite of the lateness of the hour, I made my way there. It was open and a lot of people were milling about. A lot of vehicles coming and going. Some of those vehicles were being driven by people that had been in this room less then twelve hours before."

The other DOD agents had drifted away. One flipped through Gerald's papers, another dialed the phone and the third looked at the two partial samples that Gerald had floating in formaldehyde.

"I don't remember inviting you to go though my notes."

"After you discovered the strange goings on at the funeral home," Special Agent Douglas pressed, "did you contact the local authorities?"

Gerald shook his head, "Not yet. It was still too fantastic to believe. I turned around and headed back to the morgue, where strange things were happening as well. I asked a nurse about it and she explained to me that the power had gone out in the critical care wing. For some reason, the back-up generators had never come on line and eight patients had died. The Sheriff was there and he told me that there had been a rash of robberies and kidnappings. The mayor's family and several other prominent townsfolk were missing."

"Had there been any ransom demands?"

"No, and in my view, no reason to expect any."

Special Agent Douglas regarded Gerald oddly as he itched under the brim of his fedora, "Why?"

"It made no sense. Why kidnap the citizens of a tiny little Oregon town? Certainly not for money. The Sheriff and I both suspected something far worse."

"And were those suspicions confirmed?"

"The next morning. At the cemetery."

"Ah. The grave robbings."

"Desecrations." Gerald spat. "The town has one cemetery. Every grave less than a decade old had been dug up, the coffins destroyed and the bodies removed."

"Was a crime like this really the bailiwick of the CDC?"

"No, but I knew it was all connected somehow."

"Intuition?"

"Exactly."

Special Agent Douglas frowned, "I don't believe in intuition."

"Great." Gerald peeled off the stained surgical gloves, "But what's our next course of action? The surviving members of the town have barricaded themselves inside the high school gymnasium."

"How did you kill so many of the walking dead?"

"Hate to say it, but . . . intuition. I happened to look over at one of the groundskeepers. He was standing nearby, leaning on a shovel. The pinky finger on his right hand was bent at a weird angle, I could see a nub of bone protruding from the skin."

"Was he in pain?"

"No. He was just standing there listening to me talk to the Sheriff and his men."

"That must have looked odd."

"Very odd. When I confronted him about it, he said it didn't really hurt and tried to turn away. I managed to get a better look at the hand and I could see his fingertips were blue and his lips were a pale color. I began to suspect that he was one of the walking dead. I asked the Sheriff to restrain him and that's when he started fighting and trying to get away."

"Is that when the deputy was killed?"

"Yes. When that happened, the Sheriff drew his revolver and opened fire. The first shot blew a hole right though the groundskeeper's head. It should have killed him but instead he started running. The Sheriff fired twice more, hitting the son of a bitch in both legs. He went down but he still kept moving, crawling away. The surviving deputy, the Sheriff and I caught up to him easily at this point. They emptied the remains of their revolvers into the groundskeeper. That stopped him. One of the bullets blew a hole into the small of his back and out the stomach. That's when we saw the foreign matter. The stuff your associate has in the formaldehyde there."

Special Agent Douglas walked over to the jar his underling was examining. It looked as though someone had chopped up a lobster and set it swirling in a jar of treacle. "Intriguing."

"You've seen this sort of thing before haven't you?"

"I can't comment on that."

"I head rumors that seven years ago you downed an alien craft in New Mexico."

"I said I can't comment on that." Special Agent Douglas set the specimen jar down next to the corpse, "But please continue your story."

Chapter Four

"Things fell into place pretty quickly after that. Once we realized what was going on, the Sheriff got a group of armed locals and set fire to the funeral home. We killed a few more of the things and after some investigation, I realized that the life forms controlling the corpses were arthropod-like in composition." Gerald gave them a self-satisfied smile, "That's when I realized that DDT might be effective against them. We got a volunteer to spray the junk on one of the walking dead and it collapsed within ten seconds of exposure. Once we knew that, we combined the DDT with a few other chemical compounds and started fumigating. With the right equipment, it was no trouble at all. The Sheriff and the others are out now cleaning up the rest of their "nests." I don't know why I'm telling you all this -- it's all there in my report."

"Weren't you worried about harming innocent townsfolk?" Special Agent Douglas had returned to examining the corpse.

"Look what we were up against!" Gerald stood next to him and jabbed a pointer at the thing entwined around the corpse's lower spinal cord. Its flesh was pale and milky; its body segmented and insect-like. It didn't look dead as much as it looked coiled, prepared to leap out at them in retaliation for being disturbed. "We had to act quickly before they spread. Think about it, we could be fighting an enemy that would never need to eat or sleep and could replenish its ranks by simply by raiding the local cemetery!"

"Did you ever find out where these things came from?"

"No." Gerald waved his hand dismissively, "There was a man who claimed he knew . . . but he couldn't be trusted."

"Then the queen is safe."

"Queen?" Gerald rounded on him, "You do know what's going on here!"

The other three agents began closing in on Dr. Becker. Special Agent Douglas removed his hat, revealing that the front third of his skull had been torn away somehow. The exposed ridges of his skull were yellowish-gray, his brain had become a writhing nest of maggots. They boiled out of the wound and crawled down over his too-pale features.

"Kriely was merely a test, a test to see if our invasion plan was feasible for a species like yours. You have shown us that if we are to attempt a full scale invasion, we must be more subtle, and quick to gain control of your civil authorities."

There was a crash as Gerald toppled the tray table in his attempt to run. The silent DOD agents that were not DOD agents pulled him down to the floor and held him. Their cold hands tore at his clothes, stripping him to the waist. The thing that was not Special Agent Douglas retrieved the dirty scalpel from the floor, and loomed over him, raining grubs onto his bare chest. "As a token of our gratitude we will release you from the burden of having to see your woefully limited species conquered and enslaved."

The quivering pink flesh of Gerald Becker's neck puckered around the tip of the scalpel and slowly gave way . . .

Introduction

This chapter lists and describes a number of different items that Cast Members will find useful in their attempts to survive the dark worlds of *All Flesh Must Be Eaten*. Clearly, the list is not absolute. Zombie Masters can devise any item for any time period and world setting desired, by consulting the list of examples given, and exercising a modicum of creativity. Further, the equipment listed here is generic; special items, custom objects or setting-specific details must be individually created, unless they are described in the setting write-up.

All items include a description, Encumbrance Value, Cost, and Availability. Others, such as weapons and armor, present additional features, such as damage imposed or Armor Value.

Encumbrance Value (EV) measures an item's weight, plus an additional factor to represent bulk. Both interfere with movement and cost Endurance. A character may carry up to half his maximum weight allowance (see Strength, p. 30) without penalty. Above that point, to 125% of carrying capacity, the character is lightly encumbered, and suffers a -1 penalty to Speed and to all Tests or Tasks that involve movement (such as Stealth or initiative rolls). Further, at that weight level, D4(2) Endurance Points are lost per ten minutes. Medium encumbrance runs between 126% and 150% of that weight, imposes a -2 penalty to movement, and costs D4(2) Endurance Points per five minutes. Heavy encumbrance arises at between 151% and 175%, imposes a -3 penalty to movement, and costs D4(2) Endurance Points per two minutes. Extra heavy encumbrance arises at maximum weight allowance, imposes a -5 penalty to movement, and costs D4(2) Endurance Points per minute. EV is expressed in two numbers separated by a slash; the first number is for those using US measurements, the second is for those using the metric system.

Cost is expressed in late-20th Century dollars. This amount is average for a modern setting (but could vary by as much as 50 to 300%), before or just after the zombie hordes have arisen. Double or triple Cost for a war setting, where the zombies and humans are locked in pitched combat over the fate of the world. In a post-apocalyptic setting, after the zombies have triumphed over all but isolated survivors, Cost is irrelevant. If the item can be found, and other "suitors" driven off, it may be kept. This feature must be modified significantly, or ignored completely, in other settings, particularly archaic or fantastic ones.

Availability (Aval) represents the difficulty in locating the item. Common (C) objects may be found in most places with relatively little effort. Uncommon (U) items are more difficult to track down, but may be secured with some effort. Rare (R) equipment is found only in a limited number of places, requiring serious effort to locate. Again, this feature may be altered or eliminated for certain settings.

The Barter Economy

In some All Flesh Must Be Eaten settings, civilization as we know it has collapsed or been significantly shattered. In such circumstances, paper money may be worthless. This does not mean that trade stops, however. Those who wish to exchange goods -- instead of just fighting over them -- work on a barter system. The costs given in this chapter may be used to determine a rough value comparison, but many other factors arise. Perceived need, local scarcity, time of day, mood and other circumstances impact the negotiation. A character's Haggling Skill is of vital importance. The final price of goods is whatever deal is worked out between the barterers.

In areas where a semblance of civilization has resurfaced or remained, a rough currency may arise. Materials with some intrinsic worth outside barter, like ammo, cigarettes and canned goods, may be substituted for money. Prices in these new currencies may have no relation to the dollar cost suggested, however. Again, it's the desires of the traders, and the Haggling Skill, that sets the final price.

Electronic Gear

	EV	Cost	Aval
Cellular Phone	1/1	$200	C
Hands Free Radio/Phone	1/1	$200	U
Laptop Computer	10/5	$2500	C
Personal Radio	1/1	$150	C
Vehicle Radio	25/12	$1000	U

Medical Gear

	EV	Cost	Aval
Auto Injector	1/1	$100	U
Doctor's Bag	10/5	$1000	U
First Aid Kit	2/1	$100	C
Medic's Kit	6/3	$250	U

Scientific Gear

	EV	Cost	Aval
Biohazard Suit	30/15	$1000	R
Geiger Counter	1/1	$200	U
Quarantine Tent	100/50	$3500	R
Radiation Suit	50/25	$2500	R
Specimen Jars and Collection Tools	10/5	$100	U

Surveillance Gear

	EV	Cost	Aval
Binoculars	2/1	$100	C
Camera (professional)	2/1	$800	C
Goggles, Infrared	2/1	$250	U
Goggles, Nightvision	4/2	$3000	U
Tape Recorder (professional)	2/1	$300	C
Telescope	4/2	$300	C
Video Camera (professional)	6/3	$2000	U

Survival Gear

	EV	Cost	Aval
Backpack	4/2	$75	C
Camouflage Fatigues	8/4	$200	C
Climbing Gear	10/5	$200	C
Combat Webbing	2/1	$15	C
Compass	1/1	$50	C
Flare Gun	2/1	$100	C
Flashlight	2/1	$150	C
Gas Mask	4/2	$200	C
Multitool	1/1	$20	C
Raft, Inflatable	60/30	$500	U
Rope	2/1	$20	C
SCUBA Gear	20/10	$500	U
Sleeping Bag	2/1	$50	C
Survival Rations	1/1	$10	C
Tent	30/15	$150	C
Water Purifier	2/1	$100	C

Misc Gear

	EV	Cost	Aval
Cutting Torch	2/1	$75	C
Fire Extinguisher	4/2	$50	C
Handcuffs	1/1	$50	C
Lockpick Set	1/1	$200	U
Metal Detector	2/1	$250	U
Toolkit	20/10	$1000	C

Electronics

All battery-power devices may be recharged from a wall outlet in the same amount of time as the battery life -- if a working outlet exits in the zombie-ravaged world, that is.

Cellular Phone: This phone is identical to a standard commercial cellular phone. Any character can get a cellular phone at any electronics outlet -- if there are any free from undead. Battery life is roughly 6 hours.

Hands-Free Radio: This is a small, concealable radio transceiver that may be strapped to the head to allow free use of the hands. The speaker is worn in the ear like a hearing aid, and the microphone is attached to the wearer's clothing, usually the lapel or collar. The radio is voice-activated, and turns itself on and off as necessary. A battery pack is strapped to the waist and wired to the earpiece and mic. These radios are commonly used by members of bodyguard and security forces to keep in touch with one another. It has a range of 3/4 of a mile (one kilometer). Battery life is roughly 6 hours. A scrambling unit may be added for $200.

Laptop Computer: The laptop is a powerful computer, including telecommunications software and a cellular modem. The computer is installed with the software needed to communicate with any modern network or telecommunication system, and the hardware necessary to connect to phone jacks, pay phones, network connections, even phone taps. The computer can run off its internal batteries for about 6 hours, or it can be plugged into any outlet for unlimited use.

Personal Radio: The personal radio (also known as a walkie-talkie) is a durable transceiver with a range of approximately 30 miles (45 kilometers). Signals my be encrypted with a special enhancement costing $100. Battery life is roughly one day; additional batteries cost $25.

Vehicle Radio: Vehicle radios are large radio transceivers installed in a vehicle that run off the vehicle's battery. Vehicle radios have a range of approximately 60 miles (90 kilometers). Scrambling components cost an additional $150.

Medical

Auto Injector: The injector is for the delivery of a drug or other substance into a body. It is essentially a reusable reservoir and needle that can be filled whatever the user desires, at dosages ranging from a fraction of a cc to a teaspoon (5ml). No medical training is necessary to use the item, but without such knowledge dosages will be a hit or miss proposition. 'Course, if the goal is to fill a Sacred Soil Zombie with Super Agent Orange, dosage concerns are minimal. Striking with an auto injector requires an improvised weapon close combat hit, and does no damage other than the effects of the substance injected.

Doctor's Bag: This bag contains the tools and drugs needed to examine and treat minor ailments and injuries with the Medicine skill. Without the equipment and supplies provided in the doctor's bag, any Medicine Task suffers a -3 penalty. Each bag contains one vial of tranquilizers.

First Aid Kit: The small kit is used to administer first aid, including bandages, antibiotics, and burn salves. Using First Aid without a kit incurs a -2 penalty. The kit contains enough supplies for six uses.

Medic's Kit: A medic's kit contains standard issue equipment for Emergency Medical Technicians. Using the kit grants a +2 bonus to First Aid Tasks or Medicine Tasks for stabilization purposes only. The kit only contains enough supplies for six uses.

Scientific

Biohazard Suit: This is a large one-size-fits-all plastic overall including rubber boots, gloves, and gas mask. A biohazard suit protects the wearer from harmful gases, microorganisms, chemicals and weak acids. The suits are quite sturdy, but by no means armored. If any weapon succeeds in hitting and doing any amount of lethal damage, the suit's integrity is breached and must be patched immediately to avoid contamination. For this purpose, scientists working in hazardous environments often wear pre-cut lengths of duct tape attached to the legs of the suit to act as instant patches. Regardless of Strength, wearing a biohazard suit lightly encumbers the wearer.

Geiger Counter: The Geiger counter is a small hand-held gauge that measures radiation levels. The unit has effectively no range and only measures radiation in the immediate area.

Quarantine Tent: A large, inflatable, airtight tent for the containment of large specimens or individuals suspected of contamination with possibly hazardous agents. The tent is equipped with an airlock to allow safe entrance and exit. It is large enough for four individuals to work comfortably on a single subject. The tent takes about 15 minutes to set up completely and includes four biohazard suits. When deflated, the tent is small enough to squeeze into the back of an SUV.

Radiation Suit: Radiation suits are heavy-duty lead-lined suits used to protect workers from lethal levels of ionizing radiation. The suit is fully filtered and enclosed and as such provides the same protection from chemicals and microorganisms as the biohazard suit. In addition, the lead lining and thick material of the suit itself protects against levels of radiation and heat that would otherwise be lethal in seconds. The thickness and durability of the suit also provides a D6 + 4(7) Armor Value. Regardless of Strength, wearing a radiation suit causes medium encumbrance.

Specimen Jars and Collection Tools: A set of small sealable specimen jars for holding biological, chemical, or organic specimens and the tweezers, razors, and glass slides used to collect those specimens.

Surveillance

Binoculars: These devices come in many shapes and sizes. Binoculars can magnify distant images 25 times, so an object 500 yards (meters) away may be examined as if it were 20 yards (meters) away.

Camera: This is a professional quality camera with all accessories including telephoto lenses, tripods, filters, and flashes. Although anyone can use a camera to document a scene, a skilled photographer is capable of recording elements that may have been missed by other observers. In addition to the standard camera, several specialty models are available, though only a skilled photographer will be familiar with their use. These include micro (36 exposures), infrared (requires infrared flash or other infrared light source), submersible (waterproof), starlight (pictures may be take in any light level, no matter how dim) and thermographic (objects appear in different colors depending on how hot they are). Except as noted, all cameras are loaded with film good for about 50 exposures.

Goggles, Infrared: These goggles allow the wearer to see in the infrared spectrum instead of the normal visual spectrum. This allows the wearer to view a clear monochrome image of his surroundings, even in complete darkness, providing he has a source of infrared light (such as a flashlight or spotlight). infrared goggles do not restrict normal vision.

Goggles, Nightvision: Nightvision goggles operate in much the same way starlight telephoto lens and rifle sights do, by amplifying existing, although minimal, light. The goggles allow the wearer to see clearly in near complete darkness, providing there is any light available at all, regardless how dim. The goggles do restrict the wearer's field of vision, however, imposing a -2 penalty to any Perception Tests or Notice Tasks. They run on their own battery with a 12 hour lifetime.

Tape Recorder: This device is a professional quality audio tape recorder that can record directly from an integral microphone or from any number of audio receivers such as bugs, wire taps, or headset and shotgun microphones. The recorder is loaded with long-term 24-hour spools of audio tape for extended surveillance operations.

Telescope: This small (approximately 1 yard/meter long) telescope is useful for long-distance surveillance, providing a clear view up to 30 miles (20 kilometers) away. The telescope is mounted on a gyro-stabilized tripod for clear and steady viewing even at extreme range. It includes an integral laser rangefinder that displays inside the scope's view.

Video Camera: These are the large, professional quality video cameras used by television news crews and direct-to-video filmmakers. The video camera is capable of professional quality production, but only in the hands of a skilled videographer. The cameras require videotape to record, but all such cameras are capable of transmitting their picture to a receiver up to half a mile (3/4ths kilometer) away.

Survival

Backpack: A simple, waterproof, multi-compartment sack attached on a metal alloy frame. Depending on size, they can hold up between 15 and 70 pounds (25 to 100 kilograms) of supplies and other miscellaneous gear.

Camouflage Fatigues: These are standard military-issue combat fatigues. It includes boots, gloves, poncho and so on. The garments contain numerous pockets to store incidental gear. Stealth tests gain a +2 bonus when wearing fatigues appropriate for the terrain. Available for forest, jungle, desert, arctic, and night (black) surroundings.

Climbing Gear: This includes all equipment necessary for climbing and rappelling down sheer surfaces, including both mountain cliffs and urban buildings. Ropes, pitons, crampons, hammers, picks, and grappling hooks are all provided. Such gear provides a +4 bonus to Climbing Tasks.

Combat Webbing: A padded suspender/harness with various pouches and pockets. It also has attachment points for carrying weapons, equipment and supplies.

Compass: This basic device always points to the magnetic North Pole. Useful for determining which way to run.

Flare Gun: This small pistol has a large barrel and is used for firing bright flares. The flares travel several hundred yards (meters) in the air and illuminate a 100-yard (meter) diameter area (centered directly below it) with dim, shadowy light. Areas already shadowy or brighter are unaffected. When a flare is fired, anyone who does not take precautions (shielding their eyes) must make a Simple Dexterity Test, or reflexively look at the flare, temporarily blinding them for the duration of the flare plus D6 Turns. Being shoot with a flare causes D6 x 3(9) points of regular damage; if 10 or more damage is inflicted the flare lodges in the body or clothing. The target also suffers burns from the intense heat of D10(5) points per Turn. Flare guns come with 6 cartridges. An additional 12 cartridges cost $30.

Flashlight: A large, waterproof, industrial strength flashlight with a range of roughly 50 yards (meters).

Gas Mask: This is a rubber mask that filters out toxic gases such as smoke, tear gas, and most nerve gasses. It protects the eyes, nose and mouth (the areas most vulnerable to toxic gases). Wearing the mask restricts the wearer's vision, imposing a -2 to all Perception Tests or Notice Tasks.

Multitool: This common, multi-purpose tool has pliers, saw, knife, etc. It may be used as a small knife.

Raft, Inflatable: A typical inflatable raft can hold four adult-sized humans, and comes with a pair of paddles. Inflatable rafts allow unpowered movement across water.

Rope: A synthetic, hemp or nylon cord (synthetic lines are stronger and lighter than natural rope of similar size). Available in a variety of colors and lengths. Rappelling is impossible without a rope.

SCUBA Gear: This is a Self Contained Underwater Breathing Apparatus, and includes mask, flippers, weight belt, snorkel, and oxygen tanks. The oxygen tanks last for up to an hour underwater.

Sleeping Bag: A good quality sleeping bag is made of composite and polymer, and folds down to a handy packet size. Modern sleeping bags can protect against both heat and cold.

Survival Rations: These rations provide all the nutrients a person needs for one meal. They come in a variety of flavors (even curried chicken) but their taste leaves a lot to be desired. Rations can remain edible in their container for up to two years.

Tent: Available in a large variety of materials (cotton, nylon, polymer or carbonate fiber), the tent provides a primitive but tough shelter against the elements. A standard tent can fit two mid-sized individuals comfortably, but larger models can house more. Tents are generally quick to set up and can be anchored to the ground in case of bad weather. When collapsed, they take up very little space.

Water Purifier: The water purifier is used to produce drinkable water from any contaminated, mineral-heavy or tainted water source. The unit has its own power supply that can last up to 2 months with light use, 1 month with heavy. The power supply and filter must be replaced at roughly the same time, and cost $50 and $20, respectively.

Misc

Cutting Torch: This hand-held unit projects a nearly invisible flame of intense heat. In time, it will cut through nearly any substance, including the hardest metal. Applied to living or dead flesh, the torch causes D10 damage per Turn, but requires an improvised weapon close combat strike.

Fire Extinguisher: An industrial-sized unit designed to extinguish any type of fire with a white foam. Each unit contains enough foam to put out a moderately large fire.

Handcuffs: These are your basic metal police-quality handcuffs. A key or Escape Task is required to get free. It's possible that a Difficult Strength Test with a -5 modifier could be used, but at least D8 + 4 points of damage would be suffered in the process. A zombie will free itself in 10 Turns regardless of the damage caused.

Lock Pick Set: Lock picks are the traditional locksmith and burglar's tool. The set consists of a number of picks and tension bars that allow someone skilled in their use to open virtually any key lock. The picks are rolled into a soft black cloth lined with pockets.

Metal Detector: This hand-held unit chimes, bings, peeps or lights up when any metal object is brought within the field of detection. It has a range of only a yard (meter), and runs off a 6-hour battery.

Tool Kit: All tool kits are contained in large but portable metal cases. The tool kits allow the use of the corresponding Craft, Electronics or Mechanics skill without penalty.

All Flesh Must Be Eaten

Close Combat Weapons Table

Weapon Type	Damage	EV	Cost	Aval
Punch	D4(2) x Strength*	n/a	n/a	n/a
Kick	D4(2) x (Strength + 1)*	n/a	n/a	n/a
Small Knife	D4(2) x (Strength - 1)**	1/1	$10	C
Large Knife	D4(2) x Strength**	1/1	$25	C
Short Sword/Huge Knife	D6(3) x Strength**	2/1	$50	C
Fencing Foil	D6(3) x Strength**	2/1	$75	U
Broadsword	D8(4) x Strength**&	4/2	$150	R
Bastard Sword	D10(5) x Strength**&	4/2	$200	R
Greatsword	D12(6) x (Strength + 1)**@	8/4	$250	R
Rapier, Edge	D6(3) x Strength**&	2/1	$150	U
Rapier, Point	D8(4) x Strength**&	2/1	$150	U
Katana	D10(5) x Strength**&	2/1	$500	U
Spear	D6(3) x Strength**&	4/2	$150	R
Spear Charge	D8(4) x (Strength + 1)**&	4/2	$150	R
Staff (Short Punch)	D6(3) x Strength	4/2	$75	U
Staff (Swing)	D8(4) x (Strength + 1)@	4/2	$75	U
Small Mace	D8(4) x Strength	2/1	$50	R
Mace	D10(5) x Strength&	4/2	$100	R
Large Mace	D12(6) x (Strength + 1)&	6/3	$150	R
Wood Axe	D8(4) x Strength**&	1/1	$25	C
Battle Axe	(D8 + 1)(5) x Strength**&	4/2	$100	R
Greataxe	D12(6) x (Strength + 1)**@	6/3	$200	R
Halberd	D12(6) x (Strength + 2)**@	10/5	$250	R
Small Club/Stick	D6(3) x (Strength - 1)	1/1	n/a	C
Police Baton/Large Stick	D6(3) x Strength	2/1	$10	C
Bat/Club/Pipe/Chair	D8(4) x Strength&	2/1	$25	C
Chainsaw	D10(5) x Strength**&	20/10	$100	C
Broken Bottle	(D4 - 1)(1) x Strength**	n/a	n/a	n/a

* Does Life Points damage, unless Endurance damage rules are used.

** Indicates a stabbing/slashing weapon. Damage is calculated normally, and then armor protection is subtracted. Remaining penetrating damage is doubled.

& Weapon may be used two-handed, raising the character's effective Strength by 1 when calculating damage. For example, the Spear does D6(3) x Strength one-handed, and D6(3) x (Strength + 1) two-handed.

@ Weapon must be used two-handed. Damage modifiers have already been accounted for in the formula.

Chapter Four

Axe: An axe is a familiar object, quickly recognized for its lethal edge. It may be used as a domestic tool and fighting weapon. A wood axe is usually over one foot (30 centimeters) long. A battle axe is twice that size, and is double-bladed or has a spike opposite the blade. A great axe is a double-bladed, two handed weapon over four feet (1.3 meters) long.

Club: The club can be regarded as the first purpose-made weapon. Not much more to say.

Chainsaw: A powerful electric or gas-powered tool generally used to cut down trees and persistent zombies. Chains are dangerous but unwieldy weapons.

Halberds: A long haft weapon, as tall as a man, with a bladed weapon on one end.

Knife: A conventional, alloyed-bladed weapon. A simple cutting weapon, held in one hand. A small knife is less than a foot long (30 centimeters); a large knife is up to two feet long (60 centimeters); a huge knife is two feet or longer.

Mace: Maces are made of iron or steel. Sometimes, the heads have a set of spikes, or flanges. A standard mace is roughly two feet (60 centimeters) long. Strangely enough, small maces are shorter and large maces are bigger. Go figure.

Spear: A spear is a wooden pole with a pointed metal tip at one end. It varies between 3 and 6 feet (1 to 2 meters) in length.

Staff: A long, two-handed wooden weapon, roughly 4 to 6 feet (1 to 2 meters) long.

Sword: The concept of the sword is very simple; it is a long blade with a grip on one end used for thrusting or cutting attacks. A broad sword a straight, double-edged weapon, roughly three feet (one meter) long. A bastard sword is wide-bladed, may be used with one or two hands and is often four feet (1.3 meters) long. A great sword is even wider and longer and must be used with two hands. A foil is a long, pointed, unedged weapon at least three feet (one meter) long. A rapier is long and narrow, single edged weapon of similar length. A katana is a slightly curved, finely made blade roughly three feet (one meter) in length.

Ranged Weapon Table

For all ranged weapons statistics, ballpark figures have been used. Weapons experts should feel free to pencil in any more accurate ranges, or plug in the latest *Guns and Ammo* statistics, depending on the specific weapon employed. Note that bullet type modifies damage.

Weapon	Range	Damage	Cap	EV	Cost	Aval
Thrown Rocks	3/7/10/13/20	1 x Strength	n/a	1/1	n/a	C
Thrown Knifes	3/5/8/10/13	D4(2) x (Strength -1)	n/a	1/1	$25	C
Short Bows	5/13/40/65/100	D6(3) x (Strength)	1	6/3	$200	C
Long/Composite Bows	10/30/50/100/200	D8(4) x (Strength)	1	8/4	$300	C
Crossbows	7/40/65/150/250	D10(5) x (Strength)	1	6/3	$250	U
Handguns	3/10/20/60/120					
.22 caliber		D4 x 2(4)	8-10	1/1	$200	C
.32 caliber		D6 x 2(6)	6-9	1/1	$250	C
.38 caliber		D6 x 3(9)	6-8	1/1	$300	C
9 mm		D6 x 4(12)	10-15	1/1	$500	C
10 mm		D6 x 5(15)	10-15	1/1	$600	C
.45 caliber		D8 x 4(16)	7-10	2/1	$750	C
High-Velocity Handguns	4/15/30/90/180					
.357 magnum		D8 x 4(16)	6-10	1/1	$800	C
.44 magnum		D6 x 6(18)	6-10	2/1	$900	U
Submachine Guns**	3/15/30/100/200					
9 mm		D6 x 4(12)	20-40	6/3	$700	U
Civilian Rifles*	10/50/150/600/1000					
.22 LR		D4 x 4(8)	1-10	8/4	$500	C
5.56 mm		D8 x 4(16)	1-30	10/5	$600	C
.30-06		D8 x 6(24)	1-10	8/4	$700	C
7.62 mm		D8 x 5(20)	1-30	8/4	$800	C
Shotguns (12 gauge)				8/4	$500	C
Birdshot	10/30/50/75/100	D6 x 5(15)	1-8			
Buckshot	10/30/50/100/200	D8 x 6(24)	1-8			
Slug	5/50/100/200/300	D8 x 5(20)	1-8			
Assault Rifles**	10/50/150/600/1000					
5.56 mm		D8 x 4(16)	20-30	8/4	$1200	U
7.62 mm		D8 x 5(20)	20-30	10/5	$1500	U
Sniper Rifles						
7.62 mm	15/75/225/900/1000	D8 x 5(20)	20	10/5	$1500	U
.50 caliber	15/75/250/1200/5000	D10 x 6(30)	10	28/14	$1800	R

* Single shot or semi-automatic.

** Capable of burst and automatic fire.

Chapter Four

Weapon	Range	Damage	Cap	EV	COST	Aval
Machine Guns@						
5.56 mm	10/100/300/1000/3000	D8 x 4(16)	200	22/11#	$1800	R
7.62 mm	10/150/300/1000/4000	D8 x 5(20)	100	24/12#	$2000	R
.50 caliber	15/200/400/2000/6000	D10 x 6(30)	100	84/42&	$4000	R

@ Capable of burst and automatic fire.

EV includes bipod (1/1) and ammo (6/3).

& EV includes tripod (40/20) making this exclusively a vehicle or stationary weapon.

Range: These numbers are expressed in yards (meters) and reflect point-blank, short, medium, long and extreme range. The ranges listed are the limits: anything below the limit is considered to be in that range, anything beyond it goes to the next range level. Note that bullets may continue to travel some distance after going past extreme range and may still be lethal, but the chance of hitting the designated target is basically nil.

Damage: The damage imposed by the most popular bullets for a given type of gun are given.

Cap: The magazine capacity indicates how many bullets are contained in a fully loaded gun. There is a lot of variation out there, however. At almost any given caliber, for example, a rifle can be a single-shot bolt action or break-open action, or a semi-automatic with a 30-bullet clip. Revolvers have 5-6 shots, while semi-automatics can have as many as 15 to 17 rounds (recent laws in the U.S. restricting magazine size to 10 rounds are in effect, but are easily avoided). A range is given, from the smaller magazines and revolvers to the biggest available in the market.

WWII Weapons

The following weapons were the basic sidearms and rifles of WWII. For ease of use, the weapon stats for grenades are the same for the modern era and WWII.

Colt Pistol: This U.S. officer's sidearm uses the same range, damage and EV as the modern .45 caliber handgun. The capacity was 7 shots.

Luger Pistol: This German officer's sidearm uses the same range, damage and EV as the modern 9mm caliber handgun. The capacity was 8.

M1 Carbine: This U.S. officer's rifle used a short .30 caliber round with less punching power and range than the Garand. Use the damage of a 9mm bullet. The range is 10/30/60/200/1000, the EV 6/3, and a 15 or 30 (1945) capacity.

M1 Garand: This U.S. soldier's rifle was semiautomatic and uses the same range, damage and EV as the .30-06 civilian rifle. The capacity is 8.

Mauser Rifle: This German soldier's rifle was bolt-action and uses the same range, damage and EV as the 7.62 caliber civilian rifle. The capacity is 5.

.30 Machine Gun: This U.S. heavy weapon was mounted on a tripod and had a three man team (firer, loader and spotter). Range: 10/150/300/2000/6000, Damage: D8 x 6(24), Cap: 240, EV: 30/15(gun); 30/15(tripod).

MG42 Machine Gun: This German heavy weapon uses the same stats as its U.S. counterpart.

Grenades and Explosives

Blowing up zombies from afar is clearly the best way to fight them. Finding such deadly weaponry may be a problem, depending on the setting, however. Grenades and mortars are discussed here.

Grenades

Regular grenades are triggered and thrown, exploding on contact or after a timed fuse has run. They appear in Offensive and Defensive types. Offensive grenades actually pack less "punch" than Defensive ones. Defensive grenades are meant to be used by troops in trenches or other fortifications; their blast radius is often greater than the distance that they can be thrown, so users have to toss them and then duck under cover. Offensive grenades are meant to be used by troops who are relatively in the open; they have a smaller blast radius so that the attackers are not caught in the blast as they approach the objective.

Grenades use a Strength and Thrown (Sphere) Task. More than three Success Levels places the target in contact at Ground Zero. Three Success Levels place the target at Ground Zero, but not in contact. Two Success Levels produce the General Effect damage, and a single Success Level does only Maximum Range damage. If the Task or Test is failed, the grenade bounces far enough away to do no damage to the target. It may land close enough to someone else to do damage, however, at the Zombie Master's discretion.

40mm grenades are launched from a weapon and explode on contact. The weapons come in two basic forms. The first is a single-shot launcher that must be broken open, like a shotgun, to reload. The second is attached under the barrel of an assault rifle. Both have the same range, capacity and cost. All grenade launchers have a minimum safe firing range of 30 yards (meters); closer than that, the firer risks being caught in the blast.

Launched grenades use a Dexterity and Guns (Launcher) Task. Hand grenade scatter rules apply.

Mortars

Mortars consist of a tube, a tripod and shells. The tube is aimed by adjusting the tripod. The shell is then dropped into the tube, and is lobbed high in the air to drop down on the target. Differences in ranges are largely irrelevant to a mortar shot; treat all ranges as medium. All mortars have a minimum firing range of 100 yards (meters). For safety reasons, the tube cannot be tilted higher; otherwise, the firer risks being caught in the explosion. Mortars are fired with a Perception and Guns (Mortar) Task. Hand grenade scatter rules apply.

Explosive Weapon Table

Weapon	Range	Cap	EV	COST	Aval
Thrown Grenade	3/7/10/13/20	1	1/1	$100	R
Grenade Launcher	30/50/100/200/350	1	4/1	$600	R
60mm Mortar	100 to 3500	1	40/20	$5000	R

Explosive Areas of Effect Table

These areas are expressed with a yard (meter) radius.

Explosive Type	Ground Zero	General Effect	Maximum Range
Offensive Grenade	1	3	5
Defensive Grenade	2	6	10
40mm Grenade	2	6	10
Mortar Shell	3	8	15

Explosive Damage Table

Each weapon has three damage numbers applying to each of the three ranges. If a bomb, shell or grenade explodes in direct contact with the target, Ground Zero damage is doubled against that target.

Weapon Type	Ground Zero	General Effect	Maximum Range
Offensive Grenade	D6 x 8(24)	D6 x 6(18)	D6 x 2(3)
Defensive Grenade	D6 x 10(30)	D6 x 8(24)	D6 x 3(9)
40mm Grenade	D6 x 12(36)	D6 x 10(30)	D6 x 4(12)
Mortar Shell	D8 x 10(40)	D8 x 8(32)	D8 x 4(16)

Incendiary Weapons

Incendiary weapons cause fire and heat damage. They come in variety of forms, from phosphorus grenades to napalm bombs. Few of these weapons are readily available, however. Among the settings provided in this book, only "Molotov cocktails" and flamethrowers will likely be encountered.

Molotov Cocktail: This home-made bomb consists of a bottle or other breakable container filled with gas and stuffed with a rag wick. When ignited and thrown, the container breaks, spreading the flaming liquid in an area three yards in diameter. Molotov cocktails may be thrown at ranges similar to a thrown grenade. Anyone in contact with the flaming liquid takes D4(2) points of damage per Turn. Anyone at ground zero when the bomb explodes is engulfed in flames and takes D6(3) points per Turn. Molotov cocktails use a Strength and Thrown (Sphere) Task.

Flamethrower: This weapon consists of a rifle-sized gun attached to one or more tanks of incendiary gel. The gel is propelled out of the gun and ignited, creating a stream of flame. The burning liquid splatters, runs and ignites any flammable liquid. Flamethrower ranges are 30/40/50/60/65 for modern weapons, and 10/20/30/40/50 for WWII-era weapons. The unit has an EV of 50/25, and automatically causes medium encumbrance.

Gel may be fired in bursts, and no more than three bursts may be fired in a Turn (each counts as a separate action). If a burst of flaming gel contacts a person, he takes D6(3) points of damage per Turn. The gel may also be sprayed at one or more targets at medium range or less by continually depressing the trigger. The latter expends D6 bursts per Turn; each Success Level in the Dexterity and Guns (Flamethrower) Task means one burst hits (the firer decides how many hits are allocated to each target in range). Those engulfed in flaming gel (being hit with 3 or more bursts) take D6 x 2(6) points of damage per Turn. Flaming gel is very difficult to extinguish. Each tank contains 10 "bursts" worth of gel.

Flamethrowers are very vulnerable. Those targeting the tanks with piercing/slashing/bullet weapon attacks suffer a -2 to the Task, and must overcome an AV of 6. Still, penetration almost guarantees explosion. Roll D10, only on a 1 or 2 is the wearer safe. Exploding tanks engulf the wearer in flames, and hit all those within 5 yards with a burst. A bulky protective suit (EV25/12; automatically causes at least light encumbrance) is available to modern-day soldiers that reduces damage from the burning gel to 1 point per Turn. U.S. troops are not equiped with flamethrowers, but those from other countries are.

Body Armor Table

Cloth and leather provide some protection against close combat weapons, but little protection against firearms. Modern "bulletproof" vests and limb protection are made of Kevlar and composite materials. Class I, IIa and II armors are heavy but flexible, and may be added to clothing. Class III and IIIa are thicker, heavier and more rigid plastic-like armors, and can only be concealed by loose or bulky clothing. Class IV is more like a breast plate for the torso, or plate greaves for the limbs. Class IV armor is theoretically able to stop .308 armor piercing rounds.

The U.S. Army's body armor is Class IV for combat units (torso), with a Class III helmet. SWAT and FBI assault teams have Class III or IV body armor, helmets and limb protection. The costs given below are for vests; double the price for both torso and limb protection.

Armor Type	Armor Value	EV	Cost	AV
Padded/Quilted Cloth Armor	D4 - 1(1)	1/1	$200	U
Leather Jacket	D4(2)	2/1	$200	C
Leather Armor	D6 + 1(4)	10/5@	n/a	R*
Chain Mail	D6 + 6(9)	40/20#	n/a	R*
Plate and Mail	(D8 x 2) + 8(16)	50/25%	n/a	R*
Plate Armor	(D8 x 3) + 8(20)	70/35&	n/a	R*
Leather Helmet	D6 + 1(4)	2/1	n/a	R*
Metal Helmet	(D8 x 2) + 8(16)	8/4	n/a	R*
Class I Armor	D6 + 7(10)	4/2	$300	C
Class IIa Armor	(D6 x 2) + 9(15)	4/2	$425	U
Class II Armor	(D6 x 2) + 14(20)	8/4@	$475	U
Class IIIa Armor	(D8 x 2) + 17(25)	10/5#	$525	R~
Class III Armor	(D8 x 3) + 18(30)	12/6#	$650	R~
Class IV Armor	(D8 x 5) + 20(40)	16/8#	$800	R~
Riot Shield	(D8 x 2) + 17(25)	8/4	$100	U~
Helmet	Use Type I-IV Armor	2/1	$100	U~

@ Regardless of EV, this item lightly encumbers a character when worn.

Regardless of EV, this item mediumly encumbers a character when worn.

% Regardless of EV, this item heavily encumbers a character when worn.

& Regardless of EV, this item extra heavily encumbers a character when worn.

* Outside the Society for Creative Anachronisms, this armor is very hard to find in a modern setting. Zombie Masters may decide that it is only available in ancient settings, such as Dead at 1000 (see p. 196). Archaic and soft armors (cloth and leather) are not designed to stop high-velocity bullets. For such armor, divide the AV by 2 when attacked by normal bullets, and by 3 when using armor-piercing. Do not double the AV when struck by hollow-point bullets.

~ Civilians will have a hard time getting anything heavier than a Class IIIa vest (anything beyond that level is hard to conceal, and the authorities will certainly investigate people purchasing heavy combat armor).

All Flesh Must Be Eaten
Vehicles

Given the various settings and time periods, a large number and variety of vehicles could come into play during the course of an *All Flesh Must Be Eaten* game. Basic stats for some of these vehicles are provided here. An explanation for these stats maybe found in Chapter Three: Shambling 101 (p. 115).

Bicycle
Weight: 30/15
Speed: 20/12
Acceleration: Str x 2
Range: *
Toughness: 1
Handling: 6
DC: 20
AV: 0
Accuracy: n/a
Cost: $300
Availability: C

* Range is based on the fitness of the rider. Endurance loss is 1 point per 10 minutes of normal riding. This can be modified based on terrain, weather, etc. Hard riding at maximum speed drains D4(2) Endurance Points per Turn

Motorcycle
Weight: 500
Speed: 160/70
Acceleration: 45
Range: 225
Toughness: 1
Handling: 5
DC: 33
AV: 2
Accuracy: n/a
Cost: $10,000
Availability: C

Sedan
Weight: 2500
Speed: 130/65
Acceleration: 30
Range: 550
Toughness: 2
Handling: 4
DC: 45
AV: 2-5
Accuracy: n/a
Cost: $25,000
Availability: C

Pick-up
Weight: 3500
Speed: 110/65
Acceleration: 25
Range: 450
Toughness: 3
Handling: 3
DC: 51
AV: 2-5
Accuracy: n/a
Cost: $20,000
Availability: C

Implements of Destruction

18-Wheeler

Weight: 20,000 **DC:** 150
Speed: 90/60 **AV:** 4-6
Acceleration: 15 **Accuracy:** n/a
Range: 350 **Cost:** $40,000
Toughness: 4 **Availability:** U
Handling: 2

Bus

Weight: 25,000 **DC:** 150
Speed: 90/60 **AV:** 4-6
Acceleration: 15 **Accuracy:** n/a
Range: 400 **Cost:** $50,000
Toughness: 4 **Availability:** U
Handling: 2

Jeep

Weight: 2000 **DC:** 70
Speed: 70/50 **AV:** 2
Acceleration: 20 **Accuracy:** n/a
Range: 320 **Cost:** $15,000
Toughness: 4 **Availability:** U
Handling: 3

Van

Weight: 4500 **DC:** 57
Speed: 110/65 **AV:** 2-5
Acceleration: 20 **Accuracy:** n/a
Range: 450 **Cost:** $30,000
Toughness: 2 **Availability:** C
Handling: 2

Military Truck (Deuce and a Half)

Weight: 12,000 **DC:** 170
Speed: 60/40 **AV:** 6-8
Acceleration: 15 **Accuracy:** n/a
Range: 350 **Cost:** n/a
Toughness: 4 **Availability:** U
Handling: 2

Armored Personnel Carrier

Weight: 25,000	**DC:** 300
Speed: 45/30	**AV:** 75 + D10 x 2 (85)
Acceleration: 15	**Accuracy:** n/a
Range: 320	**Cost:** n/a
Toughness: 5	**Availability:** R
Handling: 2	

Armament:
 .50 Machine Gun

Hum-Vee

Weight: 6000	**DC:** 110
Speed: 80/50	**AV:** 4
Acceleration: 15	**Accuracy:** n/a
Range: 320	**Cost:** n/a
Toughness: 5	**Availability:** U
Handling: 3	

Armament:
 M60 Machine Gun
  Range: 125, Damage: D8 x 5 (20), Cap: 100

Huey Helicopter

Weight: 5000	**DC:** 100
Speed: 130/90	**AV:** 5
Acceleration: 40	**Accuracy:** n/a
Range: 250	**Cost:** n/a
Toughness: 4	**Availability:** R
Handling: 4	

Armament:
 .50 Machine Gun

For Dead at 1000, the basic means of transportation were foot, boat and horse. Sample horse stats are provided below.

Riding Horse

Strength 4-6 Dexterity 3-5
Constitution 2-4 Intelligence 0-1(animal)
Perception 3-4 Willpower 2-5
Life Points: ([Strength + Constitution] x 5) + 15
Speed: ([Dexterity + Constitution] x 2) + 15
Attack: D8(4) x Strength
Skills: Brawling 2; Notice 3

War Horse

Strength 6-9 Dexterity 3-5 Constitution 4-6 Intelligence 0-1(animal)
Perception 3-4 Willpower 2-5
Life Points: ([Strength + Constitution] x 5) + 20
Speed: ([Dexterity + Constitution] x 2) + 20
Attack: D10(5) x (Strength +1)
Skills: Brawling 4; Notice 3

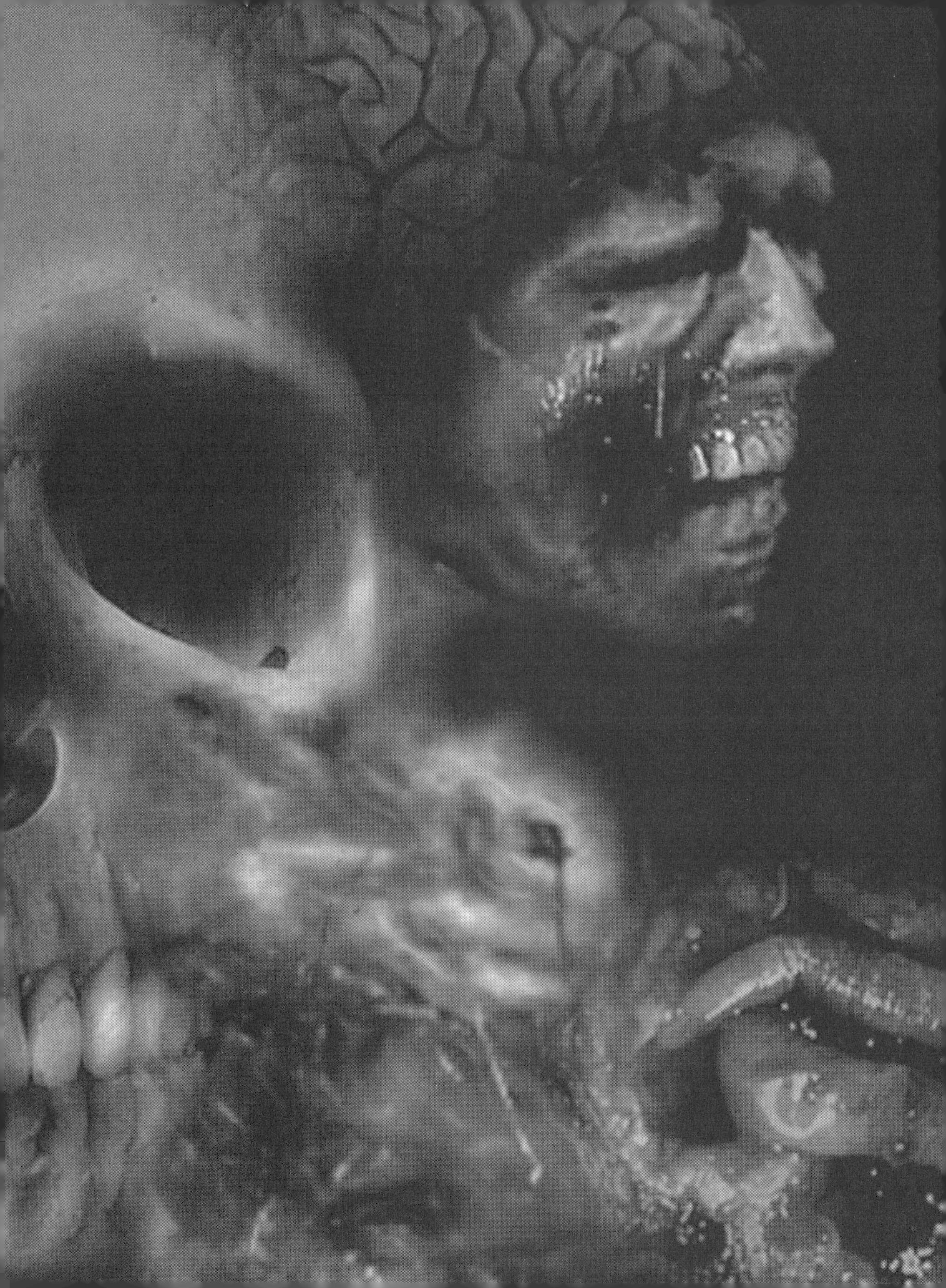

Chapter Five
Anatomy of a Zombie

"The brain is the engine, the motor that drives them. They don't need any blood flow, don't need any of their internal organs"

--Day of the Dead

All Flesh Must Be Eaten

My husband and I couldn't leave the city with the rest of the evacuees.

We both tested positive for the PHADE virus. That gave us two years to live, three tops. Christ, we probably would have been killed on the spot if not for the President's insistence on treating infected Americans "humanely." Humane or not, only citizens with a clean bill of health got to go to the quarantine zones in the Midwest. My husband, I and all the rest were forced to stay in the city, observed by scientists who viewed us as a bunch of lab rats and protected by soldiers that were afraid to touch us.

I still can't believe it. AIDS would have been enough but when I think of what PHADE will do to me . . . my body rotting from the inside out, my skin peeling like old wallpaper, and when my heart finally gives in to the virus, the real funs starts. Somehow PHADE will jump start my nervous system and make me into something not quite alive and not quite dead. I've seen the videos of what the press had dubbed "PHADE zombies." I've seen what they do, how they feed. I don't know what's worse, to be the consumer or to be consumed.

Maybe it's knowing that in the end I'll be both.

A few months ago, the military declared martial law and relocated all of us to a series of high rise tenements on the East Side. They said that they would be able to protect us more easily this way. The apartments here are larger and nicer than anything we could have afforded, so I tried to make the best of it. My husband Brian, however, insisted day in and day out that we were only here so that when the time came they could liquidate us more easily. Ever since we tested positive, Brian hasn't exactly been the best company.

Our marriage was a troubled one and neither of us was exactly the picture of fidelity. I know that Brian blames me for this. He still loves me, I think, but he won't touch me, not even in passing. It's like he thinks I'm more diseased than he is! I sleep in one bedroom, he sleeps in another. Not that anyone around here gets much sleep anyway. Most of the people here take catnaps in the morning and afternoon. Nobody sleeps here at night anymore.

You see, the zombies know where we are and every night they come to try and get us. From dusk 'til dawn, all we hear is gunfire and the occasional scream of an unlucky soldier. I think that's why we started having the Gatherings. It wasn't a conscious decision, you understand, it's just that these nights are too terrible to experience alone.

At first we grouped together in clusters of people that knew each other. But as the zombies continued their unending nighttime assaults, the clusters started coming together. Soon all fifty or so of us were congregating nightly in the penthouse. We would cook and drink and laugh and try to shut out the horrors going on outside as well as the nightmare going on inside our bodies. Most nights Brian would sit on the balcony of whoever's apartment we were using and drink.

One nice thing about our keepers, they are pretty generous with booze and food. What the hell, I guess, it's not like any of us are going to die of a heart attack, right?

Tonight's gathering was going along nicely. Someone had dug up a karaoke machine from someplace and we were all "four sheets to the wind," doing our best to belt out the songs of our glory days.

All except for Brian, of course. He was out on the balcony. Occasionally, I would glance over and catch him glaring reproachfully at us. I would wave for him to join in, but he would only look away.

Chapter Five

About halfway though a rambling version of "Paradise by The Dashboard Lights," Brian started screaming. For a moment, I had a vision of him hurling himself over the banister, but he was still there. He was pointing and gesturing to the darkened horizon. I ran out to see what he was pointing at; several others followed.

Zombies, thousands of them. They were converging on us.

The streets were clogged with them, every street! They were just walls of dead flesh moving toward us. The soldiers were shooting at them, but there was no way they would have enough bullets. They were even using the machine guns they kept on the tanks, but for every zombie they cut to ribbons, four more stepped over it to get to us.

Somebody actually started singing "Amazing Grace." Instinctually, I reached for Brian. He pulled away with an angry growl.

I don't know, I guess something snapped inside me. I just wanted him to hold me. Was that so much to ask? I shoved past him and stormed into the middle of the apartment. I grabbed the karoke microphone and said . . . hell, I don't remember exactly, but it was something to the effect of, "You know this is it! You know those helicopters we're hearing aren't here to rescue us! There just gonna take the soldiers and the doctors and leave us here!"

I slammed down a whole glass of something alcoholic and said, "Let's live tonight 'cause we'll all be dead by morning!"

Then I grabbed the nearest man and kissed him hard. Fear and desperation fueled our reactions. We fell back onto an overstuffed chair, tearing at each other's clothes. There was no thought, we were like animals.

It was like a floodgate had opened. We were joined by another couple on the floor and then another. It was surreal, half of the gathering on the balcony praying while the other half was having a damn orgy. I became lost in an erotic fog. I think we all did. We were all trying to lose ourselves in a sea of strangers' hands and faces. For a while we did.

A few hours later, we lay exhausted. The military and the undead were still going at it. Talk about staying power. Brian was gone. For a moment, I gloried in the thought of how the sight of me in the arms of another must have burned him. Then another thought occurred to me. It was just a small worry, but it was enough to send me running half-dressed down the hall to our apartment.

It was too late, of course. I found Brian in the bathtub with his wrists slit. The expression on his face was the most peaceful I'd ever seen.

There are procedures for when someone infected with the PHADE virus dies. For us it was relative simple: you call the soldiers, they bundle up the corpse for a swift cremation and then send you an army chaplain-slash-grief councilor. I didn't do that. I got up and went into the bedroom.

The sound of gunfire is still going on outside. To pass the time, I wondered who was winning. I've been waiting now for almost two hours. The PHADE virus should be just about done with Brian by now and any moment now he's going to come in that door looking for me.

And he's going to touch me.

One last time.

Introduction

All zombies are not created equal. In fact, zombie is as general a term as vampire or werewolf: it can describe a number of different monsters that all fall into the same basic category of walking corpses. Aside from the fact that all zombies were dead at one time, there are a myriad of ways the living dead can manifest themselves. This chapter attempts to categorize a number of different Aspects of zombies and provide game stats for these Aspects. This allows Zombie Masters to build their own zombies from the ground up (or, if you prefer, from six feet underground up).

The process is simple. Zombie Aspects separate into a number of categories ranging from how to kill them, to what they feed on, to any special powers they might possess, etc. Read through each section and choose the Aspect that bests serves the undead's needs. Put them all together and a complete zombie is ready to terrorize local residents, tourists, and Cast Members at a moment's notice.

For the number crunchers out there, each Aspect has a Power number assigned to it (comparable to character points). The higher the number, the more powerful the Aspect (and thus the tougher the final zombie). This allows Zombie Masters to judge the strength of their walking dead. In the roughest sense, a Cast Member can handle a number of zombies with a Power level equal to the character points used to build the character. Also, for an evening's fun, two or more players with teams of zombies can fight to the second death (especially compatible with the Dawn of the Zombie Lords background, p. 206). Give each player a set number of points to spend designing zombies, then let the brain munching begin!

The Basics

The basic zombie is no world beater. It relies on numbers, not talent. The -2 Intelligence means the zombie has no language, no tool use, no problem-solving and no long-term memory capacity. Its subhuman intelligence allows it to shuffle around, look for food and get up when knocked down. They have Dead Points (DPs), but this is basically the same as Life Points for characters. Finally, no zombie worries about endurance; just not in character.

The additional features listed are detailed in the course of this chapter. Alternatives may be taken to increase the zombie's Power.

Basic Zombie

Str: 2 Dex: 1 Con: 2
Int: -2 Per: 1 Wil: 2

DPs: 26
EPs: n/a
Spd: 2
Essence: 6
Skills: Brawling 2
Attack: Bite damage D4 x 2 (4) slashing
Weak Spot: All
Getting Around: Slow And Steady
Strength: Dead Joe Average
Senses: Like the Dead
Sustenance: Daily; All Flesh Must Be Eaten
Intelligence: Dumb As Dead Wood
Spreading the Love: Only The Dead
Power: 5

All Flesh Must Be Eaten
Flesh Notes

As is well known, zombies suffer damage a bit differently from normal people. Unless there is something unusual going on, they don't suffer from shock, pain or bleeding. Severed limbs, decapitation, and maiming are all in a day's work for a zombie. The following rules apply when battling zombies.

Hit Location

It is often important to know where a Cast Member has hit a zombie. For those who have a single weak spot, like the brain, it's crucial to the Cast Member's survival. If necessary to the game, once a zombie has been hit, use the Hit Location Diagram nearby to determine where. Of course, most will not leave it to chance. If a Cast Member knows about a zombie's weak spot, she may specifically target that area and apply the proper modifier to her skill roll (see Weak Spot, p. 148).

> **Hit Location Diagram**
> Head/Neck: 1
> Right Arm/Wrist/Hand: 2
> Left Arm/Wrist/Hand: 3
> Torso: 4-6
> Right Leg/Ankle/Foot: 7-8
> Left Leg/Ankle/Foot: 9-10

Effects of Damage

Now comes the good part -- trashing the shambling monster. First, the regular damage value is calculated as usual. Then, multipliers for the type of attack (fire, chemicals, etc.) are applied. Note that these multipliers arise from weaknesses of the zombie (see p. 148); regular modifiers, such as bullet type, slashing, etc., are not used (unless specified in the particular world setting). Finally, the effects of the damage vary depending where the zombie got punked.

Head: If the Brain is the zombie's Weak Spot, regular Dead Point damage is suffered. If the cumulative damage exceeds the zombie's Dead Point capacity, the creature falls down and stays down. If the Brain is not the zombie's Weak Spot, damage is generally ignored. 20 Dead Points inflicted in a single blow or bullet decapitates the zombie. Note that this has no effect on performance (although it does eliminate any bite attack).

Arms: Damage is ignored unless 15 Dead Points are inflicted in a single blow or bullet. If so, the arm is severed. Zombies missing both arms lose any punch or claw attack, and suffer a -2 on any bite attack. Their manual dexterity also goes down hill in a big way . . . that is, if they had any to begin with.

Legs: Damage is ignored unless 15 Dead Points are inflicted in a single blow or bullet. If so, the leg is severed. Zombies missing one leg lose half Speed, and suffer -2 on all attacks. Zombies missing both legs can drag themselves around at Speed 1, and suffer a -4 on all attacks.

Torso: If the Heart or Spine are the zombie's Weak Spot and are specifically targeted, regular Dead Point damage is suffered. If the cumulative damage exceeds the zombie's Dead Point capacity, the creature drops and deceases. Otherwise, damage to the torso generally has no effect. 20 Dead Points inflicted in a single blow or bullet knocks the zombie down. Once it takes a Turn to rise, however, it is none the worse for the wear (other than looks, but those weren't too good in the first place).

Other Damage

Bludgeoning, slashing and poking damage is not the only way to down a zombie. Burning, chemical baths and mincing are also effective, if a very thorough job is done. Any non-bullet, non-weapon damage that causes 100 Dead Points of cumulative damage completely destroys the zombie. Any knife, sword or other slashing weapon that does 200 Dead Points of cumulative damage minces the monster sufficiently to stop it. Remember that, for zombies, slashing damage gains no modification.

Anatomy of a Zombie

The Weak Spot

The characteristic that most defines how a zombie threatens the living is its toughness. Traditionally, zombies can only be stopped by damaging the brain, either with a bullet or some other piercing attack. There are of course many other options that can make zombies both more dangerous and less predictable.

If more than one positive Power level Weak Spot is chosen, additional Weak Spots after the first subtract one Power level. For example, if the Heart and Spine Weak Spots are taken, the Heart is worth +7, and the Spine becomes -1.

All — Power: 0

Any attack that harms the living harms the dead. No particular area is susceptible. They all suffer Dead Point damage until the zombie falls over, again. Just go ahead and bash them.

None — Power: +10

It could be that the zombie has no weak spot at all. Whatever force has animated it has animated every bit of it. Thus, each cell of the undead monster operates under its own supernatural power. Chop off the head and the rest of the body keeps coming. Even the decapitated head will bite, if one gets too close. Amputated limbs squirm around on their own, desperately searching for something. Destroying one of these zombies requires either cutting it into so many pieces that they can't do any harm or burning it to ashes. A large vat of acid works well too, if there is one lying around. Dead Points are inapplicable (see Other Damage, p. 147).

Brain — Power: +6

The classic weak spot, this one never goes out of style. Even in death the brain remains the seat of consciousness, such as it is. Damage to the brain means that the undead can no longer send signals to the rest of the body telling it what to do. Technically, if someone wanted to graft a new head onto the old reanimated body, it would work again, but this seems terribly unlikely. -5 to hit when targeting the head. Dead Points are all located in the head, and less than complete destruction of parts other than the head has no effect on zombie performance. Dead Points are 15.

Heart — Power: +7

What really keeps a zombie going? The heart is responsible for pumping whatever blood the monster has left in it to the reanimated limbs and head. In that frame of mind, a stake through the heart works well, although a couple of bullets probably does the trick quicker and easier. -6 to hit when targeting the heart. Dead Points are all located in the heart, and less than complete destruction of parts other than heart has no effect on zombie performance. Dead Points are 15.

Spine — Power: +5

The spine holds the whole body together. Even if everything else is dead, the neurons still have to tell the muscles when and how to move in order to bring down that tasty living morsel over there. Lose the head and the body can keep on going. After all, these things usually work on instinct anyway. However, sever the spinal cord and suddenly the neurons aren't firing any more. This is easier said than done. The blade of a shovel to the lower back works well, if the zombie will hold still for it. Likewise, enough bullets fired in the right region would do the trick. The problem isn't made any easier by the fact that the best way to get at the spine is to get behind a zombie and most of the time they are not so cooperative. -4 to hit when targeting the spine from rear; -5 to hit when targeting the spine from front. Dead Points are all located in the spine, and less than complete destruction of parts other than the spine has no effect on zombie performance. Dead Points are 15.

Fire — Power: -5

Death has a way of drying the skin and no amount of moisturizer helps. Some zombies are particularly susceptible to fire attacks. A little gasoline or napalm and they flame up like the Fourth of July. Just because these zombies burn quicker than a normal human does not mean death is immediate. Also, while a human on fire tends to run around on the panic or roll on the ground, zombies hardly notice the flames consuming their flesh. They keep right on coming. This means that for a few minutes anyway, the zombie is on fire and can set fire to other things as it walks around, like characters. Double damage from fire-based attacks.

Chemicals   Power: Varies

Acid works well on most zombies, at least if large enough quantities are available. It is somewhat disgusting when a zombie melts down to slime, though. Some zombies are particularly susceptible to specific kinds of chemicals. The voodoo masters have powders and potions for pulling the life back out of a zombie. Certain neuro-toxins might effectively paralyze a zombie (and who can really tell the difference between a paralyzed zombie and a corpse?). In some cases merely exposing the zombie's flesh to the chemical will do the trick. Other times they must actually be injected with it. Double damage from chemical-based attacks, or D8(4) per Turn from chemicals that don't normally do damage. Exact chemicals and delivery method must be specified. Power: -1 to -10 depending on range of chemicals, their destructiveness, their availability and difficulty of delivery method.

Blessed Objects   Power: Varies

There are some zombies who rise again for purely religious reasons. In their case, the only way to stop them might be something blessed by God or other higher power. For example, kosher bullets might harm a zombie just like they would harm a living being while holy water might act like acid. Zombies susceptible to such methods usually have trouble attacking those of great faith, destroying churches, and generally are respectful of sacred locations. On the other hand, sometimes they aren't. Double damage from blessed objects. Exact object, blessing process, and delivery method must be specified. Power: -1 to -10 depending on exact object, blessing process and the difficulty of delivery method.

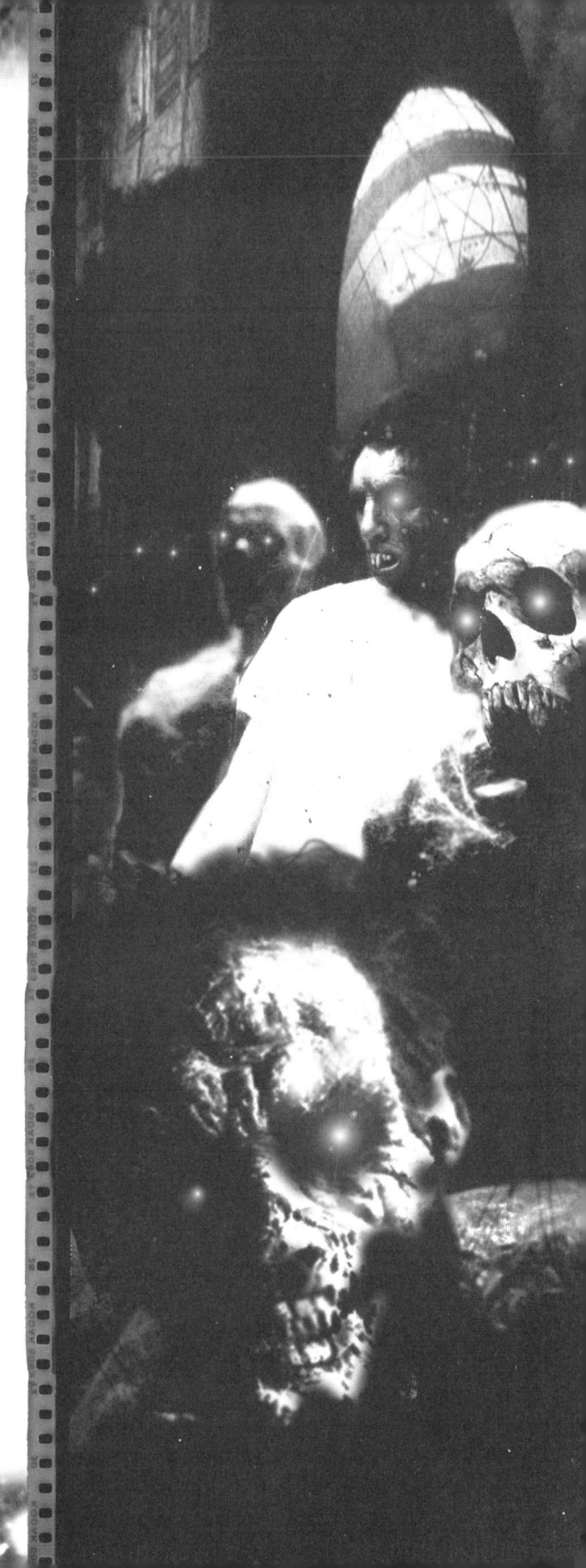

Getting Around

One of the first things one notices about a zombie (aside from how really gross it is and whether or not it's trying to kill you) is how it moves. For the most part, zombies tend to be kind of sluggish. They shamble along slowly, dragging themselves from place to place. The main reason for this is that zombies have less than ideal joint flexibility. Try walking around without being able to bend at the knees and ankles and hips (go on try it, no one's looking) -- that's what a zombie moves like. Not all zombies have such deficient joints, however. Some move just as well as humans, and some move even better. First choose one of the three basic speeds. Then choose any additional special movement abilities desired.

Slow And Steady   Power: 0

These traditional undead cannot run and even when they walk they do so at much less than normal human speed. On the other hand, like all zombies, they never, ever get tired. Dexterity 1; Speed 2.

Life-Like   Power: +3

The zombie has the same basic mobility as a living human. Usually this is accompanied by ominous creakings and crackings from the zombies dead joints and bones, but the dead don't seem to mind, so why should you? Even though these zombies can move around like humans when walking, they still cannot run well. The typical zombie does not have the best sense of balance and running tends to throw them off rather quickly. The zombie can walk quickly however, usually half as fast as the average walking pace for living folks. Dexterity 2; Speed 4.

The Quick Dead   Power: +10

These zombies can actually move faster and better than normal humans. This makes them particularly dangerous. Quick moving zombies often look strange to the living because their movements are not normal. They flail their arms wildly and move like they had rubber bands for limbs. Their run is a kind of loping gait. It may sound funny, but it's not when there's a pack of them closing in. Dexterity 3; Speed 18.

Special Movement Features
Burrowing   Power: +3

Most zombies start off unlife buried six feet under. It's only natural that some of them would develop a talent for moving like moles (or the worms that dine on their unliving flesh). The zombie has the ability to tunnel underneath the ground for great distances. This may not be the fastest means of traveling -- usually no more than a couple of feet per minute and only through sand and dirt (not rock). It can still come as an awful shock to the living when zombies start coming up from beneath the floorboards or through the basement wall.

Leaping   Power: +3

Few zombies possess this high flying movement technique, but it is not unheard of. The zombie can literally leap up great heights or forward great distances. This frog-like movement technique is used primarily for attacking prey or getting over obstacles. It is a product of the zombie's animated musculature more than actual speed. Preparing for the jump might still be a slow process if the leaper is a slow zombie. However, once airborne, the laws of physics take over and it moves fast and high. Can leap obstacles up to 6 feet (2 meters) in height. Can leap forward up to 12 feet (4 meters).

The Lunge   Power: +3

Zombies shamble about in their unlife with no haste or hurry. All that can change however once it gets near delicious, living human flesh. Then instinct takes over and the thing becomes capable of quick bursts of speed. Much like a cat stalking its prey, the zombie moves at regular speed until it is within striking distance. Then, like a flash, it can lunge forward (up to three yards/meters on average) as quick as a cat. This often catches the living off guard the first time, but if they survive this surprise attack, they will likely not make the same mistake again. +2 Initiative in close combat.

Aquatic — Power: +2

Most zombies don't do very well with water. They either float around helplessly or sink to the bottom like a rock and get mired in the mud. There are those undead, however, who can deal with the watery depths admirably. These zombies either swim at a slow pace or, since they do not need to breathe, walk along the bottom as they please. The important thing is that this ability allows them to do both. Thus, unlike some undead, they won't get trapped in the deep end of the pool. Gain Swimming 2 skill. Underwater Speed: 3.

Climbing — Power: +2

As a general rule of thumb, zombies do not climb. First, they tend to think in two dimensions (food and more food) and second, climbing usually requires more coordination and dexterity than the zombie will ever have. In this case, the zombie has the ability to climb through a combination of heightened dexterity and undead strength. The zombie can scale surfaces that would give pause to an experienced mountain climber simply by not caring about pain and using its strength to claw into whatever surface it needs to climb. Thus the zombie can easily scale things like chain link fences, wooden barricades, and even the walls of some houses and buildings. It cannot climb vertical concrete, the glass walls of skyscrapers or any other very tough surface. Gain Climbing 2 skill. Climbing Speed: 3 feet (one meter) per Turn.

Strength

Now that the zombie can be destroyed and can walk around, it's time to decide how strong it really is. Death does funny things to people, especially the part of death where the corpse reanimates and tries to kill the living. In some zombies, the reanimation leaves them drained, just a shadow of their former physical prowess. In others, it causes no change, while some even grow stronger, sometimes much stronger than they ever were before.

In this section, first chose a level of Strength. Then, any of the special strength-related abilities may be used to further supplement the zombie's potency.

Ninety-Pound Weakling — Power: −3

There's nothing like dying to shed those unsightly pounds. Unfortunately, as we all know, muscle disappears a lot faster than fat. Zombies of this low caliber fall below human average when it comes to strength. However, these weaker zombies are often faster than others and may have special abilities to make up for their lack of strength. Either that or they come in very large numbers. Strength 1.

Dead Joe Average — Power: 0

These walking dead returned with all the muscle fiber of a regular joe (or jane). Nothing special here, but not below average either. Strength 2.

Strong Like Bull — Power: +5

This zombie has returned with a great deal more going on in the strength department. While much stronger than average, the zombie is still not beyond human range or experience -- at least with respect to strength. Strength 4.

Monstrous Strength — Power: +10

Reanimation has made the zombie something quite special indeed, something capable of breaking rocks over its own head, punching through walls, and bending iron bars. Zombies this pumped up would win the World's Strongest Man competition hand's down and not even break a sweat. Strength 7.

Special Strength Features

Damage Resistant — Power: +5

Death has made the zombie's flesh and bones more resistant to damage. The skin is tough as leather, the muscles resilient as vulcanized rubber. Even the bones have grown harder, almost as tough as rocks. This makes it much harder to destroy the zombie, even if it has a weak spot like the brain. All weapons except fire and chemicals do half damage.

Flame Resistant — Power: +1/+3

Being buried next to an abandoned asbestos factory can have its advantages. Whatever the reason, the zombie is now resistant to fire in all its many forms. Zombie takes half (+1) or no (+3) damage from fire. Zombies who have fire as their Weak Spot cannot have this special feature.

Iron Grip — Power: +1

Once the zombie grabs hold of something with one of its hands, nothing is going to make it let go. Forcibly breaking the grasp is nearly impossible, no matter how many cool aikido moves are thrown. The only way to make a zombie let go is to cut its fingers off one at a time. Even if its hand gets severed from the rest of its body, it keeps on holding on. Of course the zombie can let go anytime it wants, but that seldom happens once it has its hands on some tasty morsel of flesh. Strength for gripping equal to 10.

Claws — Power: +8

Humans are not naturally the most impressive fighting machines. They have no real built in weapons for killing prey. Some zombies have, in their undeath, developed more potent mechanisms for destruction, usually in the form of claws. Sometimes the claws are merely the tough fingernails of the risen dead. More often the zombie actually chews off the flesh on the ends of its fingers, revealing an inch or so of bone. These bone tips become preternaturally sharp and capable of tearing through flesh, leather, and even thin sheet metal (like the roof of a car). No modifier to hit in close combat. D6(3) x Strength in armor-piercing, slashing damage.

Teeth — Power: +4

Of course, if zombies could talk they would call them fangs because it sounds scarier, but basically these are just your average human chompers with a few modifications. Most notable is that the strength of the jaw has increased dramatically. As a result, the zombie's bite has all the same advantages of the special ability Iron Grip (it's just a little harder to bite something than it is to grab it). The zombie's bite also does extra damage when it latches on to a target. It continues to cause damage each Turn until the zombie runs out of flesh to eat or somehow gets removed (a welding torch works well for this). -3 to hit in close combat. Damage equals 6 per Turn.

The Hug of Death — Power: +8

It shambles forward, arms outstretched. A week ago he was a loved one. Then he drowned in a terrible ice fishing mishap. Still, he hasn't lost any of his affection. All he wants now is a hug . . . of death. The zombie needs to get both its arms around the target, but once it does there's no getting out of it. The zombie grasps its prey in a bear hug and starts squeezing the life out of her. The two usually fall to the ground as the zombie even wraps its legs around the target, causing damage each round until something stops it. Even if the zombie is destroyed, it still holds on (although it no longer squeezes). Better cut it free before the next one arrives. -2 to hit in close combat to establish hug. Strength once hugging equal to 10; hug damage equals D4(2) x 10 per Turn.

Senses

Okay, the zombie can move around, it can be destroyed, and it can beat the crap out of people, but how is it going to find the people? Well, a few years or even months in the grave can wreak havoc with one's eyesight, especially once the maggots get in. Still, for some reason most zombies retain a pretty decent ability to track down likely sources of food.

First decide at what level the zombie's basic senses function. Then, add in extra special senses to make it even more deadly.

Like The Dead — Power: 0

A few days/months/years underground hasn't exactly done wonders for the zombie's senses. They are significantly less than human standard. The zombie can only make out dim forms moving around -- just the outline of a human figure for instance. Their senses of smell and touch are gone completely and their sense of hearing is pretty shabby. Basically, the zombie will chase down anything that moves without too much discrimination. Even so, it will not attack other zombies. A zombie always knows a brother living dead. Perception 1.

Like The Living — Power: +1

This zombie returns with the perception of an average human. The better to see you, my dear! There is a drawback to this -- since the zombie retains its sense of touch, it can also feel pain. While attacks to nonvital parts cause no real damage, it still feels like they do. As a result, the zombie becomes temporarily distracted every time it takes significant damage. It is unable to act the Turn after it suffers 10+ Dead Points in a single attack. Perception 2.

Like A Hawk   Power: +2

The rejuvenation process was better than complete and the zombie retained all of its senses at better than average human level. Again, the zombie feels pain (see Like The Living). On the plus side, its vision is good enough to see exactly who's doing the shooting and exact appropriate vengeance. Perception 3.

Like Nothing You've Ever Seen   Power: +10

Death has given the zombie a clarity of senses unparalleled in nature. The zombie has eyes like a zoom lens and hearing like an FBI bug. Hardly anything escapes its notice, especially if it's living and breathing. In fact, it can hear breathing from a hundred yards away. These super-perceptive zombies make deadly hunters, but do feel pain (see Like the Living). Perception 7.

Special Senses Features
X-ray Vision   Power: Perception x2

The zombie has the ability to see through walls, trees, and anything less than three feet (one meter) thick that is not lead. In fact, the zombie probably sees the world this way all of the time -- a series of solid and semi-transparent objects, some of which move around and look especially delicious. Range equals ten times Perception in yards.

Life Sense   Power: Perception x2

These zombies always know where their next meal is going to come from -- right around that corner. Being dead has given the walking corpse the ability to sense the presence of living beings within a certain range, no matter what obstructions lie between it and its moving dinner. Of course, being able to sense a living thing does not mean the zombie can get to it. Zombies are simple creatures, however, and once they find a nearby source of food they tend to stay as close as possible. Thus, holing up in the old barn is not such a great idea. The zombies cannot get in (at the moment), but they keep massing outside, waiting for you to come out. They know there's food inside and they are hungry! Range equals ten times Perception in yards.

Scent Tracking — Power: Perception

Like a well trained bloodhound, the zombie has a nose for human flesh. Even if the zombie's senses are normally terrible, when it comes to sniffing out prey, there's no stopping this reanimated cadaver. It can follow the scents of living beings that are up to 24 hours old. Like any tracker, it loses the scent if the target passes through water -- although if it's just a stream, the zombie can probably already smell the scent from the opposite bank. Zombies tend to follow these scent trails around until they find something to eat. Once a zombie encounters potential prey, it often single-mindedly follows that particular scent until it finds the prey once more. Perception times 2 for purposes of smelling (minimum 4).

Infravision — Power: Perception x2

No, zombie elves or dwarves are not the only ones to come back with Infravision. These zombies home in on the heat given off by living creatures, just like a guided missile. In fact, most zombies with this ability can only tell the living from the dead because of the heat signature. This allows them to hunt day or night, but can cause some problems on a really hot day when even zombie bodies reach temperatures over 98 degrees. Also, the zombies can be distracted by high heat sources. Range equals ten times Perception in yards.

Sustenance

Remember, death doesn't always stop those hunger pangs. Zombies still crave something to fill their atrophied stomachs or just satiate that infantile need to have something in their mouth. Most living dead actually do need some source of energy to keep them going. The exact nature of this energy source depends on the reason they came back from the dead in the first place. Whatever the cause, these zombies need to eat if they want to continue to unlive long and productive unlives.

Need To Feed

The first step in this Aspect is choosing how often the zombies need to feed. What exactly they are consuming is discussed later.

Daily — Power: 0

Everyone needs three square meals a day to make the most out of life and these zombies are no exception. They don't need to eat a whole lot but they must consume at least 10 ounces of whatever it is they crave each day. After a day without eating, the zombie starts to lose Strength. For every day of starvation, the zombie loses one quarter of its original Strength rating (round up for purposes of using the Attribute) to a minimum of zero. Once Strength drops below one, the creature is very weak and can do little more than drag itself slowly along. Lack of food will not destroy the zombie, but it will render it unable to do anything but lie around and moan "Braiiiiiins . . ."

Occasionally — Power: +2

The zombie can go up to three days without eating, but every fourth day it needs to consume at least 16 ounces of its preferred nutrient. It doesn't have to eat all 16 ounces at once, but it does need at least that much each three day period. Each day after that, the zombie starts suffering Strength loss (see Daily).

Weekly — Power: +4

The zombie can keep going with even the smallest amount of food. Once a week it needs to have a nice big meal of at least 24 ounces or it starts to suffer the effects of starvation (see Daily).

Who Needs Food? — Power: +8

These rare zombies have no need to feed at all. They kill just for the fun of it. Often these zombies are powered by something in the environment, such as sunlight or massive amounts of radioactivity. Should the zombie ever be cut off from its seemingly endless source of reanimatory energy, it will lose its Strength as if it were starving (see Daily).

The Menu

The one thing that almost all zombies have in common is a need to feed on the living. It's part of that whole cosmic cycle thing, the nature of the beast, and so forth. Different zombies have penchants for particular parts of the living human, some of which are easier to get at than others.

All Flesh Must Be Eaten　　Power: 0

Many zombies just aren't too particular -- they'll take any meaty bit of living flesh they can sink their teeth into. This diet works well for zombies who need to eat a lot.

Braiiiiins　　Power: -3

The classic zombie fare; the living dead love the tender taste of human brains. Often it's all they can think of, repeating that same word over and over. The tricky part is getting the skull open, so only zombies with either high strength or the ability to use tools should have brains as their main source of nutrition.

Sweet Breads　　Power: -3

Most know these as organs. Pick a particular human organ that the zombie is fond of and have them literally tear in. The liver is always popular, but one kidney is never enough to satisfy a hungry zombie. Then there's the heart, a perennial favorite with the sentimental living dead.

Blood　　Power: -2

It's not just for vampires anymore. The zombie needs to drink fresh human blood to keep going. Unlike certain suave bloodsuckers who can take a little and leave the victim living, zombies tend to break the skin and just get as much as they can, as quickly as they can. Just for future reference, the larger the holes in the victim, the more blood available for a hungry ungrowing undead.

Soul Sucker　　Power: +5

For the more supernaturally oriented zombies out there, the flesh of the living does not do the trick. They hunger for something greater: the immortal human soul. Devouring the souls of the living usually requires some sort of physical attack. Examples include a big messy kiss, tearing out the throat, or simply squeezing the life out of the victim. Whatever the method of retrieval, it's invariably painful and may leave the victim quite, quite dead (until they rise again, that is). The zombie drains Essence points equal to double its Willpower, but only consumes (gains the benefit of) half that (the rest is wasted). Each Essence Point consumed is equal to one ounce of sustenance for purposes of the starvation rules.

Intelligence

No matter what it needs to eat, how it moves around, what it sees, or how strong it is, the one factor guiding all of a zombie's activities is its intellect (or lack thereof). Some zombies are purely creatures of instinct, shambling around, feeding, and moving on to the next closest target. Others retain some of their old intellect. As often as not, these intellectual abilities come in fragments -- they can talk but they don't remember how to drive a car. One thing that tends to make zombies manageable for humans to fight is that they are very, very stupid. In fact, most zombies are in the none-too-bright category. Zombies smarter than the average cadaver must be built slowly, brain power by brain power.

Dumb as Dead Wood　　Power: 0

This is the basic zombie intelligence. It detects something alive and it tries to kill it, end of story. It cannot open doors or climb over things real well, or do much more than walk in straight lines and knock things down. The zombie has Intelligence -2 regardless of how bright it was in life, and cannot use language or tools.

Language   Power: +1

The zombie can still talk, although it is not a pretty sound. Further, it can understand what others are saying, whether they be zombies or humans. Of course, its language skills are restricted to whatever abilities it had when alive. Talking zombies can cooperate with one another and even make deals with the living. Furthermore, they can read and understand the dangers of words like "flammable" and "explosive." At the very least, they can get on the phone and call for more ambulances. Add Language (local area) 5.

Tool Use   Power: +3 per level

There are three levels to this intellectual ability. Tool use is a combination of intellect and manual dexterity. Even if a zombie is smart enough to talk, it does not necessarily have the ability to drive a car because it can't make its body work that way. At level 1, the zombie can use simple tools like clubs, doorknobs, melee weapons and anything else that does not require too much thinking. At level 2, the zombie can operate machines that require some thinking, such as telephones, electrical switches, and firearms. At level 3, the zombie can operate complex machines that require it do several things at once, like driving a car or operating a computer. Any level also grants Intelligence 1.

Animal Cunning   Power: +2/+4

These zombies are able to puzzle out certain things, and do learn from experiences. At the lower level (+2 Power), the zombie gains Intelligence 0, and knows to use a more direct path to cut off prey, to lie in ambush, and to avoid harmful attacks. At the higher level (+4 Power), the zombie's Intelligence becomes 1 but it can only act as an intelligent animal. It can open doors by pushing, lift things without grasping, or leave crude traps to get at prey. These abilities may include crude communication and teamwork, but nothing beyond the capacity of a relatively smart animal. Tool use of any sort is not possible.

Teamwork   Power: +4

Some zombies seem to communicate with one another with a kind of ESP. They always know just how to work together when in a group, whether it be to bust down a door by combining their strength or to surround some poor human and close in for the kill. This natural teamwork capability requires no verbal communication between the zombies. Range of communication is 20 yards.

Long-term Memory   Power: +5

The living dead with this capability learn from their mistakes and the mistakes of others. Thus, if they see that their buddies attacking the humans through a certain doorway are mostly getting their heads shot off, they will try to find a safer way to get at the tasty, well-armed morsel. Likewise, they can remember where a human is hiding, go off and get a club, and come back and use it to help bash down the door. Zombies with this feature are much easier to train since they actually remember instructions given to them and know that when they do what they're told, they receive a reward (punishment does not work well since most zombies don't feel pain). This feature is a prerequisite to retaining skills from life (each such skill level adds to Power level). Zombies gain Intelligence 2 for purposes of memory (no language).

Problem Solving   Power: +15

The zombie is capable of advanced leaps of logic when it comes to getting at its next victim. For instance, it might realize that the dead mall security guard has a key to open the door that those three tasty humans are hiding behind. Or something even simpler like moving a box next to a window in order to climb up high enough to break the glass and crawl through. Most zombies, even tool users, don't think this far ahead, preferring to move (mentally and physically) in straight lines. The zombie gains Intelligence 2 for purposes of problem solving only (no language or memory). Includes the Tool Use feature at level 3 for free, and allows for increases in Intelligence up to level held during life (each level adds to Power level).

Chapter Five

Spreading the Love

Where did I come from, mommy?

Well dear, first you were bitten by daddy and then you died . . .

Although most zombies start off their undeath in the grave, once the world starts crawling with living dead, it usually doesn't take much to make more zombies. The exact way in which old zombies create new zombies varies. Choose or modify one of the following (variations may be found in Chapter Six: Worlds in Hell), or devise one more fitting to the campaign setting used.

Only the Dead   Power: –2

The zombie has to actually kill its victims in order for them to come back as a member of the club. Anyone killed by a zombie rises again within a few hours. Of course, if the victim falls prey to a pack of zombies seeking fresh meat, there may not be much of her left to rise up again. However, most zombies stop the feeding once a person dies so there's usually only a few pounds of meat missing, not enough to really make a difference.

One Bite and You're Hooked
Power: +2

The zombie need only bite a living being and the chain reaction begins. The process usually takes a day or so to finally set in, during which time it might be possible to reverse the effects if a skilled research doctor treats the victim. Otherwise, the bitten goes straight from living to undead without ever really passing out and dying.

Bury the Body   Power: –2

Sometimes its not the zombie that reanimates the corpse but rather something in the very soil or air. In order to rise again, a body has to be buried under the ground or stored in some container, or coated with some chemical. Zombies created this way have a natural instinct to bury their victims, or otherwise prepare the body, and thus enlarge the undead community every step of the way. Rising from the shallow grave, or awakening after embalment usually takes between six and twelve hours, but sometimes occurs much more quickly.

Special Zombie Features

Now that the myriad basic Aspects of the zombie are determined, the creature's destructive power can be augmented with any number of special abilities. These are usually special attacks of one sort or another. Some of these powers may not even exist in all of the zombies, just a lucky few that will give the Cast Members an extra challenge.

Acid Blood — Power: Varies

The zombie's blood would make a vampire need dentures. It is highly corrosive and will eat through any biological material and some metals. The zombie itself cannot use its blood in an offensive way, but it makes things dangerous for anyone in close combat with the creature. Oddly enough, the zombie's flesh is immune to the acid blood, even after the zombie is destroyed. Zombie fighters searching for protective wear may choose to garb themselves in the flesh of their foes for added, but gruesome protection. Acid does regular damage per Turn equal to double the Power level of this feature.

Diseased Corpse — Power: +3

Corpses are renowned for their unsanitary nature. Zombies with this ability carry some dread disease along the lines of the bubonic plague or the ebola virus (although it could be something as mundane as a really bad flu). Any contact with one of these zombies carries a risk of catching the disease, even if the zombie does not successfully attack the person. In fact, the disease often proves a more deadly killer than the zombies themselves. Disease rules are discussed in Chapter Three: Shambling 101 (p. 108).

Noxious Odor — Power: +5

No corpse really smells good, but these zombies stink to high heaven. In fact, the stink is so great that anyone coming within six feet (two meters) of the festering cadaver is almost immediately overcome by the odor. Living folk begin to vomit uncontrollably and may even pass out if exposed to the smell for too long. Nearby characters must make a Difficult Constitution Test or be rendered unconscious or otherwise incapacitated.

Nest — Power: Varies

Although most zombies have maggots and worms living in their bodies, these zombies have developed a special, symbiotic relationship with some of the parasites. Feeding off the undead flesh has turned the insects into zombies of a sort. They work in conjunction with the living dead that hosts them, swarming out and attacking anything that comes close (close combat distance) to the creature. They can be biting ants, stinging wasps, pinching beetles, even deadly spiders. Whatever they are, it's sure to creep the Cast Members out the first time they come swarming forth. Creatures do regular damage per Turn equal to the Power level on this feature (they ignore armor).

Spitter — Power: Varies

The zombie can spit some sort of toxic fluid. Often this is a mixture of saliva, embalming fluid, and other unidentifiable internal liquids. The substance causes living skin to itch and burn, much like a very bad case of poison ivy or jellyfish stings. The real threat from this spitting attack is if the zombie manages to hit the target in the face and the toxin gets in her eyes. The burning sensation effectively blinds the target for D4(2) hours unless she can somehow rinse the fluid from her eyes with lots of running water. Range equals half Constitution in yards (meters). Spit does regular damage per Turn equal to half the Power level of this feature (armor is ignored if face is targeted).

Spew Flame — Power: Varies

Through a curious chemical process that results from the production of methane gas as the body decomposes, the zombie is able to actually open its mouth and release a short range blast of flame, much like the fire eaters at carnivals and renaissance festivals the world over. The zombie can only do this once every six hours, and often does so uncontrollably, although it will save the flaming belch for a living target if one is nearby. Even worse, because the flame is powered by methane, the stench of the belch can be debilitating even if the flame misses. Range equals Constitution in yards (meters). The attack requires a Resisted Test between the zombie's Dexterity and Perception, and the target's Dodge and Dexterity Task (or Difficult Dexterity). Flame does regular damage per Turn equal to the Power level of this feature.

Detachable Body Parts
Power: Varies, but at least +10

The zombie has the bizarre ability to actually separate off parts of its body and let them act on their own. The most common use of this power is removing a hand and letting it crawl about, like Thing in search of prey. The zombie has full control over what the detached body parts do and can even sense what it senses (which is usually only by touch). Tool-using zombies can use this ability to sneak their hands through a hole or window, and have the crawling thing unlock a door from the inside. Others throw their hands like weapons and have them latch onto the necks of prey that are trying to run away. Of course, the zombie can detach any part of the body, including internal organs. Thus small intestines become animated, constricting snakes and so forth. The possible uses are endless. The specifics of this feature, including any special damage are left to the Zombie Master's discretion.

Explosive Personality
Power: +2/+5

When this zombie returns to the dead (the kind that does not move, that is), it does so with a bang . . . literally. Once the zombie's Dead Points are exceeded, its body parts, at least those that remain, fly apart with a loud and messy explosion. At the lower level (+2 Power), the parts spread over a 4 yard (meter) radius. This causes no damage to those caught in the blast, but does force a Fear Test at -4 (at least for the first dozen or so times it is witnessed). At the higher level (+5 Power), the flying guts cause D6(3) points of damage to all those in the explosion radius, and a Fear Test for those who witness it.

Regeneration   Power: +2/+5

These zombies have the special ability to recover from the damage done to them. This does not mean that ineffective holes or partially missing limbs are repaired. That is window dressing that gives the zombie a real visual *ummph*. This regenerative ability is limited to Dead Point damage that will ultimately force the zombie to stop moving around and eating. At the lower level (+2 Power), the zombie regains 1 Dead Point per minute. At the higher level (+5 Power), 1 Dead Point is gained per Turn.

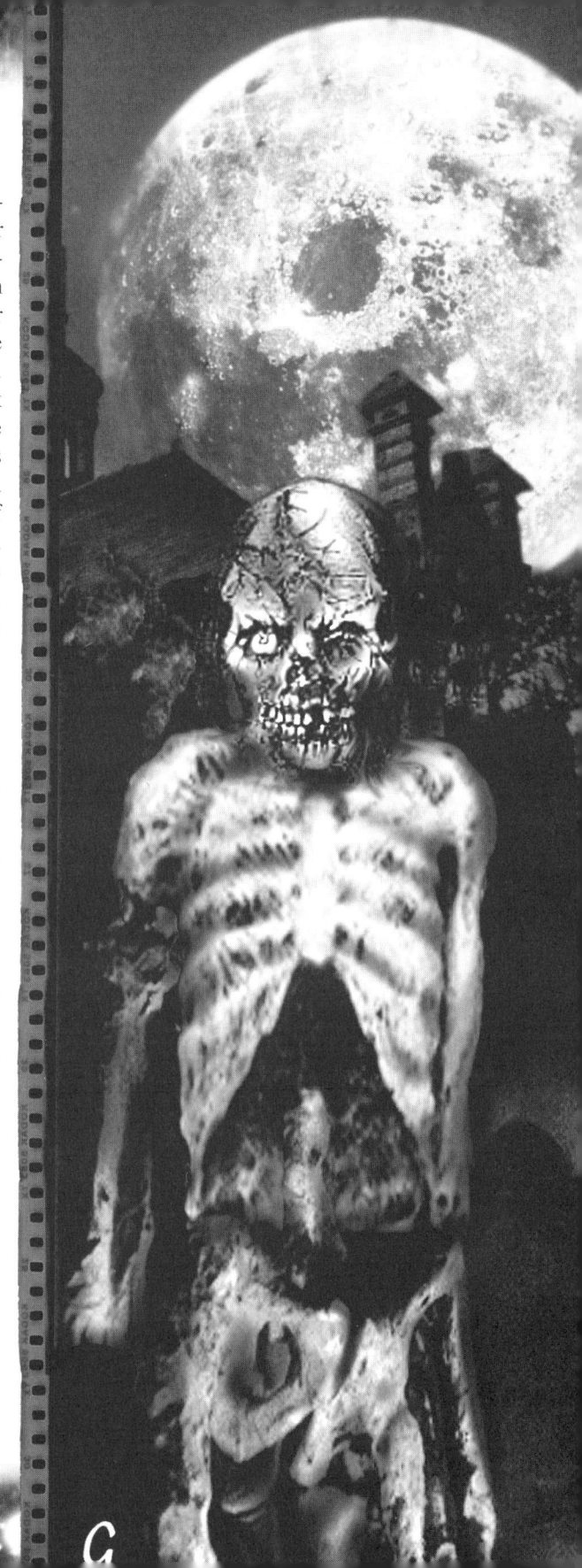

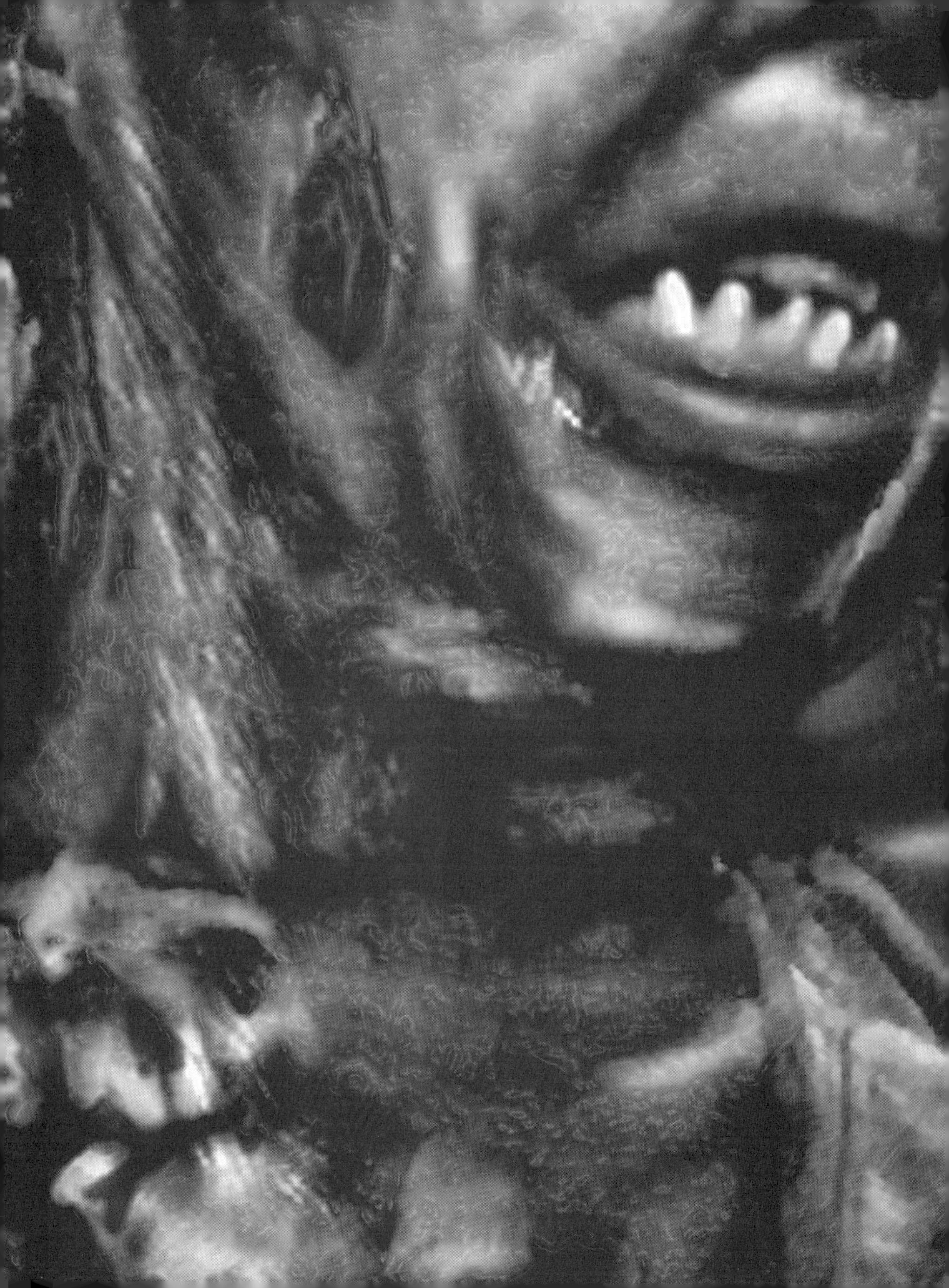

Chapter Six
Worlds in Hell

"When there's no more room in **hell** the dead will **walk** the Earth"

—Dawn of the Dead

Introduction

There's more to a zombie than just a walking corpse. While it's busy busting down the front door and scooping out your sister's brains, there's not much time to think about that. But later, when the action slows, there's some time to reflect in the basement, while you hope that door doesn't give way. Aside from wondering how much food is around, your thoughts turn to considering just where these damn dead guys came from. After all, the dead don't rise up and start consuming the flesh of the living for no reason at all. Behind every good zombie story, there's a good (or at least amusing) back story. In this chapter, eleven of them are presented.

Each of the following worlds gives an entirely different reason for the dead to rise. Zombie Masters can use the portions of this chapter in a number of different ways. To play *All Flesh Must Be Eaten* as a stand alone game, Zombie Masters should read through each world, choose a setting and have the players make characters. Alternately, one of these settings may be incorporated into an existing, on-going campaign. There's nothing that confuses a regular group of Gifted, an Aegis Cell, some vampires, a pirate gang, or an adventuring party of heroes more than having the dead rise up against them en masse.

Each world description contains four distinct sections. First, there's a little bit of fiction to set the mood for the piece. For the most part, these are stories told by someone experiencing this particular zombie crisis first hand, or some sort of news account. The Zombie Masters could photocopy and let the players read them when the Cast Members met someone who could tell the story.

Next comes the history section, where all the background about why the zombies are rising is revealed. In general, the players should not have access to this information, since part of the fun of many of these scenarios is figuring out why the dead keep eating people.

The third section details the current state of affairs. Feel free to set scenarios back further in the setting history, if desired. That gets more "normal" world description going, before the zombies come a'callin'. This description is simply a suggestion about what the world is like when a typical game of *All Flesh Must Be Eaten* gets under way. Usually this is just after the zombies have risen and started all kinds of panic somewhere. This section also gives some details about just how these particular zombies operate: their strengths and weaknesses and so forth.

The final section contains story hooks to give some direction when running the game. Some of these require the players to create certain types of characters, so make sure to take this into consideration before playing.

Before moving to the zombies, however, there's one matter still to discuss . . .

Chapter Six

Intraparty Conflict

A central feature of many zombie stories -- conflict among the party members -- has not yet been addressed. Blowing away zombies is all well and good, but the constant danger of becoming zombie chow tends to set people on edge. After a while, personality quirks, mental debilities, biases and downright orneriness surface from the depths of a person's psyche. For some, these conflict-causing features aren't so far down -- they come up at the first chomp of trouble. As just one example, in the *Day of the Dead* movie, the military types are at loggerheads with the scientists over "harvesting" zombies for study. In one encounter, a soldier dies. The leader blames the "pencil-necks" and the tension (and outright conflict) between the two groups hastens the death of all but a few.

For brave Zombie Masters with experienced roleplayers, or those looking for something different in their gaming sessions, such intraplay can be emphasized. This tension can add an unique element to an *All Flesh Must Be Eaten* game. It can supplement the battle against the undead hordes and the search for a cure, or become the heart of the Story itself.

A Word of Warning

Inserting and emphasizing intraparty conflict should not be done lightly, or without consultation with all the players. As any reasonably experienced gamer knows, the easiest way to get everyone killed is to start fighting among the Cast Members. This might not be so bad -- in fact, it may be the point of the Zombie Master's storytelling efforts. On the other hand, even tension and abuse short of character death can leave hard feelings between friends who are supposed to be playing a game. All in all, a Zombie Master who is interested in keeping the party alive long enough to get to the end of the adventure will need to plan carefully and allow for events that diffuse tension, or force it in another direction (e.g., at the shambling dead). So, if interested in adding the intraparty conflict element, prepare well -- you have been warned.

Character Creation

Interparty conflict best starts at character creation. As the players are formulating their Cast Members, or picking their Archetypes, make sure they discuss adding potentially conflicting features. One might take a Minority Drawback, while another takes Delusions: Prejudice against that minority. A Cast Member might choose to be addicted to something that another has a Level 3 Honorable Drawback against. At the least extreme, one character could be Cowardly, while another is Reckless. By seeding the party in this way, conflicts can be predicted and more easily roleplayed (and prepared for).

Stress and Essence Loss

Setting the Cast Members up with certain Drawbacks during character creation, and beginning play may be sufficient to sow the seeds of intraparty tension. Optionally, this process may be encouraged by tightening the screws. Use the stress Essence loss rules (see Essence Loss, p. 116). As Cast Members slowly lose Essence due to stress, their Drawbacks become more pronounced. Rather than having little emotional reaction, those with less than half Essence wind up with emotional hair-triggers. Any Simple Willpower Test required to set aside the Drawback becomes Difficult, or suffers a -1 to -6 penalty. Further, during tense moments (like combat), the Zombie Master may call for a Willpower Test at such a penalty in order to not succumb to temptation. For example, if a Cowardly Cast Member with half Essence was told to guard a door to keep out zombies, the Zombie Master might call for a Willpower Test. If failed, the character might just go back through, lock the door and throw away the keys. Depending on the circumstances, this might substantially decrease the survival odds of the rest of the group.

Rewards

Good roleplaying of any kind deserves a bonus when awarding experience points (see Experience, p. 120). When intraparty conflict is at issue, a Zombie Master may award another point. Of course, if such conflict results in the death of party members, the experience award may not be so meaningful. Again, no one said intraparty conflict was going to be pretty.

Rise of the Walking Dead

I was born in this town, grew up here, lived here every day of my thirty-three years. A small farming community like this, you get to know most everybody pretty well and you always help your friends and neighbors out when they need it. So when I saw Frank Jenkins stumbling down Rabbit Run Road, I stopped my truck and got out to see if I could help him. He looked like hell, all beat up and even bitten in a few places, like some animal had attacked him.

"Frank! Jesus, what happened to you?" I yelled as I caught him up in my arms just before he collapsed. His eyes were wild, unfocused. He didn't even recognize me. "What happened to you Frank? What happened?"

"Ron . . ." he gasped, "Ron Bloom?"

"Huh? Ron Bloom's dead, Frank!" Ron had been my best friend. He died in a car accident on New Year's Eve.

"No he ain't. I seen him." Frank started coughing, spitting up blood. The spasms seemed to last forever, but when they stopped Frank was dead. I laid him down gently, my hands covered in blood. I'd never seen a man die before.

I jumped at a sound from the bushes off to the left, the way Frank had come. I turned and stared in disbelief. It was Ron. At least, it looked like Ron. His face hung limp, his skin pale, his clothes covered in blood and mud. I reeled backwards towards my truck. Ron just kept coming, groaning mindlessly. All of a sudden my leg was on fire with pain. Frank was biting me, drawing blood. I kicked him away and ran back to the truck. I got in and drove straight to the sheriff's.

Then I had to sit down. My leg was killing me, and I started feeling awful . . .

All Flesh Must Be Eaten

History

This is the classic zombie story seen a hundred times before. One fine day, for no explicable reason, the dead start clawing their way out of their graves. Of course, there is a reason, but no one knows what it is just yet. They're too busy worrying about what the damn things are doing. The problem centers around a small town in upstate New York. This quiet rural community named Argos is noteworthy for just about nothing, except the nearby system of natural caves that extend miles into the ground.

Thirty years ago, the government decided these caves were the perfect place to store containers of spent uranium and other nuclear waste. They bought the land, buried tons of radioactive sludge deep in the cave system and, once they thought it full, sealed the whole thing off. They didn't plan on the containers leaking and getting into the local soil and water table. And no one could have imagined the effect this radiation would have on the local population, particularly the local *dead* population.

Some said the radiation became a tool of the spirits or demonic forces, particularly those who remembered that the native Americans who once lived in the region held the caves as sacred. Others maintained that it was the radiation itself, somehow jump-starting the dead nervous system, creating brain-dead beasts who could only act on the most basic instinct: find food. Whatever the cause, it didn't discriminate about who it raised from the dead. Every deceased creature, animal or human, within fifty miles of those caves became one of the walking dead.

It probably spread slowly, raising a few dead animals. No one really noticed until it hit the small Lutheran Church outside of town, the one with its own graveyard. They were the first people to rise, some of them decades old. They clawed their way into the early evening air and quickly killed the groundskeeper and his wife.

By morning, the radiation had spread to the town cemetery and hundreds more began to rise. The sheriff got word that some sort of gang was attacking the town. He called over to Albany for help. By the next day, all contact with the town had been lost. State troopers sent to investigate never returned. That's when the military stepped in.

The State of Things Today

The zombies have overrun all of Argos. At least ninety percent of the residents have been killed, partially eaten, and subsequently turned into zombies.

The bodily fluids of these creatures are completely irradiated. Anyone killed by a zombie is infected by these deadly toxins and returns as another zombie. Even those who just get bitten may be infected. If they survive the initial attack, the infected die within a few days if they do not get a full blood transfusion. The zombies are completely mindless. They cannot understand language, nor do they work together. However, they never attack one another. Their craving for human flesh is limited to the flesh of the living.

Within the town and the surrounding countryside, a few pockets of humanity have managed to hole up in safety for a while. Unfortunately, the zombies have an unerring ability to home in on the flesh of the living. For the moment they are busy consuming livestock, pets, and other easily accessible sources of fresh meat. These animals become zombies as well, and they can be just as deadly as their human counterparts, sometimes more so.

The few remaining live residents of Argos are scared to walk the zombie-infested streets. Yet, the longer they stay in place, the greater the population of zombies becomes. The slow-moving animated corpses seem easy to avoid, but in large numbers they can stop a car or surround a human on foot. What's more, weapons don't seem to hurt them, at least not for the most part. Only a blow that pierces the zombie's brain has any chance of successfully bringing it down. Some still cling to the hope that outside help is on the way.

As indeed it is, in a manner of speaking. The national guard, the Centers for Disease Control, the EPA, and the U.S. Army are all on the scene, but none of them have entered the town as of yet. No one outside of Argos knows what is really going on in the town and the few reports they've had are too unbelievable to be true. Helicopter flybys have shown that the local population is out in the streets, but behaving strangely. For now, the government forces are concentrating on sealing the area and making sure whatever it is that's going on does not spread any further.

Worlds In Hell

The government is currently putting together a team of scientists and soldiers to send into the town and investigate. The team will collect blood, air, soil, and water samples, and if possible capture and isolate one of the infected residents. No one is allowed to leave the town under any circumstances, and the team will wear full body protective gear at all times. With any luck, they can contain and eliminate this problem before it spreads too far.

Unfortunately they are already too late. Although no human zombies have breached the military cordon, several zombified animals have already made their way out and into surrounding communities. The plague has already begun to spread, but no one knows it. Perhaps the living can stop the rise of the dead before it is too late. Perhaps not.

Experimental Weapon

If the Zombie Master wishes, the following weapon can be introduced after some study of the Zombies.

XM-27
Range: 3/30/60/180/350
Damage: D4 x 5(10)*
Cap: 6   EV: 20/10
Cost: $3400   Availability: R

The XM-27 is called a cryorifle. It fires a projectile that injects a liquid nitrogen gel into the target.

* If the brain of a zombie is targeted, the gell renders it "unconscious" for D8 + 2(6) minutes, allowing transfer to a scientific facility for study. For living creatures, the gell instantly kills with a head shot, or destroys any limb it hits.

Story Ideas
Escape From Argos

This traditional zombie scenario offers a number of different gruesome options for Zombie Masters to inflict on their players. The classic tale centers around a group of living humans caught within a town full of zombies. Perhaps the players are just passing through and stopped in Argos to refuel their car and get a bite to eat. On the other hand, they might be locals, confronted by the walking corpses of their friends, family, and loved ones. Either way the object is the same: get out of town alive.

Unfortunately, getting out of town is not as easy as it would seem. The zombies tend to stick with what they know, the habits that were ingrained in them when they were still alive. Thus, they clog the streets and alleys of Argos, hunting for any sign of the living. This makes driving very problematic. Furthermore, most of the roads out of town are blocked by cars whose drivers stopped rather than running down their next door neighbor (who they obviously didn't realize was already dead). Abandoned cars with broken windows and bloodstained upholstery give testament to the sad fate of these overly conscientious drivers.

Some may prefer to fortify a position and wait for the cavalry to come. Anyone who has spent any time in town will have seen the military helicopters flying overhead. Presumably, it is only a matter of time before the army marches on Argos. Sadly, it is also only a matter of time before the zombies kill every living thing in Argos and converge upon the characters with unerring accuracy. Hopefully, the heroes can hold out long enough.

Even if they do manage to escape through town and the surrounding countryside, they still have to deal with the military presence. Frightened national guardsmen are just as likely to shoot at the characters as at zombies. The CDC scientists no doubt would love to get their hands on someone who managed to survive this "outbreak." Of course, the zombies were not contained, so the adventure can continue. While the heroes are examined and debriefed, the zombie plague spreads inexorably across the country.

Into the Fire

Alternately, the players can create Cast Members who are part of the government task force sent in to investigate the local cadaver problem. In this role, the characters receive excellent equipment and support as soldiers, scientists, doctors, and possibly even local law enforcement officers drafted as guides. Their mission: enter Argos, collect samples, and figure out just what the hell is going on.

The team encounters the same problem as those trying to escape, only in reverse. Their first priority should be to save and quarantine any survivors found in the town. After that, they have to capture at least one zombie and bring it back "alive" (i.e., still kicking and biting). Additionally, the heroes must collect soil, air, and water samples in an effort to determine how this "disease" is spreading. Meanwhile, the hundreds of zombies in the town draw in closer and closer around the heroes, making their job all the more difficult. The high radiation levels in the soil wreak havoc with radio systems, making communication with headquarters spotty at best.

Eventually, by analyzing soil samples and the blood of any zombie, the heroes can trace the source of the zombie effect back to the government-owned cave system. Perhaps a survivor informs them that the living dead first appeared out by the old Lutheran graveyard. A nightmare journey into the caves, plagued by zombie animals and mutated creatures, leads to the leaking waste storage facility and the cause of all this trouble.

As an optional, added complication, the Cast Members' radio calls for back-up go unanswered. While the team was away, the zombies overran a portion of the quarantine line. Soon enough the entire on-sight force is either a zombie or fighting for its life -- certainly too busy to come and help the stranded investigators. Now the heroes are in much the same boat as the residents of Argos: they must fight to survive against the encroaching zombie hordes while they look for the source of the contagion, or an avenue of escape.

Soldier
Supporting Cast/Adversary

Strength 3 **Constitution** 3
Dexterity 2 **Intelligence** 2
Perception 2 **Willpower** 2
Life Points 34 **Speed** 10
Endurance Points 29 **Essence Pool** 14

Qualities/Drawbacks

Contacts (Military), Contacts (Police)

Skills

Brawling 2, Climbing 2, Demolitions 2, Dodge 2, Driving (Car) 2, First Aid 1, Guns (Assault Rifle) 2, Guns (Handgun) 2, Hand Weapon (Knife) 2, Stealth 2, Survival (Forest) 2, Swimming 2

Equipment

Backpack, Camouflage Fatigues, Compass, Rations, Flashlight, 5.56 Assault Rifle with Underbarrel Grenade Launcher, Class IV torso armor, Class III helmet

CDC Scientist
Supporting Cast/Adversary

Strength 2 **Constitution** 3
Dexterity 2 **Intelligence** 3
Perception 3 **Willpower** 2
Life Points 26 **Speed** 8
Endurance Points 23 **Essence Pool** 14

Qualities/Drawbacks

Contacts (University) 2, Contacts (Hospital) 2, Contacts (Government) 2

Skills

Bureaucracy 2, Computers 3, Driving (Car) 1, Engineer (Biological) 2, Humanities (Psychology) 2, Research/Investigation 2, Sciences (Biology) 3, Writing (Scientific) 2

Equipment

Laptop Computer, Doctor's Bag, Specimen Jars and Collection Tools

Rise of the Walking Dead Zombies

Strength 2　　**Constitution** 2
Dexterity 1　　**Intelligence** -2
Perception 1　　**Willpower** 2
Dead Points 15　　**Speed** 2
Endurance Points n/a　　**Essence Pool** 8

Attack: Bite damage D4 x 2(4) slashing

Zombies attempt to grab the living and bite them. This is handled as a close combat attack with a Resisted Test. If a number of zombies attack at the same time, the character may defend against all (and suffer the multiple action penalties), or ignore some of them. If ignored, a zombie grabs and bites with a Simple Dexterity Test.

Weak Spot: Brain
Getting Around: Slow and Steady
Strength: Dead Joe Average
Senses: Like the Dead; Life Sense
Sustenance: Daily; All Flesh Must Be Eaten
Intelligence: Dumb As Dead Wood
Spreading the Love: Special (see sidebar)
Power: 15

Spreading the Love

No matter who or what the zombie is, it infects the living in the same way. People who are bitten must make a Constitution Test, with a +2 bonus for a scratch or a light wound (9 points or less), no penalty for a deep bite or wound (more than 10 points of damage), and -1 for severe injuries (more than 20 points of damage). The Zombie Master may wish to make these rolls in secret. If infected, the victim suffers a wasting disease which imposes a cumulative -1 penalty per day to all Tasks or Tests (i.e., -2 on the second day, -3 on the third day, etc.). After (Constitution + Willpower)/2 days, the character dies. If a character is killed by a zombie bite, he will rise up as another undead in 3-30 minutes (3D10).

Chapter Six

All Flesh Must Be Eaten

Zombie Rat

Strength 0   **Constitution** 2
Dexterity 3   **Intelligence** -2
Perception 2   **Willpower** 2
Dead Points 15   **Speed** 10
Endurance Points n/a   **Essence Pool** 8
Attack: Bite damage D4(2) slashing
Weak Spot: Brain
Getting Around: Special
Strength: Special

Senses: Like The Living; Life Sense
Sustenance: Daily; All Flesh Must Be Eaten
Intelligence: Dumb As Dead Wood
Spreading the Love: Special (see sidebar)
Power: 20

Zombie Dog

Strength 2   **Constitution** 2
Dexterity 2   **Intelligence** -2
Perception 2   **Willpower** 2
Dead Points 15   **Speed** 8
Endurance Points n/a   **Essence Pool** 10
Attack: Bite damage D4 x 2(4) slashing
Weak Spot: Brain
Getting Around: Special
Strength: Special

Senses: Like The Living; Life Sense
Sustenance: Daily; All Flesh Must Be Eaten
Intelligence: Dumb As Dead Wood
Spreading the Love: Special (see sidebar)
Power: 21

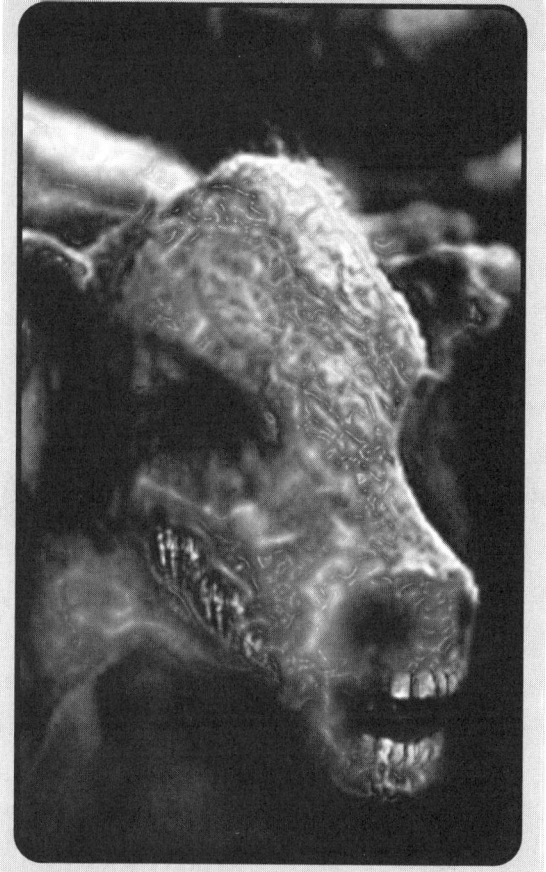

Zombie Cow

Strength 6   **Constitution** 2
Dexterity 1   **Intelligence** -2
Perception 1   **Willpower** 2
Dead Points 15   **Speed** 6
Endurance Points n/a   **Essence Pool** 12
Attack: Bite damage D4 x 6(12) slashing
Weak Spot: Brain
Getting Around: Special
Strength: Special

Senses: Like the Dead; Life Sense
Sustenance: Daily; All Flesh Must Be Eaten
Intelligence: Dumb As Dead Wood
Spreading the Love: Special (see sidebar)
Power: 25

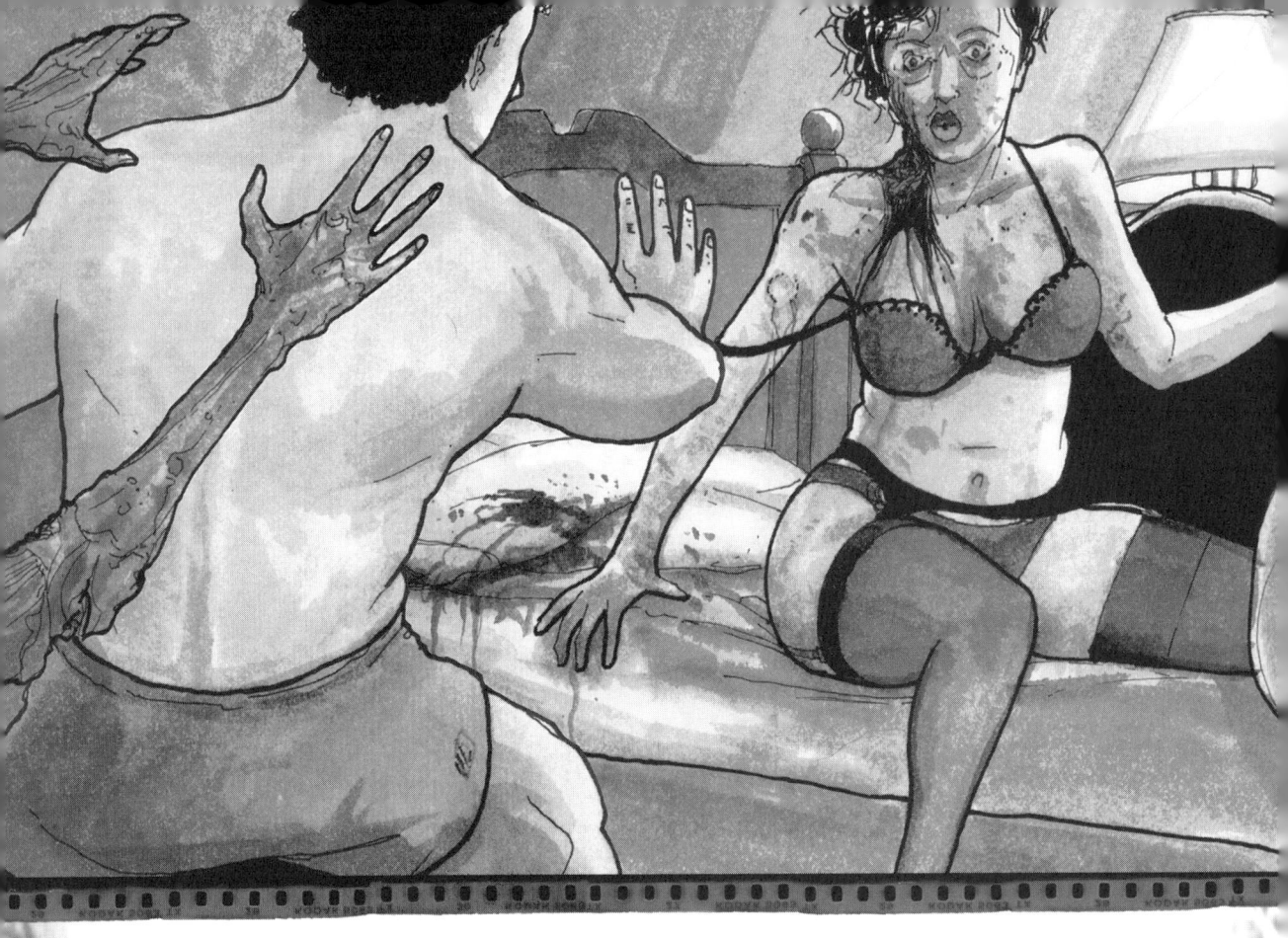

PHADE to Black

Fate can be so cruel. They say the worst thing that can happen to a mother is to see her own children die before her. That's what happened to me. With the coming of AIDS, sex became unsafe. With the AIDS vaccine, suddenly people started getting overconfident. No one worried about other diseases, and no one had ever heard of the PHADE virus. My son Philip was one of the first to die from it. It had lain dormant within him for years, then one day it decided to kill him . . . him and several million others.

Horrified, despondent, depressed beyond all salvation, I threw myself into the battle to find a cure for this deadly disease. The loved ones of the dead built a monument to the fallen, and my son, the first to die, lay entombed within it. I and thousands of others attended the dedication ceremony, where I was to deliver a eulogy for my son and a call for more funding for PHADE research. No one had even figured out how to test to see if someone was a carrier yet. Who knew how many more would die if no cure could be found?

As I ascended the rostrum in front of the marble monument, the crowd quieted. I opened my mouth to speak, and heard a loud crash from inside Philip's tomb. Horrified that someone would desecrate his memory, I wheeled around to see the culprit. The bronze door swung open silently and there in the shadows stood an unmistakable figure: my son. Startled beyond belief, I stood dumbfounded as he slowly moved forward. Partially decayed, stinking of embalming fluid and rotten flesh, I could smell him from twenty feet away. A security guard moved to intercept him. My son -- my loving, caring, sweet son -- grasp him in freakishly powerful, dead arms and tore his throat out.

I started to run into the screaming crowd. Then I realized how truly cruel fate can be. There is one thing worse for a mother than seeing her son die: seeing him raised from the dead as a monster.

Chapter Six

All Flesh Must Be Eaten

History

The PHADE virus is more than just another sexually transmitted disease. It is in fact a recipe for zombification. Zombies have always been with us in one form or another. Many cultures, including modern voodoo practitioners, have theories about the process of animating the dead through magical potions, elixirs, and rituals. In the modern information age, the details of such practices are more accessible to the common man, or in this case, the common high school student.

Philip Harrison was your average sixteen year old -- young, handsome, and desperately in love for the first time in his life. The object of his affection, Jenna Filipachi, was fond of him as well, but she was also quite a party girl. Only fifteen, she had already discovered cocaine and heroin. She was also not overly chaste and had tragically been infected with AIDS. Worse still, one night at a party, she discovered the real power of drugs -- she overdosed and died.

Distraught and disbelieving, Philip sought to conquer death, and after months of cruising the internet and frequenting voodoo chat rooms, he learned all he needed to know to raise lovely Jenna from the grave. Quite mad by this time, Philip raised the decaying girl and consummated his love with her. When he woke up the next morning, the handsome young man came to his senses and decided that the Jenna corpse wasn't nearly as desirable as the living thing. He disposed of the hapless zombie and got on with his life. By then, it was too late. He had contracted PHADE, a zombie STD that Jenna's body created when her AIDS-infected corpse rose from the dead.

On the rebound, Philip started making up for lost time with the local female population. The next fall, he went to a huge state university and started to really sow his wild oats. Never one to listen to authority figures, he was not the world's foremost practitioner of safe sex. Spring break in Amsterdam did not help matters, and soon carriers were spreading PHADE all over the world. Unfortunately for the world, the disease did not manifest itself for another four years. More easily transmissible than AIDS, millions now had the deadly virus lurking in their blood.

Philip was the first to die and hundreds of thousands more followed in the next few months. A year later, a million people had died. The world was in shock, and the public demanded a solution. A flurry of government programs and private organizations arose to try and fight this new sexually transmitted menace. Then the true horror of the disease made itself evident. Over a period of several months, those who died from the disease began getting up again. Panic filled the streets as thousands of zombies in every city surged forth from the graveyards and converged on the local population.

Semi-intelligent, these zombies worked in packs to hunt down and destroy the living. Those who died at their hands rose hours or days later to join the undead hordes. The creatures seemed bent on destruction for its own sake, not only killing, but destroying buildings and anything else that got in their path. In less than a week, the world became embroiled in a fight for survival: living pitted against the dead with humanity's very survival at stake.

PHADE in on the Present

Today the living fight an ongoing battle just to survive. The PHADE zombies took everyone by surprise and gained a great deal of ground before the living gathered together the wherewithal to respond. Many regions of the world have fallen into complete or partial chaos, chiefly because the zombies have an annoying habit of pulling down phone and power lines as well as destroying power plants and electrical substations. As a result, many communities have no power or phones and the cell phones are quickly running low on batteries.

The panic among the populace at large has only made matters worse. Many people saw the videotape of Philip Harrison's remarkable resurrection and subsequent attack. Harrison was destroyed -- torn to pieces by gunfire on national television -- but only after killing half a dozen police and onlookers. Many went outright mad at the sight of their friends and relatives returning from the grave and others fled to the rural areas. With millions of zombies now on the loose, looting and even outright robbery of the living have become commonplace.

The PHADE zombies are not making things easy. Althought the resurrection has not changed their appearance, they are much stronger than in their living days. Also, they are very difficult to stop. The key to a PHADE zombie is its blood. As long as its undead body keeps pumping blood through the body, it keeps on killing. That means in order to stop one of these things, its heart must be destroyed. Holes in the head don't bother them at all, and the only advantage to taking the head clean off is that the monstrosity cannot see, hear, or bite.

The zombie body does not heal, but it does compensate for wounds by quickly closing off blood flow to a damaged area. Thus, should a zombie lose a limb, the severed veins and arteries automatically seal shut to prevent loss of blood. As long as there is an ounce of blood in the zombie's body, it keeps on going at full strength. Fire causes only superficial damage, but it can eventually consume one of these creatures if it's hot enough and burns long enough.

The living dead show a rudimentary intelligence. They know enough to get out of the way of speeding cars, build simple roadblocks, open and unlock doors, and other straightforward tasks. They cannot speak nor do they seem to understand human speech, yet they have shown an amazing ability to work together, especially when it comes to hunting down the living. Their favorite tactic is to surround a poor victim and then move in for the kill simultaneously.

Despite their strength, their movements are slow and stiff and none seem capable of moving with great speed except over very short distances. They can lunge forward up to about nine feet (three meters), but if they do not strike their target, they usually fall to the ground.

Once a zombie has brought down its prey, it starts to feed. Much like a vampire, the zombie's primary goal is lapping up the target's blood from open wounds. The zombies can go for long periods without feeding, although they constantly thirst for fresh blood. Eventually, they will fall dormant after a month without sustenance.

In the process of feeding, the zombie's own bodily fluids and blood usually mix with that of the poor victim. This infects the living with the virus. If given its way, zombies always feed until the victim dies or they do. Those who die from a zombie bite rise themselves within a few hours. Those that somehow manage to survive the attack become carriers of the PHADE virus, which will remain dormant for several months or even years.

Story Ideas
Fighting for Home

Much of the living population is currently concerned with carving out safe zones free of PHADE zombies. Many have chosen to head for rural areas, but merely getting out of the cities can be quite a challenge. With their rudimentary intelligence, the zombies have managed to block most of the roads out of town. Undead wait in ambush, taking down the steady stream of living humans trying to make their way out. Meanwhile, zombie packs roam the city streets looking for fresh blood.

The Cast Members start in any major city, somewhere towards the center of things. When the zombie outbreaks began, the local authorities declared martial law and ordered 24-hour a day curfews. Everyone was to remain in their homes, locked up tight while the government took care of the situation. Then, the power went out, the looting began, and all hell broke loose. Torn between fighting zombies, stopping the looters, and enforcing the curfew, the government forces were overcome and disintegrated. Now its up to the people to defend themselves.

The characters begin with what they might find around the house. The adventure can take on several forms. The characters can try to fortify a region of the city and look for other survivors to help them out. Some of these survivors may well turn out to be less than trustworthy. Street gangs and other criminal elements are taking advantage of the chaos to further their own ends. Scattered military personnel can be of assistance if the characters can convince them to help.

Ultimately the heroes must fortify their position and either wait for help or ride the problem out -- which could take a long time.

Alternatively, the heroes try to fight their way out of the city, embarking on a nightmare journey through the streets of the dead. Zombies lurk around every corner. Constant cries for help are heard. Is it a trap or someone in need of their assistance? Is the approaching group of figures a street gang, an undead horde, or possible help? What happens when the army decides the best way to solve the problem is destroy the entire city?

The PHADE Vaccine

Another story idea centers around the heroes as government employees whose job it is to test a vaccine against the zombie virus. This experimental drug should inoculate people against becoming zombies once they have been bitten. It works in the lab, but now its time to try it in the field. The heroes venture into a city overrun with zombies, armed with hypodermic needles filled with the vaccine.

Noble and very brave souls may decide to use the vaccine on themselves and then let themselves be munched on a bit. This risks both poisoning from the vaccine or infection instead of vaccination, as well as the dangers of zombie dentures and blood. More prudent and merciless operatives could do things differently. They might find some living volunteers, preferably from the street gangs, vaccinate them, and then expose them to the virus. They must let enough zombies at them to make sure they get bit, and then pull their fat from the fire and transport them to the nearest prepared government laboratory. Meanwhile, the zombies, and no doubt the "test subjects" may have different ideas.

If it works after all this, the heroes are assigned the job of vaccinating as many people in the city as possible, thus preventing the creation of more zombies. They must set up a clinic, fortify it heavily, and offer help to anyone still in the city (or force them into the clinic to receive the vaccine). Meanwhile, everyone in the area around the city receives mandatory vaccinations. Once the first step towards victory -- vaccination -- is completed, or even while it is going on, it's just a matter of destroying a few million walking corpses.

PHADE to Black Zombies

Strength 4 **Constitution** 2
Dexterity 2 **Intelligence** 1
Perception 2 **Willpower** 2
Dead Points 15 **Speed** 4
Endurance Points n/a **Essence Pool** 13

Attack: As normal human or according to weapon type. Once the zombie causes an open wound (anything over 5 Life Points of damage), it moves its head to drink or suck blood. Feeding causes D4 points of damage per Turn. Given the zombie's great Strength, it is difficult to dislodge a feeding zombie (Resisted Strength Test).

Weak Spot: Heart

Getting Around: Life-Like; The Lunge

Strength: Strong Like Bull

Senses: Like The Living

Sustenance: Weekly; Blood

Intelligence: Tool Use; Team Work

Spreading the Love: One Bite and You're Hooked
Mixing bodily fluids or blood with a zombie infects the living. Those infected carry the virus, which remains dormant for D6 x 3(9) months. If the victim dies from the damage sustained in the zombie's attack, he rises from the dead in D6 hours.

Power: 35

Grave Impact

I have just informed the United Nations and our NATO allies of a recent discovery made by American scientists in Flagstaff, Arizona. A previously unidentified planetoid is on a collision course with earth. Unless we find a way to prevent this body from impacting on our world, life as we know it will cease to exist. Fortunately, our best scientists and technicians at NASA and in the United States Military have been working on solutions to this problem for several years. My advisors assure me that we can avert disaster. Rest assured, life will go on and we will emerge from this crisis better and stronger.

-Presidential Speech, October 12, 1999

I am proud to be the first to tell the world to breathe easily. Operation Gaia's Shield has succeeded and the Earth is safe! At 17:23 Eastern Standard time, combined U.S., Russian, and Chinese missiles impacted with the Nemesis comet, effectively shattering it into hundreds of thousands of harmless pieces. Over the next few days, we can expect to see no effects more noticeable than brilliant but harmless meteor showers around the globe. This incident proves that we can work together for the safety of all humanity. God bless us, every one.

-Presidential Speech, May 28, 2000

I'm here this evening at Arlington National Cemetery, where Memorial Day remembrances have been going on throughout the day. This evening a large crowd has gathered for a free evening concert and fireworks display, a tribute to our brave men and women who died protecting this country. The occasion is made all the more special by the spectacular meteor shower that is lighting up the sky even as I speak. The President is scheduled to start speaking in just a few moments . . . Hold on a second . . . there seems to be some sort of commotion down by the graves . . . people running and screaming . . . let's get over there Tom. Alright, I'm standing here overlooking the cemetery, there appears to be some sort of brawl going on . . . Oh my God! Sweet Jesus what is that?!?

-CNN Live, May 29, 2000

Chapter Six

History

Millions of years ago and hundreds of light years from our own world, an ancient civilization toyed with forces better left undisturbed. Their own dead rose up against them as the result of a series of diabolic necromantic experiments. The only way they could save themselves was to literally blow a chunk of their world off into space, ridding the planet of any trace of the zombie taint. Ever since then the zombie planetoid has traveled through space, unbeknownst to anyone, on a direct collision course with Earth.

American scientists detected the incoming chunk of rock, although they had no clue as to its true origins or deadly purpose. Fearing the end of life on Earth, the nuclear powers of the world combined their arsenals, modified their missiles, and sent millions of megatons flying into space. Already eroded by millions of other impacts in its long history, the zombie planet burst apart under the nuclear onslaught. The Earth thought itself safe.

Then the irradiated pieces of the planet came hurtling down to Earth, burning up and dissolving into the atmosphere. As a result of prevailing winds and the widespread dispersal pattern of the dust, hardly a corner of the planet escaped exposure. As the dust settled to the ground it began immediately to seep into the soil, water, and even the air. The result was all too horrible and predictable -- the ancient powers awoke the dead from their eternal rest.

Without a doubt the most dramatic and public instance of the living dead rising from their graves occurred at Virginia's Arlington Cemetery during the year 2000 Memorial Day services. With over 200,000 dead soldiers dating back to 1864 buried there, the cemetery became an instant army of the dead, counting skeletal civil war generals, badly maimed soldiers from a over a century of warfare, and even some ex-presidents among its number. All sense of patriotism long gone from their dead brains, these cadaverous warriors clawed their way to freedom with just one thing in mind: consuming the flesh of the living. Best of all, it happened on live television.

While the president and his staff escaped unscathed, thousands of others died in the ensuing mayhem. The roads out of the cemetery became clogged with traffic and the zombies had free reign to slay the attending veterans and their families. All over the world similar scenes began to play themselves out. The horror had just begun. The army moved in on Arlington to try and seal the area off. Despite what they had seen with their own eyes, at first no one wanted to believe the truth about what was really going on in.

All found out the truth soon enough, however. The army's, and everyone else's, guns were almost useless against the mindless, walking corpses. Contrary to popular movies, shots to the head did nothing to stop these monsters. The only way to stop them was to burn them. The army soon figured out that the desiccated bodies were surprisingly flammable, except when wet. They caught fire and burned completely in a matter of minutes. Unfortunately, they remained animated until the fire destroyed them.

As a result, these walking torches spread the cause of their own destruction with them. Well-meaning citizens using home-made fire bombs ended up causing more damage to their homes than the zombies. Many of the major and minor cities suffered from fires that swept through block after block. In many places, the firefighters could not do their job for fear of the ever-growing zombie population. Thousands more died in house fires and flamming apartment buildings. The worst part was that those who weren't totally consumed in the fires soon rose up themselves.

As The World Turns

The national infrastructure has collapsed. Telephones, power, and even water are all off-line or on their way to being so. The flaming cities became deathtraps for millions, caught on congested roads by either fire, or zombies, or both. With many cemeteries located on the outskirts of towns, zombies have already flooded into rural areas and suburbs. There seems to be no way of stopping this endless tide of walking dead. It simply grows larger and larger with every passing hour.

The military has begun making tactical air strikes against large concentrations of zombies. While this seems to have been somewhat effective at destroying the monsters, it also has caused significant damage to the surrounding buildings. Also, it has exacerbated the fires raging in these areas. The most panic-stricken among the politicians and military personnel have begun talking about using nuclear weapons against the creatures. Fortunately, saner minds have realized that any such use would kill as many citizens as zombies. As the zombie scourge drives out the living from certain areas, "life-free" zones are created and nuclear weapon use becomes more viable.

The President has declared martial law and begun to order the establishment of safe zones where the living can seek refuge. With so many of the country's cities in flames, most of these safe zones are in rural areas. It is now widely known that anyone who dies will soon rise again unless their body is cremated immediately. Everyone has begun to stockpile gasoline and the military is trying to concentrate all of its incendiary weapons in the safe zones.

One problem with these rural safe zones, at least in some parts of the country, is that they are threatened by another danger besides the zombies. The zombie invasion happened to strike at a time of severe drought in many areas of the world. Particularly in the western United States, forest fires and brush fires have consumed many areas. These massive fires may help curtail the zombies, but they continue to cause significant damage since there are few fire fighters willing and able to contain them.

Some of the safe zone compounds are already at their maximum capacity. The soldiers and civilian volunteers guarding them are refusing to admit any more refugees. This has led to several instances of violence and even murder as those trying to escape the zombies clash with frightened guards inside the safe zone compounds.

The zombies created by the disintegrated planetoid are of the slow and stupid variety. They cannot think past making a straight line towards any source of living flesh they see, hear, or smell. They move slowly, and stiffly but are incredibly strong. Once one of these mindless monsters gets its hands on a victim, it is almost impossible to escape. The most dangerous thing about them is that they are almost impossible to kill with anything but fire. Hacking them to pieces just leaves you with a lot of animated pieces, which might seem harmless but can actually cause significant damage. The pieces also hinder the living in the face of other, more complete, zombies.

Once a zombie latches onto a victim, it begins to consume the poor soul's flesh while the victim is still alive. Eventually the victim dies of shock or blood loss, but is usually horribly mutilated afterwards. The zombies immediately lose interest in the victim once he dies. Anyone who dies anywhere on the planet that has been exposed to the planetoid dust (meaning anywhere but sealed rooms) rises from the dead within ten minutes to an hour of their passing on. Those who actually die from a zombie attack turn into one of the undead almost immediately. Those who somehow survive an attack continue on as normal (although other diseases might infect them).

Story Ideas
We Are The World

This zombie scenario works well with a rather specialized evening of roleplaying in mind. The GM should hide the true nature of the evening's entertainment from the players. Have them generate characters as normal, but instead of making up fictional personas, have them create themselves. This in and of itself can be fun as the play group discusses each person's statistics and skills. Once the players have defined themselves in game terms, let the fun begin.

Start off the story with the impending destruction of the comet by the nuclear assault. Make the players think that the adventure is going to center around what they would do if a giant asteroid were about to strike the earth (something we've all thought about of late, no doubt). Then, once the asteroid is destroyed, move on to the Memorial Day party the next day. Where are the players when the meteor showers begin? Perhaps they gather at a friend's house to view the magnificent light show.

Then, of course, the dead start to rise. Since the adventure is set wherever you and your players live it should be easy to set the scene. Get a map and find all the local cemeteries and hospitals. Now the chaos really begins as sporadic reports come in. If they are watching television, they can see for themselves just what happens at the Arlington National Cemetery. Being overly imaginative, gamers they no doubt see the possibilities and repercussions and start doing their best to prepare for the worst. From there its just a matter of following the players' lead and throwing zombies and dead friends, teachers, and employers at them as they try to reach safety.

The President's Daughter

For those who want a little more action and heavy firepower in their evening's entertainment, the players can make soldiers tasked with journeying into a city to rescue someone, the President's daughter for instance. Armed with flamethrowers, incendiary grenades, and other weapons, the heroes must fight their way through zombies, burning buildings, and God knows what else to save the hapless girl before the walking dead rip the flesh from her body and make her one of their own.

Just finding her should be hard enough, and then they have to get her back out alive. What happens when they return to find their former base overrun by zombies or the President himself turning into one of the living dead? Perhaps it is left to them to fire the tactical nuke that will take out the city, killing many innocent living people but destroying millions of zombies in the process. If they survive and escape, somewhere, somehow, there's got to be a place where they feel safe, if only they can find it.

Grave Impact Zombies

Strength 4   **Constitution** 2
Dexterity 1   **Intelligence** -2
Perception 2   **Willpower** 2
Dead Points 15   **Speed** 2
Endurance Points n/a   **Essence Pool** 9
Attack: Bite damage D4 x 2(4) slashing

The zombie first attempts to grab the victim. Unless the Cast Member is surprised, this requires a Resisted Dexterity Test. Zombie Masters should assign modifiers to the Cast Member's roll depending on the number of zombies crowding around (-1 per) and the number of zombie parts interfering with the Cast Member (-1 per). Once the zombie grabs the victim, the Iron Grip strength takes over.

Weak Spot: None; Fire

Any damage inflicted is ignored (other than gruesome graphic descriptions) unless it is fire damage. Severed limbs, heads and bodies remain active and seek to interfere with any victims nearby. Five points of fire damage to a limb or head will destroy that part.

Getting Around: Slow and Steady
Strength: Strong Like Bull; Iron Grip
Senses: Like the Living
Sustenance: Who Needs Food?; All Flesh Must Be Eaten
Intelligence: Dumb as Dead Wood
Spreading the Love: Only the Dead

Anyone who dies anywhere (except in sealed rooms) from any cause rises from the dead in D10 x 6(30) minutes. Those who die from a zombie attack turn into one of the undead in D10 minutes.

Power: 23

Sacred Soil

    I don't understand it, I really don't. I mean, I was so sure I was on the right side of all these issues. Nuclear Power, the whales, vegetarianism, PETA, pesticides, organic foods, yoga, all of that stuff. All of us were so sure that we were right, that the rest of the world had it all wrong. Well . . . we were half right. The rest of you had it all wrong, but then again, so did we. Who would have thought that our effort to create healthier crops and decrease our reliance on meat would lead to, well, all this?

    When the backlash came against pesticides and chemical fertilizers, my organic farm was suddenly in high demand. I added more acreage and produced plenty of natural foods. But then, as demand rose I found that I was having a hard time meeting the needs of the market. I needed to grow more, and keep the damn bugs from eating it before harvest. Suddenly, I understood why the old school farmers depended on that nasty stuff. Luckily for me (or so thought), OrganoCore came along and saved the day.

    OrganoCore's fertilizers and pesticides met with all my demands for an environmentally safe product. I used the stuff for two years and my crop yields increased by forty percent. I was happy as a clam. Then two weeks ago, I started using the new and improved formula and that's when it happened.

    I had a dog, a big ole' German shepherd named Shep. When he got hit by a car three weeks ago, I buried him out by the lettuce fields. One night, I hear a scratching at the front door, just like Shep used to do when he wanted in. I open the door and there he is -- his rotting corpse stinking to high heaven. I thought it was some sick joke but then the corpse moved. It lunged at me, biting for my leg. I screamed and kicked him away but the damned thing kept coming. I finally made it to the kitchen and, well, I defended myself with a butcher's knife. It wasn't pretty, and worst of all, the damn dog bled everywhere. The blood wasn't what bothered me, though. What bothered me was that he bled green.

Chapter Six

The Flora Fight Back

OrganoCore corporation had its heart in the right place. They wanted to protect the environment and the consumer from harmful toxins found in some fertilizers and most pesticides. So, they developed a line of safe, healthy alternatives for the organic farmer. The problem was, these safe alternatives did not work nearly as well as the toxic ones. They cost more, and thus organic foods remained too costly for the average consumer. OrganoCore realized that it needed to be better than its toxic competitors if it wanted to make a real difference.

Funded in part by various environmental groups, the company embarked on a groundbreaking research project which ultimately yielded them some amazing results. Combining a number of tribal and ancient folk remedies with newly found ingredients imported from the jungles of the Carribean and Indonesia, the researchers managed to create some astounding products. Their new fertilizers and pesticides worked just as well or better than the artificial varieties and they were entirely harmless to the environment.

Once the OrganoCore products hit the market, they were a smash success, and farms across the country and around the world began using them. When OrganoCore recently announced its new line of improved products, it was estimated that fully three quarters of America's farm acreage planned on using them. That's exactly what happened. OrganoCore became a Fortune 500 company, but the results were more disastrous than anyone could imagine.

The new products, again using formulas derived from ancient Caribbean and Indonesian rituals, were more effective than the original formula and seemed just as safe. Indeed, by themselves they were safe, but when combined with the older formula, they awakened a previously untapped potential within the soil. Some say they awakened the vengeful soul of mother Earth herself and now she has chosen to strike down the animals that have oppressed her for so long. Others say that the chemicals spurred some speedy and powerful mutation in plant life, effectively jumping it ahead millions of evolutionary years.

Whatever the true cause, the result was obvious: the dead were coming back to life all across the country, wherever corpses and OrganoCore products mixed. The alchemical mixture gave the world's plants a new life and new purpose. Growing with incredible speed, the vegetation sent tendrils into the bodies of the dead humans and animals buried beneath the ground. These plant tendrils replaced the veins and nervous system of the dead bodies but kept the bones and muscles strong. Thus, vegetatively animated, the dead began to rise and do the deadly work of their plant overlords.

Driven by a kind of communal but primitive plant mind, these organically certified zombies seek to destroy everything that humanity has ever built, starting with the humans themselves. Rising from their graves, the zombies descended first upon the rural communities throughout America. In many places, whole towns fell before them before anyone knew what was happening. Reports came in from across the country of mass murders and the destruction of farms, grain silos, and the release of herds of cattle into the wild.

Then the horror struck the nation's cities as well. The fertilizer took a little longer to make its way into the carefully manicured lawns of the urban graveyards, but when it did, all hell broke loose. The zombies rose up, their eyes glowing green with hate and blood lust. All the while, the number of zombies increased. The zombies buried their dead victims in the foul soil that had spawned them, creating more plant-infested cadavers.

Weeding The Living

The people are in a state of panic. When the government finally realized and accepted what was happening, a state of national emergency was declared. Government troops sealed off the cities and did their best to drive the zombies out. This turned out to be easier than might be imagined. Many of the newly risen zombies headed for the countryside rather than into the city, naturally seeking refuge amongst their fellow plants.

Now the cities are becoming the only safe zones on the planet, fortresses of urbanity amidst the terrors that lurk in the wilderness. Not only humans, but animals as well, are rising from the dead. In fact, the zombies have been killing larger mammals with as much vigor as they kill humans, creating herds of undead cattle, packs of cadaverous dogs, and even swarms of zombie rats. As time passes, the rural environment becomes more and more deadly.

Inside the cities, food is quickly becoming very scarce. No fresh produce, meats, or dairy products can be brought into towns. As soon as the panic set in, desperate shoppers cleared the stores of canned goods and preserved foods. Now each family or group jealously guards their own food stores while eyeing those of their neighbors. The government has distributed most of its own reserves, except for the necessary rations for feeding the military. Even those won't last much longer than a few months. Unless something can be done about the zombies, the nation will starve to death.

Nor can America expect help from overseas. The OrganoCore fertilizers were already in use in much of the world, and the problem is spreading quickly. European regions used the fertilizer as heavily as the U.S. and now face the same problems. Further, the food grown with the fertilizers seems to retain the deadly zombie toxin. U.S. foodstuffs sent abroad have already infected the soil, creating breeding grounds for more zombies. In heavily forested areas of South America, Africa, and Indonesia, the zombies have begun to show up as well, both in human and animal form. If the world cannot find a solution to its problems, humanity will starve or be torn to shreds by the undead hordes.

These organic zombies are difficult but not impossible to destroy. The brain remains the center of control and enough damage to the head does manage to knock one of these monsters out of commission. Herbicides and toxic chemicals also work very well against the OrganoCore zombies. Of course, a spray bottle of weed killer doesn't bother them a bit, but products similar to Agent Orange will do the trick. Likewise, large amounts of chlorine, acids, and other nasty chemicals work. Fire also destroys these zombies, although they are no more susceptible to it than a normal human body would be. In fact, they keep fighting longer because they feel no pain and do not need to breathe. Once the fire consumes them however, they are destroyed forever.

Once a zombie kills a living being, its first thought it to look around for more victims. Once there are no likely targets within sight, the zombie instinctually buries the dead body in soil that has been infected with OrganoCore products. A body buried in such soil rises again within the hour. The zombies themselves can infect soil by simply lying down on the ground for a period of at least an hour. While lying thus, tendrils extend from the zombie into the earth, secreting powerful, dead-raising compounds. In this way, the zombies spread their source of creation and ranks over the whole earth.

Story Ideas
Bastions of Life

This zombie scenario turns the typical living dead story on its ear. Instead of fleeing the cities, now the cities are the place to be at least for the time being. The first thing to do is clear the zombies out of the city streets and keep them out. The play begins as the dead start to rise and the heroes find their neighborhoods plagued with small bands of living dead. Through cooperation, they can clear a number of safe zones and eventually save the entire urban area. That's when things start to get really tough.

At that point, the problem becomes not only keeping the zombies outside the city limits but trying to find enough food and water to survive. Soon, the humans are turning on each other in a way that makes the zombies look good. Ultimately, the characters may have to flee the city and search for food and safety elsewhere. This exodus results in a corpse-filled journey through rural America where the plants have gone wild, growing at an extraordinary rate. There's plenty of food and plenty of monsters who think the heroes are food.

All Flesh Must Be Eaten

Thank God for DDT

In this scenario, the heroes have the task of finding a powerful defoliant that might stop the zombies for good. Developed by the military, this is the next generation of Agent Orange, the most powerful plant killer ever designed. The army stockpiled its resources of the stuff, and the technology to make more, in a base outside of the Cast Members' city. The Cast Members could be either military ordered to retrieve the toxin, or civilians who hear about it and realize that it is their only hope for survival.

Unfortunately, the zombies have already overrun the military base in question. They are using the base as a breeding ground for new zombies since the soil there is particularly rich in OrganoCore products (the result of EPA-mandated environmental standards on all U.S. government property). The heroes have to fight their way past both the base security and the undead hordes that guard it. Once they recover the tanks, they are equipped with a chemical which destroys a zombie with only a tablespoon of liquid. Get out the super squirt guns and get ready to rock and roll. Perhaps humanity has a chance after all . . . once all the plants are gone.

Sacred Soil Zombies

Strength 2	**Constitution** 2
Dexterity 2	**Intelligence** -2
Perception 1	**Willpower** 2
Dead Points 15	**Speed** 4
Endurance Points n/a	**Essence Pool** 7

Attack: As normal human or according to weapon type
Weak Spot: Brain; Chemicals
Getting Around: Life-Like
Strength: Dead Joe Average
Senses: Like the Dead
Sustenance: Who Needs Food?; All Flesh Must Be Eaten
Intelligence: Dumb As Dead Wood; Teamwork
Spreading the Love: Bury the Body

Regardless of the cause of death, once a zombie finds a corpse, it buries the body in the nearest soil infected with OrganoCore products. Such a buried body rises again in D10 x 6 (30) minutes.

Power: 14

Delivery Systems

The chemicals that harm Sacred Soil zombies may be delivered in a number of ways, including dumping buckets on them. For those that wish to remain some distance away, however, the following item may be used.

SuperSquirter 2000
Range: 2/5/7/10/15
Damage: By contents
Cap: 10*   Cost: $30   Aval: C

* One capacity (6 ounces) of liquid is expended per "shot" at short range, two at medium range, three at long range, and four at extreme range. Multiple "shots" cause no recoil or multi-action penalties.

Cow, dog and rat basic stats can be found in the Rise of the Walking Dead section (p. 169). Their other abilities are the same as those of the Sacred Soil zombie.

Chemicals

The Zombie Master may devise any number of chemicals that can harm Sacred Soil Zombies using the Corrosive Poisons rules (p. 106). The following is just one example.

Super Agent Orange

This powerful anti-foliant acts as a Strength Rating 6 poison against the Sacred Soil zombies (doubled damage: D6 x 4 (12) per 6 ounces). It must be handled carefully, however, as it is a Strength Rating 3 poison for humans (damage: D6(3) per 6 ounces).

Worlds In Hell

They Came From Beyond

I woke up to what sounded like a muffled scream. I wasn't sure though, it might have been an animal scrounging around outside, or maybe even a dream. I wasn't used to this "life in the country" thing, and the commonest noises still kind of freaked me out.

Then I heard a door creak from down the hall -- my mother's room. My wife and I had moved out here with her for her health, thinking the country air and peace would do her some good. Without waking my wife, I got out of bed and crept down the hall to make sure mom was okay. I found the door slightly ajar so I looked inside. Something was not right.

Her neck was twisted in an impossible angle. I ran towards the bed, thinking "Oh My God, someone's killed mother!" Then she sat up in bed. I was so relieved. She stepped out of the bed, her head still at that weird angle. What the hell! Mom hadn't walked in three years. Before I could say anything, her hands wrapped around my throat, trying to squeeze the life out of me. I pushed her away, then backed towards the open door. Staggering slightly, she came after me.

Then I heard my wife scream from our room. Worse, the shriek suddenly muffled and cut off. I turned and ran back down the hall. Throwing the door to our room open, I was just in time to see some sort of thing, like a giant centipede, crawling down my wife's throat. She was desperately trying to pull it out, but was clearly losing the fight. Blood was all over everything. I lunged forward to help her but I got hit from behind. It was mother. I kicked and punched at her. I didn't know what the hell was going on, but I had to save my wife.

Just as I escaped mom's grasp, the struggling on the bed stopped. My wife sat up in the blood-drenched bed as calm as could be. It was then that I knew I had lost her too. She sprang at me, knocking out my front tooth and sending me sprawling. I don't know how I managed to get out of there, but I did.

God help me. God help us all.

Chapter Six

History

For them, names have no meaning. For them, there is simply the Race, and the Others. The Race came from far beyond our solar system, an intelligent species millions of years more advanced than our own. The Others, well, the Others are any that are not the Race. The Race attacks, conquers, and uses up the Others before moving on to the next one. Over countless eons, the Race has traveled space, searching for new worlds to host their bloody needs. They never stay in one place for more than a few centuries, just long enough to destroy one civilization and find a new one to invade.

The Race's biology does not conform to any of the Earth standards, but it most closely resembles the insect family, particularly when it comes to community and social structures. Great Brood Queens rule the race. They are giant, amorphous beings, immensely intelligent but almost entirely helpless on their own. Thousands of drones serve each Queen, depending on her for guidance and a sense of purpose. The Race consists of several hundred of these Brood Queens, and although they do not always get along, they seldom actively fight against one another. They save those aggressive feelings for the Others.

The drones in their natural state look like foot-long centipedes with four pairs of two-foot tentacles running down the sides of their bodies. By themselves, the creatures seem harmless enough -- certainly not capable of bringing death and destruction down upon countless different worlds. In fact, the Race cannot conquer anything without a little help; namely, the recently dead bodies of the Others. The drones can insert themselves into any dead body and fully reanimate it. Although they gain none of the cadaver's memories, they gain almost full function over its body. What's more, the body works solely on the power of the drone's psychic energy, making it immune to the effects of most attacks.

Time and again, the Race has repeated its horrifyingly effective tactics. Using the psychic powers of the Brood Queens, the Race teleports itself from one world to the next, a process that requires a vast expenditure of energy, leaving the Queens nearly powerless for several years. While the Queens lie hidden in safety, they expand their awareness to learn about the local culture and dominant species. Once they have a read on the situation, they send out their drones to quietly begin taking over bodies. Once they have recovered somewhat, they start producing more drones as more bodies become available, building secret armies of the dead all over the planet. When the time is right, they attack, sweeping away all who stand before them.

Once the Race subdues all potential opposition, they rule over the world as tyrants, forcing species to serve them, and breeding them and killing them to create new hosts for their drones. As the Brood Queens recover from the exertion of teleporting, they grow hungry, hungry for energy and hungry for living flesh. Eventually they consume all that the world has to offer. With the planet used up, they send their consciousness out into the universe to look for a new target. Most recently, they found Earth and they are already here among us. In the face of these zombies from beyond, the future of humanity looks bleak.

Sightings

As events stand now, the Race's operations are at their most delicate point. The queens have begun to make their move, taking over corpses, but they do not yet have overwhelming force. Indeed, they are far from it. In order for a drone to take over a body, the corpse cannot have been dead more than two days. Also, the body cannot have been subjected to embalming fluids; such treatment makes the body inhospitable for the drone. Thus, the drones cannot simply raid the graveyards for a ready-made army of walking dead; they must depend on the morgues and what they themselves kill (their primary avenue for expanding their ranks).

There are currently 307 Brood Queens on Earth, secreted in underground lairs all over the planet, usually near major population centers. All over the world, hospitals and police agencies have reported an unexplained rash of missing bodies. What at first seemed coincidence is now becoming downright eerie. With thousands of dead bodies missing all over the world, the people of Earth have started to grow nervous. No one knows what this could mean.

Now that they have built up their core offensive units, the Brood Queens are ready to make their move. At the same time across the planet, the undead armies rise from their underground lairs and begin to attack the local populations. From all over, reports of mass murders, riots, and attacks by gangs of "drug fiends" come pouring in. At this stage, the drones concentrate on killing as many people, as quickly as they can, in order to build up the number of potential hosts. New drones inhabit the freshly dead and the tide of carnage sweeps forward. Within hours, the zombie armies nearly quadruple in size.

The drones can reanimate a corpse in just a few minutes. The drone crawls into the body, usually through the mouth, and then extends its physical and psychic tendrils into the corpse. The animated body usually retains much of its original manual dexterity and agility while under drone control. The drone can also use weapons, including firearms with the body, but their aim is generally very poor. The body remains functional until the drone itself is killed, even if it loses arms, legs, or the head (the drone sees psychically, not through the body's eyes). While controlling the corpse, the drone curls up along the spine. Thus, the vulnerable spot on these zombies is along the spine where any significant damage harms the drone as well. Once a drone dies in a body, no other drone can inhabit that body.

Now, as humanity draws together to face this threat, they must discover why the dead seem to be rising and how to stop them. The military has recovered from the initial shock and is organizing a defense. The Race plans to simply sweep forward and destroy anything that stands in their way, since most rifle shots don't even slow them down. The only sure way of defeating them is to destroy the Brood Queens in their hidden lairs. Once a Brood Queen dies, all of its drones die as well and their corpse shells become inanimate for good. Unfortunately for humankind, no one actually knows this crucial bit of information. Right now, the humans are fighting just to survive a few more days.

Story Ideas
Fight to Survive

The fight against the drone-controlled zombies offers a different challenge than most presented in this book. These zombies know how to pick up a weapon and use it, albeit not with the greatest of accuracy. Furthermore, they work together in teams, trying to overwhelm targets. They engage the living not only with sheer numbers, but by maneuvering as well. In the fight to survive, the heroes must deal with all these problems, and somehow discover that the weak spot on these beasts is along their spine.

The basic fight centers around the need to find someplace safe. For the most part, that means either heading for the countryside or seeking shelter with the military. Since the military concentrations are at the top of the list of the Race's targets, those areas won't be safe for long. The countryside offers its own problems as well. The drones can take over animals as well as humans. What's more, perhaps that safe looking cave system isn't so safe after all, maybe its the entrance to a Brood Queen's lair.

Killing the Brood Queen

This adventure idea begins with the characters either part of the military, or the army being in such desperate straits that they'll take any help they can get. The heroes witness or partake in an autopsy of a destroyed zombie, or are briefed on its result. They discover the creature attached to the body's spine. From the way the zombies work together without any apparent means of communication, some may venture to guess that they are somehow telepathically connected. Certainly, their mere presence in the body offers no explanation as to how they manage to make the dead rise and fight.

Someone can make the logical leap that perhaps there is some outside source controlling these things. Once that is done, it's just a matter of finding the Queen and killing it. An examination of reports of missing bodies and the sites of the first attacks should give the players a pretty good idea of the general area where the Queen might be found. Then, it's a matter of journeying to the area (well behind enemy lines of course), and looking around. Simple, no?

The easiest way to find the lair's location is to try and follow some of the zombies as they come and go. This is no mean feat, since the psychic drones are instantly aware of any living being that comes within thirty yards (meters) of them. The heroes will have to keep their distance, while ensuring that they don't lose their mark.

If they do manage to trail the zombies, they discover that live humans and animals are being collected, and brought into some sort of cave system. Worse still, the Queens use their meager but steadily increasing telepathic powers to slowly carve the caves when they first arrive. By the time the drones are ready to strike, whatever natural caves exist in the region are expanded to form a extensive network of warrens.

Descending into the lair is like venturing onto another world, a maze of weirdly lit, psychically carved caves, crawling with zombies of all sorts. The Brood Queen emits numerous foul odors as it sits in its lair, surrounded by drones in and out of their zombie bodies. Once they fight off the guards they must deal with the Queen herself, whose psychic powers can play tricks on their minds, arouse intense emotions, and even directly assault the brain. Of course, a few pounds of explosive will put an end to all of that right quick.

> Cow, dog and rat basic stats can be found in the Rise of the Walking Dead section (p. 169). Their remaining abilities are the same as those of the They Came From Beyond zombie. This includes their ability to work as a team with other zombies, and problem-solve as well as their physical limitations will allow (no hands!). These corpses are animated by psychic drones just like the human zombies.

They Came From Beyond Zombies

Strength 2 **Constitution** 2
Dexterity 2 **Intelligence** 2
Perception 3 **Willpower** 2
Dead Points 15 **Speed** 4
Endurance Points n/a **Essence Pool** 13

Attack: As normal human or according to weapon type
Weak Spot: Spine
Getting Around: Life-Like; Climbing; Aquatic
Strength: Dead Joe Average
Senses: Like the Living; Life Sense
Sustenance: Who Needs Food?; All Flesh Must Be Eaten
Intelligence: Teamwork; Problem Solving
Spreading the Love: Only the Dead

Zombies only kill. They do not create new zombies. That is the job of the drones.

Power: 40

They Came From Beyond Drone

Strength 1 **Constitution** 1
Dexterity 3 **Intelligence** 2
Perception 3 **Willpower** 1
Life Points 5 **Speed** 10
Endurance Points 10 **Essence Pool** 11

Attack: Bite damage D6(3) slashing

If the creature's Essence Pool is exhausted for any reason, it stops moving and curls into a ball.

The drone is small and very fast. While not very tough, it is hard to hit (effective Dodge 4 skill). In close combat, it crawls up the victim's body and attacks the nose and mouth area, trying to worm its way inside. The drone uses psychic abilities to graft itself to the host and animate it. This ability does not use Essence. The drone has no other psychic powers or abilities.

They Came From Beyond Brood Queen

Strength 8	**Constitution** 4
Dexterity 5	**Intelligence** 4
Perception 3	**Willpower** 6
Life Points 100	**Speed** 6
Endurance Points 200	**Essence Pool** 50

Attack: Claw damage D4 x 8(16)

The Queen has a number of clawed appendages sprouting from various parts of her bloated, elongated body. She can attack with up to six of these claws per Turn, but can target a single character with only two. Like all her ilk, the Queen tries to kill without damaging the body too much. There is always a drone near the Queen to inhabit any freshly killed corpse.

The Queen also emits an odor that is highly offensive to humans. Unless serious precautions are taken (gas mask, perfume soaked rag, etc.), all humans within 30 yards (meters) of her presence suffer -2 to all Tests and Tasks. On the upside, this scent permeates all but the outermost areas of a Queen's cave complex and gets stronger as the character gets closer. Any Cast Member can use the scent to locate the Queen inside her lair by making a number of different Difficult Perception Tests.

Brood Queen Psychic Powers

Each of the Queen's psychic abilities has two elements: Strength and Art. The Strength represents her raw metaphysical power. This governs how far away the Queen can reach others with her abilities, the amount of damage she can inflict, and how lasting the effects she creates are. The Art represents the degree of expertise the Queen has in using her abilities.

Mindtalk
Strength 16; Art 5

The Queen uses this power to keep the lines of communication open with her brood, to a range of 150 miles. While she is alive, all of her own spawn can communicate with her and with each other. This power forms the basis for the drones teamwork ability. The Queen cannot communicate with drones from other Queens, but she can talk to other Queens. Also, given the alien mindframe and nature of communication, the Queen cannot converse with humans.

Mindtalk can also be used to "scream" into the mind of an enemy. This requires a Resisted Task -- the Queen's Willpower and Mindtalk Art against the victim's Difficult Willpower Test. If successful, the target loses D4 x 4(8) Essence Points (see Essence Point Loss, p. 114). Further, the victim loses all his actions for one Turn, and suffers a penalty of -4 to all Tests or Tasks the next Turn. The "scream" has a range of 42 yards (meters).

Mindrule
Strength 5; Art 5

This is the power to influence or control the minds of others. The Queen can create illusions, trigger emotions and even command others to do her bidding. Making a character do something that goes completely against his personality (making someone murder a loved one, for example) is much more difficult to accomplish than "pushing" somebody into doing something they were considering doing anyway (like convincing an already-scared attacker to run away).

For the power to be effective, the Queen must be within line of sight of the target. The victim must also be aware of the Queen's presence.

Mindrule causes a Resisted Task, using the Queen's Willpower and Mindrule Art against a Difficult Willpower Test on the part of the victim. If the illusion, feelings or orders are totally contrary to what the victim would normally believe, feel, or do, the victim gets a bonus of +3 to +7 to the Willpower Test. If the Queen is successful, the effect varies depending on what she intends.

Illusions: The Queen can create realistic sights, sounds and textures. These must be individually tailored to the situation at hand, but usually distract the Cast Member, or lead to the character injuring himself or his comrades. Examples might be creating a drone crawling up the back of a comrade, covering a crevice with solid-looking ground, having an image of a friend urge the character to leave the area or lay down his weapons.

Emotions: The Cast Member feels an overwhelming emotion, like anger/pleasure, fear or revulsion. Anger or pleasure will distract the character, imposing a -4 to all actions for as long as the Queen concentrates. Fear causes the character to flea the area. Revulsion renders the character incapable of action for one Turn. Other effects can be determined as the Zombie Master desires.

Control: The Queen takes over the Cast Member's mind for a short period of time. For one Turn, the victim can be made to follow a one sentence command to the letter. Regardless of the command, the Queen suffers a -3 penalty when using this ability.

Using Essence Defensively

The Inspired can defend against the Queen's attacks by using their Essence. Each point of Essence released grants the Inspired a +1 bonus to his Resisted Test. As usual, the Inspired's faith allows him to use as much of his Essence Pool in defense as he desires. Further, it hardly need be said, but any fight against a Brood Queen automatically qualifies as service to one's Lord.

Mein Zombie

Yeah, I was at Omaha Beach. I came in on the fourth wave. We thought we were lucky -- that the other guys would have cleared the place for us by the time we landed. Riiiight . . . no such luck. As we piled outta the boat, Heine machine gun fire ripped up the water, mud, and soldiers all around me. Me and only about two-thirds of the company made it to cover.

We thought we were the first ones to actually make a go at flushing those damn machine gun nests. I mean, if anyone had any balls they would have taken those things out by now, right? That's what we told ourselves anyway. We broke through the Jerrie line and in behind 'em. My sergeant was in the lead as we came at the pillbox from behind. There were half a dozen Krauts just standin' there -- like they didn't have a care in the world.

On the counta three, we jumped out and gunned 'em all down. Or thought we did, anyway. The bastards took the bullets like they were mosquito bites. They just turned around, raised their rifles and charged. We shot 'em as they came on. I musta hit one guy a dozen times before he got to me. Then, it was hand to hand and things got ugly. While we're wrestlin' with these guys, tryin' to figure out why they won't go down, we start takin' fire from off to the left.

There's a damn squad of Jerries shootin' right into the brawl, not carin' if they hit us or their own guys. We got the worst of it. These unkillable soldiers took down half of us and the snipers took down the rest. When I saw one of the Krauts bitin' and eatin' my buddy Ryan, I just turned tail and ran back for the beach. Fuck this, I said. I took a hit in the leg on my way out. What the fuck happened up there, sir? What the fuck is goin' on?

History

The year was 1944 and the war had begun to turn against Nazi Germany. Its early successes were a thing of the past, and its armies began to give way before the combined assaults of the Soviet Union in the east and the United States and Great Britain in the west. Hitler, desperate to prove the superiority of the German people, searched for any weapon he could use against the oncoming Allied armies. While some scientists developed rockets and assault rifles or strove to unlock the secrets of the atom, a secret Nazi research team was working on an entirely different line of inquiry.

From its earliest days, the Nazi party had been affiliated with occult organizations. Hitler himself was obsessed with mystical matters. His quests for objects of occult significance from the Holy Grail to the Ark of the Covenant are legendary. What was not so legendary was the evil dictator's fascination with overcoming the inevitability of death. "Conquer death and we shall conquer the world," he would proclaim to his supernatural researchers as they combed through confiscated ancient texts stolen from countless libraries across Nazi-occupied Europe.

As the Allies prepared for D-Day, Hitler's top-secret Occult Corps got ready to repulse the invasion. The researchers had, in a matter of speaking, conquered death. Although the secret to immortally still eluded them, they had achieved the next best thing: the living dead. Based on ancient formulae and magic rituals, the Nazis developed a serum that would raise their soldiers from the dead once they had fallen in battle. The result: an army that could never be stopped.

D-Day finally came and Allied troops swarmed onto the beaches of Normandy, facing fortified German positions. Up and down the beaches of western France, the American and British troops fought their way forward and into the German lines. Then, they discovered the most horrifying fact of all on this bloodiest of days: the damn Germans weren't dying. Undead soldiers continued to fight on, taking ten or twenty shots to the chest without stopping. Although they could not reload their empty rifles, they could use their bayonets with deadly power.

The Allies held the advantage in the air, but the German zombies drove the ground forces back onto the beaches and into the water. Some discovered that a well-placed shot to the brain felled these undead soldiers, but this did little to assuage the panic and fear most felt at the sight of dead soldiers who kept on fighting. Given the pure terror value of such troops, the invasion was a failure and Germany held on to all of occupied France.

Hitler was more than pleased with his new weapon. Careful use of propaganda and the complete victory against the allied invasion helped him convince his living soldiers of the value of these terrifying undead soldiers. Soon, the German chemical industry began mass producing the zombie serum for all of Germany to use. Hitler was letting the world know that no one would ever take back what he had conquered, that the Germans would keep on fighting until long after they died. This war was not going to end anytime soon.

Op Sit

The date is 1945 and the war in Europe stands at a stalemate. After repulsing the Allied forces on D-Day, the Germans turned east and stalled the Soviet Army advance, thanks again to the hordes of living dead soldiers. Now the two armies lie locked in continuing combat in the Ukraine. On the Western Front, the Allies are fighting on in Italy, but the Germans have launched a massive counter-offensive led, of course, by zombie troops.

Within Germany and occupied France, the Nazi propaganda machine is in overdrive, expounding upon the new super serum that makes its soldiers invincible in combat. Since this is the first time in a long while that the German army is advancing rather than retreating, the people seem satisfied with their government's lies. Few know the truth about the serum and those that hear the stories fear placing any credit in such tales.

The Allies have captured several zombie bodies and are working hard trying to analyze the foreign substance in their blood. They have not yet managed to capture a still-functional zombie, something they would very much like to do in order to discover the creature's weaknesses. For now, General Eisenhower has decreed that the truth about these zombies must remain a secret, although thousands of wounded and frightened servicemen have already spread the tale all over England and sent letters home about the horrors they saw at Normandy. The papers have run several stories about German super-soldiers who would not die no matter how many times they were shot.

Hitler wants every German inoculated with the serum and the chemical companies are all working overtime to refit their factories for the drug's production. Meanwhile, Allied spies and a few defectors (men and women too horrified by the zombies to keep on with the Nazis) have reported Hitler's plan. The Allies have intensified their efforts to bomb the factories as much as possible, but many of them have already been moved far inland, either out of range or at the extreme range of Allied bombers.

The troops in Italy and Russia are getting plenty of first-hand experience in facing these zombies. The Germans usually march the living dead soldiers in tight formation, armed with rifles and bayonets. The zombies can fire the rifles, although with little accuracy, but they have trouble reloading them. They are pretty effective at smashing and slashing with their rifle butts and bayonets, however. The live troops, equipped with machine guns and explosives, come in behind the dead ones, using them as cover. Simple as this tactic is, again and again it has shown itself to be effective in forcing the Allies back.

Destroying a zombie requires putting a bullet through its brain. Nothing else seems to bother them. They lose limbs, have gaping holes blown in their chests, and still they keep on coming. They have a limited intelligence. They do not attack anyone wearing a German uniform and they follow the chain of command from when they were living soldiers. Thus, German officers can still give their dead soldiers orders and expect them to be obeyed. They can use simple tools like rifles and doorknobs, but aren't quite together enough to drive a tank or operate a radio. Another favorite tactic is to cut a hole in a zombie's chest, fill it with explosives and then run it at the enemy with a detonator. The zombie can follow instructions well enough to activate the bomb when it gets within range of the enemy.

Only those who have received an injection of the zombie serum have the potential of returning from the dead upon death. The serum must be administered at least once a month in order to retain its potency.

The zombies do still need to eat, and like most of their kind their tastes run towards the flesh of the living. Usually, the Nazi walking dead feast on the corpses of their fallen enemies once the battle is done. While the problem hasn't arisen thus far, should the zombies run out of fresh food (say, for instance, from lack of combat), they might well turn on their masters.

Story Ideas
Bring 'em Back Dead

The heroes are a group of soldiers on the Italian front, fighting squads of zombies and live German troops. A few firefights with the zombie menace should give the heroes an idea of what they're up against. Then they draw an important mission: capture one of these zombies "alive" and bring it back for closer study. The Germans know better than to let the Allies capture any active zombies if they can help it, so this is not going to be an easy job.

Capturing a zombie requires that the heroes immobilize it. On its own, this probably would not be much of a problem since the Nazi zombies are no stronger than they were when alive. However, the Germans always keep their zombie troops in large packs, knowing that their fighting power increases dramatically when they work in such numbers, much like the ancient Greek Phalanxes. Also, the heroes have to deal with live snipers in the rear, picking off anyone trying to steal their undead comrades.

The army would prefer it if the heroes brought the zombie back intact, i.e., without blowing off its legs and arms. They are provided with heavy duty manacles and leg chains as well as a leather hood for covering the zombie's face and dangerous mouth. Once they get back with the creature, the testing begins, but one is never enough for a truly scientific investigation. The heroes may be out in the field again soon.

Blowing the Chemical Plants

This is a deep cover raid into enemy territory. The heroes must journey into Germany itself, deep behind enemy lines, and try to destroy one of the factories manufacturing the zombie serum. If possible, they should confiscate some of the serum as well, and gather intelligence on just how the stuff is actually made. This means breaking into the factory and snooping around, all the while avoiding both living and undead guards.

The adventure can become more complicated if they meet a German scientist who wants to defect to the Allies. He can reveal every secret behind the Nazi zombie project, including all of its weaknesses and how the zombies are made. The trouble is, how do they get this frail old man out of German? That's up to the heroes to figure out. We can't tell them everything!

Mein Zombies

Strength 2 **Constitution** 2
Dexterity 2 **Intelligence** 2
Perception 2 **Willpower** 2
Dead Points 15 **Speed** 4
Endurance Points n/a **Essence Pool** 12

Attack: As normal human or according to weapon type. The zombie punches, kicks, bites and shoots a rifle just like a normal human. It has a skill level 1 in whatever activity is involved.

Weak Spot: Brain
Getting Around: Life-Like
Strength: Dead Joe Average
Senses: Like The Living
Sustenance: Daily; All Flesh Must Be Eaten
Intelligence: Tool Use 1; Long-term Memory
Spreading The Love: Special (see sidebar)
Power: 20

Allied/German Soldier
Supporting Cast/Adversary

Strength 2 **Constitution** 2
Dexterity 2 **Intelligence** 2
Perception 2 **Willpower** 2
Life Points 26 **Speed** 8
Endurance Points 23 **Essence Pool** 12

Skills

Brawling 2, Climbing 2, Demolitions 2, Dodge 2, Driving (Car/Jeep) 1, First Aid 1, Guns (Rifle) 2, Hand Weapon (Knife) 2, Stealth 2, Survival (Forest) 2, Swimming 2

Equipment

Colt Pistol/Luger Pistol (officers), M1 Garand or Mauser Rifle (enlisted), rations

---

Spreading the Love

Unlike most undead in this book, Mein Zombies do not spread the love. They simply kill and eat. To create a Mein Zombie, a living person must have regular injections of the Nazi serum and then be killed.

Character Creation

Given the time setting of Mein Zombies, character creation choices must be modified. The money values of the Resources Quality should be divided by five. The Minority Drawback is worth 3 points. The Computers, Computer Hacking, Computer Programming and Electronic Surveillance skills are generally unavailable. Finally, the Archetypes presented in Chapter Two: Survivors cannot be used.

After the Bomb

The elders of the tribe, those who remembered life before The Fall, warned us against going into the city. At the same time, they told us tales of how things once were, of all the wonders people had not so long ago. My brother and I, we wanted to see it for ourselves, or . . . at least what remained. We had always seen the steel mountains of the city from afar. Now we would see them up close.

Paul and I set out thinking we were ready for anything. Armed with our best bows and finest arrows, I also had the long knife my father had given me before he died. Paul had his faithful hatchet -- he never went anywhere without it. We were sure we could handle anyone who tried to bother us. It took us two days to reach the outskirts of the city. We were closer than we'd ever been before. It was more frightening and wondrous than I had imagined. How had people lived in such a place?

We entered the city streets and wandered around for half a day, amazed at the wreckage. Then Paul heard something and motioned me to be silent. There, in the shadows was a human figure, hunched over, chewing on something. It stopped when it noticed us. All three of us stood still as rocks for a long time. Then it leaped at Paul, moving faster than a scared rabbit. It was a man, but a huge, deformed man. Paul's arrow struck him through the throat but the beast didn't care. My arrow lodged in his thigh and he didn't even notice.

A moment later, Paul was dead before he hit the ground, his neck twisted horribly. I heard the crack of breaking bones. Then the creature bit into Paul's neck with his horribly deformed jaw, tearing away at the flesh. I turned and ran, only to hear it drop Paul's corpse and come crashing after me. I ran without looking back, without stopping, until I reached the edge of the city. Then it gave up. The elders were right. Don't go into the damned city. You'll die. The monster there will kill you. Just like Paul.

History

The trouble began with China. Right-wing pundits had been warning about it for years and, surprisingly enough, they turned out to be correct. China did have a growing nuclear arsenal and they were making better missiles thanks to stolen U.S. technology. What no one suspected was that Chinese scientists had managed to make their own variations on the nuclear payload. It was a highly radioactive, low destructive yield device that would kill millions but leave the buildings intact. The plan, presumably, was to rid the planet of the other populations and make more room for the Middle Kingdom.

Of course, China had no intention of starting a war, at least not when it did. However, as usual, things got out of hand when relations with the island of Formosa, known throughout the world as Taiwan, soured. It started when a notorious Chinese serial killer escaped custody and fled to Taiwan. In a fit of uncooperativeness, the Taiwanese refused to extradite the man back to mainland China. The Chinese sent in a special forces team to bring the murderer home but the Taiwanese military intercepted the team on its way in, killing them to a man. The Chinese Navy blockaded Taiwan, the U.S. Navy moved in to break up the blockade and one trigger-happy captain ended up firing on another.

The war began with the U.S. Navy and Chinese Air Force exchanging missile attacks, some of which started landing in Taiwan. The Taiwanese, believing themselves under attack, responded in kind. They launched a very special missile they had bought from the Russians: one with a nuclear tip. Thus World War III began and the Chinese and Americans started bombing each other into the stone age. Soon India, Pakistan, Russia and Europe got dragged into the fray and when the dust settled, the Earth was in the depths of nuclear winter and civilization as we know it had come to an end.

The specially designed Chinese radiation bombs had their desired effect, killing millions of Americans and European civilians but leaving the cities mostly intact for those few survivors who could take advantage of them. Now, thirty years later, the world is beginning to see that the bombs had another, rather interesting effect: they mutated the living and the unborn in strange and unpredictable ways. Some were born with missing or extra limbs and other malformations, but a few came into this world with radiation literally flowing through their veins. Some have theorized that this was an evolutionary solution to the new hostile world environment.

The result: a race of humans that can survive radiation just fine, live, grow old, and die in it. The problem is, once they die, they don't stay dead. The dead rise again, stronger, meaner, and more deadly than they ever were in life. The true legacy of the Chinese bombs is that now, thirty years after they detonated, they still manage to create new and terrifying ways of killing the living. These radiation zombies may not be overwhelming the world with their numbers, but they make up for that with pure strength and brutality.

Mutant Zombies R Us

Civilization as we know it no longer exists on Earth. Thirty years after the nuclear holocaust destroyed much of the planet's life, only a few million humans exist, spread out over five continents. Most of the cities were either destroyed in the war or made uninhabitable by radiation.

Human society now centers around small family and tribal groups, usually numbering no more than two or three dozen. Some have settled down in small fortress communities where they grow crops and raise animals under harsh conditions. Few species can survive in the harsh climates of the modern world. The northern climes are too cold for any but the bravest or most foolish of men, and even the southern regions suffer from crippling cold in the winter months, thanks to the cloud of dust that still chokes the atmosphere and blocks much of the sun's life-giving warmth.

Recently, the newly radiation-resistant humans have begun to creep back into the cities. There they hope to find storehouses of food, weapons, and technology to help the rebuild a shattered world. Those that dare to venture back into the urban areas indeed are discovering all manner of wonders, from canned food to working batteries to generators. They have even found riot gear, assault rifles and grenades in police stations, sporting goods stores and old army bases. The problem is, in many places, the radiation was still strong enough to kill those with radiation resistance. Even worse, those early explorers did not stay dead, or rather they didn't let a little thing like death stop them. The radiation zombies thrive on the same deadly energy that killed them. As long as the rads keep coming, they fight on.

These zombies have mutated, gaining incredible strength and even above-human agility. Although they still look basically human, many have horribly deformed features, oversized limbs, and nauseating blisters covering their flesh. Undead, they are nearly impossible to kill without sustained effort by a group of hunters. Dismembering them at least keeps the different parts from working together, and destroying their eyes does blind them. Even blind, they can still be deadly, and very quick. The only way to destroy one of these things for good is either to burn it to cinders or remove it from the radiation-filled city which gave it birth.

Some explorers go to the trouble of carrying around large lead lined containers. Forcing a zombie into one of these things and then sealing it cuts off the flow of radiation. Of course, as soon as they open it again, the beast starts to revive if there is any significant source of radiation nearby. However, for those first few minutes, the zombie's strength is reduced, making it easier to dismember and burn.

Story Ideas
The Quest for Firearms

In this Story, the characters are the most adventurous members of a small tribe of survivors living several dozen miles from a major city. Character creation is modified slightly (see sidebar on the next page). Also, most characters were born after the war and are thus subject to becoming zombies once they die.

The characters should have no idea that zombies exist or where they come from. They learn, either from a traveler or a fellow tribesman, the location of a large cache of firearms and weapons located within the city. Meanwhile, a neighboring tribe has been making continuous, and increasingly deadly, raids on the characters' tribe. Getting ahold of these guns could well turn the tide of this inter-tribal war.

The heroes, armed with primitive weapons and possibly one firearm with a limited number of bullets (say, six), must journey into the city and find this hidden weapons cache. In the course of their desperate venture, they encounter other humans scavenging for artifacts from the city. Some might prove helpful, others attack, while the rest just want to be left alone. They also hear tales of the powerful zombies that prowl the streets, something none of them have encountered before. Finally a group of malevolent scavengers attack the heroes. The characters fight them off, killing at least one of them.

Of course, those the characters killed soon rise from the dead and come after them again, and this time they are much harder to put down. Eventually, the characters locate the weapons cache only to learn that it is guarded by a group of very large and tough zombies. Although the zombies do not use guns, they are deadly and very tough to kill. If the characters succeed, however, the pay off is immense: rifles, ammo, grenades, and other weapons.

Out of the Vault

The heroes are a small group or family that has lived inside a bomb shelter for the last thirty years. The shelter was state-of-the-art, prepared by a nearly insane but tragically foresightful weapons manufacturer magnate (who died shortly after the shelter was sealed by his hand-picked "chosen"). Character creation proceeds as normal, except Riding, Driving and other skills that require large outdoor areas are unavailable for the youngsters. The oldtimers may remember these skills but they will be very rusty.

Now the exterior radiation sensors have declared it safe to venture forth into the outside. Unfortunately, that outside is right in the middle of a huge city populated chiefly by the living dead. Armed with plenty of weapons, ammo and armor, the heroes are just now running out of food and certain supplies. First things first, they have to deal with zombies attracted to the smell of fresh meat.

The heroes have to fight their way out of the city and make their peace with one of the farming communities in the rural regions. Their guns give them a big advantage, so they can arrive as conquerors or in peace. Either way, they now have to set up a new life, one filled with both zombies and tribes of humans.

All We Need is Zombiedome

A group of survivors has found a wonderful new way to entertain themselves. They have constructed a large, dome-shaped cage with makeshift bleachers surrounding it. They go into the city in large groups to capture zombies and bring them back to the cage. There, just on the edge of the city's radiation belt, they make criminals and slaves (and anyone else they don't like) fight the zombies for their amusement.

The heroes can come into this Story from two directions. They can be part of the group that runs the arena, journeying into the city to capture zombies for the games and scavenge weapons for the victims to use in the arena (chainsaws are a big favorite with the crowd). Alternately, the heroes themselves are prisoners of the arena owners and they must fight zombies in the cage. This latter course is sure to kill off a character or two, but is fun if you enjoy bloody, graphic combat.

After The Bomb Zombies

Strength 7
Dexterity 3
Perception 3
Dead Points n/a
Endurance Points n/a
Constitution 4
Intelligence 1
Willpower 2
Speed 18
Essence Pool 20

Attack: As normal human or according to weapon type.

Weak Spot: None

Getting Around: The Quick Dead

Strength: Monstrous Strength

Senses: Like A Hawk; Scent Tracking

Sustenance: Who Needs Food?; All Flesh Must Be Eaten

The zombies are animated by the heavy radiation still present in the cities. The level of radiation trails off outside the cities and the zombie gets weaker and weaker as it travels away from the center of the city. The creatures realize this as soon as it happens and return to the city environs.

Intelligence: Tool Use 1

Spreading the Love: Special (see sidebar)

Power: 50

Special: This large, powerful zombie inspires fear in those around it. Apply a Fear Test with a -2 modifier when the zombie is near.

Also, each is relatively unique. For that reason, Zombie Masters should pick and choose their Getting Around and Strength special features and modify the Power level accordingly.

Spreading the Love

After the Bomb Zombies do not spread the love. They simply kill and eat. These zombies arise when a radiation-resistant human dies inside the heavily irradiated cities. The transformation takes 3D10 hours and hideously deforms the person.

Character Creation

If the characters were born in the waste (few if any oldtimers have survived the harsh years since the war), character creation choices must be modified. The Resources and Multiple Identities Qualities are unavailable. The Computers, Computer Hacking, Computer Programming and Electronic Surveillance skills are almost entirely unavailable, and the Guns skill is usually nonexistent. Instead, Hand Weapon (Knife) or Hand Weapon (Bow) are very common. Finally, the Archetypes presented in Chapter Two: Survivors cannot be used.

Dead at 1000

My parents sent me to be cared for by the monks when I was but twelve. I have spent every one of my thirty-six years since studying the mysteries of my faith. I even became something of a specialist in the holy writing concerning to the apocalypse. I have always known that someday the Lord would choose to invoke his final Judgment, but I never dreamed that I would be alive to see it happen. All my life, I looked forward to an eternity in paradise. Tragically, I find myself trapped in a hell on earth.

It began for me in the middle of mass. Abbot Geoffrey was leading thirty of us in solemn prayer, celebrating the feast of Saint John. Suddenly, from the rear of the chapel came the resounding crash of heavy stone on stone. Unable to ignore such an interruption, and fearing that perhaps the chapel itself was collapsing, we all rushed back to see what had happened. Our first thought was that some heathen had desecrated the tomb of Brother Stephen, the founder of our monastery. And indeed, his marble sarcophagus was open -- the heavy stone lid cracked.

Horrifying as the thought of a desecrated tomb was, the truth was far worse. We saw Brother Stephen himself, risen from the dead. Unlike the Lord's son, however, his body was horribly decayed, wearing the moldering vestment in which he'd been buried decades ago. He clawed his way out of the tomb, accompanied by such a horrible stench that many of began retching. Only Abbot Geoffrey seemed unaffected, filled with the bravery of the Lord. He knelt down in prayer, asking in Latin for the risen monk to bless him.

We watched in horrified fascination as the dead brother shambled forward and grasped the abbot's head between his desiccated, rotting hands. The thing pulled upwards, forcing the abbot to come to his feet. No divine rapture came from that touch, however. It leaned forward and began tearing at the Abbot's cheek with its teeth. He screamed, and feebly tried to break away from the demonic thing's grip. The rest of us turned and ran, many like myself screaming to God for mercy. Since then, things have gotten much, much worse.

All Flesh Must Be Eaten

History

This scenario is all about history. In fact, the clock must be turned back 1000 years before things get started in earnest. Everyone knows about the pre-millennium panic in the late 1990s, but what about when people were really scared, back in the 990s. The European Christians felt certain that the world was going to end any day -- that the Lord would come down and rescue the pious and punish the wicked. This setting assumes that at least part of this belief turned out to be true: the world is coming to an end, in a manner of speaking anyway.

The cause of this end of the world scenario is a far cry from God, however. No, here the culprit is a man, although not a normal one by any means. His name is Lucius Mordecai, a disenfranchised Venetian nobleman with a vendetta and an abiding interest in the black arts. Mordecai grew up in Venice, at the time a growing power in Europe thanks to its extensive commercial contacts with the Middle East. He took advantage of the city's worldly connections to buy mystic texts from as far away as India and China, along with the means to translate them.

Intrigued by what he learned, Mordecai decided to put some of these dark rituals to the test. He performed demonic summoning and sacrificed animals and even humans in the privacy of his family palazzo. Unfortunately, the neighbors learned of this and decided to burn the lovely Mordecai family home to the ground, with Lucius in it. The dabbler in satanic rites managed to slip out barely singed and fled Venice in disgust. He traveled all over Europe searching for a place to call home, where he could offer up the blood of virgins to his dark gods in peace.

Alas, he found no such place. Eventually, he decided that the time had come to show the world what he was really capable of. If they were not going to give him any peace, then by Lucifer, no one would ever have peace again. An ancient Sanskrit manuscript had outlined for him a ritual that he had not previously dared to attempt. Now, in anger and desperation, he turned to it and made the necessary preparations.

Mordecai chose the city of Paris as the site of his ritual. On a moonless night, he gathered his coven in the city cemetery, along with thirteen sacrificial virgins. The neighbors huddled in their beds in terror as lighting flashed, thunder roared, and the smell of brimstone filled the air. The blood of innocents spilled to the ground and awakened the bodies of those who lay at rest. At the command of the Italian magician, the dead clawed their way from their graves, hungering for the flesh of the living.

Mordecai's own followers were the first to fall to the decaying claws and rotting teeth of the undead. The creatures then descended on Paris, breaking down doors and consuming the living. Too frightened to do much more than pray, many died without a fight. The local nobles and their soldiers put up more of a fight, but they found it well nigh impossible to kill the undead army besieging them. Some managed to wall themselves up in their castles, but most were not so lucky. From Paris, the power of Mordecai's spell spread with each new death, engulfing much of France and beginning to creep into the neighboring lands. Unless it is somehow stopped, the whole world shall some day succumb to the tide of living dead.

Anno Domini

The kingdoms of Europe are reeling in reaction to the reports coming out of France. Many believe that this truly is the end of the world. Religious fanaticism has spread like wildfire. The peasants leave the fields untilled as they flock to the churches to pray night and day. Many of the nobles are doing the exact same thing, donating all their worldly possessions to the Church in hopes of buying their way into heaven before the living dead reach them.

Surprisingly enough, the calmest heads are located in the Vatican, where there is much skepticism about what is truly going on. There, Pope Silvester II has his own feelings on what is happening in France. A man who believes in his own papal infallibility, the Pope is sure that if the end of the world really were at hand, God would have told him. Therefore, he suspects the undead hordes are the work of the Devil, not God. Moreover, the Pope has received reports that the notorious black magician Lucius Mordecai was in Paris around the time the dead began to rise. Mordecai has quite a reputation within the church, having long ago been excommunicated for his dreadful and damned activities.

Thus, Rome has become an island of sanity in the face of the growing panic that is sweeping through Europe. Pope Silvester preaches daily that this is not the end of the world, but the work of the Devil. Moreover, he has issued a Papal Bull declaring that the events in France are the work of sinful miscreants and black magicians and that the Lord will deliver the faithful if they have the strength to get up and fight for themselves. Slowly, Silvester is rallying the nobles to his cause, planning a great crusade against the undead armies of France. However, time grows short and the zombies numbers keep growing.

The zombies themselves are the slow moving, stupid variety. They hunger for living flesh, and have an innate ability to home in on any living being nearby. They cannot communicate with one another and do not really work in concert, although it may seem so since they often gang up on individual living beings. The only way to stop these zombies is to destroy their brain or cut their brain from the rest of the body. Arrows or crossbow bolts through the eye or that penetrate the skull stop a zombie cold, as does a sword strike that severs head from neck. Anyone who dies at the hands of a zombie will rise up again to become one of the living dead. This takes only a matter of minutes to happen. Then, the newly dead and mangled corpse seeks out living flesh to satiate its own undying hunger.

At the center of it all sits Lucius Mordecai, ruling over a Paris in which few living things stir but himself. Out of touch with the rest of the world, totally mad, and loving every minute of it, Mordecai has finally realized his dream of revenge against all who mocked him. He continues his dark experiments, hoping to find new and even more terrifying horrors to unleash on the unsuspecting world.

Story Ideas
Last Stand at Saint John's

The characters are simple medieval folk from whatever European town, city, parish or berg the Zombie Master chooses to set the adventure in. Word has spread that the end of the world is nigh and everyone and their mother is heading for the churches. The Cast Members get swept up in the tide of panicked humanity. The whole town is gathered in the local cathedral, listening to the bishop's endless prayers in Latin. Then, the horror begins.

Unfortunately for the Cast Members, most churches have crypts within them. The faithful get their first dose of terror when the long dead bishops, noblemen, and saints start crawling their way out of their marble caskets, looking for human flesh to devour. The heroes are right there to help fight the monsters off, but things only get worse when the rest of the zombies come knocking at the front door. This is a classic zombie scenario of living folks under siege by dead ones, with the added twist that there are no guns, cars or electricity, just steel, brains and brawn.

In preparation, the bishop may have allowed the faithful to bring picks, axes, hoes, rakes and scythes. Alternatively, he may have trusted to God and barred all potential weapons from the home of the Lord. If so, the Cast Members must find weapons among the braziers, candlesticks, benches and other trappings in the church. Their best bet is a very unChristian-like behavior of placing the panicked faithful between them and the zombies as they escape through a secret passage with the bishop. The outside world is hardly the safest of places at the moment, however.

The Great Crusade

For an adventure with a more epic feel, start the Cast Members off in Rome. They have journeyed to the Holy See to answer a call from the Pope for brave souls willing to risk their lives to fight the undead French menace. Pope Silvester is gathering together a great army to march into the Gallic nightmare realm and cleanse the Devil's influence from it forever. The ultimate goal, of course, is the destruction of the evil warlock, Lucius Mordecai.

All Flesh Must Be Eaten

The characters, heroes that they are, draw the job of scouting ahead and trying to find out where Mordecai is. Is he still in Paris or has he moved on? Unbeknownst to the Pope or the Cast Members, Mordecai still has living agents in the world, cultists totally devoted to the mad magician now that he has displayed his awesome power. These cultists try their best to end the heroes' mission before it begins by assassinating them. Should the heroes manage to capture one of the cultists and make him talk, they learn that Mordecai has provided a route of safe passage back into Paris that the heroes could take to get that much closer to the evil necromancer.

By following the secret path north through France, the heroes make their way to Paris without too much trouble, physically at least. The sights they see along the way are horrifying enough -- whole villages destroyed, covered in blood and gore but bereft of a single dead body. Once they arrive in the city itself they must sneak and fight their way through the streets, pitting themselves against zombies and Mordecai's cultists. Finally, they confront Mordecai, who may have summoned a demon just to make things interesting, and in a final clash the heroes either die or save the world. Destroying Mordecai causes the zombies to drop dead where they stand (or just halt the creation of new ones if the Zombie Master wants to prolong the storyline in that way). If the Cast Members die, the Zombie Master has a choice to make. Does the Pope send another team, do the Papal armies drive the monstrous hordes back, or does the world eventually succumb to the undead lust for human flesh?

Character Creation

Character creation is much more limited in Dead at 1000. The Resources Quality should be removed -- priests and nobles have as much money as they want, peasants have none. The Computers, Computer Hacking, Computer Programming, Demolitions, Driving, Electronic Surveillance, Electronics, Guns, Mechanic and Piloting skills are unavailable. Martial Arts would be exceedingly rare and would require some background explanation. Medicine (of any kind) and First Aid were practiced but were largely ineffective (and often caused more harm than good). Finally, the Archetypes presented in Chapter Two: Survivors cannot be used.

Dead at 1000 Zombies

These undead use the same basic stats as the Rise of the Walking Dead Zombies (see p. 168). The differences are that no zombie animals exist and the living become zombies only by being killed (there is no wasting disease). Further, the Dead at 1000 zombies are vulnerable to Blessed Objects. They take double damage from Blessed weapons, and will not willingly come within 10 yards (meters) of a Blessed item. Finally, Holy Fire does double damage to zombies. Their Power is 10.

Mordecai's Patron

At the Zombie Master's discretion, Mordecai's powers can stem from a Dark Patron -- a near god-like entity bent on global domination. This Patron may intervene on Mordecai's behalf as the storyline demands. Cutting the link between Mordecai and this Patron may be the best way to defeat him, if the characters can figure out how to do that. Finally, it may be that Mordecai is wholly unaware of his powerful benefactor, and will disbelieve and even resent the "intrusion" if made aware of it.

Worlds In Hell

Character Templates

The following templates may be used as Adversaries or Supporting Cast Members, or tailored by adding more character points to become Archetypes.

Noble
Character Type: Survivor

Strength 4	Constitution 4
Dexterity 3	Intelligence 2
Perception 2	Willpower 3
Life Points 45	Speed 14
Endurance Points 38	Essence Pool 18

Qualities/Drawbacks

Hard to Kill 1, Fast Reaction Time

Skills

Brawling 3, Dodge 2, Gambling 2, Hand Weapon (Bow) 2, Hand Weapon (Knife) 2, Hand Weapon (Sword) 4, Intimidation 2, Riding (Horse) 4, Survival (Forest) 2, Tracking 2

Character Points Used: Attributes 18; Qualities 3; Skills 25

Priest
Character Type: Inspired

Strength 2	Constitution 3
Dexterity 3	Intelligence 3
Perception 3	Willpower 4
Life Points 30	Speed 12
Endurance Points 32	Essence Pool 38

Qualities/Drawbacks

Charisma 1, Gift, Increased Essence (4), Inspiration

Skills

Bureaucracy 1, Dodge 2, Fine Arts (Illuminated Manuscripts) 2, Humanities (Catholic Theology) 4, Humanities (History) 2, Instruction 2, Intimidation 2, Language (Latin) 3, Medicine 1, Riding (Horse) 1, Rituals (Catholic) 4, Singing 2, Smooth Talking 2, Writing (Latin) 1

Metaphysics

Blessing, The Binding, Touch of Healing

Character Points Used: Attributes 18; Qualities 15; Skills 29; Metaphysics 15

Bard/Jester/Storyteller
Character Type: Survivor

Strength 2	Constitution 2
Dexterity 3	Intelligence 2
Perception 4	Willpower 3
Life Points 26	Speed 10
Endurance Points 26	Essence Pool 17

Qualities

Charisma 2, Showoff

Skills

Acrobatics 2, Acting 2, Brawling 1, Dancing 2, Disguise 1, Dodge 2, Haggling 2, Hand Weapon (Knife) 2, Myth and Legend 2, Play Instrument (any two) 3, Singing 2, Sleight of Hand 2, Smooth Talking 1, Stealth 2, Storytelling 4, Survival (Forest) 2

Character Points Used: Attributes 17; Qualities 2; Drawbacks 2; Skills 35

Peasant
Character Type: Norm

Strength 2	Constitution 2
Dexterity 2	Intelligence 2
Perception 2	Willpower 2
Life Points 26	Speed 8
Endurance Points 23	Essence Pool 12

Skills

Brawling 2, Cheating 1, Climbing 1, Craft (Farming) 2, Dodge 2, Gambling 2, Hand Weapon (Farming Tools) 2, Hand Weapon (Knife) 2, Snares 2, Survival (Forest) 2, Stealth 2, Tracking 2, Traps 2

Character Points Used: Attributes 12; Qualities 0; Skills 24

Chapter Six

Lucian Mordecai

Strength 4
Dexterity 5
Perception 6
Life Points 46
Endurance Points 50
Constitution 5
Intelligence 4
Willpower 6
Speed 20
Essence Pool 155

Qualities/Drawbacks

Charisma 2, Contacts (Zealots) 4, Cruel 2, Gift, Increased Taint (25), Obsession, Paranoid, Showoff

Skills

Bureaucracy 1, Brawling 1, Dodge 2, Humanities (History) 2, Intimidation 4, Language (Latin) 3, Occult Knowledge 3, Research/Investigation 2, Rituals (Dark Arts) 4

Metaphysics

Unlike the Inspired who look to a greater power for their mystical might, Mordecai relies on his own dark, twisted abilities. He practices Black Magic, with a bitter, corrupted form of Essence called Taint.

To perform an Invocation, Mordecai must first gather the necessary Taint. He can draw on 10 of his Taint Points per Turn. While he does this, he must cause pain to himself or to someone around him (he usually keeps one or two disciples around just for that purpose). Once he has built up the requisite amount of Taint, the dark mage must make a Focus Task, using Willpower and his Invocation skill level. Failure means the Invocation does not manifest.

Mordecai's most commonly used Invocations are listed below. Zombie Masters may devise new ones based on these descriptions, or consult other books in the Unisystem family of games.

Affect the Psyche 3: This effect creates an impression of power and control around Mordecai, making others unwilling to oppose him. He gains a +2 bonus on most social interaction Tasks, with an additional bonus equal to the Success Levels of the Focus Task. People who have a reason to dislike or hate the Magician resist with a Simple Willpower Test. This effect costs 2 Taint and lasts 5 minutes per Success Level; at the end of that time, the Invocation must be repeated.

Soulfire 3: This Invocation allows Mordecai to fire bolts of pure Taint. Soulfire inflicts D6(3) x Taint Points of damage. Survivors struck by Soulfire lose 1 Essence Point for every 3 points of damage inflicted by the attack. Inspired lose Essence on a one-for-one basis. Soulfire can strike any target within line of sight. Survivors cannot Dodge the attack because the Soulfire is invisible; Inspired can see Soulfire and may Dodge normally.

Spirit Mastery 3: With this Invocation, Mordecai can summon his own personal "demon." The Invocation requires a day's preparation and six hours of ritual. Further, a living human must be killed to draw the monster.

If successful (any roll but a 1), Mordecai's demon appears in a cloud of brimstone. It will obey Mordecai's commands for 5 Turns. Each Turn after that, Mordecai must make a Willpower and Spirit Mastery Task at a cumulative -1 penalty. Failing this Task results in the demon turning on its master. So, if the Cast Members can just hold out long enough, and Mordecai messes up his rolls, and . . . ah . . . never mind.

Mordecai's Demon

This monstrous creature has a deformed humanoid form covered with boils, open wounds and rolls of fat. It has leathery skin (Armor Value 5), sharp claws (D4(2) x 6 slashing damage), and a grinning, slobbering maw (D4(2) x 3 slashing damage).

Strength 6 Dexterity 6 Constitution 6
Intelligence 1 Perception 4 Willpower 2
Life Points 58 Endurance Points: n/a Speed 24 Essence Pool 25
Skills: Brawling 3, Tracking 3

Until the Ending of the World

"And I saw the dead, great and small, standing before the throne, and books were opened. And also another book was opened, which was the book of life. And the dead were judged by what was written in the books, by what they had done. And the sea gave up the dead in it, Death and Hades gave up the dead in them, and all were judged by what they had done. Then Death and Hades were thrown into the lake of fire. This is the second death, the lake of fire; and if anyone's name was not found written in the book of life, he was thrown into the lake of fire."

"Thus endeth the lesson," intoned the priest, as he had done daily for the past fifty years. Now though, the words carried new and terrible import. Outside the church, he could hear the screams of the dying and the fall of the great city. Worse than that, however, were the other sounds -- the sounds of the risen dead as they shuffled and clawed their way toward the final judgment, sweeping the living before them. "The end has come and God in his wrath holds us accountable for our sins. Let us pray for his forgiveness."

As one, the congregation began to chant, "Our Father, who art in heaven, Hallowed be thy name."

History

Prophecy is a funny thing. It often turns out that what you thought it said is quite different from what it actually meant. For years, liberal-minded Christian priests and scholars had argued that the controversial Book of Revelations was just metaphor and myth, that it did not describe an actual future event. For the most part, people believed this since few really wanted to contemplate the end of the world and their own final judgment. After all, the Bible is a book like any other, and over the years it has seen some editing and revising and even rewriting.

The truth of the matter is, the Book of Revelations got it all right, at least in its original presentation. Unfortunately, the Church fathers did a little messing around with the contents and some important facts got reworked to make them sound more mysterious and well, poetic. Saint John's original text read more like a Stephen King novel than a holy text. Even so, the book retained its monsters and cataclysms, many of which were in fact metaphors for what was really going to happen.

God, being omnipotent, omniscient, and as it turns out, very judgmental, knows that the best way to punish humanity is to let it punish itself. When God decides the world is done stewing in its own sin, it will be time to pull the plug and start over again. All the good souls go to heaven; all the bad ones go straight to hell. Those unfortunate enough to fall into the latter category (which turns out to be most of the folks on Earth) get to go out in a most gruesome way. God intends for this final end to be an object lesson for those who dwell in the next world, the reincarnated souls of the saved who en masse get another shot at what Adam and Eve screwed up.

The Divine being still has something of a soft spot for humans. Those left alive on Earth when the end comes still have a chance to redeem themselves and join the rest of the lucky souls up in heaven. If they can survive the terrors of the end days and do so with love, charity, and goodwill (i.e. without killing their neighbors so that they may survive), they earn a ticket to heaven. In order to promote this kind of behavior, God will protect those who show real faith, at least to a certain degree.

So what is this horrible fate that awaits humanity in the end days. Church scholars have known of it for centuries but no one ever really thought out the whole repercussions. The teachings say that on Judgment Day, the dead will rise from their graves to be judged by the second coming of Christ. It's just this scene that Michelangelo depicted on the wall of the Sistine Chapel. Those teachings are sadly based on a mistranslation of a passive verb that should have been active. The dead will rise on judgment Day not to be judged, but to do the judging themselves. In other words, the dead will rise to bring holy terror to every living thing on the planet.

A Day In the Faith

It was a day like any other. Who can fathom why God chose this moment to end the world? Not surprisingly, the end began in Israel, the site of so many important events in religious history. First, there were reports of mobs of attackers killing people near cemeteries just after dawn. Then came the even wilder reports that the mobs, far from being the Palestinian separatists the news services originally blamed, were in fact the living dead. From there, panic spread through the streets of Jerusalem and out into the rest of the world, thanks in large part to the omnipresent CNN cameras.

As dawn crept across the world from Israel west, the dead rose in its wake. As soon as the sun's first light touched upon their graves the corpses animated and began to claw their way out. Twenty-four hours later, the dead had risen everywhere and the slaughter began in earnest. Fear gripped all who tried to face the undead hordes. Few places were able to establish any kind of resistance to the flesh-consuming monstrosities that were once friends and neighbors.

Now it is day two and people are starting to ask why. Many rightly assume that the end of the world has come. Others are more skeptical, looking in vain for scientific reasons. One thing that all discovered was that there were safe places in the world, places where the hordes of zombies would not go: the churches and holy places of all faiths. In many regions, word of these safe havens spread quickly and the churches quickly overflowed. Then, disaster struck. When panicked individuals began to force their way in through violence, all found the sanctity of the church had suddenly vanished. A church defiled by sin no longer kept the dead at bay and mass slaughter ensued.

God has imbued the corpses with a need to destroy and tear down anything relating to humanity. They not only terrorize people, but tear down structures as well. They possess a strength beyond that of their living days and large groups of zombies are more effective than a wrecking ball at demolishing concrete and wooden structures. A living person wishing to fight one of these monsters must somehow immobilize it, or douse it in flame or holy water. Only then will it die a second death.

When these zombies kill a person, the victim's soul is immediately judged and sent on to the appropriate afterlife. The body then rises up and joins the ranks of the undead. Inexorably, more and more of God's zombie agents spread the wrath and judgment of the lord all over the planet.

Those with strong personal faith can walk amongst the undead without fear, as long as they maintain a state of divine devotion and do not embark upon any sinful acts. Thus, a man of faith might walk out into a horde of undead to rescue a child and return with her to safety. Were he to pull a revolver and start shooting at other living things or even the zombies themselves, however, God's aegis would quickly vanish. Likewise, the faithful have an obligation to help those in need. Standing by and watching others suffer while doing nothing is just as much a sin as performing the sinful act itself.

Much of the world still has not yet found faith, although the world around them shows every sign of having literally gone to hell. They fight to survive at all costs, destroying not only zombies but any of the living who get in their way. The armies of the world have organized in small groups to defend against undead incursions. For now they can hold territory but they have made little headway in their attempts to contain the growing number of zombies. Ultimately, it seems impossible to hold back the tide forever. The question now becomes not whether death comes, but when and how.

Story Ideas

In this seting, the Cast Members' main goal is not to survive so much as to ensure their own salvation. Of course, first they need to figure this out. The Zombie Master can have a kindly priest explain the situation to them, or let them work it out on their own. There are plenty of hints: churches provide sanctuary, holy water hurts zombies, those of obvious faith seem immune to attack. Now all the characters have to do is find a way to make their own belief work for them, or barring that, to make the best deal they can with the other side of this end game.

Servants of the Light

The Cast Members must try to do as many good deeds as possible in the short time they have left on Earth. Some basic acts of goodness include rescuing people from the zombie hordes and bringing them safely to church, clearing areas of zombies and with the help of a holy person consecrating new ground to whichever incarnation of God they are devoted to, and fighting off those evil folks who would do harm to the world or work hand in hand with the devil. Once the heroes have accomplished enough good to redeem their sinful lives, they can go on into the light and exist happily ever after. Then again, this means succumbing to the zombie hordes -- none too pleasant, at least while it's going on.

Servants of the Dark

Less pious-minded Cast Members might decide that it's better to be a prince in hell than a slave in heaven. In this case, they do their best to make things worse. In fact, the devil himself might offer them a deal. They need to try and stop the zombies from destroying the Earth precisely because that is what God wishes. Despite the horror of dying at the claws of the undead, it gives people a last chance at performing some good deed and offers a true test of faith. The devil wants as few people to pass that test of faith as possible. Thus, the Cast Members fight both the zombies and the do-gooders, trying to prolong the horror as long as possible so that more survivors lose their faith. Granted this course is not very appealing, but some folks go in for this sort of thing.

The Middle Path

Most folks never really settle on one side or the other in the battle between good and evil. Most folks just want to get along, and be left alone. The Cast Members might fall into this category -- simple people just trying to fight on as long as they can and cling to life. In this case, they not only have to deal with the hordes of undead as in traditional zombie stories, they also have to face the religious zealots from both sides. The good guys want to save them, which might mean forcing them to leave their fortified shopping mall and venturing outside through packs of zombies. The bad guys want to damn them, which might mean any number of horrible fates. Then again, no one said Armageddon was going to be easy.

Until the Ending of the World Zombies

Strength 4
Constitution 2
Dexterity 2
Intelligence 1
Perception 1
Willpower 2
Dead Points 34
Speed 4
Endurance Points n/a
Essence Pool 12
Attack: As normal human or by weapon

Zombies are unable to use ranged weapons.

Weak Spot: Blessed Objects

Blessed weapons do double damage. Holy water is created as any other blessed object, and damages the zombie as fire does. Zombies react to Holy Symbols as described in Chapter Two: Survivors (p. 66). Otherwise, the zombie must be hacked into small pieces to be stopped.

Getting Around: Life-Like

Strength: Strong Like Bull

Senses: Like the Dead; Life Sense

Sustenance: Who Needs Food?; All Flesh Must Be Eaten

Intelligence: Tool Use 1

Spreading the Love: Only the Dead
When the zombies kill a person, the victim's soul leaves the body for judgment. The corpse rises in D10 minutes as a new agent of God's justice.

Power: 20

The Faithful

Those with strong personal faith gain several advantages in this setting. Acquiring that faith requires at a minimum some level of the Humanities (Theology) skill. Even then, the Zombie Master must determine how sincere the Cast Member is.

The Faithful may walk among the undead without fear, or harm. They may use Prayer, and may invest Holy Symbols (crosses, rosaries, etc.) (see Chapter Two: Survivors, p. 66). In either case, the Task or Test is modified according to the Cast Member's sincerity: -10 (for a foxhole convert) to +10 (for a truly saintly person).

Dawn of the Zombie Lords

We fled into the mountains when it began. At first we couldn't believe it, that the dead were rising to consume the flesh of the living. Then again, you only have to see one of those things before you become a believer, and I've seen a whole lot more than that. About fifty of us ended up hiding out up there. We hunted, we grew potatoes and other food. We managed to eke out a living for years. Every time we sent a few folks down to have a look around, they never came back. Soon enough, we stopped trying. We learned that when someone dies, you decapitate them and then burn the body or else you're gonna have one flesh-eating corpse on your hands before too long. Our lives were good enough I suppose, better than being down there among those monsters. Better than they are now.

Then they came. It had been years since we'd seen a zombie. Then all of a sudden there came a pack of 'em. They were on us before we knew it. In the end, they made seven of us their own before we destroyed them all. I was afraid our powder would have gone bad, but luckily it didn't. Otherwise, we would've been left with bows and arrows and hatchets, although there was some of that as well.

We thought that was that. We increased our guards and tried to get back to what had become our normal lives. Then, three nights later, they came again. This time there were hundreds of them. They clawed their way past all of our barriers, pits, and traps. Soon they had us walled up in the long house, just a dozen of us left alive. That's when we heard the voice. A human, living voice. "If you surrender now, none of you will be harmed." Well, we'd never heard of a zombie talking before. After talking with that strange voice a bit, we decided to risk it and give up. We were as good as dead anyway.

We walked out of the house, hands behind our heads as we were told. There we saw him -- a man in some kind of red and black military uniform carrying a shotgun and a cattle prod. Around him were scores of zombies, all of them standing stock-still like soldiers on parade. I couldn't believe what I was seeing. The zombies weren't attacking!

Another pair of living, breathing soldiers came out of the trees and took our weapons. Then we made the long march down the hill. We could already see that our fallen comrades had joined the ranks of the truly dead. They had each been shot in the head, execution style. We marched in silence for days, our guards talking to each other in some other language so none of us could understand what they were saying. They gave us food and water when we needed it. Even as hungry as I was though, it was hard to eat under the gaze of those dead-eyed monstrosities that guarded our every step. They were like robots, obeying simple commands in whatever language the living soldiers spoke.

Our journey ended here, in this camp. I don't know what's going to happen any more than you do, but I have a feeling it isn't gonna be good for any of us.

Chapter Six

All Flesh Must Be Eaten

History

This adventure is set in a world not too different from our own, sometime in the near future. It can even follow up one of the other zombie scenarios presented earlier in this section. Several years ago, the dead rose from their graves and began to spread terror, panic, and death among the peoples of the Earth. Humanity seemed doomed, but as so often happens, they found a way to survive. Now a century later, the earth is a nightmare planet ruled by those who have mastered the ability to control the undead and force them to do their bidding.

The first of the Zombie Lords came from the Caribbean, a master of Voodoo who had a long tradition of dealing with the undead. He called himself Lord Obatala, named for an ancient god of his people. He had the ability to control the undead through sheer force of will, causing them not only to leave him unharmed in their midst, but to attack his enemies. Soon the entire island of Hispaniola was under his sway thanks to his zombie armies.

Around the world, others began to exhibit similar abilities to control the undead. Some theorized that it was a latent psychic ability that only a few choice humans were lucky enough to possess. Others claimed to have been touched by God or the spirits, or whatever higher power they had devoted themselves to. A few of these zombie controllers used their powers for good, creating safe zones where no undead could enter and the living could find shelter and peace. Most seemed to have a dark streak to them, however, a need to rule over others. Perhaps it was this very need that gave them the power to control the living dead.

The shattered governments of the world tried in vain to stand up against these new lords of the dead. Lord Obatala created a fleet of ships, crewed by living sailors but filled to the brim with undead warriors. He invaded the United States and quickly his armies grew as the American dead fell under his sway. Near Atlanta, he fought a great battle with the remnants of the U.S. Army. Well over two million zombies engaged twenty thousand well-equipped and armed soldiers. Explosives, fire, shots to the head, all of these took their toll on the zombie force, wiping out over three quarters of a million of the undead. But the living could not stop the advance. The army of life made a fighting retreat all the way back to Ohio. Finally though, the weight of numbers overcame the soldiers and they too joined the ranks of the dead.

The same story repeated itself all over the world. In Europe, Count von Stults took control of much of the continent. In China, a mysterious figure calling herself the Lady of the Yellow Springs rose to power at the head of an army of undead.

Those willing to swear their allegiance to the Zombie Lords continued to live, although they gave up all freedom and all rights. The Zombie Lords became absolute monarchs, and it wasn't long before they started eyeing each other jealously as well. That's when the great Zombie Wars began.

Zombie Wars

Now that the Zombie Lords have established their mastery over the Earth, they have begun to look for ways to expand their own power. Billions died in the course of the zombie uprising and subsequent battles, with the result that the current human population is about 1.2 billion living and 7 billion living dead. Most, but not all, of these zombies are under the direct control of one of the world's three dozen Zombie Lords.

Zombie Lords can control their subjects through force of will alone. When in line of sight of a zombie, they can command its every action with a thought and give detailed orders to large groups at a time. They can also issue long-term orders, effectively programming their zombie subjects much like one might program a robot or computer. Once a zombie has fallen under the sway of a Zombie Lord, it is very difficult for another Lord to control that particular walking corpse. Reconditioning another Lord's zombie requires intense, individual concentration, easy enough to do when faced with one recalcitrant zombie, but impossible against an army of thousands.

The zombies do menial tasks like carrying heavy objects and even some simple farming. They also stand guard, ready to attack anyone who does not have the appropriate seal of protection. Zombie Lords issue these seals to their living and dead subjects. The seals are mental imprints that identify the holder as property of a specific Zombie Lord. None of that Lord's zombies attack someone with the right seal. All zombies attack humans without a seal unless specifically ordered not to. A Zombie Lord can bestow or remove a seal on anyone within his line of sight. It is possible to have seals from more than one Zombie Lord, but a Lord can always tell if more than one seal has been granted to a person.

The living serve in higher capacities for the Zombie Lords, but live in constant fear of falling out of favor. Most of the world's cities contain thousands if not millions of walking dead, and any living being without a seal will soon get devoured and end up a zombie themselves. There are, of course, some resistance groups, and a few isolated communities trying to make due far from the protection and tyranny of a Zombie Lord. When one of the Lords discovers such a community, he invariably descends upon it with an army of zombies. Those that resist are destroyed; the rest may join the Lord's service. Such independent living sets a bad example.

The zombies themselves are of the typical sort: slow moving, of normal human strength, but only vulnerable to attacks that harm their brains. Whenever anyone dies, they come back as a zombie unless cremated, no matter what the cause of death might be. When two Zombie Lords fight, they do so with huge armies of the living dead supported by a few live soldiers using weapons. Zombies themselves cannot use anything more complicated than a simple melee weapon. They do know to to bash in an opponent's undead skull. The living troops rain down artillery and explosives from the rear, often unconcerned with who gets hit. Thus far, the wars have mostly been stalemates. Only when one Lord has an overwhelming army of zombies is a victory recorded.

Zombie Lords

There are at least three dozen Zombie Lords known to exist. Each has his own personality, skills and talents. One example is presented here: Lord Obatala, ruler of Eastern United States.

Story Ideas
Servants of the Zombie Lords

In this option, the Cast Members are loyal to one of the many Zombie Lords. The characters can be assigned any number of different missions on behalf of their master. One of the more exciting possibilities is an attempt to assassinate a rival Zombie Lord. The Cast Members have their seals removed so they can sneak into the enemy territory and offer their services to the rival Lord. Then they must try to kill the Lord and escape with their hides intact. Once a Lord dies, all of his zombies go wild, attacking any living thing within their reach. They no longer work in concert. Alternately, the characters can seek to overthrow their own Zombie Lord from within. This is a dangerous proposition as it makes for a lot of angry, uncontrolled and very hungry zombies.

On Their Own

Another option centers around the Cast Members living in isolation without the protection of any Zombie Lord. They begin in some remote, rural area. When the dead started rising, they fled to the mountains and haven't been in contact with the rest of the world. They are self-sufficient and want no trouble from anyone. Unfortunately, trouble comes looking for them in the form of a party of zombie ravagers -- zombies programmed to hunt down and exterminate unaligned living ones.

The heroes succeed in defending their small community, but now the Zombie Lord is aware of their presence. He sends more zombies, this time under live leaders, to investigate. The characters must choose between defending their freedom or fleeing to a different location. Either path may lead to succumbing to the tyrannical rule of the local Lord of the Undead. If the characters are strong enough, they might even be able to play one Zombie Lord against another, hiring themselves out as mercenaries or freelance zombie hunters. Alternately, they might try and seek out one of the few benevolent Zombie Lords who offer both freedom and security.

All Flesh Must Be Eaten

A New Lord Rises

This scenario revolves around a single character who has the ability to control zombies just like a Zombie Lord. As play begins, the power is weak, but the more he uses it, the more powerful he becomes. With the help of the other characters, the group can assemble its own army of zombies to challenge the local Zombie Lord. From there, who knows where the Cast Members' power will lead them. Perhaps they will be the ones to finally unite a dying world under one great Zombie Lord, either for good or for evil.

Dawn of the Zombie Lords Zombies

Strength 2
Constitution 2
Dexterity 1
Intelligence 1
Perception 2
Willpower 2
Dead Points 15
Speed 2
Endurance Points n/a
Essence Pool 10

Attack: As normal human or by weapon

Weak Spot: Brain

Getting Around: Slow and Steady

Strength: Dead Joe Average

Senses: Like the Living

Sustenance: Who Needs Food?; All Flesh Must Be Eaten

Intelligence: Tool Use 1

Spreading the Love: Whenever a human dies, regardless of cause, they come back as a zombie within D6(3) days. This can only be prevented by cremation.

Power: 15

"Typical" Zombie

The stats given here are for a typical zombie in a Dawn of the Zombie Lords game. If used as a follow-up to another setting, carry over the stats of those zombies. Note that if the zombie stats are vastly different from those detailed here (such as using an After the Bomb Zombie), this may change the nature of the Dawn of the Zombie Lords campaign.

Lord Obatala

Strength 3
Constitution 4
Dexterity 3
Intelligence 4
Perception 3
Willpower 4
Life Points 250
Speed 14
Endurance Points 38
Essence Pool 46

Qualities/Drawbacks

Charisma 3, Cruel 2, Delusions (Loa's Avatar), Gift, Hard to Kill 4, Increased Essence 5

Skills

Brawling 1, Bureaucracy 2, Dancing 2, Dodge 2, First Aid 2, Haggling 3, Hand Weapon (Knife) 2, Intimidation 2, Myth and Legend 3, Occult Knowledge 2, Rituals (Voodoo) 4, Smooth Talking 3, Survival (Jungle) 3, Tracking 2

Powers

Might of the Dead: A Zombie Lord's connection to the undead grants him a toughness beyond mortal ken. This grants him 200 extra Life Points.

Seal the Dead: A Zombie Lord may imprint a zombie or living human with his own identifying mark at the cost of 1 Essence Point. The zombie will not resist. A human may resist through a Resisted Simple Willpower Test. Any person killed by a sealed zombie rises similarly marked. Zombies will not attack those similarly sealed, living or dead. Removing a seal from the living takes one Turn, and costs no Essence; removing one from a zombie takes 10 minutes of intense concentration, and costs 5 Essence.

Rule the Dead: A Zombie Lord and any sealed human may converse or command any sealed zombie within earshot. Simple commands or questions to less than 5 zombies costs 1 Essence Point. Detailed commands or commanding large groups of zombies costs 2 Essence Points. Large groups of zombies may not be given detailed command. In all cases, the zombies will obey until given another command, even if the object of the commands no longer exists or further activity would do more harm that good.

Worlds In Hell

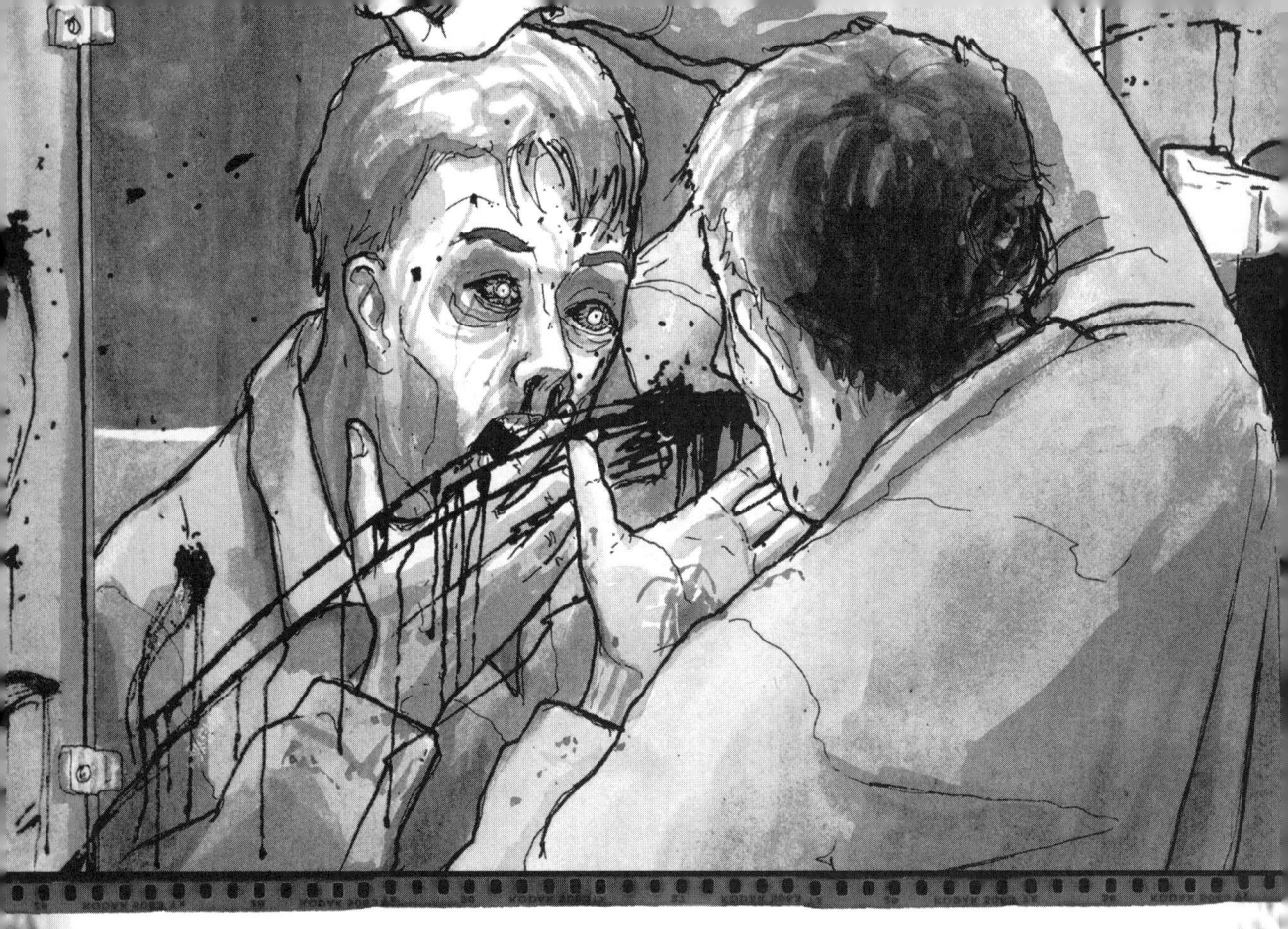

Rebirth Into Death

    I remember passing out in the back seat of Mike's van, drunk off my ass. I didn't wake up when the tires started screeching, or when the van shot off the highway, or when it plunged of the cliff. I was dead before I knew what had happened.

    It was just like they said -- this bright white light drew me up into the heavens. I floated upwards and looked down at my mangled body amid the wreckage of the van. Oddly, I didn't give a damn at all. I just felt good, peaceful, warm and fuzzy. I'm pretty sure it wasn't the beer talking, either. I thought, hey this ain't half bad.

    For what seemed like forever and yet no time at all, I was in the bright light. I could feel my friends with me too, floating around, all of us feeling like a million bucks. Then this black hole opened up, just like that old Disney movie, and sucked me right back down into the darkness.

    Everything was black but I felt like I had a body again. I could move my arms and legs but not very far. I started to panic when I realized I was in some kind of box. I tried to scream but only a low moan came out. That's when I realized I wasn't breathing. It seemed I didn't need to breathe. I started banging away at the box side in front of me. After a few blows, my fists went through the flimsy wood and into the dirt. I kept digging and pounding and clawing. I was moving through the dirt, certain that I was heading for the surface. The other weird thing was that all this scraping and digging didn't hurt at all.

    Suddenly the darkness vanished and light was everywhere. I looked around and saw a graveyard. All around me others were busy working their way out of the ground too. Seems we had all just dug ourselves out of our own graves. Suddenly, I began to feel very hungry . . . hungry for flesh.

Chapter Six

History

As it turns out, the Buddhists were right about a few things the Christians got totally wrong. At the same time, the Buddhists didn't know the whole story either. As might be expected, the reality of life and death actually turned out to be different than anyone suspected. This in and of itself wasn't really a problem. The problem came when the system began to break down.

The human soul is indeed an eternal force, transcending all of time and space. Actually, to call the soul human is to demean life, since all living things share the same basic life essence. Every time a soul dies, it is reborn into another living being. In the forgotten mists of time, the reincarnation process turned out to be pretty random. The soul just flitted from some dying creature to a nearby newborn, or waited around until a likely opportunity presented itself.

However, evolution did its work and more and more lifeforms became available. Eventually, truly thinking beings like dolphins, whales, apes, and humans came onto the scene. As their awareness grew, they carried this knowledge with them into the afterlife. Eventually, some of those souls learned to control which body they would be born into, thus ensuring countless lives among the "higher" species. All this was well and good until a few powerful souls learned how to maintain a state of disembodied consciousness, and later, how to control what bodies other souls were reborn into. In effect, this handful of powerful souls became gods.

In a fit of benevolence, these gods decided that they should work to make the world a better place. They would do this by shaping the flow of birth and rebirth in the world. They decided to promote certain souls into sentient bodies over others. At the same time, they decided to make sure that particularly loathsome souls didn't get the chance to become sentient again. Thus, Hitler might be reborn, but only as a particularly racist badger. That was the theory anyway. In practice, it didn't seem to do much good, at least in the grand scheme of things. Humanity kept on basically the same, if not getting worse.

Part of the problem was that the gods themselves did not always agree on what the best course of action was in any given situation. After all, they had all been human once, and still suffered from the same kinds of frailties as humans (no matter how loathe they might be to admit this fact). Over the millennia, there have been fights, disputes, and even outright wars amongst the gods. Most recently, things have gotten much worse. The problem: some of the gods have finally found their way into paradise (heaven, nirvana or what-have-you), and they don't want to share the knowledge with everyone else.

So the gods went to war in earnest and left humanity in the lurch. This might not have been a problem except that the gods left in place their rather arcane system of judging and assigning new bodies to old souls. Now that process has broken down and no one is doing anything to fix it, at least for the moment. As a result, the unthinkable is happening: souls are being reborn into bodies that are already dead.

Soul Train

As if the world weren't crazy enough at the turn of the millennium, now the gods have to go and disappear. The chaos began to set in almost immediately. Not surprisingly, it started in India, always a hotbed for reincarnation. The bodies in the public morgues were the first to rise up and walk out. Dazed, confused, and hungry, the dead killed the few morgue attendees, lurched into the streets, and then dispersed among the population in dead-eyed wonderment.

The zombies did not go on an immediate killing rampage. In fact, for a while, they simply went about business as normal, to a certain extent. They fell into old habits, riding buses, walking streets, and going to work. Soon, however, people started to recognize their dead relatives and friends, especially when they came home to dinner and then tried to eat their own widowed spouses. Over the next few days, the trend spread to the rest of the planet and chaos and terror settled in just as one would imagine.

With dead bodies crawling their way out of graves and morgues all over the world, the U.S. government was surprisingly slow to react. It had a harder time dealing with the panicky living, who either fled or looted the cities in mobs. Unlike in the movies, the zombies did not kill mindlessly, nor did they shamble about slowly. They seemed to have some sort of basic intelligence left over from their living days, including the wherewithal to hide from large troops of soldiers intent on putting a bullet in their brains.

The truth is, the human souls reborn into zombie bodies are still very much aware. Unfortunately, being reborn into a dead body is not like true reincarnation. The cadaver reacts poorly to mental commands, no matter how astute the soul controlling it. The zombies can walk and even run in a shambling way, and can use simple tools that do not require much manual dexterity (like a doorknob or a club). The most significant thing they can't do is talk, at least not to the living. Since their souls have not firmly latched onto the new bodies in the normal manner, they do retain the telepathic ability of disembodied spirits. The zombies can communicate with one another and possibly with human psychics.

The other unfortunate side effect is that they crave the flesh of the living on a daily basis. This craving is irresistible and no matter how repugnant they find it, the zombies eventually give in to the need. The flesh does not have to be human, but it does have to be living and breathing as it is being consumed. Unfortunately, in the feeding frenzy that overcomes a zombie, they often have a hard time distinguishing between old friends and fresh meat.

New zombies are being born all the time. Essentially, whenever any human dies, they are reborn in a nearby dead body within a few hours. As a result, it almost never occurs that a person rises again in the same body they had in their most recent incarnation. There are always several souls waiting in line for the next available corpse. People who die together often end up being reborn in bodies close by, so it is possible for friends to come back and be near their old chums, just with new, undead bodies.

As it turns out, the brain really is the seat of the soul, and thus bodies with severe brain damage do not receive new souls. Likewise, any attack that shatters the integrity of the brain forces the soul right out of the body. Of course, from there it moves on to another dead body if any are available. Otherwise, it might just as well become a gnat, cat, or trout since humans still do get reborn into lower animals on occasion, especially if they've already been reincarnated once as a zombie.

Story Ideas

From the point of view of the living, this story of zombie rebirth is not all that different from the ones already examined. The big change here is that instead of playing humans desperately trying to survive in the face of undead hordes, the Cast Members are the zombies. They get to see what it's like when the shoe's on the other foot. Shotgun crazy humans skilled at head shots try their damnedest to bring the player-zombies down. All the characters can say in protest is "Uuuuuungh" or possibly "Braaaaaiiiiinss."

The Cast Members do have an unfortunate hunger for living flesh, and in fact they must consume at least 10 ounces of live meat every twenty-four hours. After about ten hours without eating, the hunger starts to overcome them and their instincts take over. They do all they can to find food, and after fifteen hours they cannot discriminate between humans and lesser animals when it comes to finding sustenance. With their dulled motor control, the zombies can only use melee weapons effectively, but they can operate simple machinery (driving a car is possible but problematic -- straight lines are okay, but turning tends to be difficult). On the plus side, they do not feel any pain whatsoever and suffer no ill effects from damage anywhere but the brain.

In their fight to survive against marauding bands of soldiers and vigilante citizens, the zombies can communicate with one another and work in concert. Indeed, they will have to if they are going to survive, since everyone knows zombies are at their strongest when in large groups. They must locate zones that are free of the living so they have somewhere safe to hide. Then again, large concentrations of undead become favorite targets for military air strikes.

At some point, the player-zombies might try to find a way to communicate with the living and tell them just what's going on. Unlike most people who get reincarnated, the zombies still have full memories of their most recent past life. They retain their basic language skills, even if they can't talk. They can clumsily type or write if they can get anyone to sit down and read their notes.

Then it's a matter of getting the humans to accept them. After all, the undead don't smell naturally sweet. As noted, they are lousy conversationalists. For some, their eating habits are highly objectionable. Finally, there's nothing more disconcerting than hearing "You've Got Mail" and discovering email from your recently departed cousin Fred.

In time, the dead may find advocates among the breathing humans, someone willing to stand up for living-impaired rights. Alternately, they can decide to just kill all the humans, devour their flesh, and live in a world free of the pesky living.

Character Generation

As might be imagined, no set group of Rebirth into Death Zombie stats exist. Each zombie is as individual as the person who died to give rise to it. Rebirth into Death Zombies are created using the following system.

Players start with the base zombie stats listed in the beginning of Chapter Five: Anatomy of a Zombie (p. 146). The zombie Cast Member is then supplement by 75 character points worth of aspects as detailed in that chapter. For purposes of this character creation, the Power of an aspect is its cost in character points. Note that skills may be purchased (at one point per level), but only after the Long-Term Memory aspect has been paid for. Then again, some of these skills may not be used unless some level of the Tool Use aspect is purchased (e.g., Driving, Electronic Surveillance).

Then, the player may spend 10 character points on Qualities, and may take up to 10 points in Drawbacks. The points granted by Drawbacks may be spent on zombie aspects or other Qualities (or Miracles if Gift and Inspired are purchased -- yes, zombies can be among the ranks of the Inspired).

Appendix

Zombie Comics

Army of Darkness Comic Series (Dark Horse 1992-3)

Dead in the West Comic Series (Dark Horse 1993-4)

Deadworld Comic Series (Arrow Comics 1988)

The Night of the Living Dead Comic Series (FantaCo Enterprises 1991-1993)

The Official Night of the Living Dead Comic Series

Clive Barker's Night of the Living Dead: London
- King of the Dead
- Night of the Living Dead (New Series)
- Legends of the Living Dead

Zombie War (FantaCo Enterprises)
- Zombie War
- Zombie War: Earth Must Be Destroyed
- Zombie War Trading Cards

Zombie World (Dark horse 1997-1998)
- Champion of the Worms
- Home for the Holidays
- Dead End
- Eat Your Heart Out
- Winter's Dregs

Zombie Books

Dawn of the Dead Novel (by George A. Romero and Susanna Sparrow)

The Fog (Written by Dennis Etchison, Based on a motion picture written by John Carpenter and Debra Hill, Bantam Books, Inc. February 1980)

The Mammoth Book of Zombies (Edited by Stephen Jones, Carroll & Graf edition 1993)

Night of the Living Dead Novel (Written by John Russo, First Pocket Books Printing, January 1981; Reprint edition (October 1997))

Resident Evil Novels (Written by S. D. Perry, Capcom, First Printing October 1998)

Return of the Living Dead Novel (Written by John Russo, Dale Books, Inc. First edition, 1978)

The Serpent and the Rainbow (by Wade Davis First Printing, April 1987)

The Ultimate Zombie (Edited by Byron Preiss & John Betancourt, Dell Publishing, October 1993)

Zombie! (by Peter Tremayne)

Zombie Movies
(Listed Alphabetically)

A
The Alchemist, 1981
Alien Dead, 1980
Alien Massacre, 1967
Army of Darkness, 1993
The Astro-Zombies, 1969
Attack of the Beast Creatures, 1985

B
Black Magic II, 1976
Blood Nasty, 1989
The Bloodeaters, 1990
Bloodsuckers from Outer Space, 1986
Bloody New Year, 1987
Bowery at Midnight, 1942
Bride of Re-Animator, 1990
Burial Ground, 1980

C
Cast a Deadly Spell, 1991 TV
Cemetery Man, 1994
Children Shouldn't Play With Dead Things, 1972
The Child, 1977
The Children, 1980
Chillers, 1988
The Chilling, 1989
Chopper Chicks in Zombietown, 1992
City of the Living Dead, 1980
City of the Walking Dead, 1983
Creature of the Walking Dead, 1960
Creature with the Atom Brain, 1955
Curse of the Living Corpse, 1964
Curse of the Living Dead, 1989

D
The Dark Power, 1985
Dawn of the Dead, 1978
Dawn of the Mummy, 1981
The Day It Came to Earth, 1977
Day of the Dead, 1985
Dead Alive, 1992 (aka Braindead)
Dead and Buried, 1981
The Dead Don't Die, 1975
Dead Heat, 1988
Dead Men Don't Die, 1991
The Dead Next Door, 1988
Dead Pit, 1989
Deadly Friend, 1986
Death Becomes Her, 1992
The Death Curse of Tartu, 1966
Deathdream, 1972
Demon Wind, 1990
Devil Kiss, 1977
Doctor Blood's Coffin, 1961

E
The Earth Dies Screaming, 1964
Ed and His Dead Mother, 1993
The Evil Dead, 1982
Evil Dead II, 1987
Evil Town, 1987

F
Flesh Eating Mothers, 1989
Flesh Eater, 1994
From a Whisper to a Scream, 1986

G
Garden of the Dead, 1972
The Ghost Breakers, 1940
The Ghost Brigade, 1993
The Ghoul, 1933
Gore Whore, 1994
The Granny, 1994

H
The Hanging Woman, 1972
Hard Rock Zombies, 1985
Hellgate, 1989
Horror of the Zombies, 1974
House of the Living Dead, 1973

I
I Eat Your Skin, 1964
I Walked with a Zombie, 1943
I Was a Teenage Zombie, 1987
Idle Hands, 1999
The Incredibly Strange Creatures Who Stopped Living and Became Mixed-Up Zombies, 1963
Invasion of the Zombies, 1961
Invisible Invaders, 1959

J
The Jitters, 1988

K
The Killing Box, 1993
King of the Zombies, 1941

M
The Mad Ghoul, 1943
Messiah of Evil, 1974
My Boyfriend's Back, 1993

N
Neon Maniacs, 1986
Night Life, 1990
Night of the Comet, 1984
Night of the Creeps, 1986
Night of the Death Cult, 1975
Night of the Ghouls, 1959
Night of the Living Babes, 1987
Night of the Living Dead, 1968

Night of the Living Dead, 1990
Night of the Living Dead, 25th Anniversary Documentary, 1993
Night of the Zombies, 1981
Night of the Zombies, 1983
Nightmare Weekend, 1986

O

Oasis of the Zombies, 1982

P

Pet Sematary, 1989
Pet Sematary II, 1992
The Plague of the Zombies, 1966
Plan 9 from Outer Space, 1958
Prince of Darkness, 1987
Prison, 1988

Q

Quartermass 2, 1957

R

Raw Force, 1982
Re-Animator, 1985
Redneck Zombies, 1987
Return of the Evil Dead, 1975
Return of the Living Dead, 1985
Return of the Living Dead 2, 1988
Return of the Living Dead 3, 1993
Revenge of the Zombies, 1943
Revolt of the Zombies, 1936

S

Seedpeople, 1992
The Serpent and the Rainbow, 1988
Seven Doors of Death, 1982
Shatter Dead, 1994
Shock Waves, 1977
Sole Survivor, 1984

Steps from Hell, 1992
The Stuff, 1985
Surf 2, 1984

T

Teenage Zombies, 1958
They Saved Hitler's Brain, 1964
Thriller, 1983 (made for video short)
Tomb of the Undead, 1972
Tombs of the Blind Dead, 1972
Torture Chamber of Baron Blood, 1972

V

Vengeance of the Zombies, 1972
Video Dead, 1987
Virgin Among the Living Dead, 1971
Voodoo Man, 1944

W

The Walking Dead, 1936
Weekend at Bernie's II, 1992
White Zombie, 1932

Z

Zombie, 1981
Zombie 4: After Death, 1988
Zombie 90: Extreme Pestilence, 1991
The Zombie Army, 1991
Zombie Creeping Flesh, 1981
Zombie Cop, 1991
Zombie Holocaust, 1979
Zombie Island Massacre, 1984
Zombie Lake, 1984
Zombie Nightmare, 1986
Zombies of Mora Tau, 1957
Zombies of the Stratosphere, 1952
Zombies on Broadway, 1945
Zombie Rampage, 1992
Zombiethon, 1986

French Films
Le Lac des Morts Vivants (Zombie Lake), 1980

German Films
Nur Uber Meine Leiche (Over My Dead Body), 1995

Italian Films
E Tu Vivrai nel Terrore - L'aldila (Seven Doors of Death), 1981
Inferno dei Morti-Viventi (Zombie Creeping Flesh), 1981
Le Notti del Terrore (Zombie 3: Burial Ground), 1980
Le Notti Erotiche dei Morti Viventi (Erotic Nights of the Living Dead), 1979
Paura Nella Citta dei Morti Viventi (Fear in the City of the Living Dead), 1980
Ultimi Zombi, Gli (Zombie 2: The Dead Are Among Us), 1979

Spanish Films
Ataque de los Muertos Sin Ojos (Return of the Evil Dead), 1972
El Buque maldito (The Ghost Galleon), 1974
Fin de Semana para los Muertos (Don't Open the Window), 1974
La Invasion de los Zombies Atomicas (City of the Walking Dead), 1980
La Noche del Terror Ciego (Night of the Blind Dead), 1971
Santo Contra los Zombies (Santo vs. The Zombies), 1961
La Tumba de los Muertos Vivientes (Oasis of the Zombies), 1983

All Flesh Must Be Eaten

Appendix

Glossary

Adversaries: Supporting Cast characters who oppose the Cast Members' actions. Adversaries are the enemies to be beaten, the rivals that provide drama, and the opponents that challenge the players.

Aspect: A feature of a zombie.

Attribute: A physical or mental trait of the character. See Primary Attributes and Secondary Attributes.

Attribute Test: See Test.

Cast Members: Also known as player-controlled characters or player characters (PCs for short). Cast Members are characters whose actions, thoughts and responses are controlled by the players, who usually also create them. In a movie, they would be the main roles, each played by a different actor.

Character Points: The points used to build a character. The specific numbers and categories are dictated by the Character Type, and the Optional Skill Point Generation System, if used.

Character Type: A character's classification. This book presents three Character Types: Norm, Survivor and Inspired.

Close Combat: Any fight conducted at arm's length by people using fists, feet, or hand weapons (such as knives, swords and sticks).

Difficult Test: A Test in which only one Attribute applies and it is not doubled.

Drawback: A special negative aspect of a character that imposes limitations or hindrances. Drawbacks are chosen during character creation and provide extra Attribute, Quality, Skill or Metaphysics Points as the player chooses. No character can take more than 10 points in Drawbacks.

Essence: Beyond matter and energy, Essence is the basic building block of Reality. It is present in all things, living and unliving. It also flows invisibly in pure form, undetected by most living things except on a primal, emotional level. Inspired and others who know the mystic Arts manipulate Essence to change the world.

Experience Points: Points awarded during the play of *All Flesh Must Be Eaten* that may be used to improve a character's capacities.

Game Time: Time as it passes in a game or session of *All Flesh Must Be Eaten*. Game Time rarely corresponds directly with Real Time.

Inspiration: The power to perform Miracles in the service of a Greater Entity.

Inspired: A Character Type -- those with the Power of Inspiration. This Character Type has fewer skills and innate abilities than Survivors, but gains access to Metaphysics.

Initiative: The order in which characters act during Turns. The character with the highest initiative acts first, and the remaining characters act in descending order of initiative. Initiative may be determined by the Zombie Master or through random means.

Metaphysics: Any of a number of supernatural abilities used to manipulate the world. Most use Essence in some manner.

Miracles: A supernatural effect, powered by Essence, caused by the will of an Inspired.

Multiplier: The number by which a set or range of points is multiplied before arriving at the final result.

Norm: A Character Type -- those normal folks who are just trying to survive to tomorrow. Norms are underpowered compared to Survivors and Inspired and should not normally be mixed with those Character Types. Norm campaigns are intended for those who wish to emphasize the horror of *All Flesh Must Be Eaten*.

Outcome Table: Found in Chapter Three: Shambling 101 (p. 95), the Outcome Table specifies the Test or Task results needed to achieve certain Success Levels and the general effects of those Success Levels.

Primary Attribute: The principal numerical measures of a character's physical and mental abilities. There are six Primary Attributes: Strength, Dexterity, Constitution, Intelligence, Perception and Willpower.

Quality: A special positive aspect of a character that grants abilities or benefits. Qualities are purchased by expending Quality Points during character creation.

Ranged Combat: Ranged combat involves any sort of missile weapon, from a thrown stone to a handgun to a machinegun.

Appendix

Real Time: Time as it passes in the "real" world, as opposed to Game Time.

Regular Skill: A basic skill of average difficulty to learn and improve. Most skills in *All Flesh Must Be Eaten* are Regular Skills. Regular Skills cost 1 character point per level until level 5, and 3 points per level thereafter. See Special Skills.

Resisted Tasks or Tests: This rule applies to any situation where someone or something is trying to perform a specific action and somebody or something else is trying to prevent it, as when two or more individuals are in some sort of competition. These Tasks or Tests are resolved normally for everyone involved, and then the results are compared. The character with the highest number of Success Levels wins. Ties go to the defender, if any. If both sides fail, it means neither side won a significant advantage.

Rule of 1: If a natural 1 is rolled, roll again and subtract 5 from the new roll. If the result is greater than 1, consider the final result to be 1. If the result is below 0, replace the result with that negative number. If another 1 is rolled, replace the first roll with -5, and roll again, following the same procedure.

Rule of 10: If a natural 10 is rolled, roll again, subtract 5 from the new roll and add the result, if greater than 1, to the total roll. If another 10 is rolled, add +5 and roll again, following the same procedure.

Secondary Attribute: A physical or metaphysical trait of a character calculated from Primary Attributes. There are four Secondary Attributes: Life Points, Endurance Points, Essence Pool, and Speed.

Simple Test: A Test in which the applicable Attribute is doubled (or two different Attributes are added together).

Skill: A learned capability. Skills are purchased during character creation using Skill Points.

Skill Type: A subgroup of certain broader skills. Skill Types must be chosen when the main skill is purchased. Skill Types do not cost character points. For example, characters must choose a Type when they take the Science Skill. It may be Biology, Chemistry, Geology or any of the other disciplines of Science.

Special Skill: Skills that require additional time or dedication to master. Special Skills cost 2 character points per level until level 5, and 5 points per level thereafter. See Regular Skills.

Specialty: A narrow band of expertise in a larger skill. For example, Humanities (Criminal Law) is a Specialty of the Humanities (Law) Skill. Specialties cost 1 character point each, and add 2 levels to the generic skill level. These additional levels only apply when the character tests the Specialty.

Story: Also known as a game or, sometimes, campaign. A series of plot-linked game sessions, like the episodes of a TV series or soap opera. A good Story is the final result and the ultimate objective of any *All Flesh Must Be Eaten* game.

Success Level: A measure of how well a character performed a successful Task or Test. The higher the Task result, the higher the level of success. Success Levels are used as a bonus on other Tasks or Tests. The Outcome Table (see p. 95) details Success Levels and their effects.

Supporting Cast: Also known as non-player characters (or NPCs). These are all the characters in a game of *All Flesh Must Be Eaten* who are not Cast Members. These roles are played by the Zombie Master.

Survivor: A Character Type -- those most able to stand against the undead hordes. Survivors have more innate abilities and skills than the other Types, but have no supernatural gifts like the Inspired.

Task: A Task is any activity that requires some training to accomplish and whose outcome is in doubt. Tasks are resolved by rolling a ten-sided die and adding one of the character's Skills and one of his Primary Attributes. The Zombie Master determines which abilities apply, and any additional modifiers that are appropriate. The result, adding the die roll to all the other modifiers, skills and Attributes, must be 9 or higher to indicate success. Results higher than 9 are referenced on the Outcome Table (see p. 95 to determine Success Levels.

Tests/Attribute Tests: A Test is an activity or situation where the character's Attribute levels determine the outcome. Any activity that depends exclusively on the character's inborn talents (such as raw strength, pure intelligence and so forth) use Tests. Tests can be Simple or Difficult. A Simple Attribute Test adds the result of a ten-sided die to the appropriate Attribute, doubled, or the sum of two Attributes. The result, after any modifiers, must be 9 or higher. A Difficult Attribute Test adds the result of a ten-sided die to the appropriate Attribute, not doubled. Again, the result, after any modifiers, must be 9 or higher. Results higher than 9 are referenced on the Outcome Table (see p. 95) to determine the Success Levels.

Turn: An arbitrary measure of time designed to break combat and other time-sensitive game play into manageable pieces. A Turn represents between 1 and 5 seconds, and is just long enough for a character to perform one action.

Type: See Skill Type.

Zombie Master: Also known as a Game Master or Referee, the Zombie Master is the player who prepares the setting, guides the game, roleplays the Supporting Cast and Adversaries, and makes all the rules decisions.

Character Creation Table

The following costs are applicable only during character generation. After a campaign has started, the character improves using the Experience Point Cost Table.

Buying Primary Attributes: Each level of an Attribute costs 1 point until level 5, and 3 points per level thereafter. Humans can only buy Attributes up to level 6.

Calculating Secondary Attributes: Life Points: ((Constitution + Strength) x 4) + 10. Endurance Points: ((Constitution + Strength + Willpower) x 3) + 5. Speed: (Constitution + Dexterity) x 2. Essence Pool: Add the character's Primary Attributes together.

Buying Qualities and Acquiring Drawbacks: Qualities have different point costs, which are listed under each entry. When a Drawback is acquired, the character gains extra points in either the Attributes, Qualities, Skills or Metaphysics categories. The one limitation is that Drawback Points equal to the new Attribute level must be spent when raising Attributes with Drawback Points. This is cumulative.

Buying Skills: Regular Skills cost 1 point per level until level 5, and 3 points per level thereafter. Special skills cost 2 points per level until level 5, and 5 points per level thereafter. Specialties cost 1 point and add 2 to the base skill level.

Buying Inspired Miracles: Each Inspired Miracle costs 5 points to acquire (see p. 64).

Character Type Reference Table

Type	Attr Pts	Qual/Draw Pts	Skill Pts	Meta Pts
Inspired	20	10/10	25	15
Traits: Must purchase Gift and Inspiration Qualities (10)				
Norm	14	5/10	30	0
Traits: May not purchase certain Supernatural Qualities or Metaphysics				
Survivor	20	15/10	35	0
Traits: May not purchase certain Supernatural Qualities or Metaphysics.				

All Flesh Must Be Eaten

Quality and Drawback List by Category

Name	Cost/Type	Page
Mental		
Addiction	Variable Drawback	36
Artistic Talent	3-point Quality	37
Charisma	Variable Quality or Drawback (1 point/level)	38
Clown	1-point Drawback	38
Covetous	1- to 3-point Drawback	39
Cowardly	1- to 3-point Drawback	40
Cruel	1- or 3-point Drawback	40
Delusions	Variable Drawback	41
Emotional Problems	Variable Drawback	41
Fast Reaction Time	2-point Quality	42
Honorable	1- to 3-point Drawback	43
Humorless	1-point Drawback	43
Lazy	2-point Drawback	43
Nerves of Steel	3-point Quality	44
Obsession	2-point Drawback	44
Paranoid	2-point Drawback	44
Photographic Memory	2-point Quality	44
Reckless	2-point Drawback	45
Recurring Nightmares	1-point Drawback	45
Showoff	2-point Drawback	46
Situational Awareness	2-point Quality	46
Talentless	2-point Drawback	47
Zealot	3-point Drawback	47
Physical		
Acute/Impaired Senses	2-point Quality or Drawback	36
Attractiveness	Variable Quality or Drawback (1 point/level)	38
Hard to Kill	1 to 5-point Quality	42
Physical Disability	Variable Drawback	45
Resistance	Variable Quality	45
Social		
Adversary	Variable Drawback	37
Contacts	Variable Quality	39
Minority	1-point Drawback	44
Multiple Identities	2 points/Identity Quality	44
Resources	Variable Quality or Drawback (2 points/level)	46
Secret	Variable Drawback	46
Status	Variable Quality or Drawback (1 point/level)	46
Supernatural		
Accursed	Variable Drawback	47
Gift	5-point Quality	48
Good Luck/Bad Luck	1 points/level Quality or Drawback	48
Increased Essence Pool	1/5-point Quality	48
Inspiration	5-point Quality	49
Old Soul	4 points/level Quality	49

Appendix

Skill List

Skill	Type	Page	Skill	Type	Page
Acrobatics	Special	51	Mechanic	Regular	57
Acting	Regular	51	Medicine (Type)	Special	57
Beautician	Regular	52	Myth and Legend (Type)	Regular	57
Brawling	Regular	52	Notice	Regular	57
Bureaucracy	Regular	52	Occult Knowledge	Special	57
Cheating	Regular	52	Pick Pocket	Regular	58
Climbing	Regular	52	Piloting (Type)	Regular	58
Computer Hacking	Regular	52	Play Instrument (Type)	Regular	58
Computer Programming	Regular	53	Questioning	Regular	58
Computers	Regular	53	Research/Investigation	Regular	58
Craft (Type)	Regular	53	Riding (Type)	Regular	58
Dancing (Type)	Regular	53	Rituals (Type)	Regular	58
Demolitions	Regular	53	Running (Type)	Regular	59
Disguise	Regular	53	Sciences (Type)	Regular	59
Dodge	Regular	53	Seduction	Regular	59
Driving (Type)	Regular	53	Singing	Regular	59
Electronic Surveillance	Regular	53	Sleight of Hand	Regular	59
Electronics	Regular	54	Smooth Talking	Regular	59
Engineer (Type)	Regular	54	Sport (Type)	Regular	59
Escapism	Regular	54	Stealth	Regular	60
Fine Arts (Type)	Regular	54	Storytelling	Regular	60
First Aid	Regular	54	Streetwise	Regular	60
Gambling	Regular	54	Surveillance	Regular	60
Guns (Type)	Regular	55	Survival (Type)	Regular	60
Haggling	Regular	55	Swimming	Regular	60
Hand Weapon (Type)	Regular	55	Throwing	Regular	61
Humanities (Type)	Regular	55	Tracking	Regular	61
Instruction	Regular	56	Trance	Special	61
Intimidation	Regular	56	Traps	Regular	61
Language (Type)	Regular	56	Uncon Medicine (Type)	Regular	61
Lock Picking (Type)	Regular	56	Veterinary Medicine	Regular	61
Martial Arts	Special	56	Weight Lifting	Regular	61
			Writing (Type)	Regular	61

R: Regular **S:** Special

Appendix 222

All Flesh Must Be Eaten
Zombie Power List

Category	Name	Power	Page
The Weak Spot			
	All	0	148
	None	10	148
	Brain	6	148
	Heart	7	148
	Spine	5	148
	Fire	-5	148
	Chemicals	Varies	149
	Blessed Objects	Varies	149
Getting Around			
	Slow and Steady	0	150
	Life-Like	3	150
	The Quick Dead	10	150
	Burrowing	3	150
	Leaping	3	150
	The Lunge	3	150
	Aquatic	2	151
	Climbing	2	151
Strength			
	Ninety-Pound	-3	151
	Dead Joe Average	0	151
	Strong Like Bull	5	151
	Monstrous Strength	10	151
	Damage Resistant	5	151
	Flame Resistant	1/3	151
	Iron Grip	1	152
	Claws	8	152
	Teeth	4	152
	The Hug of Death	8	152
Senses			
	Like the Dead	0	152
	Like the Living	1	152
	Like a Hawk	2	153
	Like Nothing Seen	10	153
	X-ray Vision	Px2	153

Category	Name	Power	Page
	Life Sense	Px2	153
	Scent Tracking	P	154
	Infravision	P	154
Sustenance (Need to Feed)			
	Daily	0	154
	Occasionally	2	154
	Weekly	4	154
	Who Needs Food?	8	154
Sustenance (The Menu)			
	All Flesh Must Be Eaten	0	155
	Braiiiiins	-3	155
	Sweet Breads	-3	155
	Blood	-2	155
	Soul Sucker	5	155
Intelligence			
	Dumb As Dead Wood	0	155
	Language	1	156
	Tool Use	3/level	156
	Animal Cunning	2/4	156
	Teamwork	4	156
	Long-term Memory	5	156
	Problem Solving	15	156
Spreading the Love			
	Only the Dead	-2	157
	One Bite Hooked	2	157
	Bury the Body	-2	157
Special			
	Acid Blood	Varies	158
	Diseased Corpse	3	158
	Noxious Odor	5	158
	Nest	Varies	158
	Spitter	Varies	158
	Spew Flame	Varies	158
	Detachable Parts	Varies	159
	Explosive Personality	2/5	159
	Regeneration	2/5	159

Appendix

AFMBE Conversion Modern

This tree is a gateway. A gateway between two worlds!
—*Sleepy Hollow*

Conversion notes by Daniel R. Davis and M. Alexander Jurkat

These pages are indeed a gateway of sorts. Though they do not connect two worlds, they do connect two game systems. The following pages present methods for converting game stats from the *All Flesh Must Be Eaten* (*AFMBE*) roleplaying game to the popular modern day roleplaying game that features twenty-sided dice ( ). Indeed, there are new and interesting rules to use in any setting. It is a good idea to read through the rest of the book before using these rules to get a feel for the game in general and to become familiar with the rules that are referenced here.

Before We Begin . . .

A few rules differences should be mentioned before going on with the conversions. These are small matters for the most part, but they may cause some confusion if not addressed.

Open Game Content

All Flesh Must Be Eaten, AFMBE, **Unisystem**, *Armageddon, Terra Primate, WitchCraft*, Power, Power Points, and all graphic content are designated Product Identity pursuant to the Open Game License. Otherwise, this appendix text is Open Game Content.

Unisystem

AFMBE uses a set of rule mechanics called the **Unisystem**. The conversion notes here will work for *AFMBE* and, in general, any of its sister **Unisystem** games (*Armageddon, Terra Primate, WitchCraft*).

Turns or Rounds

In the **Unisystem**, a Turn is approximately five seconds of combat or activity. In , a round is approximately six seconds. Any time the word *Turn* is used in a **Unisystem** book it is essentially the same as a *round* of combat or activity in .

Appendix 224

Simple or Difficult Tests

The **Unisystem** often uses Simple and Difficult Tests. For purposes of the [d20] conversion treat any Simple Test as a check with a DC 10 and any Difficult Test as one with a DC 15. Any time Willpower Tests are mentioned use the Will save based on the DC indicated (e.g., Difficult = DC 15). If Dexterity Tests are required, use a Reflex save at the appropriate DC. Any Constitution Tests or Survival rolls would be done using a Fortitude save. Any Test that requires the addition of two Attributes is considered a Simple Test (DC 10), using the most appropriate ability modifiers or save for the circumstance.

Characters

AFMBE is set in the real world . . . well, as real as one with zombies and people who perform miracles regularly. Otherwise, there are no magical and mystical races. The people in *AFMBE* are of three types: Norms, Survivors, and Inspired.

In some instances, the Zombie Master (ZM) might limit a player's choices. For instance, the ZM may want to run a game where horror and ingenuity are the main focus. In this case he may dictate that the only type available is the Norm. Or perhaps the ZM decides to run a game where there are no such things as Miracles. In this case he may decide that only Survivors or Norms may be used. In the end, it all depends on the game world the ZM decides upon.

Norms are everyday people. They are just like most people in the world. These are the people who are usually depicted in horror movies, barely surviving in the end. Then, they come back in the sequel and die at the hands of the creature they thought was gone for good. But by then there's a new ingénue . . .

Survivors are more like the action-hero types. These people usually have dangerous or heroic lines of work. Survivors have an amazing habit of surviving impossible odds (that's why they are called "Survivors"). Survivors are closest to the usual Heroes in [d20].

Inspired are those who have found a Higher Power, whatever it may be. They are priests and wicca, shamans, and acolytes. These people can do things that most people today would consider Miracles. The Inspired type is a little Survivor and a little Norm with some miraculous powers thrown in for good measure.

AFMBE does not use the usual fantasy character races or classes. However, ZMs may allow other races or classes from such games if they wish. There should be no need to adjust them as far as game mechanics go, but they will change the character of any *AFMBE* campaign.

When creating a character, it is best to use the Standard Point Buy method. Characters created in this manner are closer to the characters that are normally found in the *AFMBE* settings. The Die Roll method can be used, but characters created in this manner will have higher ability scores than standard *AFMBE* characters, generally speaking.

Norms

Norms are under-powered compared to the usual [d20] character classes. Their attributes should be determined using the Planned Generation method or the Standard Point Buy method. Norms have 15 points to allocate (low-powered campaign) rather than the usual 25. Also, they are granted one less feat than other characters. Their Hit Die is one step lower than a normal [d20] class (e.g., a class that has a d10 Hit Die would have a d8 Hit Die as a Norm) to a minimum of d4.

Norms progress up levels and gain benefits as regular [d20] characters, but cannot multi-class until reaching third level. This is due to their need to actively learn and grow physically, mentally, and spiritually.

Survivors

Survivors are created just like regular [d20] character classes. The most applicable is the Tough Hero, but any may be used.

Inspired

Inspired characters should be made, for the most part, with the Dedicated Hero Class due to their devotion to a philosophy or belief in a higher power. Inspired characters in *AFMBE* possess the ability to perform Miracles. This means they are allowed a certain number of spells per day as a cleric or other divine spellcaster class. Inspired characters do not get Domain spells or abilities.

Qualities and Drawbacks

In the **Unisystem**, Qualities are special benefits the characters possess and Drawbacks are disadvantages or negative traits. The nearest comparable feature of [AFMBE] is feats. Conversion notes from Qualities to feats are discussed below. All these feats are Extraordinary abilities, unless otherwise stated.

Drawbacks from the **Unisystem** have been recast as nega-feats for the [AFMBE] system. Nega-feats allow a character to start with additional feats or talents, depending upon how much the nega-feat is worth.

One Quality does not conform well to the feat mechanic and has been converted into a Talent Tree that can be added to any class or taken as a replacement for the usual class talents available (see p. 230).

From Qualities to Feats

Acute Senses (see p. 36)
Benefit: Characters with this feat gain a +3 circumstance bonus on any checks involving one of the five basic senses (touch, taste, sight, smell, hearing). This feat must be taken separately for each sense to be heightened. Such bonuses might apply to checks for Spot, Listen, Search, and skills involving the identification of poisons, liquids, or substances.

Artistic Talent (see p. 37)
Benefit: This feat works as stated with a couple of exceptions. First, no Essence is gained for taking the Artistic Talent feat. Also, the character gains a +3 circumstance bonus on any rolls for creating a work of art in the style chosen. The DC for the creation of a Masterwork item, provided it is in the field the character has Artistic Talent, is five points lower.

Attractiveness (positive levels, see p. 38)
Benefit: Grants the character a +3 circumstance bonus on any Charisma-modified checks where the character's looks could play a role. Unlike the **Unisystem** Quality, this feat can only be taken once.

Contacts (see p. 39)
Benefit: This is treated as the Contact class feature of the Investigator advanced class. It may be taken multiple times and each costs a feat or talent slot. It is available to any class or profession.

Good Luck (see p. 48)
Benefit: Each time the Good Luck feat is taken it adds one extra Action Point to the character's pool and an additional Action Point per level. This feat may be taken more than once and the bonuses stack.

Fast Reaction Time (see p. 42)
Benefit: This feat gives the character a +3 circumstance bonus on Initiative checks. It also grants a +1 circumstance bonus to Will saves involving fear. This feat does not stack with other feats granting bonuses to Initiative.

Nerves of Steel (see p. 44)
Benefit: The character is immune to all but the most horrid or supernatural fear. When forced to make a Fear check, she gains a +4 circumstance bonus to any Will save.

Old Soul (see p. 49)
Benefit: This feat can only be taken during character creation and takes up two feat slots. When it is taken the character's Wisdom ability increases by one. When tapping into a past life to gain insight or skill that he may not ordinarily possess, the character must make a Concentration check at DC 10 (with any appropriate penalties for distraction). If successful, he may make an unskilled attempt at any skill with a rank equal to his Wisdom bonus (the Wisdom or other ability bonus is added to these ranks as usual), with a minimum bonus of +1. This is a Supernatural ability and works even with trained-only or restricted skills.

Photographic Memory (see p. 44)
Benefit: This feat works exactly as discussed, with the same bonus levels.

Resources (positive levels, see p. 46)
Benefit: This feat works like the Windfall feat in [AFMBE] for positive levels.

Situational Awareness (see p. 46)
Benefit: This feat works exactly as discussed.

Status (see p. 46)
Benefit: This is treated as the Renown feat except it may be taken multiple times and its benefits stack.

Appendix 226

Nega-feats

Drawbacks are a very important feature of **Unisystem** character creation. Everyone has a few foibles and problems that they deal with on a day-to-day basis. For *AFMBE* characters, Drawbacks are replaced by nega-feats. Nega-feats affect a character adversely and as recompense, additional feat or talent slots are provided. Some nega-feats are only worth a half-feat slot while particularly debilitating nega-feats may provide as many as two feat slots. Nega-feats can also be given to a character during game play, but do not grant any additional feats or talents in that case.

> ### Game Balance
>
> Feats are an important and powerful feature of the modern system. As nega-feats allow characters to gain more feats, they may cause some imbalance compared to regularly constructed modern characters. Further, certain feats are required by some prestige classes, and the additional feats granted may allow those classes to become available sooner than expected. For these reasons, GMs are cautioned to use nega-feats carefully and adjust the feat slots they grant depending on the particulars of their campaigns.

Accursed (see p. 47)

Penalty: There are three levels to this nega-feat. The first level is Minor and is worth a half-feat slot. The second level is Moderate and is worth one feat slot. The third is Severe and is worth one and a half-feat slots. ZMs are encouraged to make life difficult for the character who is Accursed.

Addiction (see p. 36)

Penalty: This nega-feat comes in three levels of severity. The first level is a Mild Addiction and is worth a half-feat slot. Mild Addictions are anything from habitual to heavy drinking or smoking, to light or occasional use of marijuana or other "less dangerous" drugs. Those with a Mild Addiction suffer a -2 penalty to most mental actions requiring Intelligence or Wisdom if they do not have their regular "fix." The second level of severity is Moderate and is worth one feat slot. Moderate Addictions are anything from heavy use of marijuana or LSD, to full alcoholism or habitual use of barbiturates or cocaine. Those with a Moderate Addiction suffer a -4 penalty to most mental actions requiring Intelligence or Wisdom if they do not get their regular fix (and a -2 penalty when "high"). The third level of severity is an Extreme Addiction and is worth two feat slots. This is anything from habitual to heavy use of heroin to heavy use of barbiturates or cocaine. Those suffering from an Extreme Addiction not only suffer -6 to most mental actions requiring Intelligence or Wisdom, but also suffer -4 to all physical actions due to illness, fatigue and withdrawal. Further, when they get their fix, they are severely disadvantaged (-4 to all actions) due to the "high."

Overcoming an Addiction should be difficult and must be roleplayed during the course of an adventure. A character must make a Will save every day (DC 10 for Mild, DC 15 for Moderate, and DC 20 for Extreme) with a penalty equal to the mental action penalty for the Addiction. When a character has accumulated 20 successes in a row, the Addiction drops by one level in severity (i.e., Extreme becomes Moderate, Moderate becomes Mild, Mild becomes cured). If any save is failed, all accumulated successes are lost and the count must start anew. Keep in mind that while a character is going through "detox," he still suffers the penalties for not having his fix.

Adversary (see p. 37)

Penalty: Adversaries come in all shapes and sizes. For this reason, the Adversary nega-feat can be taken at one of three levels. The first level denotes a person or organization roughly as powerful as the character (Minor). This level is worth a half-feat slot. The second level would be a person or organization roughly three Encounter Levels higher than the character (Moderate). This level is worth one feat slot. The third level would be a person or organization roughly five Encounter Levels higher than the character and is worth two feat slots (Major). If the Adversary does not show up on a regular basis (roughly every three sessions or so), the value of the nega-feat goes down one level. Thus, a Major Adversary that only shows up occasionally and is not a huge thorn in the character's side would only be worth one feat slot. The player and ZM should get together to design an appropriate Adversary for the character.

Attractiveness (negative levels, see p. 38)

Penalty: Negative Attractiveness is treated as a nega-feat. The character incurs a -3 penalty on any Charisma-based checks where the character's looks could play a role. Unlike the **Unisystem** Drawback, this feat cannot be taken more than once.

Bad Luck (see p. 48)

Penalty: Each level of Bad Luck is worth one feat slot and removes one Action Point from the character's pool. The character also gains one less Action Point per level for each level of Bad Luck possessed. This nega-feat may be taken multiple times and the penalties stack.

Clown (see p. 38)

Penalty: This nega-feat works as discussed and is worth a half-feat slot.

Covetous (see p. 39)

Penalty: There are three levels of the Covetous nega-feat, each with its own penalties. The first level is Mild and requires a DC 10 Will save anytime the character wishes to stray from her professed goal. The Mild level is worth a half-feat slot. The second level is Moderate and requires a DC 15 Will save in similar circumstances. The Moderate level is worth one feat slot. The third level is Severe and characters must make a DC 20 Will save in similar circumstances. The Severe level is worth one and a half-feat slots. If the Will save is failed, the compulsion is so strong that it dictates the character's actions. If the player can adequately explain how any given action comports with her Covetous goals, she does not need to roll a Will save.

Cowardly (see p. 40)

Penalty: The Cowardly nega-feat has three levels of severity. The first level is Mild and requires a DC 10 Will save to go against the character's cowardly nature. The Mild level is worth a half-feat slot. The second level is Moderate and requires a DC 15 Will save in similar circumstances. The Moderate level is worth one feat slot. The third level is Severe and the character must make a DC 20 Will save in similar circumstances. The Severe level is worth one and a half-feat slots.

Cruel (see p. 40)

Penalty: There are two levels to the Cruel nega-feat. The first level is worth a half-feat slot. Some who have heard of the character's exploits (a successful Reputation check) may react to them negatively (25% chance, depending upon the circumstances that the character will be viewed as Infamous). The second level is worth one feat slot and most that have heard of the character's exploits (a successful Reputation check) may react to them negatively (50% chance, depending upon the circumstances that the character will be viewed as Infamous).

Delusions (see p. 41)

Penalty: There are many different types of Delusions and each has two levels: Mild and Severe. Mild delusions are worth a half-feat slot and are generally harmless. These impose a -2 reaction penalty on any NPC Reaction checks if the NPC has seen the Delusion in action. The second level is worth one feat slot and is usually more dangerous. These impose a -4 reaction penalty on any NPC Reaction checks if the NPC has seen the Delusion in action.

Emotional Problems (see p. 41)

Penalty: Each emotional problem is worth a half-feat slot. These problems, as well as their cures, must be roleplayed.

Honorable (see p. 43)

Penalty: There are three levels of Honor. Level 1 is worth a half-feat slot, Level 2 is worth one feat slot, and Level 3 is worth one and a half-feat slots. This nega-feat works exactly as described.

Humorless (see p. 43)

Penalty: This nega-feat works as described and is worth a half-feat slot.

Impaired Senses (see p. 36)

Penalty: Characters with this nega-feat suffer a -3 penalty on any checks involving one of the five basic senses (touch, taste, sight, smell, hearing). This nega-feat is taken separately for each impaired sense. Such penalties might be applied to checks for Spot, Listen, Search, and skills involving the identification of poisons, liquids, or substances.

Lazy (see p. 43)

Penalty: This nega-feat doubles the cost of skill ranks purchased after the ranks total half of the associated ability score for class skills, and one-quarter the associated ability score for cross-class skills. Lazy is worth one feat slot.

Minority (see p. 44)

Penalty: This nega-feat is worth a half-feat slot. ZMs may raise the value to one feat slot if members of that minority are treated particularly badly.

Obsession (see p. 44)

Penalty: This nega-feat works as described and is worth a half-feat slot.

Paranoid (see p. 44)

Penalty: This nega-feat works as described and is worth a half-feat slot.

Physical Disability (see p. 45)

Penalty: This nega-feat works as described. The value of each one is as follows:

Missing or crippled arm/hand: half-feat slot.

Missing or crippled leg/foot: one feat slot.

Missing or crippled arms: one and a half-feat slots.

Missing or crippled legs: one and a half-feat slots.

Paraplegic: two feat slots.

Reckless (see p. 45)

Penalty: This nega-feat works as described and is worth a half-feat slot.

Recurring Nightmares (see p. 45)

Penalty: This nega-feat works as described and is worth a half-feat slot. The day after a night in which the character suffers from a recurring nightmare, he incurs a -2 on all attacks and checks due to mental drain. If the character suffers nightmares two nights in a row, he becomes fatigued.

Resources (negative levels, see p. 46)

Decrease the character's Wealth bonus by -3 each time this nega-feat is taken. Each level is worth one feat slot.

Secret (see p. 46)

Penalty: There are three levels to this nega-feat. The first level is Minor and is worth a half-feat slot. The second level is Moderate and is worth one feat slot. The third is Severe and is worth one and a half-feat slots. ZMs are encouraged to make life difficult for the character living with a secret.

Showoff (see p. 46)

Penalty: This nega-feat works as described and is worth a half-feat slot.

Talentless (see p. 47)

Penalty: Talentless works much like described with one exception. No matter how successful the check is, the result is still only mediocre. A Talentless character can never make masterwork items. A character cannot have both Artistic Talent and Talentless. This nega-feat is worth a one feat slot.

Zealot (see p. 47)

Penalty: This nega-feat works as described and is worth a half-feat slot.

Removing Nega-Feats

Nega-feats may be lost during game play. ZMs are encouraged to only allow the removal of nega-feats through roleplaying and character growth. However, other methods include buying off a nega-feat with a feat slot or talent allowance gained through experience. Another method allows the player to sacrifice experience point gains to remove a nega-feat. Consult the table for the actual cost to remove.

Nega-Feat Value	Experience Points
Half-feat slot	1,000
One-feat slot	3,000
One-and-a-half-feat slot	5,000
Two-feat slot	7,000

Optional Talent Tree

The following talent tree may be taken by any character class as a replacement for a normal talent choice.

Hardened Talent Tree

Hard to Kill: Each time this Talent is purchased, the character adds the roll of his best class HD type to his hit points.

Other Feats

There are a number of *AFMBE* skills that just do not exist in the system. These skills become feats according to the following list.

AFMBE Skill	Feat
Brawling	Brawl
Dodge	Dodge or Defensive Martial Arts
Guns	Personal Firearms Proficiency or Exotic Firearms Proficiency
Hand Weapon	Simple Weapons Proficiency or Archaic Weapons Proficiency
Martial Arts	Combat Martial Arts
Running	Endurance
Throwing	Simple Weapon Proficiency
Track	Track

Skill Similarities

There are many skills in *AFMBE* that have equivalents in ⬡. They are listed below.

AFMBE Skill	⬡ Skill	*AFMBE* Skill	⬡ Skill
Acrobatics	Balance or Tumble	Medicine	Profession or Treat Injury
Acting	Craft (visual arts) or Perform	Myth and Legend	Knowledge (theology and philosophy)
Beautician	Profession	Notice	Listen, Spot or Search
Bureaucracy	Knowledge (business or civics)	Occult Knowledge	Spellcraft or Knowledge (arcane lore)
Cheating	Bluff or Sense Motive	Pick Pocket	Sleight of Hand
Climbing	Climb	Piloting	Navigate or Pilot
Computer Programming	Computer Use	Play Instrument	Perform
Computer Hacking	Computer Use	Questioning	Sense Motive
Computers	Computer Use	Research/Investigation	Gather Information, Investigate or Research
Craft	Craft	Riding	Ride
Dancing	Perform	Rituals	Knowledge (arcane lore)
Demolitions	Demolitions	Sciences	Craft (chemical) or Knowledge (earth and life sciences or physical sciences)
Disguise	Disguise		
Driving	Drive		
Electronic Surveillance	Craft (electronic) or Computer Use	Seduction	Sense Motive
		Singing	Perform
Electronics	Craft (electronic), Profession or Repair	Sleight of Hand	Perform
		Smooth Talking	Bluff or Diplomacy
Engineer	Knowledge (physical sciences or technology)	Sport	Knowledge (art) or Profession
Escapism	Escape Artist	Stealth	Hide or Move Silently
Fine Arts	Perform	Storytelling	Perform
First Aid	Treat Injury	Streetwise	Gather Information
Gambling	Gamble	Surveillance	Hide
Haggling	Sense Motive	Survival	Survival
Humanities	Knowledge (art, behavioral sciences, business, civics, current events, history, popular culture, or theology and philosophy)	Swimming	Swim
		Tracking	Survival
		Traps	Craft (electronic or mechanical), Disable Device or Survival
Instruction	Profession		
Intimidation	Intimidate	Unconventional Medicine	Knowledge (earth and life sciences) or Profession
Language	Read/Write Language or Speak Language	Veterinary Medicine	Knowledge (earth and life sciences) or Profession
Lock Picking	Disable Device		
Mechanic	Craft (mechanical), Profession or Repair	Writing	Craft (writing)

Appendix

Trance

The Trance Skill from *AFMBE* becomes a feat in 🎲. The character must succeed in a Concentration check (minimum DC 10) to benefit from the trance. External factors can affect the DC, like loud distraction, combat, and other annoyances. If the roll is successful the feat grants the same benefits as the **Unisystem** skill (see p. 61).

Weight Lifting

The Weight Lifting skill in *AFMBE* requires some special rules in the 🎲 format. Whenever a character needs to make a Strength check to lift heavy objects, she may add her Weight Lifting ranks to her roll. Keep in mind however, that being able to lift heavy objects is quite different from being able to do anything with the object other than carry it around slowly. The ZM is the final arbiter on the difficulty and how much weight is too much, however, a good rule of thumb is +5 DC for every 50 pounds over two times the character's max load. The penalties for carrying two times the max load still apply.

> ### Skill Ranks
>
> As the modern system uses a 20-sided die and the Unisystem uses a 10-sided die, a rough comparison can be set by equating one level in a Unisystem skill to two levels in a comparable modern skill. But this equation ignores character balance within the modern system. Our recommendation is to determine the level equivalence of the Unisystem character to be converted (see p. 236) and from there, determine how many modern skill points she has to allocate. Then scatter those skill points among the converted skills as desired. That ensures the proper allocation of skill ranks for the modern system.

Optional Rules

All of the following rules can be used in any 🎲 setting as an interesting change of pace, but are not essential for the use of this conversion. Use all, some or none, as desired.

Alternate Skill Methods

Some players may want to continue to use *AFMBE* skills that normally become feats in the 🎲 rules. Here are some suggestions.

Martial Arts: Martial Arts is a Special Skill in the **Unisystem** and could be treated as a cross-class skill in a 🎲 setting. It works in all respects as the description on p. 56. So, if a character has three ranks of Martial Arts skill his punches and kicks do three more points of damage than normal. A character with Martial Arts 3 and Strength 14 punches for 1d3 + 5 (two for the Strength modifier and three for the Martial Arts bonus).

Weapon Skills: Weapons skills from *AFMBE* remain the same with one exception. The character's Base Attack Bonus equals the appropriate Weapon Skill - 2. Thus, a character with four ranks of Guns (Handgun) skill would have a Base Attack Bonus of +2 with handguns. The Attack Bonuses on the character class table are ignored under this rule. Weapon Proficiency feats are no longer necessary. The character gains additional attacks in the same manner as normal in the 🎲 rules. Thus, at +6 he gains an additional attack at +1. If his weapon skill goes up at that point, he would have +7/+2. On the downside, players must keep track of separate attack bonuses for each weapon skill category. Brawling would also work in this manner, but only for unarmed combat. For conversions from 🎲 to **Unisystem**, simply grant four skill points for each Weapon Proficiency feat the character possesses. However, these points must be split up among as many Hand Weapon/Gun skills as possible.

Dodge: Using a Dodge skill does not eliminate the desirability of the Dodge feat. When a character attempts to dodge, she rolls a d20 + Dodge Ranks + Dexterity modifier against a DC 5. For each five points over the DC she achieves, she gains a +1 on her Defense. So, if a character with two ranks of

Dodge skill and Dexterity 14 rolls 10, she adds a +2 onto her Defense to avoid the blow. If the character had rolled a 16, she would add +4 to her Defense. If the ZM wishes, this maneuver can be simplified by allowing only one Dodge check against all attacks in the round. The Dodge skill is considered a cross-class skill due to the difficulty in reading and judging an attacker's movements during a combat situation.

Alternate Movement Rate

Not all characters move at the same rate. To determine the movement rate of a converted character, add her **Unisystem** Dexterity and Constitution together and multiply by two (the result is the character's mile per hour movement). Then consult the Movement Rate table nearby. For example, a character with Dexterity 4 and Constitution 3 could travel at 14 mph, and would have a speed of 30 ft.

Movement Rate

Unisystem	mph	
2		5 ft
4		10 ft
6		15 ft
8		20 ft
10		25 ft
12		27 ft
14		30 ft
16		35 ft
18		40 ft
20		45 ft
22		50 ft
24		55 ft

Miracles

Miracles are a big part of the Inspired character's capabilities. They are mystical powers that come from her faith in a belief system. Miracles become divine spells in the system and their mechanics are detailed below.

Miracles should only be available for use against supernatural forces or when the Inspired or another's life is in great peril. The ZM is the final judge on whether a Miracle can be used in certain situations. The Lord (whoever that may be) works in mysterious ways and may not feel that using a Miracle is necessary to accomplish a task.

Divine Blessing

Enchantment

Level: Insp 1, Clr 1
Components: V, S
Casting Time: 1 action
Range: Touch
Target: 1 creature or item
Duration: Until used
Saving Throw: Will negates
Spell Resistance: Yes (harmless)

This spell allows the caster to imbue a target with a luck bonus of +1 per two levels of the caster starting at first level (e.g., 1st/+1; 3rd/+2; 5th/+3) to a maximum of +5. The recipient can use this luck bonus as an attack or a skill check bonus. If the Blessing is used on an item, it can be used in the same way by the wielder of the item. Some supernatural creatures are particularly susceptible to blessed weapons (zombies, ghosts, and the like). In that case, this bonus applies not only to the attack roll, but also to damage. An item blessed in this manner is treated as magical against creatures that can only be hit by magical weapons. The recipient can hold the bonus until needed, but the Inspired loses the spell slot until the bonus is used. A Blessed holy symbol may make certain supernatural creatures recoil in fear from the mere sight of it (Will save DC 10 + caster level). Using the holy symbol in this manner does not discharge the magic.

The Binding

Enchantment (Compulsion)

Level: Insp 1, Clr 1

Components: V, S

Casting Time: 1 action

Range: Medium (100 +10 ft./level)

Target: 1 supernatural creature or zombie +1 additional per Wisdom bonus

Duration: 1 round +1 per Wisdom bonus

Saving Throw: Will negates

Spell Resistance: Yes

This spell binds zombies or other supernatural creatures temporarily in place. If the being is not truly evil as dictated by the Inspired's religion, the creature has a +2 bonus to resist the spell.

Divine Sight

Divination

Level: Insp 3, Clr 3

Components: V, S

Casting Time: 1 action

Range: Personal

Target: You

Duration: 1 minute/level

Saving Throw: None/Special

Spell Resistance: Yes

The spell functions exactly like Divine Sight (see p. 64). The spell does not allow the caster to detect magically hidden doors or to see through illusions (unless those illusions are specifically masking the appearance of a humanoid or supernatural being). It also does not confer the ability to see through normal or magical darkness, nor will it see through any magic that protects from scrying or mental probing. However, such protections can be perceived by the divine sight spell. *Divine sight* works to a range of 120 ft. from the caster.

The Touch of Healing

Conjuration (Healing)

Level: Insp 1, Clr 1

Components: V, S

Casting Time: 1 action

Range: Touch

Target: Creature touched

Duration: Instantaneous

Saving Throw: None

Spell Resistance: Yes (harmless)

The spell functions a little differently the more powerful the Inspired gets. Beginning at first level the Inspired can cure 1d4 damage +1 per caster level. When the Inspired reaches 3rd level, he can cure mild diseases or purge mild poisons or narcotics using *the touch of healing*. At 5th level, the caster can cure moderate diseases or purge moderate poisons or narcotics. At 7th level, the caster can cure serious diseases or purge serious poisons or narcotics. At 10th level, the caster can cure terminal diseases. The Inspired can only do one type of cure per application of the spell (i.e., damage, disease, poison). *The touch of healing* may only be used under extraordinary circumstances and is generally only used on the faithful.

Holy Fire

Evocation

Level: Insp 1, Clr 3

Components: V, S

Casting Time: 1 Action

Range: Long (400 ft. + 40 ft./level)

Target: 1 target

Duration: Instantaneous

Saving Throw: Reflex half

Spell Resistance: Yes

If bards are part of an AFMBE campaign, they may roll a Use Magic Device skill check at DC 20 + the level of the caster to mask the bard's true nature from *divine sight*. However, the bard must first be aware that the spell is being used.

The exact form the spell takes depends on the Inspired's preference or belief system. It could appear as a column of fire, a bolt of lightning from the heavens, a ray of sunlight, or a giant foot coming from above to squash the target. Inspired can use this spell at first level to cause 1d6 damage. At second level, the caster can do either 1d6 or 2d6 at their option. Once the Inspired has reached third level, the spell can fill either a 1st-level spell slot (doing 1d6 or 2d6 damage) or a 2nd-level spell slot (doing 3d6 damage). At fourth level, the caster can do up to 4d6 with the 2nd-level spell slot. A 5th-level Inspired has the added option to insert the spell into 3rd-level spell slot (doing 5d6 damage). After that level, the spell increases by 1d6 per caster level but must fill a 3rd-level spell slot if used to cause more than 4d6 damage. The spell only damages evil outsiders and the undead.

Strength of Ten

This spell is essentially the same as the *bull's strength* spell.

Visions

The Visions Miracle converts to a supernatural feat. The possessor of the feat must roll a successful Concentration check at DC 15 (plus penalties for distractions) to gain divine insight as described in the Miracle (see p. 65). ZMs can visit divine visions upon the character at any time, even if the character was not actively seeking guidance.

The Power of Prayer

In some *AFMBE* settings, Prayer can benefit any type of character. The character must roll a successful Knowledge (theology or rituals) check at a base DC 15 with the bonuses or penalties as discussed on p. 66. If successful, the character receives +1 bonus to any one skill check or attack roll (not damage) plus an additional +1 for every five points that the roll exceeded the DC, as long as the roll contributes to the survival or advancement of the faithful.

Conversions

Some players may wish to convert existing *AFMBE* characters into [d20] or vice-versa. Below is a system for doing so.

Attributes and Abilities

The basic capacities of a character are called Attributes in the **Unisystem** and abilities in [d20]. The tables below show the correspondence between Attributes and abilities.

Abilities to Attributes

[d20]	Unisystem
Strength	Strength
Dexterity	Dexterity
Constitution	Constitution
Intelligence	Intelligence
Wisdom+Intelligence/2 (round down)	Perception
Wisdom+Charisma/2 (round down)	Willpower

Attributes to Abilities

Unisystem	[d20]
Strength	Strength
Dexterity	Dexterity
Constitution	Constitution
Intelligence	Intelligence
Perception+Willpower/2 (round down)	Wisdom
Strength+Constitution+Intelligence/3 (round down)	Charisma

Once the proper calculations are made, apply the numbers to the table below to convert scales. For example, a character with Intelligence 4 in **Unisystem** would have Intelligence 14 in [d20], and vice-versa. A **Unisystem** character with a Perception 3 and Willpower 2 would have Wisdom 10 in [d20].

Attributes/Abilities Correspondence

[d20]	Unisystem
1-3	-2
4-6	-1
7-8	0
9	1
10-11	2
12-13	3
14-15	4
16-17	5
18-19	6
20-21	7
22-23	8
24-25	9
26-27	10
28-29	11
30-31	12
+2	+1

What Level Am I?

The **Unisystem** does not use levels, so this aspect of the conversion to [d20] is at best an estimate. The easiest method for figuring out what level the character would begin at is by looking at each individual character and his Attributes and abilities and comparing them to the class that most fits the character. This material uses the Police Officer (see p. 74) to walk players through the process of conversion.

First things first. Take each of the **Unisystem** character's Attributes and convert them to abilities. The Police Officer Attributes come out something like this: Str 12, Dex 10, Con 14, Int 12, Wis 14, Chr 12.

Next, choose the most appropriate class and profession for the character. The Police Officer best fits the Tough Hero class and the Law Enforcement occupation.

Next total up how many feat slots and talents the character possesses. Start with the **Unisystem** character's Qualities and Drawbacks. You may also need to look at the character's skills, as some skills become feats in [d20].

Applying the materials already discussed, the Police Officer has two new feats (Nerves of Steel and Situational Awareness). The Hand Weapon (Club) skill transfers over to the free Simple Weapon Proficiency feat that all Tough Heroes begin with. The Police Officer has two Gun skills that transfer into the Personal Firearms Proficiency feat that can be taken with the Law Enforcement Profession. The Police Officer also has the Dodge skill, which is a feat in *Modern*. Finally, the Brawling skill becomes the Simple Weapon Proficiency feat. So, the feats that the Police Officer possesses are: Simple Weapon Proficiency (gained from Tough Hero Class), Personal Firearms Proficiency (gained from Law Enforcement Profession), Nerves of Steel (starting feat), Situational Awareness (starting feat), and Dodge (level dependent).

The Police Officer has Contacts per the Investigator special feature but available to any class as a feat or talent. He also has the Hard to Kill talent. So, our Police Officer takes the following as talents: Contacts and Hard to Kill.

At this point we can see that the converted Police Officer should be at least 3rd level, since he has one extra talent and one extra feat. Now that a definitive level is known, the rest of the character is built using the rules in the description of the class, with skills, hit points, BAB, RAB, Defense and Reputation bonuses. All **Unisystem** skills must be changed to their *Modern* equivalents and at least one *Modern* skill point should be spent in each (this provides the player with an opportunity to rearrange skill ranks as desired). Speed becomes 30 ft. unless the ZM is using the Alternate Movement Rate rules (see p. 233).

Although there are some judgement calls and detective work in converting a **Unisystem** character, it will become easier with practice. No conversion is 100% infallible and all should be passed by the ZM before play begins. Keep in mind when converting Norms that they begin the game with lower abilities and feats than normal Hero classes. Also, all Inspired should be converted into the Dedicated Hero class.

Combat

Weapons

Specific weapons and firearms are detailed in *Modern* and *AFMBE*. Simply use the proper stats depending on the game system employed.

> To account for the more deadly tone of AFMBE (as befits a game about survival horror), ZMs may wish to incorporate AFMBE's damage-doubling rule for slashing and stabbing/piercing weapons (se p. 105). Of course, this does not apply to damage against zombies.

Armor

Equivalents between **Unisystem** armors and *Modern* armors are presented below.

Unisystem	*Modern*
Light	
Padded/Quilted Cloth Armor	Padded Armor
Leather Jacket	Leather Jacket
Leather Armor	Leather Armor
Class I	Undercover Vest
Leather Helmet	Armor Bonus: +1 (head only); Armor Pen. 0 (Perception-based skills)
Helmet	Armor Bonus: Class I +2; Class II +3; Class III +4; Class IV +5 (head only); Armor Pen. -2 (Perception-based skills)

Unisystem

Medium

Metal Helmet	Armor Bonus: +3 (head only); Armor Pen. -2 (Perception-based skills)
Chain Mail	Chainmail
Class IIa	Concealable Vest
Class II	Light Duty Vest
Class IIIa	Tactical Vest

Heavy

Plate and Mail	Half-Plate
Plate Armor	Full-Plate
Class III	Special Response Vest
Class IV	Forced Entry Unit

Shields

Riot Shield	Large Shield

Bullet Type Effects

A few bullet types are detailed here, as well as their effects on their target. More information on these bullet types can be found on p. 105.

Normal Bullets: These bullets are standard rounds and do the listed damage for each firearm.

Hollow-Point: Increase the equipment bonus of any armor worn or the hardness of an item (round down) by half (multiply by 1.5) to determine if the target takes damage. If the target is damaged, treat the attack roll as a threat and roll again for a critical hit. For example, a standard breastplate has a normal AC bonus of +5. Against hollow-point bullets it would have an AC bonus of +7 instead.

Armor-Piercing: Halve the equipment bonus of any armor worn or the hardness of objects (round down). A critical hit requires two successive natural 20 rolls regardless of the normal threat range of the firearm.

Shotgun Rounds: Slugs do the listed damage for the shotgun and hollow-point slugs work the same as hollow-point bullets above. Buckshot has a +1 to hit a target due to the spread, but armor is more effective against it (multiply equipment bonus or item hardness by 1.5). Birdshot is even better at striking the target and grants a +2 to the attack roll. However, the equipment bonus of any armor or the hardness of an object is doubled against birdshot.

Called Shots

In *AFMBE*, hitting a zombie in a specific location could mean the difference between having lunch and being lunch. Thus, the following called shot rules should be applied in an *AFMBE* game. Damage to zombie extremities follows the rules on p. 147.

Head: -4 to attack roll. Successful hit results in a threat.

Neck/Throat: -5 to hit. Successful hit results in a threat.

Arms/Legs: -2 to hit. If the attack does one third of the target's total hp in one shot, the victim must make a Fort save at DC 10 or the limb is crippled. Any extra damage beyond that is lost. Additional strikes against the same area impose a cummulative -5 to the Fort save DC.

Hand/Wrist/Foot/Ankle: -4 to hit. If the attack does one quarter of the target's total hp in one shot, the victim must make a Fort save at DC 10 or the extremity is crippled. Any extra damage beyond that is lost. Additional strikes against the same area impose a cummulative -5 to the Fort save DC.

Vital Points (heart, lungs, spine, kidneys, etc): -2 to hit (due to their propensity to mass together in one torso). Damage is normal, but the target suffers the effects of a bleeding wound. He takes an additional one hp of damage per round until the wound has been stabilized with a Heal/First Aid check. The additional damage is due to the puncture of a vital organ.

The Smell of Fear

Fear plays a huge part in any survival horror game. Being hunted by hordes of shambling undead really gets the fear response going. Whenever a character is confronted with a frightful situation, a Fear check (Will save) is required. For Norms and Survivors, the DC is 15; for Inspired it is DC 10. The ZM can set a penalty to the roll depending on how bad the cause of the Fear check is. See Fear Modifiers on p. 96 for some suggestions.

If the Fear check is failed, compare the result to the Fear Table on p. 97. The first Success Level on the Fear Table is the base failure. For each five point difference between the roll and the DC, move to the next level on the Fear Table. As always, the ZM can modify events if the table result would be inappropriate to the situation. Instead of Essence, the character who fails the Fear check loses the equivalent amount in temporary Wisdom. This temporary drop returns as normal for temporary ability loss once the character is far, far away from the cause of the fright.

Zombie Conversion

Now for the tasty sweet breads of the whole conversion section—the zombies! Those players who are not familiar with the *AFMBE* settings should look over the zombie Aspect section beginning on p. 146 before attempting to play Frankenstein with these rules, as only the conversion notes are provided here. If an Aspect is not mentioned, it can be used without conversion concerns at the same Power as indicated. Also added here are conversions of the Aspects in the *AFMBE Zombie Master's Screen*.

Base Zombie

The base *AFMBE* zombie has the following stats.

Medium-size Undead
Hit Die: 2d12 (13 hp; Mas —)
Initiative: -1 (-1 Dex)
Speed: 10 ft.
Defense: 9 (-1 Dex)
  Touch: 9 (-1 Dex)
  Flatfooted: 9 (-1 Dex)
Base Attack Bonus: +0
Grapple: +1

Attack: +1 melee (1d6+1 bite),
             +1 unarmed (1d6+1 slam)
Fighting Space: 5 ft. by 5 ft.
Reach: 5 ft.
Special Qualities: Undead, partial actions only
Saves: Fort +0, Ref -1, Will +2
Abilities: Str 13, Dex 8, Con —, Int 1, Wis 9, Cha 1
Skills: —
Feats: Brawl

Aspects
Weak Spot: All
Getting Around: Slow and Steady
Strength: Dead Joe Average
Senses: Like the Dead
Sustenance: Daily; All Flesh Must Be Eaten
Intelligence: Dumb as Dead Wood
Spreading the Love: Only the Dead
CR: 1/4

This base zombie may be modified in a number of areas as detailed in the rest of the chapter. Each Aspect has a listed Power Point modifier. Once the various Aspects have been chosen total all Power Point modifiers and consult the table nearby to determine the CR modifier. Combine that modifier with the base zombie's CR of 1/4 to get the final CR of the newly constructed zombie.

Additional Power	CR Modifier
1-10	—
11-20	1/4
21-40	1/2
41-60	3/4
61-80	1
81-95	2
96-110	3

Each additional +1 CR gained by the zombie translates into +1 HD and additional hit points (but only if the All Weak Spot is chosen; hit points do not increase for other Weak Spot zombies).

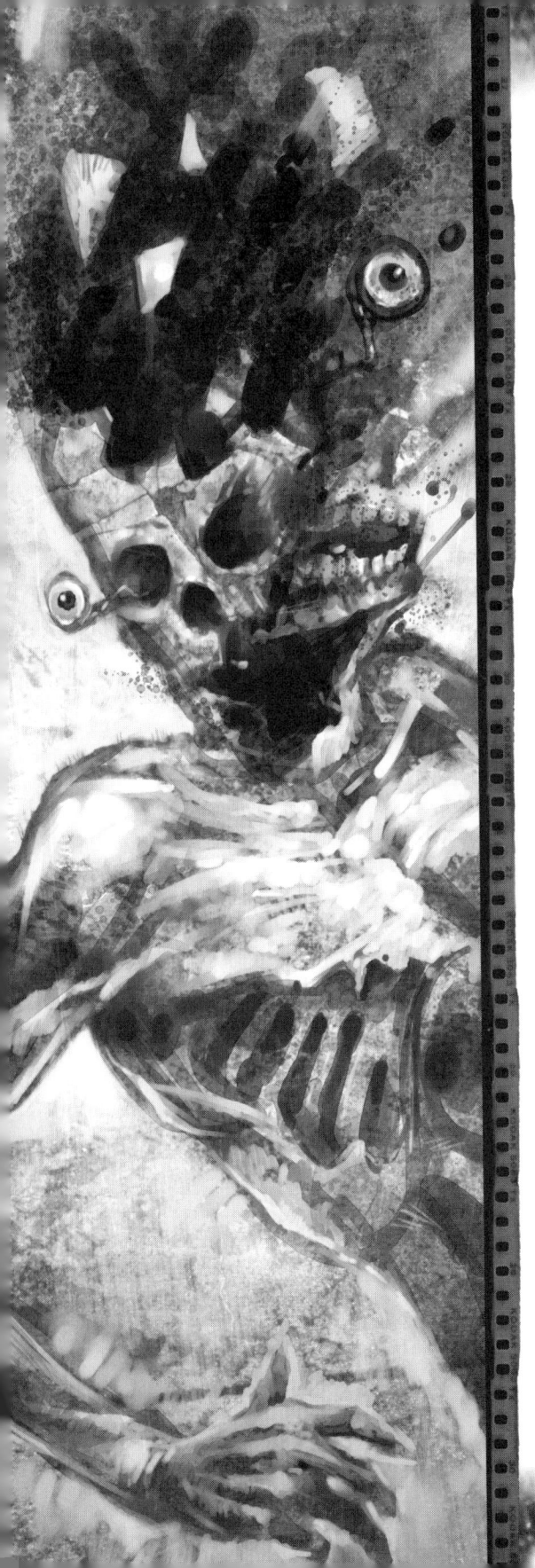

Zombies are always more dangerous in numbers. The Challenge Rating of a group of zombies is determined normally for those of CR 1 or greater. For those less than CR one, add sufficient zombies to get a group equal to CR 1. Then total such groups as normal. For example, four base zombies would have a CR 1. Eight base zombies would be treated as two CR 1 creatures.

Classes

If the proper cognitive Aspects are possessed (Long-term Memory, Problem Solving, Language), a zombie may be given any class level. The level provides regular benefits for that class, except for skill points which are gained as for an additional level (not x4). Each class level adds +1 to the zombie's CR.

Skills and Feats

Zombies can be assigned feats and skills outside of gaining a class level and each adds a certain amount of Power onto the zombie. Every two skill ranks that the zombie possesses adds +1 power. Each physically oriented feat or talent increases the zombie's power by +5. Keep in mind that a zombie cannot have any feats that would rely on cognizant thought processes without possessing the Problem Solving Aspect. Zombies with that Aspect can take mentally oriented feats at +3 power. Likewise, a zombie cannot normally possess skills unless it has the Long-Term Memory Aspect.

Zombies with both cognitive Aspects may possess all the skills, feats, and talents they enjoyed while alive, and all should be calculated into the zombie's total Power.

Zombies and Saves

Zombies follow the rules for Undead and Fort saves for the most part. However, depending on the Deadworld chosen, not all zombies are created by a spell caster. Indeed, many are accidents or the product of an environmental change. When the zombie has no caster level due to not being raised by a spell caster, the bonus to its Fort save is determined by its HD and/or level. The basic zombie above is considered a second-level creature.

Weak Spot

Some zombies need to be struck in a specific portion of the body to destroy them. Others can be taken out by hitting them anywhere (see pp. 148-149).

None   Power: +10

The zombie may only be stopped or destroyed as specified on p. 147. Additional HD add d12 hit points to the 100/200 hit point thresholds set in the main text.

Brain   Power: +6

Requires an attack roll at -5 to hit the brainpan. Hit points are 15.

Heart   Power: +7

Requires an attack roll at -6 to get to the heart of the matter. Hit points are 15.

Spine   Power: +5

Requires an attack roll at -4 to strike the spine from the rear, -5 when attacking from the front. Hit points are 15.

Fire   Power: -5

Zombies take double damage from fire-based attacks. Another Weak Spot must be chosen to give the zombie specific hit points. If Weak Spot (None) is chosen, the rules for Other Damage on page 147 still apply, but fire does double the damage it would normally do.

Chemicals   Power: Varies

Works like Weak Spot (Fire) above. If the chemicals do not normally do damage to flesh, they cause d6 points of damage per round. The Power of this Aspect varies from -1 to -10 depending on the range of effective chemicals, their destructiveness, their availability and the difficulty of the delivery method.

Blessed Objects   Power: Varies

Works like Weak Spot (Fire) above. The Power of this Aspect varies from -1 to -10 depending on the range of the blessed objects, their destructiveness, their availability and the difficulty of the delivery method.

Vulnerability   Power: Varies
(ZM Screen Aspect)

A zombie that has a Vulnerability to a substance takes one point of damage per round of contact. Like all Undead, zombies normally do not suffer from critical strikes. However, a vulnerable zombie that is struck by a weapon made of the appropriate substance will suffer a critical hit normally. Also, the threat range of a weapon made of the substance is increased by one. For example, a pistol bullet made of the substance will affect the zombie with a threat range of 19-20 instead of 20. The Power varies from -1 to -3 with the availability of the substance.

Getting Around

How does the zombie get around? These conversions create zombies that will be able to shamble into any system game (see p. 150-151).

Slow and Steady   Power: 0

Dexterity 8; Defense 9; partial actions only; movement 10 ft.

Life-Like   Power: +3

Dexterity 10 (or 11); Defense 10; partial actions only; movement 20 ft.

The Quick Dead   Power: +10

Dexterity 12 (or 13); Defense 11; movement 40 ft.

The Lunge   Power: +3

When the zombie is within 10 ft. of a target, it can lunge forward in a flash, catching its prey flat-footed and negating any attacks of opportunity. Due to this feral, hunger-induced speed they also gain a +2 to Initiative in close combat.

Aquatic   Power: +2

Gains two ranks in the Swimming skill. Underwater movement is 10 ft.

Climbing   Power: +2

Gains two Ranks in the Climb skill. Climbing movement is 3 ft.

Strength

These Aspects are used to determine the physical strength of the zombie (see p. 151-152).

Ninety-Pound Weakling   Power: -1

Strength is 9; melee attack modifier/damage modifier -1

Dead Joe Average   Power: 0

Strength is 13; melee attack modifier/damage modifier +1

Strong Like Bull   Power: +5

Strength is 15; melee attack modifier/damage modifier +2

Monstrous Strength   Power: +10

Strength is 21; melee attack modifier/damage modifier +5

Iron Grip   Power: +1

The zombie gains a grapple check modifier of +9.

Claws   Power: +8

Damage is d8 plus Strength modifiers; armor bonuses are halved. May be combined with bite attack if zombie is capable of full attack.

Teeth   Power: +4

A successful bite attack is followed by a grapple check. The zombie gains a grapple check modifier of +9. Bite damage is d8 per round as long as grapple is maintained.

The Hug of Death   Power: +8

The zombie gains a grapple check modifier of +9. Damage is d4 + 8 per round as long as grapple is maintained.

Senses

Even zombies need to sense their prey. These Aspects allow the zombie to see, smell, or hear its food source (see pp. 152-154).

Like the Dead   Power: 0

Wisdom 8 (or 9); -1 modifier to perception-based checks, including those like Search which are not normally modified by Wisdom.

Like the Living   Power: +1

Wisdom 10 (or 11); no special modifier to perception-based checks, including those like Search which are not normally modified by Wisdom.

Like a Hawk   Power: +2

Wisdom 12 (or 13); +1 modifier to perception-based checks, including those like Search which are not normally modified by Wisdom.

Like Nothing You've Ever Seen   Power: +10

Wisdom 21; +5 modifier to all perception-based checks, including those like Search which are not normally modified by Wisdom.

X-Ray Vision   Power: +2/+4/+6/+14

Power and distance depends upon the zombie's Wisdom. 8-9 = 30 ft.; 10-11 = 60 ft.; 12-13 = 90 ft.; 20-21 = 140 ft.

Life Sense   Power: +2/+4/+6/+14

Power and distance depends upon the zombie's Wisdom. 8-9 = 30 ft.; 10-11 = 60 ft.; 12-13 = 90 ft.; 20-21 = 140 ft.

Scent Tracking   Power: +1/+2/+3/+7

Grants the zombie the Scent (Ex) Special Quality with a +5 modifier to track by scent. The cost depends upon the zombie's Wisdom.

Infravision   Power: +2/+4/+6/+14

Distance and power depend upon zombie's Wisdom. 8-9 = 30 ft.; 10-11 = 60 ft.; 12-13 = 90 ft.; 20-21 = 140 ft.

Sustenance

Zombies are (or is that were?) what they eat. What does the zombie eat and how often (see p. 154-155)?

Soul Sucker   Power: +5

Grants the zombie the Energy Drain (Su) Special Quality. A zombie bestows one negative level per successful attack, or one negative level per round if a grapple is maintained. Each negative level imposed counts as two ounces of food for purposes of the starvation rules (see p. 154).

Intelligence

These Aspects make zombies much more dangerous (see pp. 156-157).

Dumb as Dead Wood   Power: 0

Intelligence 1.

Language   Power: +1

The zombie gains the ability to speak one language common to the area in which it is found each time this Aspect is taken.

Tool Use   Power: +3 per level

Intelligence 9. Level one grants the Simple Weapon Proficiency feat. Level two grants the Personal Firearm Proficiency feat.

Animal Cunning   Power: +2/+4

Intelligence 7 for +2 Power; Intelligence 9 for +4 power. Zombie gains one rank in Hide, Intimidate, Listen, Move Silently, Search, and Spot skills. Additional ranks may be purchased at an increase in the zombie's power of one each.

Long-Term Memory   Power: +5

Intelligence 11 (no language). Zombie gains the ability to purchase ranks in any skill. Each rank so purchased increases the zombie's Power by one.

Problem Solving   Power: +15

Intelligence 11 (no language or memory). Allows the purchase of any feat, at an increase in the zombie's Power of three each. A zombie must have both Long-Term Memory and Problem Solving to have full mental capabilities.

Special Features

Just when you thought the zombie couldn't get any more tougher, these features give the zombie an extra surprise punch that can really throw a PC's entire day out of whack (see pp. 158-159). Some of the Special Features listed here require a save. The save DC can be calculated using the regular Monster Abilities formula, unless a DC is already given.

Acid Blood   Power: Varies

Acid does double the Power in hit point damage per round of exposure. A character who hits the zombie may make a Reflex save for half damage but the DC is 15 due to the close proximity. Whether this avoidance attempt is successful or not, the character suffers a -2 penalty on his next attack roll (not cumulative).

Items worn by the victim may be damaged by the acidic blood. Clothes are burned through automatically. Armor and other more sturdy items must make a Fortitude save using the victim's Fortitude modifier. If the save is failed the item deteriorates. Armor drops one point from its equipment bonus, weapons take damage directly to their hit points and may break easier in combat. Magic items, armor, or weapons do not need to save.

Diseased Corpse   Power: Varies

Base Power level is 1/2 of the DC of the required Fort save. Add +3 if delivery method is inhaled. Add +3 if effects are potentially permanent.

Noxious Odor   Power: +5

Requires Fort save at DC 20.

Nest   Power: Varies

Creatures do damage per round equal to the Power chosen. The creatures ignore armor.

Spitter   Power: Varies

Range equals half Strength in feet (no increments). The zombie must succeed in only a ranged touch attack, due to proximity to the target and the splatter effect. Spit does damage equal to half the Power chosen, and burns for d6 rounds unless it is washed off or neutralized. A Reflex save by the victim results in half damage.

Spew Flame   Power: Varies

The zombie must succeed in a ranged touch attack to hit and the target may make a Reflex save to avoid the damage, unless he is grappled or otherwise unable to move out of the way. Range is equal to Strength in feet (no increments). Flame does damage equal to the Power chosen.

Explosive Personality Power: +2/+5

Damage is d6 to all those in the explosion radius. This Aspect requires a Fear check at -4 for those who witness it.

Regeneration Power: +2/+5

At the lower level, one hit point is regained per minute. At the higher level, one hit point is regained per round.

Vomit Power: Varies
(ZM Screen Aspect)

Zombie must succeed in a touch attack to hit and target may make a Reflex save to avoid the damage, unless she is grappled or otherwise unable to move out of the way. Range is equal to Strength in feet (no increments). Damage is equal to double the Power chosen. The vomit continues to burn the victim for d6 rounds unless it is quickly washed off or neutralized.

New Special Features

Natural Armor Power: +3 per level

There's nothing tackier than seeing a zombie in heavy armor. Some zombies have gotten around this problem by simply becoming physically tougher. It might be skin that has dried to the consistency of hardened leather or some strange serum or power of unknown origin that has caused the skin of the zombie to become resistant to harm. Each level of Power grants the zombie a +1 Defense bonus to a maximum of +8.

Willful Power: +5

Sometimes zombies just aren't very religious and no amount of shouting and gesturing by priests will get them to behave. Zombies with this Aspect are not subject to being turned or rebuked by anything but the most powerful artifacts.

Example Time

And now, for the coup de grace, let's make a zombie. Starting with the basic zombie (CR 1/4), we add in one level of the Toughness feat. The zombie can take this at +5 Power since it is a physical feat. Then, we purchase two levels of the Natural Armor Aspect for +6 Power. Lastly, the Like the Living Aspect is added, which raises the zombie's Wisdom. That leaves us with a close approximation of the familiar Medium-sized zombie everyone knows and loves. The additions add 12 Power and add 1/4 to the CR (making the final zombie a 1/2 CR creature).

Medium-Size Undead

Hit Die: 2d12+3 (16 hp; Mas —)

Initiative: -1 (-1 Dex)

Spd: 10 ft.

Defense: 11 (-1 Dex, +2 natural)
   Touch: 9 (-1 Dex)
   Flatfooted: 11 (-1 Dex, +2 natural)

BAB: +1

Grapple: +1

Attack: +1 melee (1d6+1 bite), +1 unarmed (1d6+1 slam)

Fighting Space: 5 ft. by 5 ft.

Reach: 5 ft.

Special Qualities: Undead, move or attack action only

Saves: Fort +0, Ref -1, Will +3

Abilities: Str 13, Dex 8, Con —, Int 1, Wis 10, Cha 1

Skills: None

Feats: Brawl, Toughness (+5)

Special Qualities

Weak Spot: All

Getting Around: Slow and Steady

Strength: Dead Joe Average

Senses: Like the Living (+1)

Sustenance: Daily; All Flesh Must Be Eaten

Intelligence: Dumb as Dead Wood

Spreading the Love: Only the Dead

Special Features: Natural Armor 2 (+6)

Additional Power: 12

CR: 1/2

OPEN GAME LICENSE Version 1.0a

The following text is the property of Wizards of the Coast, Inc. and is Copyright 2000 Wizards of the Coast, Inc ("Wizards"). All Rights Reserved.

1. Definitions: (a)"Contributors" means the copyright and/or trademark owners who have contributed Open Game Content; (b)"Derivative Material" means copyrighted material including derivative works and translations (including into other computer languages), potation, modification, correction, addition, extension, upgrade, improvement, compilation, abridgment or other form in which an existing work may be recast, transformed or adapted; (c) "Distribute" means to reproduce, license, rent, lease, sell, broadcast, publicly display, transmit or otherwise distribute; (d)"Open Game Content" means the game mechanic and includes the methods, procedures, processes and routines to the extent such content does not embody the Product Identity and is an enhancement over the prior art and any additional content clearly identified as Open Game Content by the Contributor, and means any work covered by this License, including translations and derivative works under copyright law, but specifically excludes Product Identity. (e) "Product Identity" means product and product line names, logos and identifying marks including trade dress; artifacts; creatures characters; stories, storylines, plots, thematic elements, dialogue, incidents, language, artwork, symbols, designs, depictions, likenesses, formats, poses, concepts, themes and graphic, photographic and other visual or audio representations; names and descriptions of characters, spells, enchantments, personalities, teams, personas, likenesses and special abilities; places, locations, environments, creatures, equipment, magical or supernatural abilities or effects, logos, symbols, or graphic designs; and any other trademark or registered trademark clearly identified as Product identity by the owner of the Product Identity, and which specifically excludes the Open Game Content; (f) "Trademark" means the logos, names, mark, sign, motto, designs that are used by a Contributor to identify itself or its products or the associated products contributed to the Open Game License by the Contributor (g) "Use", "Used" or "Using" means to use, Distribute, copy, edit, format, modify, translate and otherwise create Derivative Material of Open Game Content. (h) "You" or "Your" means the licensee in terms of this agreement.

2. The License: This License applies to any Open Game Content that contains a notice indicating that the Open Game Content may only be Used under and in terms of this License. You must affix such a notice to any Open Game Content that you Use. No terms may be added to or subtracted from this License except as described by the License itself. No other terms or conditions may be applied to any Open Game Content distributed using this License.

3. Offer and Acceptance: By Using the Open Game Content You indicate Your acceptance of the terms of this License.

4. Grant and Consideration: In consideration for agreeing to use this License, the Contributors grant You a perpetual, worldwide, royalty-free, non-exclusive license with the exact terms of this License to Use, the Open Game Content.

5. Representation of Authority to Contribute: If You are contributing original material as Open Game Content, You represent that Your Contributions are Your original creation and/or You have sufficient rights to grant the rights conveyed by this License.

6. Notice of License Copyright: You must update the COPYRIGHT NOTICE portion of this License to include the exact text of the COPYRIGHT NOTICE of any Open Game Content You are copying, modifying or distributing, and You must add the title, the copyright date, and the copyright holder's name to the COPYRIGHT NOTICE of any original Open Game Content you Distribute.

7. Use of Product Identity: You agree not to Use any Product Identity, including as an indication as to compatibility, except as expressly licensed in another, independent Agreement with the owner of each element of that Product Identity. You agree not to indicate compatibility or co-adaptability with any Trademark or Registered Trademark in conjunction with a work containing Open Game Content except as expressly licensed in another, independent Agreement with the owner of such Trademark or Registered Trademark. The use of any Product Identity in Open Game Content does not constitute a challenge to the ownership of that Product Identity. The owner of any Product Identity used in Open Game Content shall retain all rights, title and interest in and to that Product Identity.

8. Identification: If you distribute Open Game Content You must clearly indicate which portions of the work that you are distributing are Open Game Content.

9. Updating the License: Wizards or its designated Agents may publish updated versions of this License. You may use any authorized version of this License to copy, modify and distribute any Open Game Content originally distributed under any version of this License.

10 Copy of this License: You MUST include a copy of this License with every copy of the Open Game Content You Distribute.

11. Use of Contributor Credits: You may not market or advertise the Open Game Content using the name of any Contributor unless You have written permission from the Contributor to do so.

12 Inability to Comply: If it is impossible for You to comply with any of the terms of this License with respect to some or all of the Open Game Content due to statute, judicial order, or governmental regulation then You may not Use any Open Game Material so affected.

13 Termination: This License will terminate automatically if You fail to comply with all terms herein and fail to cure such breach within 30 days of becoming aware of the breach. All sublicenses shall survive the termination of this License.

14 Reformation: If any provision of this License is held to be unenforceable, such provision shall be reformed only to the extent necessary to make it enforceable.

15 COPYRIGHT NOTICE

Open Game License v 1.0 Copyright 2000, Wizards of the Coast, Inc.

Modern System Reference Document Copyright 2002, Wizards of the Coast, Inc.; Authors Bill Slavicsek, Jeff Grubb, Rich Redman, Charles Ryan, based on material by Jonathan Tweet, Monte Cook, Skip Williams, Richard Baker, Peter Adkison, Bruce R. Cordell, John Tynes, Andy Collins, and JD Wiker.

AFMBE Conversion Copyright 2002, Eden Studios, Inc.

Index

Archtypes..27,68-79
   Athlete..68
   Biker..69
   Cheerleader...70
   Detective...71
   Goth Chick..72
   Hacker...73
   Police Officer..74
   Priest...75
   Reporter..76
   Scientist..77
   Soldier/SWAT..78
   Video Store Clerk...79
Attributes...30-34
   Buying..30
   Constitution...31
   Dexterity..31
   Endurance Points..34
   Essence Pools..34
   Intelligence..31
   Life Points...33
   Meaning of the Numbers.................................31
   Perception...31
   Secondary..33
   Speed..34
   Strength...30
   Willpower..31
Character Creation.......................................27-67
   Archtypes..27,68-79
   Attributes..30-34
   Character Elements..27
   Character Type..27-28
   Finish Touches...67
   Metaphysics..62-66
   Possessions..67
   Qualities & Drawbacks...............................35-47
   Skills..51-61
   Supernatural Qualities & Drawbacks..........47-50
Character Type...27-28
   Norm...28
   Survivors..28
   Inspired..28
Combat...98-105
   Actions, Intentions...99
   Actions, Multiple...100
   Actions, Performance....................................100
   Armor..109-110
   Close Combat..100
   Damage..103
   Improvised Weapons......................................101
   Initiative..99
   Injury...111-112
   Ranged Combat......................................101-103
   Recuperation..113
   Special Weapon Types..................................105
   Turns...98
Damage..103-114
   Disease...108
   Endurance Loss..114
   Essence...114
   Injury...111-112
   Other Sources of Injury.................................108
   Poison...106-107
   Recuperation..113
   Special Weapon Damage..............................105
   Supernatural Healing and Poisons...............108
Deadworlds..164-213
   After the Bomb.....................................192-195
   Dawn of the Zombie Lords...................206-209
   Dead at 1000...196-201
   Grave Impact...174-177
   Mein Zombie...188-191
   PHADE to Black..................................170-173
   Rebirth Into Death................................210-213
   Rise of the Walking Dead....................164-169
   Sacred Soil..178-181
   They Came From Beyond....................182-186
   Until the Ending of the World.............202-205
Equipment..126-141
   Bartering...127
   Body Armor...138
   Close Combat Weapons........................132-133
   Electronic Gear.......................................127,128
   Explosive Area of Effect...............................136
   Explosive Damage...137
   Explosive Weapons................................136-137
   Medical Gear..127,128
   Miscellaneous Equipment......................127,131
   Ranged Weapons...................................134-135
   Scientific Equipment.............................127,129
   Surveillance Equipment..................127,129-130
   Survival Gear..127,130-131
   Vehicles...139-141
Experience..118-119
   Awarding..118
   Improving Characters...........................118-119

Appendix

Fear 96
Game Mechanics 90-96
   Basic Rule 90
   Determining Attribute Use 91
   Fear 96
   Luck 93
   Jumping 30
   Modifiers 94
   Outcome 94
   Tasks 90
   Tasks, Resisted 92
   Tests 91
   Tests, Resisted 92
   Time 96
   Unskilled Attempts 92
Glossary 218-220
Metaphysics 62-65
   Acquiring Miracles 62
   Blessing 64
   Binding 64
   Divine Sight 64
   Holy Fire 65
   Holy Symbols 66
   Inspiration 62
   Miracles 63
   Prayers 66
   Strength of Ten 65
   Tests of Faith 63
   The Denial 62
   Touch of Healing 64
   Using Miracles 62
   Visions 65
   When Miracles Clash 62
Qualities & Drawbacks 35-47
   Acute/Impaired Senses 36
   Addiction 36-37
   Adversary 37
   Artistic Talent (type) 37-38
   Attractiveness 38
   Charisma 38
   Clown 38
   Contacts 39
   Covetous 39
   Cowardly 40
   Creating 35
   Cruel 40
   Delusions 41
   Emotional Problems 41-42
   Fast Reaction Time 42
   Hard to Kill 42
   Honorable 43

Humorless 43
Lazy 43
Minority 44
Multiple Identities 44
Nerves of Steel 44
Obsession 44
Paranoid 44
Photographic Memory 44
Physical Disability 45
Recurring Nightmares 45
Resistance 45
Resources 46
Secret 46
Showoff 46
Situational Awareness 46
Status 46
Talentless 47
Zealot 47
Skills 51-61
   Acrobatics 51
   Acting 51
   Beautician 52
   Brawling 52
   Bureaucracy 52
   Cheating 52
   Climbing 52
   Computer Hacking 52
   Computer Programming 53
   Computers 53
   Craft (type) 53
   Creating New Skills 52
   Dancing (type) 53
   Demolitions 53
   Disguise 53
   Dodge 53
   Driving (type) 53
   Electronic Surveillance 53
   Electronics 54
   Engineer (type) 54
   Escapism 54
   Fine Arts (type) 54
   First Aid 54
   Gambling 54
   Guns (type) 55
   Haggling 55
   Hand Weapon (type) 55
   Humanities (type) 55-56
   Instruction 56
   Intimidation 56
   Language (type) 56
   Learning New Skills 51

Lock Picking (type)..56
Martial Arts (special)...56
Mechanic..57
Medicine (special)..57
Myth and Legend (type)...57
Notice..57
Occult Knowledge..57
Optional Skill Points..29
Pick Pocket...58
Piloting (type)...58
Play Instrument (type)..58
Questioning..58
Research/Investigation...58
Riding (type)...58
Rituals (type)..58
Running (type)..59
Sciences (type)...59
Seduction...59
Singing...59
Sleight of Hand..59
Smooth Talking..59
Specialties...51
Sport (type)..59
Stealth...60
Storytelling..60
Streetwise...60
Surveillance..60
Survival (type)...60
Swimming...60
Throwing (type)...61
Tracking..61
Trance (special)..61
Unconventional Medicine (type/special).............61
Veterinary Medicine..61
Weight Lifting..61
Writing (type)..61

Supernatural Qualities & Drawbacks................47-50
Accursed..47-48
Gift...48
Good/Bad Luck..48
Increased Essence Pool..................................48-49
Inspiration...49
Old Soul..49-50

Vehicle Rules...115-117
Air Combat..117
Attributes...115-116
Ground Combat..117
Vehicles...139-141

Zombie Master..86-89,162-163
Dice..87
Diceless..88
Diceless Damage..89

Discretion..94
Interparty Conflict...163
Random Elements...89
Running a Game..86
Story Driven...89
Using the Rules..87

Zombies
After the Bomb...195
Basic..146
Brood Queen..186-187
Cow..169
Dawn of the Zombie Lords................................209
Dead at 1000...199
Dog...169
Drone...185
Grave Impact...177
Mein Zombie..191
PHADE to Black..173
Rat...169
Rise of the Walking Dead..................................168
Sacred Soil..181
They Came From Beyond..................................185
Until the Ending of the World...........................205

Zombie, Game Mechanics...............................146-159
Effects of Damage...147
Hit Locations...147
Intelligence..155-157
Movement..150-151
Other Damage...147
Senses...152-154
Spreading Zombies..157
Special Features..158-159
Strength..151-152
Sustenance..154-155
Weak Spots..148-149

Zombie, Intelligence..155-157
Animal Cunning...156
Dumb as Dead Wood...155
Language...156
Long-term Memory...156
Problem Solving...156
Teamwork..156
Tool Use...156

Zombie, Movement...150-151
Aquatic..151
Burrowing..150
Climbing..151
Leaping..150
Life-Like...150
Lunge, The...150
Quick Dead, The...150
Slow and Steady..150

Zombie, Senses..152-154
   Infravision..154
   Life Senses..153
   Like a Hawk...153
   Like Nothing You've Ever Seen...............153
   Like the Dead...152
   Like the Living..152
   Scent Tracking..154
   X-Ray Vision...153
Zombie, Special Features..........................158-159
   Acid Blood..158
   Detachable Body Parts.............................159
   Disease Corpse...158
   Explosive Personality................................159
   Nest..158
   Noxious Odor...158
   Regeneration...159
   Spew Flame..158
   Spitter...158
Zombie, Spreading...157
   Bury the Body..157
   One Bite and You're Hooked....................157
   Only the Dead..157
Zombie, Strength.....................................151-152
   Claws..152
   Damage Resistant.....................................151
   Dead Joe Average.....................................151
   Flame Resistant...151
   Hug of Death, The......................................152
   Iron Grip...152
   Monstrous Strength...................................151
   Ninety-pound Weakling..............................151
   Strong Like Bull...151
   Teeth...152
Zombie, Sustenance..................................154-155
   All Flesh Must Be Eaten............................155
   Blood..155
   Braiiiiiins..155
   Daily...154
   Menu, The..154
   Need to Feed...154
   Occasionally..154
   Soul Sucker...155
   Sweet Breads..155
   Weekly..154
   Who Needs Food?.....................................154
Zombie, Weak Spots................................148-149
   All..148
   Blessed Objects...149
   Brain...148
   Chemicals...149

Fire...148
Heart..148
None...148
Spine..148

Charts

Addiction Point Value......................................36
Body Armor..138
Character Creation..220
Character Improvement................................119
Character Type Reference............................220
Close Combat Weapons...............................132
Common Objects Armor Value.....................110
Common Objects Damage Capacity............110
Difficulty Numbers Table................................89
Electronic Gear...127
Endurance Loss..114
Explosive Area of Effect...............................136
Explosive Damage..137
Explosive Weapons......................................136
Fear..97
Hit Location Diagram....................................147
Language Skill Level......................................57
Luck..93
Medical Gear...127
Miscellaneous Equipment............................127
Outcome Table..95
Quality and Drawback List............................221
Ranged Combat Modifiers............................102
Ranged Weapons...134
Scientific Equipment.....................................127
Skill List...222
Strength...30
Surveillance Equipment................................127
Survival Gear..127
Targeting Body Parts....................................104
Task Modifiers...94
Test Modifiers..94
Vehicles...139-141
Zombie Power List..223

All Flesh Must Be Eaten

Name:
Character Type:

CHARACTER POINTS — SPENT ☐ UNSPENT ☐

Primary Attributes

- STRENGTH ☐
- DEXTERITY ☐
- CONSTITUTION ☐
- INTELLIGENCE ☐
- PERCEPTION ☐
- WILLPOWER ☐

Secondary Attributes

- LIFE POINTS ☐
- ENDURANCE POINTS ☐
- SPEED ☐
- ESSENCE POOL ☐

Qualities	Points	Drawbacks	Points

Skill	Level	Skill	Level

© 1999-2003 Eden Studios. Permission granted to photocopy.

All Flesh Must Be Eaten

Name:

Character Type:

CHARACTER POINTS [ ] **SPENT** [ ] **UNSPENT**

Primary Attributes

- STRENGTH
- DEXTERITY
- CONSTITUTION
- INTELLIGENCE
- PERCEPTION
- WILLPOWER

Secondary Attributes

- LIFE POINTS
- ENDURANCE POINTS
- SPEED
- ESSENCE POOL

Qualities	Points	Drawbacks	Points

Skill	Level	Skill	Level

Power	Level	Power	Level

© 1999-2003 Eden Studios. Permission granted to photocopy.

All Flesh Must Be Eaten

- Sex
- Age
- Height
- Weight
- Hair
- Eyes

Weapons/Hand to Hand

Type	Range	Damage	Cap	EV

Possessions

Allies/Contacts

Character History

© 1999-2003 Eden Studios. Permission granted to photocopy.

All Flesh Must Be Eaten

Ammo Record Forms

Keeping track of ammunition is essential in a game of survival horror. Thus, the following ammo record sheets are highly suggested. Please photocopy and distribute them to the players so they may keep track of ammunition for each of their guns. Alternatively, a Zombie Master might hold these sheets and record the ammo as it is used. This enables Zombie Masters to determine exactly when their hapless zombie chow runs out of bullets.

Magazine   **Magazine**   **Magazine**   **Magazine**

Caliber_____   Caliber_____   Caliber_____   Caliber_____

Magazine   **Magazine**   **Magazine**   **Magazine**

Caliber_____   Caliber_____   Caliber_____   Caliber_____

100 Round Belt   **100 Round Belt**   **100 Round Belt**   **100 Round Belt**

Caliber_____   Caliber_____   Caliber_____   Caliber_____

© 1999-2003 Eden Studios. Permission granted to photocopy.

Expand Your Game!

Intelligent Apes...

Terra Primate Corebook
EDN8100

Fallen Angels...

Armageddon
The End Times
Corebook
EDN5000

UNISYSTEM

...Witches

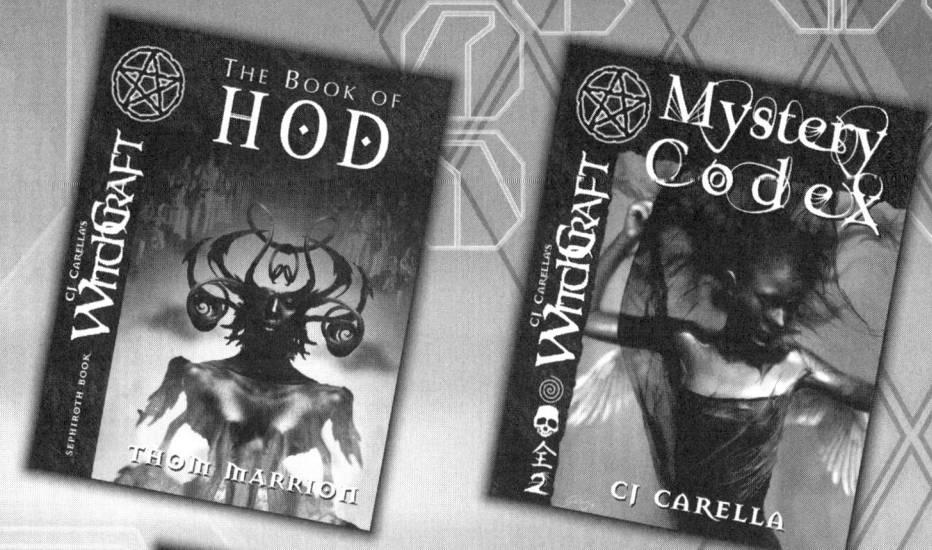

WitchCraft 2nd Ed.
Corebook
EDN4000HC

UNISYSTEM has it all

www.edenstudios.net/unisystem

Survival Horror Never Tasted This Good

All Flesh Must Be Eaten
The Zombie Survival Horror Roleplaying Game

Need seconds? We have more.

www.allflesh.com
www.edenstudios.net